EXCESSION

Also by Iain M. Banks

CONSIDER PHLEBAS
THE PLAYER OF GAMES
USE OF WEAPONS
THE STATE OF THE ART
AGAINST A DARK BACKGROUND
FEERSUM ENDJINN

Also by Iain Banks

THE WASP FACTORY
WALKING ON GLASS
THE BRIDGE
ESPEDAIR STREET
CANAL DREAMS
THE CROW ROAD
COMPLICITY
WHIT

IAIN M. BANKS

EXCESSION

ORBIT

An *Orbit* Book

First published in Great Britain by Orbit in 1996

Copyright © Iain M. Banks 1996

The moral right of the author has been asserted.

A CIP catalogue record for this book
is available from the British Library.

ISBN 1 85723 394 8

Typeset by Palimpsest Book Production Limited,
Polmont, Stirlingshire
Printed and bound in Great Britain by
Clays Ltd, St Ives plc

Orbit
A Division of
Little, Brown and Company (UK)
Brettenham House
Lancaster Place
London WC2E 7EN

To the memory of Joan Woods

Prologue

A little more than one hundred days into the fortieth year of her confinement, Dajeil Gelian was visited in her lonely tower overlooking the sea by an avatar of the great ship that was her home.

Far out amongst the heaving grey waves, beneath drifting banks of mist, the great slow bodies of some of the small sea's larger inhabitants humped and slid. Jets of vapour issued from the animals' breathing holes in exhaled blasts that rose like ghostly, insubstantial geysers amongst the flock of birds accompanying the school, causing them to climb and wheel and scream, side-slipping and fluttering in the cool air. High above, slipping in and out of pink-rubbed layers of cloud like small slow clouds themselves, other creatures moved, dirigibles and kites cruising the upper atmosphere with wings and canopies extended, warming in the watery light of a new day.

That light came from a line, not a point in the sky, because the place where Dajeil Gelian lived was not an ordinary world. The single strand of fuzzy incandescence began near the far, seaward horizon, stretched across the sky and disappeared over the foliage-strewn lip of the two-thousand-metre-high cliff a kilometre behind the beach and the single tower. At dawn, the sun-line would have appeared to rise from the horizon to starboard; at mid-day it would be directly above the tower, and at sunset it would seem to disappear into the sea to port. It was mid-morning now, and the line lay about half-way up the sky, describing a glowing arc across the vault like some vast slow-moving skipping rope forever twirling above the day.

On either side of the bar of yellow-white light the sky beyond – the real sky; the sky above the clouds – could be seen; a solid-looking brown-black over-presence that hinted at the extreme pressures and temperatures contained within, and where other animals moved in a cloudscape of chemistries entirely toxic to that below, but which in shape and density mirrored the grey, wind-ruffled sea.

Steady lines of waves broke on the grey slope of the shingle beach, beating on shattered, ground-up shells, tiny fragments of hollow animal carapaces, brittle lengths of light-blighted sea-wrack, water-smoothed slivers of wood, pitted pebbles of foamstone like dainty marbles of porous bone and a general assortment of seaside detritus collected from a handful-hundred different planets strewn across the greater galaxy. Spray lifted from where the waves fell against the shore and brought the salty smell of the sea across the beach and the tangle of scrawny plants at its margin, over the low stone wall providing some protection to the tower's seaward garden, and – wrapping around the stubby construction itself and scaling the high wall beyond – intermittently brought the sea's iodine tang to the enclosed garden within, where Dajeil Gelian tended raised carpets of bright spreadling-flowers and the rustling, half-stunted forms of barb trees and shadow-flowering wilderbush.

The woman heard the landward gate-bell tinkle, but already knew that she had a visitor because the black bird Gravious had told her, swooping from the misty sky a few minutes earlier to screech, 'Company!' at her through a writhing collection of beak-held prey before beating off again in search of more airborne insects for its winter larder. The woman had nodded at the bird's retreating form, straightening and holding the small of her back as she did so and then absently stroking her swollen abdomen through the rich fabric of the heavy dress she wore.

The message borne by the bird had not needed to be any more elaborate; throughout the four decades she had lived here alone, Dajeil had only ever had to receive one visitor, the avatar of the vessel she thought of as her host and protector, and who was now quickly and accurately pushing aside the barb-tree branches as it made its way down the path from the land-gate. The only thing that Dajeil now found surprising was that her visitor was here at this moment; the avatar had attended her regularly – entirely as though dropping casually by while on a walk along the shore – for a short visit every eight days, and habitually arrived for a longer, more formal call – at which they ate breakfast, lunch or supper, accordingly – every thirty-two days. Going by that schedule, Dajeil ought not to be expecting a visit from the ship's representative for another five days.

Dajeil carefully tucked a stray strand of her long, night-black hair back beneath her plain hair band and nodded to the tall figure making its way between the twisted trunks. 'Good morning,' she called.

The ship's avatar called itself Amorphia, which apparently meant something reasonably profound in a language Dajeil did not know and had never considered worth studying. Amorphia was a gaunt, pale, androgynous creature, almost skeletally thin and a full head taller than Dajeil, who was herself both slender and tall. For the last dozen or so years, the avatar had taken to dressing all in black, and it was in black leggings, black tunic and a short black jerkin that it appeared now, its cropped blonde hair covered by a similarly dark skull cap. It took the cap off and bowed to Dajeil, smiling as though uncertain.

'Dajeil, good morning. Are you well?'

'I'm well, thank you,' Dajeil said, who had long since given up protesting at or indeed being bothered by such probably redundant niceties. She was still convinced that the ship monitored her closely enough to know exactly how well she was – and she was anyway always in perfect health – but was nevertheless prepared to go along with the pretence that it did not watch over her so scrupulously, and so had to ask. Still, she did not respond in kind by asking after whatever might pass as the health of either a humanly formed but ship-controlled entity which functioned – as far as she knew – solely as the vessel's contact with her, or indeed the ship itself. 'Shall we go inside?' she asked.

'Yes. Thank you.'

The upper chamber of the tower was lit from above by the building's translucent glass dome – which looked up to an increasingly cloudy, grey sky – and from the edges by gently glowing in-holo'd screens, a third of which showed blue-green underwater scenes, usually featuring some of the larger mammals and fish the sea outside contained, another third of which displayed bright images of soft-looking water-vapour clouds and the huge airborne creatures which played among them, and the last third of which seemingly looked out – on frequencies inaccessible directly to the human eye – into the dense dark turmoil of the gas-giant atmosphere held compressed in the artificial sky above, where yet stranger beasts moved.

Surrounded by brightly decorated covers, cushions and wall hangings, Dajeil reached from her couch to a low table of swirlingly carved bone and poured a warmed infusion of herbal juices from a glass pitcher into a goblet of hollowed crystal contained within a filigree of silver. She sat back. Her guest, sitting awkwardly on the edge of a delicate wooden seat, picked up the brimming vessel, looked around the room and then put the goblet to its lips and drank. Dajeil smiled.

The avatar Amorphia was deliberately formed to look not simply neither male nor female but as perfectly, artificially poised between maleness and femaleness as it was possible to be, and the ship had never made any pretence that its representative was other than completely its creature, with only the most cursory intellectual existence of its own. However, it still amused the woman to find her own small ways of proving to herself that this seemingly quite human person was nothing of the kind.

It had become one of the small, private games she played with the cadaverously sexless creature; she gave it a glass, cup or goblet full to the brim of the appropriate drink – indeed sometimes full beyond the brim, with only surface tension holding the liquid in the container – and then watched Amorphia lift it to her mouth and sip it, each and every time, without either spilling a single drop or appearing to devote any special attention to the act; a feat no human she had ever encountered could have performed.

Dajeil sipped her own drink, feeling its warmth make its way down her throat. Within her, her child stirred, and she patted her belly gently, without really thinking.

The avatar's gaze seemed fixed on one particular holo screen. Dajeil twisted on the couch to look in the same direction and discovered violent action in a couple of the screens displaying the views from the gas-giant environment; a school of the habitat's food-chain-topping predators – sharp, arrow-headed things, finned like missiles, venting gas from steering orifices – were shown from different angles as they fell together out of some towering column of cloud and swept through clearer atmosphere down upon a group of vaguely bird-like grazing animals clustered near the edge of an up-welling cloud-top. The avian creatures scattered, some crumpling and falling, some beating frantically away to the side, some disappearing, balled in fright, into the cloud. The predators darted and spun amongst them, most missing their fleeing prey, a few connecting; biting, slashing and killing.

Dajeil nodded. 'Migration time, up there,' she said. 'Breeding season soon.' She watched a grazer being torn apart and gulped down by a couple of the missile-bodied predators. 'Mouths to feed,' she said quietly, looking away. She shrugged. She recognised some of the predators and had given them her own nick-names, though the creatures she was really interested in were the much bigger, slower-moving animals – generally untroubled by the predators – which were like larger, more bulbous relations of the unfortunate grazer flock.

Dajeil had on occasion discussed details of the various ecologies contained within the ship's habitats with Amorphia, who seemed politely interested and yet frankly ignorant on the subject even though the ship's knowledge of the ecosystems was, in effect, total; the creatures belonged to the vessel, after all, whether you regarded them as passengers or pets. Much like herself, Dajeil thought sometimes.

Amorphia's gaze remained fixed on the screens displaying the carnage taking place in the sky beyond the sky. 'It is beautiful, isn't it?' the avatar said, sipping at the drink again. It glanced at Dajeil, who was looking surprised. 'In a way,' Amorphia added quickly.

Dajeil nodded slowly. 'In its own way, yes of course.' She leant forward and put her goblet on to the carved-bone table. 'Why are you here today, Amorphia?' she asked.

The ship's representative looked startled. It came close, Dajeil thought, to spilling its drink.

'To see how you are,' the avatar said quickly.

Dajeil sighed. 'Well,' she said, 'we have established that I'm well, and—'

'And the child?' Amorphia asked, glancing at the woman's belly.

Dajeil rested her hand on her abdomen. 'It is . . . as ever,' she said quietly. 'It is healthy.'

'Good,' Amorphia said, folding its long arms about itself and crossing its legs. The creature glanced at the holo screens again.

Dajeil was losing patience. 'Amorphia, speaking as the ship; what is going on?'

The avatar looked at the woman with a strange, lost, wild look in its eyes, and for a moment Dajeil was worried that something had gone wrong, that the ship had suffered some terrible injury or division, that it had gone quite mad (after all, its fellows regarded it as being half-mad already, at best) and left Amorphia abandoned to its own inadequate devices. Then the black-clad creature unfolded itself from the chair and paced to the single small window that faced the sea, drawing aside curtains to inspect the view. It put its hands to its arms, hugging itself.

'Everything might be about to change, Dajeil,' the avatar said hollowly, seemingly addressing the window. It glanced back at her for a moment. It clasped its hands behind its back. 'The sea may have to become as stone, or steel; the sky, too. And you and I may have to part company.' It turned to look at her, then came over to where she sat and perched on the other end of the couch, its thin frame hardly making an impression on the cushions. It stared into her eyes.

'Become like stone?' Dajeil said, still worrying about the mental health of the avatar or the ship controlling it, or both. 'What do you mean?'

'We – that is the ship . . .' Amorphia said, placing one hand on its chest, '. . . we may finally have . . . a thing to do.'

'A thing to do?' Dajeil said. 'What sort of thing to do?'

'A thing which will require that our world here changes,' the avatar said. 'A thing which requires that – at the least – we have to put our animated guests into storage with everybody else – well, save for yourself – and then, perhaps, that we leave all our guests – *all* our guests – behind in appropriate other habitats.'

'Including me?'

'Including you, Dajeil.'

'I see.' She nodded. Leaving the tower; leaving the ship. Well, she thought, what a sudden end to my protected isolation. 'While you?' she asked the avatar. 'You go off to do . . . what?'

'Something,' Amorphia told her, without irony.

Dajeil smiled thinly. 'Which you won't tell me about.'

'Which I can't tell you about.'

'Because—'

'Because I don't yet know myself,' Amorphia said.

'Ah.' Dajeil thought for a moment, then stood up and went to one of the holo screens, where a camera drone was tracking a light-dappled school of triangular purple-winged rays across the floor of a shallow part of the sea. She knew this school, too; she had watched three generations of these huge, gentle creatures live and die; she had watched them and she had swum with them and – once – assisted in the birth of one of their young.

Huge purple wings waved in slow motion, tips intermittently disturbing little golden wisps of sand.

'This is a change indeed,' Dajeil said.

'Quite so,' the avatar said. It paused. 'And it may lead to a change in your own circumstances.'

Dajeil turned to look at the creature, which was staring intently over the couch at her with wide, unblinking eyes.

'A change?' Dajeil said, her voice betraying her in its shakiness. She stroked her belly again, then blinked and looked down at her hand as though it too had turned traitor.

'I cannot be sure,' Amorphia confessed. 'But it is possible.'

Dajeil tore off her hair-band and shook her head, setting free her long dark hair so that it half covered her face as she paced from one side of the room to the other.

'I see,' she said, staring up at the tower's dome, now sprinkled with a light, drizzling rain. She leant against the wall of holo screens, her gaze fixed on the avatar. 'When will all this happen?'

'A few small changes – inconsequential, but capable of saving us much time in the future if carried out now – are happening already,' it said. 'The rest, the main part of it . . . that will come later. In a day or two, or maybe a week or two . . . if you agree.'

Dajeil thought for a moment, her face flickering between expressions, then she smiled. 'You mean you're asking my permission for all this?'

'Sort of,' the ship's representative mumbled, looking down and playing with its fingernails.

Dajeil let it do this for a while, then she said, 'Ship, you have looked after me here, indulged me . . .' she made an effort to smile at the dark-clad creature, though it was still intently studying its nails, '. . . humoured me for all this time, and I can never express my gratitude sufficiently or hope even to begin paying you back, but I can't make your decisions for you. You must do as you see fit.'

The creature looked up immediately. 'Then we'll start tagging all the fauna now,' it said. 'That'll make it quicker to round them up when the time comes. It'll take a few more days after that before we can start the transformation process. From that point . . .' It shrugged. It was the most human gesture she had ever seen the avatar make. '. . . there may be twenty or thirty days before . . . before some sort of resolution is reached. Again, it's hard to say.'

Dajeil folded her arms across the bulge of her forty-year-old, self-perpetuated pregnancy. She nodded slowly. 'Well, thanks for telling me all this.' She smiled insincerely, and suddenly she could not hold in the emotions any longer and looked through tears and black, down-tumbled curls at the long-limbed creature arranged upon her couch and said, 'So, don't you have things you must be doing?'

From the top of the rain-blown tower, the woman watched the avatar as it retraced its steps along the narrow path through the sparsely treed water meadow to the foot of the two-kilometre cliff, which was skirted by a rough slope of scree. The thin, dark figure – filling half her field of view and grainy with magnification – negotiated a last great boulder at the base of the cliff, then disappeared. Dajeil let muscles in her eyes relax; meanwhile a set of near-instinctive routines in her brain shut down again. The view returned to normal.

Dajeil raised her gaze to the overcast. A flight of the box-kite creatures was poised in the air just under the cloud surface directly above the tower, dark rectangular shapes hanging still against the greyness as though standing sentinel over her.

She tried to imagine what they felt, what they knew. There were ways of tapping directly into their minds, ways that were virtually never used with humans and whose use even with animals was generally frowned upon in proportion to the creature's intelligence, but they did exist and the ship would let her use them if she asked. There were ways, too, for the ship to simulate all but perfectly what such creatures must be experiencing, and she had used those techniques often enough for a human equivalent of that imitative process to have transferred itself to her mind, and it was that process she invoked now, though to no avail, as it transpired; she was too agitated, too distracted by the things Amorphia had told her to be able to concentrate.

Instead, she tried to imagine the ship as a whole in that same, trained mind's eye, remembering the occasions when she had viewed the vessel from its remote machines or gone flying around it, attempting to imagine the changes it was already preparing itself for. She supposed they would be unglimpsable from the sort of distance that would let you see the whole craft.

She looked around, taking in the great cliff, the clouds and the sea, the darkness of sky. Her gaze swept round the waves, the sea-marsh, and the water meadows beneath the scree and the cliff. She rubbed her belly without thinking, as she had done for nearly forty years, and pondered on the marginality of things, and how quickly change could come, even to something that had seemed set to continue as it was in perpetuity.

But then, as she knew too well, the more fondly we imagine something will last forever, the more ephemeral it often proves to be.

She became suddenly very aware of her place here, her position. She saw herself and the tower, both within and outside the ship; outside its main hull – distinct, discrete, straight-sided and measured exactly in kilometres – but within the huge envelope of water, air and gas it encompassed within the manifold layers of its fields (she imagined the force fields sometimes as like the hooped slips, underskirts, skirts, flounces and lace of some ancient formal gown). A slab of power and substance floating in a giant spoonful of sea, most of its vast bulk exposed to the air and clouds that formed its middle layer and around which the sun-line curved each day, and all domed with the long, field-contained pressure vessel of ferocious heat, colossal pressure and crushing gravity that simulated the conditions of a gas-giant planet. A room, a cave, a hollow husk a hundred kilometres long, hurrying through space, with the ship as its vast, flattened kernel. A kernel – an enclosed world inside this world – within which she had not set foot for thirty-nine of these forty unchanging years, having no desire ever again to see that infinite catacomb of the silent undead.

All to change, Dajeil Gelian thought; all to change, and the sea and the sky to become as stone, or steel . . .

The black bird Gravious settled by her hand on the stone parapet of the tower.

'What's going on?' it croaked. 'There's something going on. I can tell. What is it, then? What's it all about?'

'Oh, ask the ship,' she told it.

'Already asked it. All it'll say is there's changes coming, like as not.' The bird shook its head once, as if trying to dislodge something distasteful from its beak. 'Don't like changes,' it said. It swivelled its head, fixing its beady gaze upon the woman. 'What sort of changes, then, eh? What we got to expect? What we got to look forward to, eh? It tell you?'

She shook her head. 'No,' she said, not looking at the bird. 'No, not really.'

'Huh.' The bird continued to look at her for a moment, then pivoted its head back to look out across the salt marsh. It ruffled its feathers and rose up on its thin black legs. 'Well,' it said, 'Winter's coming. Can't delay. Best prepare.' The bird dropped into the air. 'Fat lot of use . . .' she heard it mutter. It opened its wings and flew away on an involute course.

Dajeil Gelian looked up to the clouds again, and the sky beyond. All to change, and the sea and the sky to become as stone, or steel . . . She shook her head again, and wondered what extremity of circumstance could possibly have so galvanised the great craft that had been her home, her refuge for so long.

Whatever; after four decades in its state of self-imposed internal exile, navigating its own wayward course within its sought-out wilderness as part of the civilisation's Ulterior and functioning most famously as a repository for quiescent souls and very large animals, it sounded like the General Systems Vehicle *Sleeper Service* was again starting to think and behave a little more like a ship which belonged to the Culture.

1

Outside Context Problem

I

(GCU *Grey Area* signal sequence file #n428857/119)

.

[swept-to-tight beam, M16.4, received @ n4.28.857.3644]
xGSV *Honest Mistake*
  oGCU *Grey Area*
Take a look at this:
∞
(Signal sequence #n428855/1446, relay:)
∞

1) [skein broadcast, Mclear, received @ n4.28.855.0065+]:
   !c11505.
∞

2) [swept beam M1, received @ n4.28.855.0066-]:
   SDA.
   c2314992+52
   xFATC @ n4.28.855.
∞

3) [swept beam, M2, relay, received @ n4.28.855.0079-]:
   xGCU *Fate Amenable To Change.*
     oGSV *Ethics Gradient*
     & as requested:
   Significant developmental anomaly.
   c4629984+523
   (@n28.855.0065.43392).
∞

4) [tight beam, M16, relay, received @ n4.28.855.0085]:
   xGCU *Fate Amenable To Change,*
     oGSV *Ethics Gradient*
     & only as required:
   Developmental anomaly provisionally rated EqT, potentially jeopardising, found here c9259969+5331.
   My Status: L5 secure, moving to L6ˆ.
   Instigating all other Extreme precautions.

∞

5) [broadcast Mclear, received @ n4.28.855.01.]:
   *xGCU *Fate Amenable To Change,*
     oGSV *Ethics Gradient*
     & *broadcast*:
   Ref. 3 previous compacs & precursor broadcast.
   Panic over.
   I misinterpreted.
   It's a Scapsile Vault Craft.
   Ho hum.
   Sorry.
   Full Internal Report to follow immediately in High Embarrassment Factor code.
   BSTS. H&H. BTB.

∞

(End Signal Sequence.)

∞

   xGCU *Grey Area*
     oGSV *Honest Mistake*
   Yes. So?

∞

There is more.
The ship lied.

∞

   Let me guess; the ship was in fact subverted.
   It is no longer one of ours.

∞

No, it is believed its integrity is intact.
But it lied in that last signal, and with good reason.
We may have an OCP.
They may want your help, at any price.
Are you interested?

∞

   An Outside Context Problem? Really? Very well. Keep me informed, do.

∞

No.
This is serious.
I know no more yet, but they are worried about something.
Your presence will be required, urgently.

∞

I dare say. However I have business to complete here first.

∞

Foolish child!
Make all haste.

∞

Mm-hmm. If I did agree, where might I be required?

∞

Here.
(glyphseq. file appended.)
As you will have gathered, it is from the ITG and concerns our old friend.

∞

Indeed.
Now that *is* interesting.
I shall be there directly.

∞

(End signal file.)

II

The ship shuddered; the few remaining lights flickered, dimmed and went out. The alarms dopplered down to silence. A series of sharp impacts registered through the companionway shell walls with resonations in the craft's secondary and primary structure. The atmosphere pulsed with impact echoes; a breeze picked up, then disappeared. The shifting air brought with it a smell of burning and vaporisation; aluminium, polymers associated with carbon fibre and diamond film, superconductor cabling.

Somewhere, the drone Sisela Ytheleus could hear a human, shouting; then, radiating wildly over the electromagnetic bands came a voice signal similar to that carried by the air. It became garbled almost immediately then degraded quickly into meaning-less static. The human shout changed to a scream, then the EM signal cut off; so did the sound.

Pulses of radiation blasted in from various directions, virtually information-free. The ship's inertial field wobbled uncertainly, then drew steady and settled again. A shell of neutrinos swept through the space around the companionway. Noises faded. EM signatures murmured to silence; the ship's engines and main life support systems were off-line. The whole EM spectrum was empty of meaning. Probably the battle had now switched to the ship's AI core and back-up photonic nuclei.

Then a pulse of energy shot through a multi-purpose cable buried in the wall behind, oscillating wildly then settling back to a steady, utterly unrecognisable pattern. An internal camera patch on a structural beam nearby awakened and started scanning.

It can't be over that quickly, can it?

Hiding in the darkness, the drone suspected it was already too late. It was supposed to wait until the attack had reached a plateau phase and the aggressor thought that it was just a matter of mopping up the last dregs of opposition before it made its move, but the attack had been too sudden, too extreme, too capable. The plans the ship had made, of which it was such an important part, could only anticipate so much, only allow for so proportionally greater a technical capability on the part of the attacker. Beyond a certain point, there was simply nothing you could do; there was no brilliant plan you could draw up or cunning stratagem you could employ that would not seem laughably simple and unsophisticated to a profoundly more developed enemy. In this instance they were not perhaps quite at the juncture where resistance became genuinely without point, but – from the ease with which the Elencher ship was being taken over – they were not that far away from it, either.

Remain calm, the machine told itself. *Look at the overview; place this and yourself in context. You are prepared, you are hardened, you are proof. You will do all that you can to survive as you are or at the very least to prevail. There is a plan to be put into effect here. Play your part with skill, courage and honour and no ill will be thought of you by those who survive and succeed.*

The Elench had spent many thousands of years pitting themselves against every kind of technology and every type of civilisational artifact the vast spaces of the greater galaxy could provide, seeking always to understand rather than to overpower, to be changed rather than to enforce change upon others, to incorporate and to share rather than to infect and impose, and in that cause, and with that relatively unmenacing *modus operandi*, had become perhaps more adept than any – with the possible exception of the mainstream Culture's semi-military emissaries known as the Contact Section – at resisting outright attack without seeming to threaten it; but for all that the galaxy had been penetrated by so many different explorers in all obvious primary directions to every periphery however distant, enormous volumes of that encompassing arena remained effectively unexplored by the current crop of in-play civilisations, including the Elench (quite how utterly that region, and beyond, was comprehended by the elder species, or even whether they really cared about it at all was simply unknown). And in those swallowingly vast volumes, amongst those spaces between the spaces between the stars, around suns, dwarfs, nebulae and holes it had been determined from some distance were of no immediate interest or threat, it was of course always possible that some danger waited, some peril lurked, comparatively small measured against the physical scale of the galaxy's present active cultures, but capable – through a developmental peculiarity or as a result of some form of temporal limbo or exclusionary dormancy – of challenging and besting even a representative of a society as technologically advanced and contactually experienced as the Elench.

The drone felt calm, thinking as coldly and detachedly as it could for those few moments on the background to its current predicament. It was prepared, it was ready, and it was no ordinary machine; it was at the cutting edge of its civilisation's technology, designed to evade detection by the most sophisticated instruments, to survive in almost unimaginably hostile conditions, to take on virtually any opponent and to suffer practically any damage in concentric stages of resistance. That its ship, its own manufacturer, the one entity that probably knew it better than it knew itself, was apparently being at this moment corrupted, seduced, taken over, must not affect its judgement or its confidence.

The displacer, it thought. *All I've got to do is get near the Displace Pod, that's all* . . .

Then it felt its body scanned by a point source located near the ship's AI core, and knew its time had come. The attack was as elegant as it was ferocious and the take-over abrupt almost to the point of instantaneity, the battle-memes of the invading alien consciousness aided by the thought processes and shared knowledge of the by now obviously completely over-whelmed ship.

With no interval to provide a margin for error at all, the drone shunted its personality from its own AI core to its back-up picofoam complex and at the same time readied the signal cascade that would transfer its most important concepts, pro-grams and instructions first to electronic nanocircuitry, then to an atomechanical substrate and finally – absolutely as a last resort – to a crude little (though at several cubic centimetres also wastefully large) semi-biological brain. The drone shut off and shut down what had been its true mind, the only place it had ever really existed in all its life, and let whatever pattern of consciousness had taken root there perish for lack of energy, its collapsing consciousness impinging on the machine's new mind as a faint, informationless exhalation of neutrinos.

The drone was already moving; out from its body-niche in the wall and into the companionway space. It accelerated along the corridor, sensing the gaze of the ceiling-beam camera patch following it. Fields of radiation swept over the drone's militarised body, caressing, probing, penetrating. An inspection hatch burst open in the companionway just ahead of the drone and something exploded out of it; cables burst free, filling to overflowing with electrical power. The drone zoomed then swooped; a discharge of electricity crackled across the air immediately above the machine and blew a hole in the far wall; the drone twisted through the wreckage and powered down the corridor, turning flat to its direction of travel and extending a disc-field through the air to brake for a corner, then slamming off the far wall and accelerating up another companionway. It was one of the full cross-axis corridors, and so long; the drone quickly reached the speed of sound in the human-breathable atmosphere; an emergency door slammed shut behind it a full second after it had passed.

A space suit shot upwards out of a descending vertical tubeway near the end of the companionway, crumpled to a stop, then reared up and stumbled out to intercept the machine. The drone had already scanned the suit and knew the suit was empty and unarmed; it went straight through it, leaving it flapping halved against floor and ceiling like a collapsed balloon. The drone threw another disc of field around itself to match the companionway's diameter and rode almost to a stop on a piston of compressed air, then darted round the next corner and accelerated again.

A human figure inside a space suit lay half-way up the next corridor, which was pressurising rapidly with a distant roar of gas. Smoke was filling the companionway in the distance, then it ignited and the mixture of gases exploded down the tube. The smoke was transparent to the drone and far too cool to do it any harm, but the thickening atmosphere was going to slow it up, which was doubtless exactly the idea.

The drone scanned the human and the suit as best it could as it tore up the smoke-filled corridor towards it. It knew the person in the suit well; he had been on the ship for five years. The suit was without weaponry, its systems quiet but doubtless already taken over; the man was in shock and under fierce chemical sedation from the suit's medical unit. As the drone approached the suit it raised one arm towards the fleeing machine. To a human the arm would have appeared to move almost impossibly quickly, flicking up at the machine, but to the drone the gesture looked languid, almost leisurely; surely this could not be all the threat the suit was capable of—

The drone had only the briefest warning of the suit's holstered gun exploding; until that instant the gun hadn't even been apparent to the machine's senses, shielded somehow. There was no time to stop, no opportunity to use its own EM effector on the gun's controls to prevent it from overloading, nowhere to take cover, and – in the thick mist of gases flooding the corridor – no way of accelerating beyond the danger. At the same moment, the ship's inertial field fluctuated again, and flipped a quarter-turn; suddenly *down* was directly behind the drone, and the field strength doubled, then redoubled. The gun exploded, tearing the suit and the human it contained apart.

The drone ignored the backward tug of the ship's reoriented gravity and slammed against the ceiling, skidding along it for half a metre while producing a cone-shaped field immediately behind it.

The explosion blew the companionway's inner shell apart and punched the drone into the corridor's ceiling so hard its back-up semi-biochemical brain was reduced to a useless paste inside it; that no major pieces of shrapnel struck it counted as a minor miracle. The blast hit the drone's conical field and flattened it, though not before enough of its energy had been directed through the inner and outer fabric of the companionway shell in a fair impersonation of a shaped-charge detonation. The corridor's lining punctured and tore to provide a vent for the cloud of gases still flooding into the companionway; they erupted into the depressurised loading bay outside. The drone paused momentarily, letting debris tear past it in a hurricane of gas, then in the semi-vacuum which resulted powered off again, ignoring the escape route which had opened behind it and racing down to the next companionway junction; the off-line displacer pod the drone was making for hung outside the ship hull only ten metres round the next corner.

The drone curved through the air, bounced off another wall and the floor and raced into the hull-wall companionway to find a machine similar to itself screaming towards it.

It knew this machine, too; it was its twin. It was its closest sibling/friend/lover/comrade in all the great distributed, forever changing civilisation that was the Elench.

X-ray lasers flickered from the converging machine, only millimetres above the drone, producing detonations somewhere way behind it while it flicked on its mirrorshields, flipped in the air, ejected its old AI core and the semi-biochemical unit into the air behind it and spun around in an outside loop to continue down the companionway; the two components it had ejected flared beneath it, instantly vaporising and surrounding it with plasma. It fired its own laser at the approaching drone – the blast was mirrored off, blossoming like fiery petals which raged against and pierced the corridor walls – and effectored the displacer pod controls, powering the machinery up into a preset sequence.

The attack on its photonic nucleus came at the same moment, manifesting itself as a perceived disturbance in the space-time fabric, warping the internal structure of the drone's light-energised mind from outside normal space. *It's using the engines*, thought the drone, senses swimming, its awareness seeming to break up and evaporate somehow as it effectively began to go unconscious. *fm-am!*, cried a tiny, long-thought-out sub routine. It felt itself switch to amplitude modulation instead of frequency modulation; reality snapped back into focus again, though its senses still remained disconnected and thoughts still felt odd. *But if I don't react otherwise* . . . The other drone fired at it again, zooming towards it on an intercept course. *Ramming. How inelegant.*

The drone mirrored the rays, still refusing to adjust its internal photonic topography to allow for the wildly shifting wavelength changes demanding attention in its mind.

The displacer pod just the other side of the ship's hull hummed into life; a set of coordinates corresponding with the drone's own present position appeared flickering in the drone's awareness, describing the volume of space that would be nipped off from the surface of the normal universe and hurled far beyond the stricken Elencher ship. *Damn, might make it yet; just roll with it,* the drone thought dizzily. It rolled; literally, physically, in mid-air.

Light, bursting from all around it and bearing the signature of plasma fire, drummed into its casing with what felt like the pressure of a small nuclear blast. Its fields mirrored what they could; the rest roasted the machine to white heat and started to seep inside its body, beginning to destroy its more vulnerable components. Still it held out, completing its roll through the superheated gases around it – mostly vaporised floor-tiles, it noted – dodging the shape spearing towards it that was its murderous twin, noticing (almost lazily, now) that the displacer pod had completed its power-up and was moving to clasp/discharge . . . while its mind involuntarily registered the information contained in the blast of radiation and finally caved in under the force of the alien purpose encoded within.

It felt itself split in two, leaving behind its real personality, giving that up to the invading power of its photonic core's abducted intent and becoming slowly, balefully aware of its own abstracted echo of existence in clumsy electronic form.

The displacer on the other side of the hull wall completed its cycle; it snapped a field around and instantly swallowed a sphere of space not much bigger than the head of a human; the resulting bang would have been quite loud in anything other than the mayhem the on-board battle had created.

The drone – barely larger than two adult human hands placed together – fell smoking, glowing, to the side wall of the companionway, which was now in effect the floor.

Gravity returned to normal and the drone clunked to the floor proper, clattering onto the heat-scarred undersurface beneath the chimney that was a vertical companionway. Something was raging in the drone's real mind, behind walls of insulation. Something powerful and angry and determined. The machine produced a thought equivalent to a sigh, or a shrug of the shoulders, and interrogated its atomechanical nucleus, just for good form's sake . . . but that avenue was irredeemably heat-corrupted . . . not that it mattered; it was over.

All over.

Done . . .

Then the ship hailed it, quite normally, over its communicator. *Now why didn't you try that in the first place?*, thought the drone. *Well*, it answered itself, *because I wouldn't have replied, of course*. It found that almost funny.

But it couldn't reply; the com unit's send facility had been wasted by the heat too. So it waited.

Gas drifted, stuff cooled, other stuff condensed, making pretty designs on the floor. Things creaked, radiations played, and hazy EM indications suggested the ship's engines and major systems were back on line. The heat making its way through the drone's body dissipated slowly, leaving it alive but still crippled and incapable of movement or action. It would take it days to bootstrap the routines that would even start to replace the mechanisms that would construct the self-repair nano-units. That seemed quite funny too. The vessel made noises and signals like it was moving off through space again. Meanwhile the thing in the drone's real mind went on raging. It was like living with a noisy neighbour, or having a headache, thought the drone. It went on waiting.

Eventually a heavy maintenance unit, about the size of a human torso and escorted by a trio of small self-motivated effector side-arms appeared at the far end of the vertical companionway above it and floated down through the currents of climbing gas until they were directly over the small, pocked, smoking and splintered casing of the drone. The effector weapons' aim had stayed locked onto the drone the whole way down.

Then one of the guns powered up and fired at the small machine.

Shit. Bit summary, dammit . . . the drone had time to think.

But the effector was powered only enough to provide a two-way communication channel.

~ Hello? said the maintenance unit, through the gun.

~ Hello yourself.

~ The other machine is gone.

~ I know; my twin. Snapped. Displaced. Get thrown a long way by one of those big Displace Pods, something that small. One-off coordinates, too. Never find it—

The drone knew it was babbling, its electronic mind was probably under effector incursion but too damn stupid even to know it and so gibbering as a side effect, but it couldn't stop itself;

~ Yep, totally gone. Entity overboard. One-throw XYZs. Never find it. No point in even looking for it. Unless you want me to step into the breach too, of course; I'd go take a squint, if you like, if the pod's still up for it; personally it wouldn't be too much trouble . . .

~ Did you mean all that to happen?

The drone thought about lying, but now it could feel the effector weapon in its mind, and knew that not only the weapon and the maintenance drone but the ship and whatever had taken over all of them could *see* it was thinking about lying . . . so, feeling that it was itself again, but knowing it had no defences left, wearily it said,

~ Yes.

~ From the beginning?

~ Yes. From the beginning.

~ We can find no trace of this plan in your ship's mind.

~ Well, nar-nar-ne-fucking-nar-nar to you, then, prickbrains.

~ Illuminating insults. Are you in pain?

~ No. Look, who *are* you?

~ Your friends.

~ I don't believe this; I thought this ship was *smart*, but it gets taken over by something that talks like a Hegemonising Swarm out of an infant's tale.

~ We can discuss that later, but what was the point of displacing beyond our reach your twin machine rather than yourself? It was ours, was it not? Or did we miss something?

~ You missed something. The displacer was programmed to . . . oh, just read my brains; I'm not sore but I'm *tired*.

Silence for a moment. Then,

~ I see. The displacer copied your mind-state to the machine it ejected. That was why we found your twin so handily placed to intercept you when we realised you were not yet ours and there might be a way out via the displacer.

~ One should always be prepared for every eventuality, even if it's getting shafted by a dope with bigger guns.

~ Well, if cuttingly, put. Actually, I believe your twin machine may have been badly damaged by the plasma implosure directed at yourself, and as all you were trying to do was get away, rather than find a novel method of attacking us, the matter is anyway not of such great importance.

~ Very convincing.

~ Ah, sarcasm. Well, never mind. Come and join us now.

~ Do I have a choice in this?

~ What, you would rather die? Or do you think we would leave you to repair yourself as you are/were and hence attack us in the future?

~ Just checking.

~ We shall transcribe you into the ship's own core with the others who suffered mortality.

~ And the humans, the mammal crew?

~ What of them?

~ Are they dead, or in the core?

~ Three are solely in the core, including the one whose weapon we used to try to stop you. The rest sleep, with inactive copies of the brain-states in the core, for study. We have no intentions of destroying them, if that's what concerns you. Do you care for them particularly?

~ Never could stand the squidgy great slow lumps myself.

~ What a harsh machine you are. Come—

~ I'm a soldier drone, you cretin; what do you expect? And anyway; *I'm* harsh! You just wasted my ship and all my friends and comrades and you call *me* harsh—

~ *You* insisted upon invasionary contact, not us. And there have been no mind-state total losses at all except that brought about by your displacer. But let me explain all this in more comfort . . .

~ Look, can't you just kill me and get it o—?

But with that, the effector weapon altered its set-up momentarily, and – in effect – sucked the little machine's intellect out of its ruined and smouldering body.

III

'Byr Genar-Hofoen, my good friend, welcome!'

Colonel Alien-Befriender (first class) Fivetide Humidyear VII of the Winterhunter tribe threw four of his limbs around the human and hugged him tightly to his central mass, pursing his lip fronds and pressing his front beak to the human's cheek. 'Mmmmww*wah*! There! Ha ha!'

Genar-Hofoen felt the Diplomatic Force officer's kiss through the few millimetres' thickness of the gelfield suit as a moderately sharp impact on his jaw followed by a powerful sucking that might have led someone less experienced in the diverse and robust manifestations of Affronter friendliness to conclude that the being was either trying to suck his teeth out through his cheek or had determined to test whether a Culture Gelfield Contact/Protection Suit, Mk 12, could be ripped off its wearer by a localised partial vacuum. What the crushingly powerful four-limbed hug would have done to a human unprotected by a suit designed to withstand pressures comparable to those found at the bottom of an ocean probably did not bear thinking about, but then a human exposed without protection to the conditions required to support Affronter life would be dying in at least three excitingly different and painful ways anyway without having to worry about being crushed by a cage of leg-thick tentacles.

'Fivetide; good to see you again, you brigand!' Genar-Hofoen said, slapping the Affronter about the beak-end with the appropriate degree of enthusiastic force to indicate bonhomie.

'And you, and you!' the Affronter said. He released the man from its grasp, twirled with surprising speed and grace and – clasping one of the human's hands in a tentacle end – pulled him through the roaring crush of Affronters near the nest space entrance to a clearer part of the web membrane.

The nest space was hemispherical in shape and easily a hundred metres across. It was used mainly as a regimental mess and dining hall and so was hung with flags, banners, the hides of enemies, bits and pieces of old weapons and military paraphernalia. The curved, veined-looking walls were similarly adorned with plaques, company, battalion, division and regimental honour plaques and the heads, genitals, limbs or other acceptably distinctive body parts of old adversaries.

Genar-Hofoen had visited this particular nest space before on a few occasions. He looked up to see if the three ancient human heads which the hall sported were visible this evening; the Diplomatic Force prided itself on having the tact to order that the recognisable trophy bits of any given alien be covered over when a still animate example of that species paid a visit, but sometimes they forgot. He located the heads – scarcely more than three little dots hidden high on one sub-dividing drape-wall – and noted that they had not been covered up.

The chances were this was simply an oversight, though it was equally possible that it was entirely deliberate and either meant to be an exquisitely weighted insult carefully contrived to keep him unsettled and in his place, or intended as a subtle but profound compliment to indicate that he was being accepted as one of the boys, and not like one of those snivellingly timid aliens who got all upset and shirty just because they saw a close relative's hide gracing an occasional table.

That there was absolutely no rapid way of telling which of these possibilities was the case was exactly the sort of trait the human found most endearing in the Affront. It was, equally, just the kind of attribute the Culture in general and his predecessors in particular had found to be such a source of despair.

Genar-Hofoen found himself grinning wryly at the three distant heads, and half hoping that Fivetide would notice.

Fivetide's eye stalks swivelled. 'Waiter-scum!' he bellowed at a hovering juvenile eunuch. 'Here, wretch!'

The waiter was half the size of the big male and childishly unscarred unless you counted the stump of the creature's rear beak. The juvenile floated closer, trembling even more than politeness dictated, until it was within a tentacle reach. 'This thing,' roared Fivetide, flicking a limb-end to indicate Genar-Hofoen, 'is the alien beast-human you should already have been briefed on if your Chief is to avoid a sound thrashing. It might look like prey but it is in fact an honoured and treasured guest and it needs feeding much as we do; rush to the animals' and outworlders' serving table and fetch the sustenance prepared for it. *Now*!' Fivetide screamed, his voice producing a small visible shockwave in the mostly nitrogen atmosphere. The juvenile eunuch waiter vented away with suitable alacrity.

Fivetide turned to the human. 'As a special treat for you,' he shouted, 'we have prepared some of the disgusting glop you call food and a container of liquid based on that poisonous water stuff. God-shit, how we spoil you, eh!' He tentacle-slapped the human in the midriff. The gelfield suit absorbed the blow by stiffening; Genar-Hofoen staggered a little to one side, laughing.

'Your generosity near bowls me over.'

'Good! Do you like my new uniform?' the Affronter officer asked, sucking back a little from the human and pulling himself up to his full height. Genar-Hofoen made a show of looking the other being up and down.

The average fully grown Affronter consisted of a mass the shape of a slightly flattened ball about two metres in girth and one and a half in height, suspended under a veined, frilled gas sac which varied in diameter between one and five metres according to the Affronter's desired buoyancy and which was topped by a small sensor bump. When an Affronter was in aggressive/defensive mode, the whole sac could be deflated and covered by protective plates on the top of the central body mass. The principal eyes and ears were carried on two stalks above the fore beak covering the creature's mouth; a rear beak protected the genitals. The anus/gas vent was positioned centrally under the main body.

To the central mass were attached, congenitally, between six and eleven tentacles of varying thicknesses and lengths, at least four of which normally ended in flattened, leaf-shaped paddles. The actual number of limbs possessed by any particular adult male Affronter one encountered entirely depended on how many fights and/or hunts it had taken part in and how successful a part in them it had played; an Affronter with an impressive array of scars and more stumps than limbs was considered either an admirably dedicated sportsman or a brave but stupid and probably dangerous incompetent, depending entirely on the individual's reputation.

Fivetide himself had been born with nine limbs – considered the most propitious number amongst the best families, pro-viding one had the decency to lose at least one in duel or hunt – and had duly lost one to his fencing master while at military college in a duel over the honour of the fencing master's chief wife.

'It's a very impressive uniform, Fivetide,' Genar-Hofoen said.

'Yes, it is rather, isn't it?' the Affronter said, flexing his body.

Fivetide's uniform consisted of multitudinous broad straps and sashes of metallic-looking material which were crisscrossed over his central mass and dotted with holsters, sheaths and brackets – all occupied by weapons but sealed for the formal dinner they were here to attend – the glittering discs Genar-Hofoen knew were the equivalents of medals and decorations, and the associated portraits of particularly impressive game-animals killed and rivals seriously maimed. A group of discreetly blank portrait discs indicated the females of other clans Fivetide could honourably claim to have successfully impregnated; the discs edged with precious metals bore witness to those who had put up a struggle. Colours and patterns on the sashes indicated Fivetide's clan, rank and regiment (which was what the Diplomatic Force, to which Fivetide belonged, basically was . . . a point not wisely ignored by any species who wished to have – or just found themselves having – any dealings with the Affront).

Fivetide pirouetted, gas sac swelling and buoying him up so that he rose above the spongy surface of the nest space, limbs dangling, taking hardly any of his weight. 'Am I not . . . resplendent?' The gelfield suit's translator decided that the adjective Fivetide had chosen to describe himself should be rendered with a florid rolling of the syllables involved, making the Affronter officer sound like an overly stagey actor.

'Positively intimidating,' Genar-Hofoen agreed.

'Thank you!' Fivetide said, sinking down again so that his eye stalks were level with the human's face. The stalks' gaze rose and dipped, looking the man up and down. 'Your own apparel is . . . different, at long last, and, I'm sure, most smart by the standards of your own people.'

The posture of the Affronter's eye stalks indicated that he found something highly pleasing in this statement; probably Fivetide was congratulating himself on being incredibly diplomatic.

'Thank you, Fivetide,' Genar-Hofoen said, bowing. He thought himself rather overdressed. There was the gelfield suit itself of course, so much a second skin it was possible to forget he wore it all. Normally the suit was nowhere more than a centimetre thick and averaged only half that, yet it could keep him comfortable in environments even more extreme than that required for Affronter life.

Unfortunately, some idiot had let slip that the Culture tested such suits by Displacing them into the magma chambers of active volcanoes and letting them pop out again (not true; the laboratory tests were rather more demanding, though it had been done once and it was just the sort of thing a show-off Culture manufactory would do to impress people). This was definitely not the kind of information to bandy about in the presence of beings as inquisitive and physically exuberant as Affronters; it only put ideas into their minds, and while the Affront habitat Genar-Hofoen lived within didn't re-create conditions on a planet to the extent that it had volcanoes, there had been a couple of times after Fivetide had asked the human to confirm the volcano story when he'd thought he'd caught the Diplomatic Force officer looking at him oddly, exactly as though he was trying to work out what natural phenomena or piece of apparatus he had access to he could use to test out this remarkable and intriguing protectivity.

The gelfield suit possessed something called a node-distributed brain which was capable of translating with seeming effortlessness every nuance of Genar-Hofoen's speech to the Affronters and vice versa, as well as effectively rendering any other sonic, chemical or electromagnetic signal into human-meaningful information.

Unhappily, the processing power required for this sort of technical gee-whizzery meant that according to Culture convention the suit had to be sentient. Genar-Hofoen had insisted on a model with the intelligence fixed at the lower limit of the acceptable intellectual range, but it still meant that the suit literally had a mind of its own (even if it was 'node-distributed', – one of those technical terms Genar-Hofoen took some pride in having no idea concerning the meaning of). The result was a device which was almost as much a metaphorical pain to live with as it was in a literal sense a pleasure to live within; it looked after you perfectly but it couldn't help constantly reminding you of the fact. Typical Culture, thought Genar-Hofoen.

Ordinarily Genar-Hofoen had the suit appear milkily silver to an Affronter over most of its surface while keeping the hands and head transparent.

Only the eyes had never looked quite right; they had to bulge out a bit if he was to be able to blink normally. As a result he usually wore sunglasses when he went out, which did seem a little incongruous, submerged in the dim photochemical fog characteristic of the atmosphere a hundred kilometres beneath the sun-lit cloud-tops of the Affront's home world, but which were useful as a prop.

On top of the suit he usually wore a gilet with pockets for gadgets, gifts and bribes and a crotch-cupping hip holster containing a couple of antique but impressive-looking hand guns. In terms of offensive capability the pistols provided a sort of minimum level of respectability for Genar-Hofoen; without them no Affronter could possibly allow themselves to be seen taking so puny an outworlder seriously.

For the regimental dinner, Genar-Hofoen had reluctantly accepted the advice of the module in which he lived and dressed in what it assured him was a most fetching outfit of knee boots, tight trousers, short jacket and long cloak – worn off the shoulder – and (in addition to an even bigger pair of pistols than usual) had slung over his back a matched pair of what the module assured him were three-millimetre-calibre Heavy Micro Rifles, two millennia old but still in full working order, and very long and gleamingly impressive. He had balked at the tall, drum-shaped much betassled hat the module had suggested and they'd compromised on a dress/armoured half-helm which made it look as though something with six long metallic fingers was cradling his head from behind. Naturally, each article in this outfit was covered in its own equivalent of a gelfield, protecting it from the coldly corrosive pressure of the Affronter environment, though the module had insisted that if he wanted to fire the micro rifles for politeness' sake, they would function perfectly well.

'Sire!' yelped the eunuch juvenile waiter, skittering to a stop on the nest-space surface at Fivetide's side. Cradled in three of its limbs was a large tray full of transparent, multi-walled flasks of various sizes.

'What?' yelled Fivetide.

'The alien guest's foodstuffs, sir!'

Fivetide extended a tentacle and rummaged around on the tray, knocking things over. The waiter watched the containers topple, fall and roll on the tray it held with an expression of wide-eyed terror Genar-Hofoen needed no ambassadorial training to recognise. The genuine danger to the waiter of any of the containers breaking was probably small – implosions produced relatively little shrapnel and the Affronter-poisonous contents would freeze too quickly to present much of a danger – but the punishment awaiting a waiter who made so public a display of its incompetence was probably in proportion to that conspicuousness and the creature was right to be concerned. 'What is this?' Fivetide demanded, holding up a spherical flask three-quarters full of liquid and shaking it vigorously in front of the eunuch juvenile's beak. 'Is this a drink? Is it? Well?'

'I don't know, sir!' the waiter wailed. 'It – it looks like it is.'

'Imbecile,' muttered Fivetide, then presented the flask gracefully to Genar-Hofoen. 'Honoured guest,' he said. 'Please; tell us if our efforts please you.'

Genar-Hofoen nodded and accepted the flask.

Fivetide turned on the waiter. '*Well?*' he shouted. 'Don't just *float* there, you moron; take the rest to the Savage-Talker Battalion table!' He flicked a tentacle towards the waiter, who flinched spectacularly. Its gas sac deflated and it ran across the floor membrane for the banqueting area of the nest space, dodging the Affronters gradually making their way in that direction.

Fivetide turned briefly to acknowledge the greeting slap of a fellow Diplomatic Force officer, then rotated back, produced a bulb of fluid from one of the pockets on his uniform and clinked it carefully against the flask Genar-Hofoen held. 'To the future of Affront-Culture relations,' he rumbled. 'May our friendship be long and our wars be short!' Fivetide squeezed the fluid into his mouth beak.

'So short you could miss them entirely,' Genar-Hofoen said tiredly, more because it was the sort of thing a Culture ambassador was supposed to say rather than because he sincerely meant it. Fivetide snorted derisively and dodged briefly to one side, apparently attempting to stick one tentacle-end up the anus of a passing Fleet Captain, who wrestled the tentacle aside and snapped his beak aggressively before joining in Fivetide's laughter and exchanging the heartfelt hellos and thunderous tentacle-slaps of dear friends. There would be a lot of this sort of stuff this evening, Genar-Hofoen knew. The dinner was an all-male gathering and therefore likely to be fairly boisterous even by Affronter standards.

Genar-Hofoen put the flask's nozzle to his mouth; the gelfield suit attached itself to the nozzle, equalised pressures, opened the flask's seal and then – as Genar-Hofoen tipped his head back – had what for the suit's brain was a good long think before it permitted the liquid inside to wash through it and into the man's mouth and throat.

~ *Fifty-fifty water/alcohol plus traces of partially toxic herb-like chemicals; closest to Leisetsiker spirit,* said a voice in Genar-Hofoen's head. ~ *If I were you I'd by-pass it.*

~ If you were me, suit, you'd welcome inebriation just to mitigate the effects of having to suffer your intimate embrace, Genar-Hofoen told the thing as he drank.

~ *Oh, we're in tetchy mode are we?* said the voice.

~ I don it with your good self.

'It is good, by your bizarre criteria?' Fivetide inquired, eye stalks nodding at the flask.

Genar-Hofoen nodded as the drink warmed its way down his throat to his stomach. He coughed, which had the effect of making the gelfield ball out round his mouth like silvery chewing gum for a moment – something which he knew Fivetide thought was the second funniest thing a human could do in a gelfield suit, only beaten for amusement value by a sneeze. 'Unhealthy and poisonous,' Genar-Hofoen told the Affronter. 'Perfect copy. My compliments to the chemist.'

'I'll pass them on,' Fivetide said, crushing his drinking bulb and flicking it casually at a passing servant. 'Come now,' he said, taking the human by the hand again. 'Let's to table; my stomach's as empty as a coward's bowels before battle.'

'No no *no*, you have to *flick* it, like this, you stupid human, or the scratchounds'll get it. Watch . . .'

Affronter formal dinners were held round a collection of giant circular tables anything up to fifteen metres across, each of which looked down into a bait-pit where animal fights took place between and during courses.

In the old days, at banquets held by the military and within the higher reaches of Affront society, contests between groups of captured aliens had been a particular and reasonably regular highlight, despite the fact that mounting such fights was often hideously expensive and fraught with technical complications due to the different chemistries and pressures involved. (Not to mention frequently presenting a very real danger to the observing dinner guests; who could forget the ghastly explosion at the Deepscars' table five back in '334, when every single guest had met a messy but honourable end due to the explosion of a highly pressurised bait-pit domed to simulate the atmosphere of a gas-giant?) Indeed, amongst the people who really mattered it was one of the most frequently voiced objections to the Affront's membership of the informal association of other space-faring species that having to be nice to other, lesser species – rather than giving the brutes a chance to prove their mettle against the glorious force of Affront arms – had resulted in a distinct dulling of the average society dinner.

Still, on really special occasions these days the fights would be between two Affronters with a dispute of a suitably dishonourable nature, or between criminals. Such contests usually required that the protagonists be hobbled, tied together, and armed with sliver-knives scarcely more substantial than hat pins, thus ensuring that the fights didn't end too quickly. Genar-Hofoen had never been invited to one of those and didn't expect he ever would be; it wasn't the sort of thing one let an alien witness, and besides, the competition for seats was scarcely less ferocious than the spectacle everyone desired to witness.

For this dinner – held to commemorate the eighteen hundred and eighty-fifth anniversary of the Affront's first decent space-battle against enemies worthy of the name – the entertainment was arranged to bear some relationship to the dishes being served, so that the first fish course was accompanied by the partial flooding of the pit with ethane and the introduction into it of specially bred fighting fish. Fivetide took great pleasure in describing to the human the unique nature of the fish, which were equipped with mouth parts so specialised the fish could not feed normally and had to be raised leeching vital fluids from *another* type of fish bred specially to fit into their jaws.

The second course was of small edible animals which to Genar-Hofoen appeared furry and arguably even cute. They raced round a trench-track set into the top of the pit at the inner edge of the circular table, pursued by something long and slithery looking with a lot of teeth at each end. The cheering, hooting Affronters roared, thumped the tables, exchanged bets and insults, and stabbed at the little creatures with long forks while shovelling cooked, prepared versions of the same animals into their beaks.

Scratchounds made up the main course, and while two sets of the animals – each about the size of a corpulent human but eight-limbed – slashed and tore at each other with razor-sharp prosthetic jaw implants and strap-claws, diced scratchound was served on huge trenchers of compacted vegetable matter. The Affronters considered this the highlight of the whole banquet; one was finally allowed to use one's miniature harpoon – quite the most impressive-looking utensil in each place setting – to impale chunks of meat from the trenchers of one's fellow diners and – with the skilful flick of the attached cable which Fivetide was now trying to teach the human – transfer it to one's own trencher, beak or tentacle without losing it to the scratchounds in the pit, having it intercepted by another dinner guest en route or losing the thing entirely over the top of one's gas sac.

'The beauty of it is,' Fivetide said, throwing his harpoon at the trencher of an Admiral distracted by a failed harpoon strike of his own, 'that the clearest target is the one furthest away.' He grunted and flicked, snapping the piece of speared scratchound up and away from the other Affronter's place an instant before the officer to the Admiral's right could intercept the prize. The morsel sailed through the air in an elegant trajectory that ended with Fivetide barely having to rise from his place to snap his beak shut on it. He swivelled left and right, acknowledging appreciative applause in the form of whip-snapped tentacles, then settled back into the padded Y-shaped bracket that served as a seat. 'You see?' he said, making an obvious swallowing motion and spitting out the harpoon and its cable.

'I see,' Genar-Hofoen said, still slowly re-coiling the harpoon cable from his last attempt. He sat to Fivetide's right in a Y-bracket place modified simply by placing a board across its prongs. His feet dangled over the debris trench which circled the perimeter of the table, and which the suit assured him was reeking in the manner approved by Affronter gourmets. He flinched and dodged to one side, nearly falling off the seat, as a harpoon sailed by to his left, narrowly missing him.

Genar-Hofoen acknowledged the laughter and exaggerated apologies from the Affronter officer five along the table who had been aiming at Fivetide's plate, and politely gathered up the

harpoon and cable and passed it back. He returned to picking at the
miniature pieces of indifferent food in the pressurised containers in
front of him, transferring them to his mouth with a gelfield utensil
shaped like a little four-fingered hand, his legs swinging over the
debris trench. He felt like a child dining with adults.

'Nearly got *you* there, eh, human? Ha ha ha!' roared the
Diplomatic Force colonel his other side from Fivetide. He slapped
Genar-Hofoen on the back with a tentacle and threw him half off
the seat and onto the table. 'Oops!' the colonel said, and jerked
Genar-Hofoen back with a teeth-rattling wrench.

Genar-Hofoen smiled politely and picked his sunglasses off
the table. The Diplomatic Force colonel went by the name of
Quicktemper. It was the sort of title which the Culture found
depressingly common amongst Affronter diplomats.

Fivetide had explained the problem was that certain sections of
the Affront Old Guard were slightly ashamed their civilisation had
a Diplomatic service at all and so tried to compensate for what
they were worried might look to other species suspiciously like
a symptom of weakness by ensuring that only the most aggressive and xenophobic Affronters became diplomats, to forestall
anybody forming the dangerously preposterous idea the Affront
were going soft.

'Go on, man! Have another throw! Just because you can't eat
the damn stuff, you shouldn't let that keep you from joining in
the fun!'

A harpoon thrown from the far side of the table sailed over the
pit towards Fivetide's trencher. The Affronter intercepted it deftly
and threw it back, laughing uproariously. The harpoon's owner
ducked just in time and a passing drinks waiter got it in the sac
with a yelp and a hiss of escaping gas.

Genar-Hofoen looked at the lumps of flesh lying on Fivetide's
trencher. 'Why can't I just harpoon stuff off your plate?' he
asked.

Fivetide jerked upright. 'Your *neighbour's* plate?' he bellowed.
'That's cheating, Genar-Hofoen, or a particularly insulting invitation to a duel! Bugger me, what sort of manners do they *teach* you
in that Culture?'

'I do beg your pardon,' Genar-Hofoen said.

'Given,' Fivetide said, nodding his eye stalks, re-winding his
harpoon cable, lifting a piece of meat from his own plate to his

beak, reaching for a drink and drumming one tentacle on the table with everybody else as one of the scratchounds got another on its back and bit its neck out. 'Good play! Good play! Seven; that's my dog! Mine; I bet on that! I did! Me! You see, Gastrees? I told you! Ha ha ha!'

Genar-Hofoen shook his head slightly, grinning to himself. In all his life he had never been anywhere as unequivocally alien as here, inside a giant torus of cold, compressed gas orbiting a black hole – itself in orbit around a brown dwarf body light years from the nearest star – its exterior studded with ships – most of them the jaggedly bulbous shapes of Affront craft – and full, in the main, of happy, space-faring Affronters and their collection of associated victim-species. Still, he had never felt so thoroughly at home.

~ *Genar-Hofoen; it's me, Scopell-Afranqui*, said another voice in Genar-Hofoen's head. It was the module, speaking through the suit. ~ *I've an urgent message.*

~ Can't it wait? Genar-Hofoen thought. ~ I'm kind of busy here with matters of excruciatingly correct dining etiquette.

~ *No, it can't. Can you get back here, please? Immediately.*

~ What? No, I'm not leaving. Good grief, are you mad? I only just got here.

~ *No you didn't; you left me eighty minutes ago and you're already on the main course at that animal circus dressed up as a meal; I can see what's going on relayed through that stupid suit—*

~ *Typical!* the suit interjected.

~ *Shut up*, said the module. ~ *Genar-Hofoen; are you coming back here now or not?*

~ Not.

~ *Well then, let me check out the communication priorities here . . . Okay. Now the current state of the—*

'—bet, human-friend?' Fivetide said, slapping a tentacle on the table in front of Genar-Hofoen.

'Eh? A bet?' Genar-Hofoen said, quickly replaying in his head what the Affronter had been saying.

'Fifty sucks on the next from the red door!' Fivetide roared, glancing at his fellow officers on both sides.

Genar-Hofoen slapped the table with his hand. 'Not enough!' he shouted, and felt the suit amplify his translated voice accordingly. Several eye stalks turned in his direction. 'Two hundred on the blue hound!'

Fivetide, who was from a family of the sort that would describe itself as comfortably off rather than rich, and to whom fifty suckers was half a month's disposable income, flinched microscopically, then slapped another tentacle down on top of the first one. 'Scumpouch alien!' he shouted theatrically. 'You imply that a measly two hundred is a fit bet for an officer of my standing? Two-fifty!'

'Five hundred!' Genar-Hofoen yelled, slapping down his other arm.

'Six hundred!' Fivetide hollered, thumping down a third limb. He looked at the others, exchanging knowing looks and sharing in the general laughter; the human had been out-limbed.

Genar-Hofoen twisted in his seat and brought his left leg up to stamp its booted heel onto the table surface. 'A thousand, damn your cheap hide!'

Fivetide flicked a fourth tentacle onto the limbs already on the table in front of Genar-Hofoen, which was starting to look crowded. 'Done!' the Affronter roared. 'And think yourself lucky I took pity on you to the extent of not upping the bet again and having you unseat yourself into the debris-pit, you microscopic cripple!' Fivetide laughed louder and looked round the other officers near by. They laughed too, some of the juniors dutifully, some of the others – friends and close colleagues of Fivetide's – overloudly, with a sort of vicarious desperation; the bet was of a size that could get the average fellow into terrible trouble with his mess, his bank, his parents, or all three. Others again looked on with the sort of expression Genar-Hofoen had learned to recognise as a smirk.

Fivetide enthusiastically refilled every nearby drinking bulb and started the whole table signing the Let's-bake-the-pit-master-over-a-slow-fire-if-he-doesn't-get-a-move-on song.

~ Right, Genar-Hofoen thought. ~ Module; you were saying?

~ *That was a rather intemperate bet, if I may say so, Genar-Hofoen. A thousand! Fivetide can't afford that sort of money if he loses, and we don't want to be seen to be too profligate with our funds if he wins.*

Genar-Hofoen permitted himself a small grin. What a perfect way of annoying everybody. – Tough, he thought. So; the message?

~ *I think I can squirt it through to what passes as a brain in your suit—*

~ *I heard that*, said the suit.

~ *without our friends picking it up, Genar-Hofoen*, the module told him. ~ *Ramp up on some* quicken *and—*

~ *Excuse me*, said the suit. ~ *I think Byr Genar-Hofoen may want to think twice before glanding a drug as strong as* quicken *in the present circumstances. He is my responsibility when he's out of your immediate locality, after all, Scopell-Afranqui. I mean, be fair. It's all very well you sitting up there—*

~ *Keep out of this, you vacuous membrane*, the module told the suit.

~ *What? How dare you!*

~ Will you two *shut up!* Genar-Hofoen told them, having to stop himself from shouting out loud. Fivetide was saying something about the Culture to him and he'd already missed the first part of it while the two machines were filling his head with their squabble.

'. . . can be as exciting as this, eh, Genar-Hofoen?'

'Indeed not,' he shouted over the noise of the song. He lowered the gelfield utensil into one of the food containers and raised the food to his lips. He smiled and made a show of bulging his cheeks out while he ate. Fivetide belched, shoved a piece of meat half the size of a human head into his beak and turned back to the fun in the animal pit, where the fresh pair of scratchounds were still circling warily, sizing each other up. They looked pretty evenly matched, Genar-Hofoen thought.

~ *May I speak now?* said the module.

~ Yes, Genar-Hofoen thought. ~ Now, what is it?

~ *As I said, an urgent message.*

~ From?

~ *The GSV* Death And Gravity.

~ Oh? Genar-Hofoen was mildly impressed. ~ I thought the old scoundrel wasn't talking to me.

~ *As did we all. Apparently it is. Look, do you want this message or not?*

~ All right, but why do I have to gland *quicken*?

~ *Because it's a long message, of course . . . in fact it's an interactive message; an entire semantic-context signal-set with attached mind-state abstract capable of replying to your questions, and if you listened to the whole thing in real time you'd still be sitting there with a vacant expression on your face by the time your jovial hosts got to the hunt-the-waiter course. And I* did *say it was urgent. Genar-Hofoen, are you paying attention here?*

~ I'm *paying* fucking attention. But come on; can't you just tell me what the message is? Précis it.

~ *The message is for you, not me, Genar-Hofoen. I haven't looked at it; it'll be stream-deciphered as I transmit it.*

~ Okay, okay, I'm glanded up; shoot.

~ *I still say it's a bad idea* . . . muttered the gelfield suit.

~ *Shut UP!* the module said. ~ *Sorry, Genar-Hofoen. Here is the text of the message*:

~ *from GSV* Death And Gravity *to Seddun-Braijsa Byr Fruel Genar-Hofoen dam Ois, message begins,* the module said in its Official voice. Then another voice took over:

~ *Genar-Hofoen, I won't pretend I'm happy to be communicating with you again; however, I have been asked to do so by certain of those whose opinions and judgement I respect and admire and hence deem the situation to be such that I would be derelict in my duties if I did not oblige to the utmost of my abilities.*

Genar-Hofoen performed the mental equivalent of sighing and putting his chin in his hands while – thanks to the *quicken* now coursing through his central nervous system – everything around him seemed to happen in slow motion. The General Systems Vehicle *Death and Gravity* had been a long-winded old bore when he'd known it and it sounded like nothing had happened in the interim to alter its conversational style. Even its voice still sounded the same; pompous and monotonous at the same time.

~ *Accordingly, and with due recognition of your habitually contrary, argumentative and wilfully perverse nature I am communicating with you by sending this message in the form of an interactive signal. I see you are currently one of our ambassadors to that childishly cruel band of upstart ruffians known as the Affront; I have the unhappy feeling that while this may have been envisaged as a kind of subtle punishment for you, you will in fact have adapted with some relish to the environment if not the task, which I assume you will dispatch with your usual mixture of off-handed carelessness and casual self-interest—*

~ If this signal is interactive, interrupted Genar-Hofoen, ~ can I ask you to get to the fucking point?

He watched the two scratchounds tense together in slo-mo on either side of the pit.

~ *The point is that your hosts will have to be asked to deprive themselves of your company for a while.*

~ What? Why? Genar-Hofoen thought, immediately suspicious.

~ *The decision has been made – and I hasten to establish that I had no part in this – that your services are required elsewhere.*

~ Where? For how long?

~ *I can't tell you where exactly, or for how long.*

~ Make a stab at it.

~ *I cannot and will not.*

~ Module, end this message.

~ *Are you sure?* asked Scopell-Afranqui.

~ *Wait!*, said the voice of the GSV. ~ *Will it satisfy you if I say that we may need about eighty days of your time?*

~ No it won't. I'm quite happy here. I've been bounced into all sorts of Special Circumstances shit in the past on the strength of a Hey-come-and-do-one-little-job-for-us come-on line. (This was not in fact perfectly true; Genar-Hofoen had only ever acted for SC once before, but he'd known – or at least heard of – plenty of people who'd got more than they'd expected when they'd worked for what was in effect the Contact section's espionage and dirty tricks department.)

~ *I did not—*

~ Plus I've got a job to do here, Genar-Hofoen interrupted. ~ I've got another audience with the Grand Council in a month to tell them to be nicer to their neighbours or we're going to think about slapping their paddles. I want details of this exciting new opportunity or you can shove it.

~ *I did not say that I am speaking on behalf of Special Circumstances.*

~ Are you denying that you are?

~ *Not as such, but—*

~ So stop fucking around. Who the hell else is going to start hauling a gifted and highly effective ambassador off—?

~ *Genar-Hofoen, we are wasting time here.*

~ We?, Genar-Hofoen thought, watching the two scratchounds launch themselves at each other slowly. ~ Never mind. Go on.

~ *The task required of you is, apparently, a delicate one, which is why I personally regard you as being utterly unsuited to it, and as*

such it would be foolish to entrust the full details either to myself,
to your module, your suit or indeed to you until all these details
are required.

~ There you are; that's exactly what you can shove; all that SC
need-to-know crap. I don't care how fucking delicate the task is,
I'm not even going to consider it until I know what's involved.

The scratchounds were in mid-pounce now, both of them
twisting as they leapt. Shit, thought Genar-Hofoen; this might
be one of those scratchound bouts where the whole thing was
decided on the initial lunge, depending entirely on which beast
got its teeth into the neck of the other first.

~ *What is required,* said the message, with a fair approximation
of the way the *Death And Gravity* had always sounded when
it was exasperated, *is eighty days of your time, ninety-nine to*
ninety-nine point nine-plus per cent of which you will spend
doing nothing more onerous or demanding than being carried
from point A to point B; the first part of your journey will be
spent travelling, in considerable comfort, I imagine, aboard the
Affronter ship which we will ask (or rather pay, probably) them
to put at your disposal, the second part will be spent in guaranteed
comfort aboard a Culture GCU and will be followed by a short
visit aboard another Culture vessel whereupon the task we would
ask of you will actually be accomplished – and when I say a short
visit, I mean that it may be possible for you to carry out what is
required of you within an hour, and that certainly the assignment
should take no longer than a day. Then you will make the return
journey to take up wherever you left off with our dear friends and
allies the Affront. I take it all that doesn't sound too much like
hard work, does it?

The scratchounds were meeting in the air a metre above the
centre of the bait-pit, their jaws aimed as best they could at each
other's throats. It was still a little hard to tell, but Genar-Hofoen
didn't think it was looking too good for Fivetide's animal.

~ Yeah yeah yeah, well I've heard all this sort of thing before,
D and G. What's in it for me? Why the hell should I—? Oh,
fuck . . .

~ *What?* said the *Death And Gravity*'s message.

But Genar-Hofoen's attention was elsewhere.

The two scratchounds met and locked, falling to the floor of the
bait-pit in a tangle of slowly thrashing limbs. The blue-collared

animal had its jaws clamped around the throat of the red-collared one. Most of the Affronters were starting to cheer. Fivetide and his supporters were screaming.

Shit.

~ Suit? Genar-Hofoen thought.

~ *What is it?* said the gelfield. ~ *I thought you were talking to—?*

~ Never mind that now. See that blue scratchound?

~ *Can't take my or your eyes off the damn thing.*

~ Effectorise the fucker; get it off the other one.

~ *I can't do that! That would be cheating!*

~ Fivetide's arse is hanging way out the merry-go-round on this, suit. Do it now or take personal responsibility for a major diplomatic incident. Up to you.

~ *What? But—!*

~ Effectorise it now, suit. Come on; I know that last upgrade let you sneak it under their monitors. Oh! Look at that. Ow! Can't you just *feel* those prosthetics round your neck? Fivetide must be kissing his diplomatic career goodbye right now; probably already working out a way to challenge me to a duel. After that, doesn't really matter if I kill him or he kills me; probably come to war between—

~ *All right! All right! There!*

There was a buzzing sensation on top of Genar-Hofoen's right shoulder. The red scratchound jerked, the blue one doubled up around its midriff and loosened its grip. The red-collared beast wriggled out from underneath the other and, twisting, turned on the other beast and immediately reversed the situation, fastening its prosthetic jaws around the throat of the blue-collared animal. At Genar-Hofoen's side, still in slow motion, Fivetide was starting to rise into the air.

~ Right, D and G, what were you saying?

~ *What was the delay? What were you doing?*

~ Never mind. Like you said, time's a wasting. Get on with it.

~ *I assume it is reward you seek. What do you want?*

~ Golly, let me think. Can I have my own ship?

~ *I understand that to be negotiable.*

~ I'll bet.

~ *You may have whatever you want. There. Will that do?*

~ Oh, of course.

~ *Genar-Hofoen, please. I beg you; say you will do this thing.*

~ D and G, you're *begging* me? Genar-Hofoen asked with a laugh in his thought, as the blue-collared scratchound writhed hopelessly in the other beast's jaws and Fivetide started to turn to him.

~ *Yes, I am! Now will you agree? Time is of the essence!*

From the corner of one eye, Genar-Hofoen watched one of Fivetide's limbs begin to flip towards him. He readied his slow-reacting body for the blow.

~ I'll think about it.

~ *But—!*

~ Quit that signal, suit. Tell the module not to wait up. Now, suit – command instruction: take yourself off-line until I call on you.

Genar-Hofoen halted the effects of the *quicken*. He smiled and sighed a happy sigh as Fivetide's celebratory blow landed with a teeth-rattling thud on his back and the Culture lost a thousand suckers. Could be a fun evening.

IV

The horror came for the commandant again that night, in the grey area that was the half-light from a full moon. It was worse this time.

In the dream, he rose from his camp bed in the pale light of dawn. Down the valley, the chimneys above the charnel wagons belched dark smoke. Nothing else in the camp was moving. He walked between the silent tents and under the guard towers to the funicular, which took him up through the forests to the glaciers.

The light was blinding white and the cold, thin air rasped the back of his throat. The wind buffeted him, raising veils of snow and ice that shifted across the fractured surface of the great river of ice, contained between the jagged banks of the rock-black and snow-white mountains.

The commandant looked around. They were quarrying the deep western face now; it was the first time he had seen this latest site. The face itself lay inside a great bowl they had blasted in the glacier; men, machines and drag-lines moved like insects in the bottom of the vast cup of shining ice. The face was pure white except for a speckling of black dots which from this distance appeared just like boulders. It looked dangerously steep, he thought, but cutting it at a shallower angle would have taken longer, and they were forever being hurried along by headquarters . . .

At the top of the inclined ramp where the drag lines released their hooked cargoes, a train waited, smoke drifting blackly across the blindingly white landscape. Guards stamped their feet, engineers stood in animated discussion by the winch engine and a caravan shack disgorged another shift of stackers fresh from a break. A sledge full of face-workers was being lowered down the huge gash in the ice; he could make out the sullen, pinched faces of the men, bundled in uniforms and clothes that were little better than rags.

There was a rumble, and a vibration beneath his feet.

He looked round to the ice face again to see the entire eastern half of it crumbling away, collapsing and falling with majestic slowness in billowing clouds of whiteness onto the tiny black dots of the workers and guards below. He watched the little figures turn and run from the rushing avalanche of ice as it pressed down through the air and along the surface towards them.

A few made it. Most did not, disappearing under the huge white wave, rubbed out amongst that chalky, glittering turmoil. The noise was a roar so deep he felt it in his chest.

He ran along the lip of the face-cut to the top of the inclined plane; everybody was shouting and running around. The entire bottom of the bowl was filling with the white mist of the kicked-up snow and pulverised ice, obscuring the still-running survivors just as the ice-fall itself had those it had buried.

The winch engine laboured, making a high, screeching noise. The drag lines had stopped. He ran on to the knot of people gathering near the inclined plane.

I know what happens here, he thought. *I know what happens to me. I remember the pain. I see the girl. I know this bit. I know what happens. I must stop running. Why don't I stop running? Why can't I stop? Why can't I wake up?*

As he got to the others, the strain on the trapped drag line – still being pulled by the winch engine – proved too much. The steel hawser parted somewhere down inside the bowl of mist with a noise like a shot. The steel cable came hissing and sizzing up through the air, snaking and wriggling as it ripped up the slope towards the lip, loosing most of its grisly cargo from its hooks as it came, like drops of ice off a whip.

He screamed to the men at the top of the inclined plane, and tripped, falling onto his face in the snow.

Only one of the engineers dropped in time.

Most of the rest were cut neatly in half by the scything hawser, falling slowly to the snow in bloody sprays. Loops of the hawser smacked off the railway engine with a thunderous clanging noise and wrapped themselves around the winch housing as though with relief; other coils thumped heavily to the snow.

Something hit his upper leg with the force of a fully swung sledgehammer, breaking his bones in a cataclysm of pain. The impact rolled him over and over in the snow while the bones ground and dug and pierced; it went on for what felt like half a day. He came to rest in the snow, screaming. He was face-to-face with the thing that had hit him.

It was one of the bodies the drag line had flicked off as it tore up the slope, another corpse they had hacked and loosened and pulled like a rotten tooth from the new face of the glacier that morning, a dead witness that it was their duty to discover and remove with all dispatch and secrecy to the charnel wagons in the valley below to be turned from an accusatory body to innocent smoke and ash. What had hit him and shattered his leg was one of the bodies which had been dumped in the glacier half a generation ago, when the enemies of the Race had been expunged from the newly conquered territories.

The scream forced its way out of his lungs like something desperate to be born to the freezing air, like something aching to join the screams he could hear spread around him near the lip of the inclined plane.

The commandant's breath was gone; he stared into the rock-hard face of the body that had hit him and he sobbed for breath to scream again. It was a child's face; a girl's.

The snow burned his face. His breath would not come back. His leg was a burning brand of pain lighting up his whole body.

But not his eyes. The view began to dim.

Why is this happening to me? Why won't it stop? Why can't I stop it? Why can't I wake up? What makes me re-live these terrible memories?

Then the pain and the cold went away, seemed to be taken away, and another kind of coldness came upon him, and he found himself . . . thinking. Thinking about all that had happened. Reviewing, judging.

. . . In the desert we burned them immediately. None of this sloppiness. Was it some attempt at poetry, to bury them in the glacier? Interred where they were so far up the ice sheet, their bodies would stay in the ice for centuries. Buried too deep for anyone to find without the killing effort we had to put into it. Did our leaders begin to believe their own propaganda, that their rule would last a hundred lifetimes, and so started to think that far ahead? Could they see the melt-lakes below the glacier's ragged, dirty skirt, all those centuries from now, covered with the floating bodies released from the ice's grip? Did it start to worry them what people would think of them then? Having conquered all the present with such ruthlessness, did they embark on a campaign to defeat the future too, make it love them as we all pretend to?

. . . In the desert we burned them immediately. They came out in the long trains through the burning heat and the choking dust and the ones that hadn't died in the black trucks we offered copious water; no will could resist the thirst those baking days spent amongst death had built up in them.

They drank the poisoned water and died within hours. We incinerated the plundered bodies in solar furnaces, our offering to the insatiable sky gods of Race and Purity. And there seemed to be something pure about the way they were disposed of, as though their deaths gave them a nobility they could never have achieved in their mean, degraded lives. Their ashes fell like a lighter dust on the powderous emptiness of the desert, to be blown away together in the first storm.

The last furnace loads were the camp workers – gassed in their dormitories, mostly – and all the paperwork: every letter, every order, every requisition pad, stores sheet, file, note and memo. We were all searched, even I. Those the special police found hiding diaries were shot on the spot. Most of our effects went up in smoke, too. What we were allowed to keep had been searched so thoroughly we joked they had managed to remove each grain of sand from our uniforms, something the laundry had never been able to do.

We were split up and moved to different posts throughout the conquered territories. Reunions were not encouraged.

I thought of writing down what had happened – not to confess but to explain.

And we suffered, too. Not just in the physical conditions, though those were bad enough, but in our minds, in our consciences. There may have been a few brutes, a few monsters who gloried in it all (perhaps we kept a few murderers off the streets of our cities for all that time), but most of us went through intermittent agonies, wondering in moments of crisis if what we were doing was really right, even though in our hearts we knew it was.

So many of us had nightmares. The things we saw each day, the scenes we witnessed, the pain and terror; these things could not help but affect us.

Those we disposed of; their torment lasted a few days, maybe a month or two, then it was over as quickly and efficiently as we could make the process.

Our suffering has gone on for a generation.

I am proud of what I did. I wish it had not fallen to me to do what had to be done, but I am glad that I did it to the best of my capabilities, and I would do it again.

That was why I wanted to write down what had happened; to witness our belief and our dedication and our suffering.

I never did.

I am proud of that too.

He awoke and there was something inside his head.

He was back in reality, back in the present, back in the bedroom of his house in the retirement complex, near the sea; he could see the sunlight hitting the tiles of the balcony outside the room. His twinned hearts thumped, the scales had risen on his back, prickling him. His leg ached, echoing with the pain of that ancient injury on the glacier.

The dream had been the most vivid yet, and the longest, finally taking him to the ice-fall in the western face and the accident with the drag line (deep buried, that had been, in his memory, submerged beneath all the dread white weight of his remembered pain). As well as that, whatever he had experienced had gone beyond the normal course, the usual environment of dreams, propelled there by the reliving of the accident and the image of fighting for breath while he stared transfixed into the face of the dead girl.

He had found himself thinking, explaining, even justifying what he had done in his army career, in the most definitive part of his life.

And now he could feel something inside his head.

Whatever it was inside his head got him to close his eyes.

~ At last, it said. It was a deep, deliberately authoritative voice, its pronunciation almost too perfect.

At last? he thought. (*What was this?*)

~ I have the truth.

What truth? (*Who was this?*)

~ Of what you did. Your people.

What?

~ The evidence was everywhere; across the desert, caked in loam, lodged in plants, sunk to the bottom of lakes, and there in the cultural record too; the sudden vanishings of art works, changes in architecture and agriculture. There were a few hidden records – books, photographs, sound recordings, indices, which contradicted the re-written histories – but they still didn't directly explain why so many people, so many peoples seemed to vanish so suddenly, without any sign of assimilation.

What are you talking about? (*What* was *this in his head*?)

~ You would not believe what I am, commandant, but what I am talking about is a thing called genocide, and the proof thereof.

We did what had to be done!

~ Thank you, we've just been through all that. Your self-justifications have been noted.

I believed in what I did!

~ I know. You had the residual decency to question it occasionally, but in the end you did indeed believe in what you were doing. That is not an excuse, but it is a point.

Who are you? What gives you the right to crawl inside my brains?

~ My name would be something like *Grey Area* in your language. What gives me the right to crawl inside your brains, as you put it, is the same thing that gave you the right to do what you did to those you murdered; power. Superior power. *Vastly* superior power, in my case. However, I have been called away and I have to leave you now, but I shall return in a few months and I'll be continuing my investigations then. There are still enough of you left to construct a more . . . triangulated case.

What? he thought, trying to open his eyes.

~ Commandant, there is nothing worse I can wish upon you than to be what you already are, but you might care to reflect upon this while I'm gone:

Instantly, he was back in the dream.

He fell through the bed, the single ice-white sheet tore beneath him and tumbled him into a bottomless tank of blood; he fell down through it to light, and the desert, and the rail line through the sands; he fell into one of the trains, into one of the trucks and was there with his broken leg amongst the stinking dead and the moaning living, jammed in between the excrement-covered bodies with the weeping sores and the buzz of the flies and the white-hot rage of the thirst inside him.

He died in the cattle truck, after an infinity of agony. There was time for the briefest of glimpses of his room in the retirement complex. Even in his still-shocked, pain-maddened state he had the time and the presence of mind to think that while it felt as though a day at least must have passed while he had been submerged in the torture-dream nevertheless everything in the bedroom looked just as it had earlier. Then he was dragged under again.

He awoke entombed inside the glacier, dying of cold. He had been shot in the head but it had only paralysed him. Another endless agony.

He had a second impression of the retirement home; still the sunlight was at the same angle. He had not imagined it was possible to feel so much pain, not in such a time, not in a life-time, not in a hundred lifetimes. He found there was just time to flex his body and move a finger's width across the bed before the dream resumed.

Then he was in the hold of a ship, crammed in with thousands of other people in the darkness, surrounded again by stink and filth and screams and pain. He was already half dead two days later when the sea valves opened and those still left alive began to drown.

The cleaner found the old retired commandant twisted into a ball a little way short of the apartment's door the next morning. His hearts had given out.

The expression on his face was such that the retirement-home warden almost fainted and had to sit down quickly, but the doctor declared the end had probably been quick.

V

[tight beam, M16.4, tra. @n4.28.858.8893]
xGCU *Grey Area*
   oGSV *Honest Mistake*
There. I am on my way.
∞

   xGSV *Honest Mistake*
      oGCU *Grey Area*
   Not before time.
∞
There was work to be done.
∞

   More animal brains to be delved into?
∞
History to be unearthed. Truth to be discovered.
∞

   I would have thought that one of the last places one would have expected to find on any itinerary concerning the search for truth would be inside the minds of mere animals.
∞
When the mere animals concerned have orchestrated one of the most successful and total expungings of both a significant part of

their own species and every physical record regarding that act of genocide, one has remarkably little choice.

∞

   I'm sure no one would deny your application does you credit.

∞

Gosh, thanks. That must be why the other ships call me *Meatfucker*.

∞

   Absolutely.
   Well, let me wish you all the best with whatever it is our friends might require of you.

∞

Thank you.
My aim is to please . . .

∞

(End signal file.)

VI

He left a trail of weaponry and the liquefied remains of gambling chips. The two heavy micro rifles clattered to the absorber mat just outside the airlock door and the cloak fell just beyond them. The guns glinted in the soft light reflecting off gleaming wooden panels. The mercury gambling chips in his jacket pocket, exposed to the human-ambient heat of the module's interior, promptly melted. He felt the change happen, and stopped, mystified, to stare into his pockets. He shrugged, then turned his pockets inside out and let the mercury splash onto the mat. He yawned and walked on. Funny the module hadn't greeted him.

   The pistols bounced on the carpeted floor of the hall and lay beading with frost. He left the short jacket hanging on a piece of sculpture in the hall. He yawned again. It was not far off the time of habitat dawn. Very much time for bed. He rolled down the tops of the knee-boots and kicked them both down the corridor leading to the swimming pool.

   He was pulling down his trousers as he entered the module's

main social area, shuffling forward bent over and holding on to the wall as he cursed the garments and tried to kick them off without falling over.

There was somebody there. He stopped and stared.

It looked very much like his favourite uncle was sitting in one of the lounge's best seats.

Genar-Hofoen stood upright and swayed, staring through numerous blinks.

'Uncle Tishlin?' he said, squinting at the apparition. He leant on an antique cabinet and finally hauled his trousers off.

The figure – tall, white-maned and with a light smile playing on its craggily severe face – stood up and adjusted its long formal jacket. 'Just a pretend version, Byr,' the voice rumbled. The hologram put its head back and fixed him with a measuring, questioning look. 'They really do want you to do this thing for them, boy.'

Genar-Hofoen scratched his head and muttered something to the suit. It began to peel off around him.

'Will *you* tell me what the hell it actually *is*, Uncle?' he asked, stepping out of the gelfield and taking a deep breath of module air, more to annoy the suit than because the air tasted better. The suit gathered itself up into a head-sized ball and floated wordlessly away to clean itself.

The hologram of his uncle breathed out slowly and crossed its arms in a way Genar-Hofoen remembered from his early childhood.

'Put simply, Byr,' the image said, 'they want you to steal the soul of a dead woman.'

Genar-Hofoen stood there, quite naked, still swaying, still blinking.

'Oh,' he said, after a while.

2

Not Invented Here

I

Hup! . . . and here we are, waking up. Quick scan around, nothing immediately threatening, it would seem . . . Hmm. Floating in space. Odd. Nobody else around. That's funny. View's a bit degraded. Oh-oh, that's a bad sign. Don't feel quite right, either. Stuff missing here . . . Clock running way slow, like it's down amongst the electronics crap . . . Run full system check.

. . . Oh, good grief!

The drone drifted through the darkness of interstellar space. It really was alone. Profoundly, even frighteningly alone. It picked through the debris that had been its power, sensory and weapon systems, appalled at the wasteland it was discovering within itself. The drone felt weird. It knew who it was – it was Sisela Ytheleus 1/2, a type D4 military drone of the Explorer Ship *Peace Makes Plenty*, a vessel of the Stargazer Clan, part of the Fifth Fleet of the Zetetic Elench – but its real-time memories only began from the instant it had woken up here, a zillion klicks from anywhere, slap bang in the middle of nothing with the shit kicked out of it. What a *mess*! Who had done this? What had *happened* to it? Where were its memories? Where was its mind-state?

Actually it suspected it knew. It was functioning on the middle level of its five stepped mind-modes; the electronic.

Below lay an atomechanical complex and beneath that a bio-chemical brain. In theory the routes to both lay open; in practice both were compromised. The atomechanical mind wasn't respond-ing correctly to the system-state signals it was receiving, and the biochemical brain was simply a mush; either the drone had been doing some hard manoeuvring recently or it had been clobbered by something. It felt like dumping the whole biochemical unit into space now but it knew the cellular soup its final back-up mind-substrate had turned into might come in handy for something.

Above, where it *ought* to be right now, there were a couple of enormously wide conduits leading to the photonic nucleus and beyond that the true AI core. Both completely blocked off, and metaphorically plastered with warning signals. The equivalent of a single lit tell-tale adjacent to the photonic pipe indicated there was activity of some sort in there. The AI core was either dead, empty or just not saying.

The drone ran another systems-control check. It *seemed* to be in charge of the whole outfit, what was left of it. It wondered if the sensor and weaponry systems degradation was real. Perhaps it was an illusion; perhaps those units were in fact in perfect working order and under the control of one or both of the higher mind components. It dug deeper into the units' programming. No, it didn't look possible.

Unless the whole situation was a simulation. That was possible. A test: what would you do if you suddenly found yourself drifting alone in interstellar space, almost every system severely damaged, reduced to a level-three mind-state with no sign of help anywhere and no recollection how you got here or what happened to you? It *sounded* like a particularly nasty simulation problem; a nearly-worst-case scenario dreamt up by a Drone Training and Selection Board.

Well, there was no way of telling, and it had to act as though it was all real.

It kept looking around inside its own mind-state. *Ah ha.*

There were a couple of closed sub-cores intact within its electronic mind, sealed and labelled as potentially – though not probably – dangerous. There was a similar warning attached to the self-repair control-routine matrices. The drone let those be for the moment. It would check out everything else that it could before it started opening packages with what might prove to be nasty surprises inside.

Where the hell *was* it? It scanned the stars. A matrix of figures flashed into its consciousness. Definitely the middle of nowhere. The general volume was called the Upper Leaf-Swirl by most people; forty-five kilolights from galactic centre. The nearest star – fourteen standard light months away – was called Esperi, an old red giant which had long since swallowed up its complement of inner planets and whose insubstantial orb of gases now glowed dully upon a couple of distant, icy worlds and a distant cloud of comet nuclei. No life anywhere; just another boring, barren system like a hundred million others.

The general volume was one of the less well-visited and relatively uninhabited regions of the galaxy. Nearest major civilisation point; the Sagraeth system, forty light years away, with a stage-three lizardoid civilisation first contacted by the Culture a decade ago. Nothing special there. Voluminal influences/interests rated Creheesil 15%, Affront 10%, Culture 5% (the normal claimed minimum, the Culture's influence/interest equivalent of background radiation), and a smattering of investigations and flybys by twenty other civilisations making up a nominal 2%; otherwise not a place anybody was really interested in; a two-thirds forgotten, disregarded region of space. Never before directly investigated by the Elench, though there had been the usual deep-space remote scans from afar, showing nothing special. No clues there.

Date; n4.28.803, by the chronology the Elench still shared with the Culture. The drone's service log abstract recorded that it had been built as part of a matched pair by the *Peace Makes Plenty* in n4.13, shortly after the ship's own construction had been completed. Most recent entry; '28.725.500: ship leaving Tier habitat for a standard sweep-search of the outer reaches of the Upper Leaf-Swirl. The detailed service log was missing. The last flagged event the drone could find in its library dated from '28.802; a daily current affairs archive update. So had that been just yesterday, or could something have happened to its clock?

It scrutinised its damage reports and searched its memories. The damage profile equated to that caused by plasma fire, and – from the lack of obvious patterning – either an enormous plasma event very far away or plasma fire – possibly fusion-sourced – much closer but buffered in some way. A nearby plasma implosure was the most obvious example. Not something it could do itself. The ship could, though.

Its X-ray laser had been fired recently and its field-shields projectors had soaked up some leak-through damage. Consistent with what would have happened if something just like itself had attacked it. *Hmm.* One of a matched pair.

It thought. It searched. It could find no further mention of its twin.

It looked about itself, gauging its drift, and searching.

It was drifting at about two-eighty klicks a second, almost directly away from the Esperi system. In front of it – it focused all its damaged sensory capacity to peer ahead – nothing; it didn't appear to be aimed *at* anything.

Two-eighty klicks a second; that was somewhere just underneath the theoretical limit beyond which something of its mass would start to produce a relativistic trace on the surface of space-time, if one had perfect instrumentation. Now, was that a coincidence, or not? If not, it might have been slung out of the ship for some reason; Displaced, perhaps. It concentrated its senses backwards. No obvious point of origin, and nothing coming after it, either. Hint of something though.

The drone refocused, cursing its hopelessly degraded senses. Behind it, it found . . . gas, plasma, carbon. It widened the cone of its focus.

What it had discovered was an inflating shell of debris, drifting after it at a tenth of its speed. It ran a rewind of the debris shell's expansion; it originated at a point forty klicks behind the position where it had first woken up, eighteen fifty-three milliseconds ago.

Which implied it had been drifting totally unconscious for nearly half a second. *Scary*.

It scanned the distant shell of expanding particles. They'd been hot. Messy. That was wreckage. Battle wreckage, even. The carbon and the ions could originally have been part of itself, or part of the ship, or even part of a human. A few molecules of nitrogen and carbon dioxide. No oxygen.

But all of it doing just 10% of its own velocity. Odd, that. As though it had somehow been prioritised out of a sudden appearance of matter. Again, as though it had been Displaced, perhaps.

The drone flicked part of its attention back inside, to the sealed cores in its mind substrate with their warning notices. Can't put this off any longer, I suppose, it thought.

It interrogated the two cores. PAST, the first was labelled. The other one was simply called 2/2.

Uh-huh, it thought.

It opened the first core and found its memories.

II

Genar-Hofoen floated within the shower, buffeted from all sides by the streams of water. The fans sucking the water back out of the AG shower chamber sounded awfully loud this morning. Part of his brain told him he was running short of oxygen; he'd either have to leave the shower or grope for the air hose which was probably in the last place he'd feel for it. It was either that or open his eyes. It all seemed too much bother. He was quite comfortable where he was.

He waited to see what would give first.

It was his brain's indifference to the fact he was suffocating. Suddenly he was wide awake and flailing around like some drowning basic-human, desperate for breath but afraid to breathe in the constellation of water globules he was floating within. His eyes were wide open. He saw the air hose and grabbed it. He breathed in. Shit it was bright. His eyes dimmed the view. That was better.

He felt he'd showered enough. He mumbled, 'Off, off,' into the air hose mask a few times, but the water kept on coming. Then he remembered that the module wasn't talking to him right now because he'd told the suit to accept no more communications last night. Obviously such irresponsibility had to be punished by the module being childish. He sighed.

Luckily the shower had an Off button. The water jets cut off. Gravity was fed gently back into the chamber and he floated slowly down with the settling blobs of water. A reverser field clicked on and he looked at himself in it while the last of the water drained away, sucking in his belly and sticking out his chin while he turned his face to the best angle and smoothed down a few upstart locks of his blond curls.

'Well, I may feel like shit but I still look great,' he announced to nobody in particular. For once, probably even the module wasn't listening.

*   *   *

'Sorry to force the pace,' the representation of his uncle Tishlin said.

''s all right,' he said through a mouthful of *feyl* steak. He washed it down with some warmed-over infusion the module had always assured him was beneficial when you hadn't had enough sleep. It tasted disgusting enough to be either genuinely good for you, or just one of the module's little jokes.

'Sleep okay?' his uncle's image asked. He was, apparently, sitting across the table from Genar-Hofoen in the module's dining room, a pleasantly airy space filled with porcelain and flowers and boasting a seemingly real-time view on three sides of a sunlit mountain valley, which in reality was half a galaxy away. A small serving drone hovered near the wall behind the man.

'Good two hours,' Genar-Hofoen said. He supposed he could have stayed awake the night before when he'd first discovered his uncle's hologram waiting for him; he could have glanded something to keep him bright and awake and receptive and got all this over with then, but he'd known he'd end up paying for it eventually and besides, he wanted to show them that just because they'd gone to the trouble of persuading his favourite uncle to record a semantic-signal-mind-abstract-state or whatever the hell the module had called it, he still wasn't going to jump just because they said so. The only concession he'd made to all the urgency was deliberately not to dream; he had a whole suite of pretty splendid dream-accessible scenarios going at the moment, several of them incorporating some powerfully good and satisfying sex, and it was a positive sacrifice to miss out on any of them.

So he'd gone to bed and had a pretty good if maybe still not quite long enough sleep and Uncle Tishlin's message had just had to sit twiddling its abstract semantics in the module's AI core, waiting till he got up.

So far all they'd done was exchange a few pleasantries and talk a little about old times; partly, of course, so that Genar-Hofoen could satisfy himself that this apparition had genuinely been sent by his uncle and SC had paid him the enormous compliment of sending not one but two personality-states to him in order to argue him round to doing whatever it was they wanted from him (that the hologram might be a brilliantly researched forgery created by SC would be even more of a compliment . . . but that way lay paranoia).

'I take it you had a good evening,' Tishlin's simulation said.
'Enormous fun.'

Tishlin looked puzzled. Genar-Hofoen watched the expression form on his uncle's face and wondered how comprehensive was the duplication of his uncle's personality now encoded – living, if you wanted to look at it that way – in the module's AI core. Did whatever was in there – sent here enciphered with the specific task of persuading him to cooperate with Special Circumstances – actually *feel*? Or did it just appear to?

Shit, I must be feeling bad, Genar-Hofoen thought. I haven't bothered about that sort of shit since university.

'How can you have enormous fun with . . . aliens?' the hologram asked, eyebrows gathering.

'Attitude,' Genar-Hofoen said cryptically, slicing off more steak.

'But you can't drink with them, eat with them, can't really touch them, or want the same things . . .' Tishlin said, still frowning.

Genar-Hofoen shrugged. 'It's a kind of translation,' he said. 'You get used to it.' He munched away for a moment while his uncle's program – or whatever it was – digested this. He pointed his knife at the image. '*That's* something I'd want, in the unlikely event I agree to do whatever it is they want me to do.'

'What?' Tishlin said, leaning back, arms crossed.

'I want to become an Affronter.'

Tishlin's eyebrows elevated. 'You want *what*, boy?' he said.

'Well, some of the time,' Genar-Hofoen said, half turning his head to the drone behind him; the machine came quickly forward and refilled his glass with the infusion. 'I mean, all I want is an Affronter body, one that I can just sort of zap into and . . . well, just *be* an Affronter. You know; socialise. I don't see what the problem is, really. In fact I keep telling them it'll be a great thing for Culture-Affront relations. I'd really be able to relate to these guys; I could really be one of them. Hell; isn't that what this ambassador shit is supposed to be all about?' He belched. 'I'm sure it could be done. The module says it could but it shouldn't and says it's asked elsewhere and I know all the standard objections, but I think it'd be a great idea. I'm damn sure *I'd* enjoy it, I mean I could always sort of zap back into my own body anytime . . . this is really shocking you, isn't it, Uncle?'

The image shook its head. 'You always were the oddest child, Byr. I suppose I should have known what to expect from you.

Anybody who'd go out there to live with the Affront in the first place has to be slightly strange.'

Genar-Hofoen held his arms out wide. 'But I'm just doing what you did!' he protested.

'I only wanted to *meet* weird aliens, Byr; I didn't want to become one of them.'

'Heck, and I thought you'd be proud of me.'

'Proud but worried. Byr, are you seriously suggesting that becoming an Affronter would be part of your price for doing what SC asks?'

'Certainly,' Genar-Hofoen said, and squinted up at the hammer-beamed ceiling. 'I vaguely recall asking for a ship as well last night and the *Death And Gravity* saying yes . . .' he shook his head and laughed. 'Must have imagined it.' He finished the last of the steak.

'They've told me what they're prepared to offer, Byr,' Tishlin said. 'You didn't imagine it.'

Genar-Hofoen looked up. 'Really?' he asked.

'Really,' Tishlin said.

Genar-Hofoen nodded slowly. 'And how did they persuade you to act as go-between, Uncle?' he asked.

'They only had to ask, Byr. I may not be in Contact any more but I'm happy to help out when I can, when they have a problem.'

'This isn't Contact, Uncle, this is Special Circumstances,' Byr said quietly. 'They tend to play by slightly different rules.'

Tishlin looked serious; the image sounded defensive. 'I know that, boy. I asked around some of my contacts before I agreed to do this; everything checks out, everything seems to be . . . reliable. I suggest you do the same, obviously, but from what I can see, what I've been told is the truth.'

Genar-Hofoen was silent for a moment. 'Okay. So what have they told you, Uncle?' he asked, draining the last of the infusion. He frowned, wiped his lips and inspected the napkin. He looked at the sediment in the bottom of the glass, then glared at the servant drone. It wobbled in the drone equivalent of a shrug and took the glass from his hand.

Tishlin's representation sat forward, putting its arms on the table. 'Let me tell you a story, Byr.'

'By all means,' Genar-Hofoen said, picking something from his lips and wiping it on the napkin. The serving drone started to remove the rest of the breakfast things.

'Long ago and far away – two and a half thousand years ago,' Tishlin said, 'in a wispy tendril of suns outside the Galactic plane, nearest to Asatiel Cluster, but not really near to that or anywhere else – the *Problem Child*, an early General Contact Unit, Troubadour Class, chanced upon the ember of a very old star. The GCU started to investigate. And it found not one but two unusual things.'

Genar-Hofoen drew his gown about him and settled back in his seat, a small smile on his lips. Uncle Tish had always liked telling stories. Some of Genar-Hofoen's earliest memories were of the long, sunlit kitchen of the house at Ois, back on Seddun Orbital; his mother, the other adults of the house and his various cousins would all be milling around, chattering and laughing while he sat on his uncle's knee, being told tales. Some of them were ordinary children's stories – which he'd heard before, often, but which always sounded better when Uncle Tish told them – and some of them his uncle's own stories, from when he'd been in Contact, travelling the galaxy in a succession of ships, exploring strange new worlds and meeting all sorts of odd folk and finding any number of weird and wonderful things amongst the stars.

'Firstly,' the hologram image said, 'the dead sun gave every sign of being absurdly ancient. The techniques used to date it indicated it was getting on for a trillion years old.'

'What?' Genar-Hofoen snorted.

Uncle Tishlin spread his hands. 'The ship couldn't believe it either. To come up with this unlikely figure, it used . . .' the apparition glanced away to one side, the way Tishlin always had when he was thinking, and Genar-Hofoen found himself smiling, '. . . isotopic analysis and flux-pitting assay.'

'Technical terms,' Genar-Hofoen said, nodding. He and the hologram both smiled.

'Technical terms,' the image of Tishlin agreed. 'But no matter what it was they used or how they did their sums, it always came out that the dead star was at least fifty times older than the universe.'

'I never heard that one before,' Genar-Hofoen said, shaking his head and looking thoughtful.

'Me neither,' Tishlin agreed. 'Though as it turns out it was released publicly, just not until long after it had all happened. One reason there was no big fuss at the time was that the ship was so embarrassed about what it was coming up with it never filed a full report, just kept the results to itself, in its own mind.'

'Did they have proper Minds back then?'

Tishlin's image shrugged. 'Mind with a small "m"; AI core, we'd probably call it these days. But it was certainly sentient and the point is that the information remained in the ship's head, as it were.'

Where, of course, it would remain the ship's. Practically the only form of private property the Culture recognised was thought, and memory. Any publicly filed report or analysis was theoretically available to anybody, but your own thoughts, your own recollections – whether you were a human, a drone or a ship Mind – were regarded as private. It was considered the ultimate in bad manners even to think about trying to read somebody else's – or something else's – mind.

Personally, Genar-Hofoen had always thought it was a reasonable enough rule, although along with a lot of people over the years he'd long suspected that one of the main reasons for its existence was that it suited the purposes of the Culture's Minds in general, and those in Special Circumstances in particular.

Thanks to that taboo, everybody in the Culture could keep secrets to themselves and hatch little schemes and plots to their hearts' content. The trouble was that while in humans this sort of behaviour tended to manifest itself in practical jokes, petty jealousies, silly misunderstandings and instances of tragically unrequited love, with Minds it occasionally meant they forgot to tell everybody else about finding entire stellar civilisations, or took it upon themselves to try to alter the course of a developed culture everybody already did know about (with the almost unspeakable implication that one day they might do just that not with a culture but with *the* Culture . . . always assuming they hadn't done so already, of course).

'What about the people on board the Culture ship?' Genar-Hofoen asked.

'They knew as well, of course, but they kept quiet, too. Apart from anything else, they had *two* weirdnesses on their hands; they assumed they had to be linked in some way but they couldn't work out how, so they decided to wait and see before they told everybody else.' Tishlin shrugged. 'Understandable, I suppose; it was all so outlandish I suppose anybody would think twice about shouting it to the rooftops. You couldn't get away with such reticence these days, but this was then; the guidelines were looser.'

'What was the other unusual thing they found?'

'An artifact,' Tishlin said, sitting back in the seat. 'A perfect black-body sphere fifty klicks across, in orbit around the unfeasibly ancient star. The ship was completely unable to penetrate the artifact with its sensors, or with anything else for that matter, and the thing itself showed no signs of life. Shortly thereafter the *Problem Child* developed an engine fault – something almost unheard of, even back then – and had to leave the star and the artifact. Naturally, it left a load of satellites and sensor platforms behind it to monitor the artifact; all it had arrived with, in fact, plus a load more it had made while it was there.

'However, when a follow-up expedition arrived three years later – remember, this all happened on the galactic outskirts, and speeds were much lower then – it found nothing; no star, no artifact, and none of the sensors and remote packages the *Problem Child* had left behind; the outgoing signals apparently coming from the sentry units stopped just before the follow-up expedition arrived within monitoring range. Ripples in the gravity field near by implied the star and presumably everything else had vanished utterly the moment the *Problem Child* had been safely out of sensor range.'

'Just vanished?'

'Just vanished. Disappeared without trace,' Tishlin confirmed. 'Most damnable thing, too; nobody's ever just lost a sun before, even if it was a dead one.

'In the meantime, the General Systems Vehicle which the *Problem Child* had rendezvoused with for repairs had reported that the GCU had effectively been attacked; its engine problem wasn't the result of chance or some manufacturing flaw, it was the result of offensive action.

'Apart from that, and the still unexplained disappearance of an entire star, everything was normal for nearly two decades.' Tishlin's hand flapped once on the table. 'Oh, there were various investigations and boards of inquiry and committees and so on, but the best they could come up with was that the whole thing had been some sort of hi-tech projection, maybe produced by some previously unknown Elder civilisation with a quirky sense of humour, or, even less likely, that the sun and all the rest had popped into Hyperspace and just sped off – though they should have been able to observe that, and hadn't – but basically the whole thing remained a mystery, and after everybody had chewed it over and over till there was nothing but spit left, it just kind of died a natural death.

'Then, over the following seven decades, the *Problem Child* decided it didn't want to be part of Contact any more. It left Contact, then it left the Culture proper and joined the Ulterior – again, very unusual for its class – and meanwhile every single human who'd been on board at the time exercised what are apparently termed Unusual Life Choices.' Tishlin's dubious look indicated he wasn't totally convinced this phrase contributed enormously to the information-carrying capacity of the language. The image made a throat-clearing noise and went on: 'Roughly half of the humans opted for immortality, the other half autoeuthenised. The few remaining humans underwent subtle but exhaustive investigation, though nothing unusual was ever discovered.

'Then there were the ship's drones; they all joined the same Group Mind – again in the Ulterior – and have been incommunicado ever since. Apparently that was even more unusual. Within a century, almost all of those humans who'd opted for immortality were also dead, due to further "semi-contradictory" Unusual Life Choices. Then the Ulterior, and Special Circumstances – who'd taken an interest by this time, not surprisingly – lost touch with the *Problem Child* entirely. It just seemed to disappear, too.' The apparition shrugged. 'That was fifteen hundred years ago, Byr. To this day nobody has seen or heard of the ship. Subsequent investigations of the remains of a few of the humans concerned, using improved technology, has thrown up possible discrepancies in the nanostructure of the subjects' brains, but no further investigation has been deemed possible. The story was made public eventually, nearly a century and a half after it all happened; there was even a bit of a media fuss about it at the time, but by then it was a portrait with nobody in it: the ship, the drones, the people; they'd all gone. There was nobody to talk to, nobody to interview, nothing to do profiles of. Everybody was off-stage. And of course the principal celebrities – the star and the artifact – were the most off-stage of all.'

'Well,' Genar-Hofoen said. 'All very—'

'Hold on,' Tishlin said, holding up one finger. 'There is one loose end. A single traceable survivor from the *Problem Child* who turned up five centuries ago; somebody it might be possible to talk to, despite the fact they've spent the last twenty-four millennia trying to avoid talking.'

'Human?'

'Human,' Tishlin confirmed, nodding. 'The woman who was the vessel's formal captain.'

'They still had that sort of thing back then?' Genar-Hofoen said. He smiled. How quaint, he thought.

'It was pretty nominal, even back then,' Tishlin conceded. 'More captain of the crew than of the boat. Anyway; she's still around in a sort of abbreviated form.' Tishlin's image paused, watching Genar-Hofoen closely. 'She's in Storage aboard the General Systems Vehicle *Sleeper Service*.'

The representation paused, to let Genar-Hofoen react to the name of the ship. He didn't, not on the outside anyway.

'Just her personality is in there, unfortunately,' Tishlin continued. 'Her Stored body was destroyed in an Idiran attack on the Orbital concerned half a millennium ago. I suppose for our purposes that counts as a lucky break; she'd managed to cover her tracks so well – probably with the help of some sympathetic Mind – that if the attack hadn't occurred she'd have remained incognito to this day. It was only when the records were scrutinised carefully after her body's destruction that it was realised who she really was. But the point is that Special Circumstances thinks she might know something about the artifact. In fact, they're sure she does, though it's almost equally certain that she doesn't *know* what she knows.'

Genar-Hofoen was silent for a while, playing with the cord of his dressing gown. The *Sleeper Service*. He hadn't heard that name for a while, hadn't had to think about that old machine for a long time. He'd dreamt about it a few times, had had a nightmare or two about it even, but he'd tried to forget about those, tried to shove those echoes of memories to some distant corner of his mind and been pretty successful at it too, because it felt very strange to be turning over that name in his mind now.

'So why's this all suddenly become important after two and a half millennia?' he asked the hologram.

'Because something with similar characteristics to that artifact has turned up near a star called Esperi, in the Upper Leaf-Swirl, and SC needs all the help it can get to deal with it. There's no trillion-year-old sun-cinder this time, but an apparently identical artifact is just sitting there.'

'And what am I supposed to do?'

'Go aboard the *Sleeper Service* and talk to this woman's Mimage – that's the Mind-stored construct of her personality apparently . . .' The image looked puzzled. '. . . New one on me . . . Anyway, you're supposed to try to persuade her to be reborn; talk her into a rebirth so she can be quizzed. The *Sleeper Service* won't just release her, and it certainly won't cooperate with SC, but if she asks to be reborn, it'll let her.'

'But why—?' Genar-Hofoen started to ask.

'There's more,' Tishlin said, holding up one hand. 'Even if she won't play, even if she refuses to come back, you're to be equipped with a method of retrieving her through the link you'll forge when you talk to the Mimage, without the GSV knowing. Don't ask me how that's supposed to be accomplished, but I think it's got something to do with the ship they're going to give you to get you to the *Sleeper Service*, after the Affronter ship they're going to hire for you has rendezvoused with it at Tier.'

Genar-Hofoen did his best to look sceptical. 'Is that possible?' he asked. 'Retrieving her like that, I mean. Against the wishes of the *Sleeper*.'

'Apparently,' Tishlin said, shrugging. 'SC thinks they've got a way of doing it. But you see what I mean when I said they want you to steal the soul of a dead woman . . .'

Genar-Hofoen thought for a moment. 'Do you know what ship this might be? The one to get me to the *Sleeper*?'

'They haven't—' began the image, then paused and looked amused. 'They just told me; it's a GCU called the *Grey Area*.' The image smiled. 'Ah; I see you've heard of it, too.'

'Yeah, I've heard of it,' the man said.

The *Grey Area*. The ship that did what the other ships both deplored and despised; actually looked into the minds of other people, using its Electro Magnetic Effectors – in a sense the very, very distant descendants of electronic countermeasures equipment from your average stage three civilisation, and the most sophisticated, powerful but also precisely controllable weaponry the average Culture ship possessed – to burrow into the grisly cellular substrate of an animal consciousness and try to make sense of what it found there for its own – usually vengeful – purposes. A pariah craft; the one the other Minds called *Meatfucker* because of its revolting hobby (though not, as it were, to its face). A ship that still wanted to be part of the Culture proper and nominally still was, but which was shunned by almost all its peers; a virtual outcast amongst the great inclusionary meta-fleet that was Contact.

Genar-Hofoen had heard about the *Grey Area* all right. It was starting to make sense now. If there was one vessel that might be capable of plundering – and, more importantly, that might be willing to plunder – a Stored soul from under the nose of the *Sleeper*, the *Grey Area* was probably it. Assuming what he'd heard about the ship was true, it had spent the last decade perfecting its techniques of teasing dreams and memories out of a variety of animal species, while the *Sleeper Service* had by all accounts been technologically stagnant for the last forty years, its time taken up with the indulgence of its own scarcely less eccentric pastime.

The image of Uncle Tishlin bore a distant expression for a moment, then said, 'Apparently that's part of the beauty of it; just because the *Sleeper Service* is another oddball doesn't mean that it's any more likely than any other GSV to have the *Grey Area* aboard; the GCU will have to lie off, and that'll make this Mimage-stealing trick easier. If the *Grey Area* was actually inside the GSV at the time it probably couldn't carry it off undetected.'

Genar-Hofoen was looking thoughtful again. 'This artifact thing,' he said. 'Could almost be a what-do-you-call it, couldn't it? An Outside Context Paradox.'

'Problem,' Tishlin said. 'Outside Context Problem.'

'Hmm. Yes. One of those. Almost.'

An Outside Context Problem was the sort of thing most civilisations encountered just once, and which they tended to encounter rather in the same way a sentence encountered a full stop. The usual example given to illustrate an Outside Context Problem was imagining you were a tribe on a largish, fertile island; you'd tamed the land, invented the wheel or writing or whatever, the neighbours were cooperative or enslaved but at any rate peaceful and you were busy raising temples to yourself with all the excess productive capacity you had, you were in a position of near-absolute power and control which your hallowed ancestors could hardly have dreamed of and the whole situation was just running along nicely like a canoe on wet grass . . . when suddenly this bristling lump of iron appears sailless and trailing steam in the bay and these guys carrying long funny-looking sticks come ashore and announce you've just been discovered, you're all subjects of the Emperor now, he's keen on presents called *tax* and these bright-eyed holy men would like a word with your priests.

That was an Outside Context Problem; so was the suitably up-teched version that happened to whole planetary civilisations when somebody like the Affront chanced upon them first rather than, say, the Culture.

The Culture had had lots of minor OCPs, problems that could have proved to be terminal if they'd been handled badly, but so far it had survived them all. The Culture's ultimate OCP was popularly supposed to be likely to take the shape of a galaxy-consuming Hegemonising Swarm, an angered Elder civilisation or a sudden, indeed instant visit by neighbours from Andromeda once the expedition finally got there.

In a sense, the Culture lived with genuine OCPs all around it all the time, in the shape of those Sublimed Elder civilisations, but so far it didn't appear to have been significantly checked or controlled by any of them. However, waiting for the first real OCP was the intellectual depressant of choice for those people and Minds in the Culture determined to find the threat of catastrophe even in utopia.

'Almost. Maybe,' agreed the apparition. 'Perhaps it's a little less likely to be so with your help.'

Genar-Hofoen nodded, staring at the surface of the table. 'So who's in charge of this?' he asked, grinning. 'There's usually a Mind which acts as incident controller or whatever they call it in something like this.'

'The Incident Coordinator is a GSV called the *Not Invented Here*,' Tish told him. 'It wants you to know you can ask whatever you want of it.'

'Uh-huh.' Genar-Hofoen couldn't recall having heard of the ship. 'And why me, particularly?' he asked. He suspected he already had the answer to that one.

'The *Sleeper Service* has been behaving even more oddly than usual,' Tishlin said, looking suitably pained. 'It's altered its course schedule, it's no longer accepting people for Storage, and it's almost completely stopped communicating. But it says it will allow you on board.'

'For a brow-beating, no doubt,' Genar-Hofoen said, glancing to one side and watching a cloud pass over the meadows of the valley shown on the dining room's projector walls. 'Probably wants to give me a lecture.' He sighed, still looking round the room. He fastened his gaze on Tishlin's simulation again. 'She still there?' he asked.

The image nodded slowly.

'Shit,' Genar-Hofoen said.

III

'But it makes my brain hurt.'

'Nevertheless, Major. This is of inestimable importance.'

'I only looked at the first bit there and it's already given me a thumping case-ache.'

'Still, it has to be done. Kindly read it all carefully and then I'll explain its significance.'

'Knot my stalks, this is a terrible thing to ask of a chap after a regimental dinner.' Fivetide wondered if humans suffered so for their self-indulgence. He doubted it, no matter what they claimed; with the possibly honourable, possibly demented exception of Genar-Hofoen, they seemed a bit too stuffy and sensible willingly to submit to such self-punishment in the cause of fun. Besides, they were so insecure in their physical inheritance they had meddled with themselves in all sorts of ways; probably they thought hangovers were just annoying, rather than character-forming and so had, shortsightedly, dispensed with them.

'I realise it's early and it is the morning after the night before, Major. But please.'

The emissary – which Fivetide had met once before, and which possessed the irritating trait of looking somewhat like a better-built version of Fivetide's dear departed father – had just appeared in the nest house without notice or warning. If he hadn't known the way these things worked, Fivetide would right now be thinking of ways to torture the head of nest security. Tentacles had rolled, beaks had been separated, for less.

Lucky he'd been able to whip the bed covers round his deputy wife and both vice courtesans before the blighter had announced his/its presence by just floating into the nest.

Fivetide clapped his forebeak together a couple of times. *Tastes like I've had me beak up me arse*, he thought. 'Can't you just tell me what the damn signal means now?' he asked.

'You won't know what I'm referring to. Come now; the sooner you read it the sooner I'll be able to tell you what it means, and the sooner I'll be able to demonstrate how it is just possible that this information will – at the very least – enable you to remove the harness of Culture interference forever.'

'Hmm. I'm sure. And what'll it do at most?'

The emissary of the ship let its eye stalks dip to either side, the Affronter equivalent of a smile. 'At most, the information in this signal will lead to you being able to dominate the Culture as completely as it – if it chose to – could dominate you.' The creature paused. 'This signal could conceivably presage the start of a process which will deliver the entire Galaxy into your hands, and subsequently open up territories for expansion and exploitation beyond that which you cannot even begin to guess at. And I do *not* exaggerate. Have I your attention now, Major?'

Fivetide snorted sceptically. 'I suppose you have,' he said, shaking his limbs and rubbing his eyes. He returned his gaze to the note screen, and read the signal.

xGCU *Fate Amenable To Change*,
  oGSV *Ethics Gradient*
  & strictly as SC cleared:
Excession notice @c18519938.52314.
Constitutes formal All-ships Warning Level 0
[*(in temporary sequestration) — textual note added by GSV* Wisdom Like Silence @ *n4.28.855.0150.650001*].
Excession.
Confirmed precedent-breach. Type K7ˆ. True class non-estimal. Its status: Active. Aware. Contactiphile. Uninvasive sf. LocStatre: Esperi (star).
First ComAtt (its, following shear-by contact via my primary scanner @ n4.28.855.0065.59312) @ n4.28.855.0065.59487 in M1-a16 & Galin II by tight beam, type 4A. PTA & Handshake burst as appended, x@ 0.7Y. Suspect signal gleaned from Z-E/Ialsaer

ComBeam spread, 2nd Era. xContact callsigned 'I'. No other signals registered.

My subsequent actions: maintained course and speed, skim-de-clutched primary scanner to mimic 50% closer approach, began directed full passive HS scan (sync./start of signal sequence, as above), sent buffered Galin II pro-forma message-reception confirmation signal to contact location, dedicated track scanner @ 19% power and 300% beamspread to contact @ -5% primary scanner roll-off point, instigated ^{2}exponential slow-to-stop line manoeuvre synchronised to skein-local stop-point @ 12% of track scanner range limit, ran full systems check as detailed, executed slow/4 swing-around then retraced course to previous closest approach point and stop @ standard ^{2}ex curve. Holding there.

Excession's physical characteristics: (¡am!) sphere rad. 53.34km, mass (non-estimal by space-time fabric influence – locality ambiently planar – estimated by pan-polarity material density norms at) 1.45×8^{13}t. Layered fractal matter-type-intricate structure, self supporting, open to (field-filtered) vacuum, anomalous field presence inferred from 8^{21} kHz leakage. Affirm K7ˆ category by HS topology & eG links (inf. & ult.). eG link details non-estimal. DiaGlyph files attached.

Associated anomalous materials presence: several highly dis-persed detritus clouds all within 28 minutes, three consistent with staged destruction of >.1m^3 near-equiv-tech entity, another ditto approx 3^8 partially exhausted M-DAWS .1cal rounds, another consisting of general hi-soph level (O_2-atmosphered) ship-internal combat debris. Latter drifting directly away from excession's current position. Retracks of debris clouds' expansion profiles indicates mutual age of 52.5 days. Combat debris cloud implicitly originating @ a point 948 milliseconds from excession's current position. DiaGlyph files attached.

No other presences apparent to within 30 years.

My status: H&H, unTouched. L8 secure post system-scour (100%). ATDPSs engaged. CRTTDPSs engaged.

Repeat:

Excession eG (inf. & ult.) linked, confirmed.

eGrid link details non-estimal.

True class non-estimal.

Awaiting.

@ n4.28.855.0073.64523 . . .

.

. . . PS:
Gulp.

Fivetide shook his stalks. Gods, this hangover was fierce.

'All right,' he said, 'I've read, but I still don't understand.'

The emissary of the war vessel *Attitude Adjuster* smiled again. 'Allow me to explain.'

3
Uninvited Guests

I

The battle of Boustrago had taken place on Xlephier Prime thirteen thousand years earlier. It had been the final, decisive battle in the Archipelagic War (though it had, inappropriately, been fought near to the centre of a continent), a twenty-year conflict between that world's first two great imperial nation states. The muzzle-loading cannon and rifle were state-of-the-art munitions at the time, though the cavalry charge was still very much regarded as both the most decisive battlefield manoeuvre and quite the finest and most stirring sight that warfare had to offer by the military high commands on each side. The combination of modern ordnance and outdated tactics had, as ever, created enormous casualties on both sides.

Amorphia wandered amongst the dead and dying of Hill 4. The battle had by this time moved on; the few defenders who'd survived and repelled the initial rush had been ordered to pull back just as the next wave of opposing troops had appeared out of the cannon smoke and fallen upon them; they had been slaughtered almost to a man and the victors had swept on to the next redoubt across the shallow valley beyond. Shattered palisades, lines of stakes and bunkers had been chewed up by the initial bombardment and later by the hooves of the cavalry. Bodies lay scattered like twisted, shredded leaves amongst the torn-up grassland and the rich brown-red soil. The blood of men and animals saturated the grass in places, making it thick and glossy, and collected in little hollows like pools of dark ink.

The sun was high in the cloudless sky; the only cover was the wispy remnants of cannon smoke. Already a few carrion birds – no longer too concerned by the noise of the battle near by – had landed and started to investigate the corpses and the shattered bodies of the wounded.

The soldiers wore brightly coloured, cheery-looking uniforms with lots of metal buckle-work and very tall hats. Their guns were long, simple-looking things; their pikes, swords and bayonets lay glittering in the sunlight. The animals lying tangled amongst the traces of the smashed cannon trains were big, thick-set beasts, almost unadorned; the cavalry mounts were almost as gaily decorated as their riders. They all lay together, some with the collapsed shapelessness of death, some in a pool of their own internal organs, some missing limbs, some in a posture appropriate to a still vital suffering, caught in expressions appropriate to their agony, thrashing or writhing or – in the case of some of the soldiers – supporting themselves on one limb and reaching out to plead for help, or water, or a *coup de grâce* to end their torment.

It was all quite still, frozen like a three-dimensional photograph, and it all lay, spread out like some military society's model scene made real, in General Bay Three Inner of the GSV *Sleeper Service*.

The ship's avatar achieved the top of the low hill and looked out over the battle-scene beyond. It stretched for kilometres in all directions across the sunlit rolling downland; a grand confusion of posed men, dashing mounts, cavalry charges, cannons and smoke and shadows.

Getting the smoke right had been the hardest part. The landscape was simplicity itself; a covering of artificial flora on a thin layer of sterilised soil lying on a structure of foametal. The great majority of the animals were simply very good sculptures the ship had created. The people were real, of course, though the ones who'd been disembowelled or particularly severely mutilated were generally sculptures too.

The details of the scene were as authentic as the ship could make them; it had studied every painting, etching and sketch of the battle and read every account, military and media report of it, even taking the trouble to track down the records of the diary entries of individual soldiers, while at the same time undertaking exhaustive research into the whole historical period concerned including the uniforms, weaponry and tactics in use when the battle had taken place. For what it was worth after so much time, a drone team had visited the preserved battle site itself and conducted their own deep-scan of the ground. The fact that Xlephier Prime was one of the twenty or so planets that could fairly claim to have been one of the home worlds of the Culture – not that it really admitted to having such things – made the task easier.

The GSV had studied the real-time recordings Contact craft

and their emissaries had taken over the years of battles fought by humanoid societies with similar technology, to get a feel for the way such events really looked and felt without the possibly prejudiced and partial eyes and memories of the participants or spectators getting in the way.

And it had, eventually, got the smoke right. It had taken a while, and eventually it had had to resort to a rather higher-tech solution than it would have preferred, but it had done it. The smoke was real, each particle held and isolated in the grip of a localised anti-gravity field produced by projectors hidden underneath the landscape. The ship was quietly proud of the smoke.

Even the fact that the scene still wasn't perfect – many of the soldiers looked female, and/or foreign, or indeed alien, when you looked closely at them, and even the males of the appropriate and not-too-meddled-with genetic stock were too big and too generally healthy to be right for the time – didn't really disturb the ship. The people hadn't been the most difficult thing to get right, but they were the most important component of the scene; they were the reason it was all here.

It had all started eighty years ago, on a very small scale.

Every Culture habitat – whether it was an Orbital or other large structure, a ship, a Rock, or a planet – possessed Storage facilities. Storage was where some people went when they had reached a certain age, or if they had just grown tired of living. It was one of the choices that Culture humans faced towards the end of their artificially extended three-and-a-half to four centuries of life. They could opt for rejuvenation and/or complete immortality, they could become part of a group mind, they could simply die when the time came, they could transfer out of the Culture altogether, bravely accepting one of the open but essentially inscrutable invitations left by certain Elder civilisations, or they could go into Storage, with whatever revival criterion they desired.

Some people slept for – say – a hundred years at a time then lived a single day before returning to their undreaming, unageing slumbers, some wanted simply to be woken after a set time had passed to see what had changed while they'd been gone, some desired to come back when something especially interesting was happening (content to leave that judgement to others), and some only wanted to be brought back if and when the Culture finally became one of the Elders itself.

That was a decision the Culture had been putting off for many millennia; in theory it could have sublimed anything up to ten thousand years ago, but – while individuals and small groups of people and Minds did sublime all the time, and other parts of the society had hived off and split away, to make their own decisions on the matter – the bulk of the Culture had chosen not to, determining instead to surf a line across the ever-breaking wave of galactic life continuation.

Partly it was a kind of curiosity that no doubt seemed childish to any sublimed species; a feeling that there was still more to discover in base reality, even if its laws and rules were all perfectly known (and besides, what of other galaxies, what of other universes? Did the Elders have access to these but none of them had ever seen fit to communicate the truth to the unsublimed? Or did all such considerations simply cease to matter, post-sublimation?).

Partly it was an expression of the Culture's extrovertly concerned morality; the sublimed Elders, become as gods to all intents and purposes, seemed to be derelict in the duties which the more naive and less developed societies they left behind ascribed to such entities. With certain very limited exceptions, the Elder species subsequently took almost nothing to do with the rest of life in the galaxy whose physical trappings they invariably left behind; tyrants went unchecked, hegemonies went unchallenged, genocides went unstopped and whole nascent civilisations were snuffed out just because their planet suffered a comet-strike or happened to be too near a super-nova, even though these events occurred under the metaphorical noses of the sublimed ones.

The implication was that the very ideas, the actual concepts of good, of fairness and of justice just ceased to matter once one had gone for sublimation, no matter how creditable, progressive and unselfish one's behaviour had been as a species pre-sublimation. In a curiously puritanical way for society seemingly so hell-bent on the ruthless pursuit of pleasure, the Culture thought this was itself wrong, and so decided to attempt to accomplish what the gods, it seemed, could not be bothered with; discovering, judging and encouraging – or discouraging – the behaviour of those to whom its own powers were scarcely less than those of a deity. Its own Elderhood would come eventually, it had no doubt, but it would be damned if it would let that happen until it had grown tired of doing (what it hoped was) good.

For those who wished to await that judgment day without having to live through every other day in between, Storage was the answer, as it was for others, for all those other reasons.

The rate of technological change in the Culture, at least at the level which directly affected the humans within it, was fairly modest. For millennia the accepted and normal method of Storing a human was to place each in a coffin-like box a little over two metres long, just under one across and half a metre deep; such units were easy to make and suitably reliable. However, even such unglamorous staples of Culture existence couldn't escape improvement and refinement for ever. Eventually, along with the development of the gelfield suit, it became possible to put people into the stasis of long-term Storage within a covering that was even more reliable than the old coffin-boxes, and yet scarcely thicker than a second skin or a layer of clothing.

The *Sleeper Service* – which was not called that then – had simply been the first ship fully to take advantage of this development. When it Stored people it usually did so in small tableaux after the manner of famous paintings, at first, or humorous poses; the Storage suits allowed their occupants to be posed in any way that would have been natural for a human, and it was a simple matter to add a pigmentation layer to the surface which did such a good job of impersonating skin that a human would have to look very closely indeed to spot the difference. Of course, the ship had always asked the permission of the Storees in question before it used their sleeping forms in this way, and respected the wishes of the few people who preferred not to be Stored in a situation where they might be gazed upon as though they were figures in a painting, or sculptures.

Back then, the GSV had been called the *Quietly Confident*, and it had been run, as ships of that class normally were, by not one but three Minds. What happened next depended on who you believed.

The official version was that when one of the three Minds had decided it wanted to quit the Culture the other two Minds had argued with it and then made the unusual decision to leave the structure of the GSV to the single dissenting Mind, rather than, as would have been more normal, just giving it a smaller ship.

The perhaps more plausible and certainly more interesting rumour was that there had been a good old-fashioned wing-ding battle between the Minds, two against one, and the two had lost, very much against the odds. The two losing Minds had been kicked out, taking to commandeered GCUs like officers given life boats after a mutiny. And that was why, this version went, the whole of the *Quietly Confident* – which promptly renamed itself the *Sleeper Service*, had been turned over to the single dissident Mind; it hadn't been some gentlepeople's agreement; it had been a revolution.

Whatever version you chose to believe, it was no secret that the Culture proper had chosen to dedicate another, smaller, GSV to the task of following the *Sleeper Service* wherever it went, presumably to keep an eye on it.

Following its renaming, and paying no apparent heed to the craft now tailing it, the *Sleeper Service*'s next step was to evacuate everybody else remaining aboard. Most of the ships had already gone, and the rest were asked to leave. Then the drones, aliens and all the human personnel and their pets were deposited on the first Orbital it came to. The only people left aboard were those in Storage.

After that the ship went in search of others (and one other in particular), and let it be known throughout the Culture, through its information network, that it was willing to travel anywhere to pick up those who might wish to join it, so long as they were in Storage and happy to be set amongst one of its tableaux.

People were reluctant at first; this was definitely the sort of behaviour that earned a ship the title Eccentric, and Eccentric ships had been known to do odd, even dangerous things. Still, the Culture had its share of brave souls, and a few took up the craft's strange invitation, without apparent ill effect. When the first few people who had been Stored aboard the GSV were safely returned on the realisation of their revival criteria, again without seeming to have suffered for the strangeness of their temporary lodgings, the slow trickle of adventurous individuals began to turn into a steady stream of slightly perverse or just romantic ones; as the reputation of the *Sleeper Service* spread, and it released holograms of its more and more ambitious tableaux (important historical incidents, then small battles and details from greater conflicts), so more and more people thought it rather amusing to be Stored within this eccentric Eccentric, where they might be said to be forming part of a work of art even while they slept, rather than just plonked in a boring box somewhere underneath their local Plate.

And so taking a ride aboard the *Sleeper Service* as a kind of vicariously wandering soul became nothing less than fashionable, and the ship slowly filled with undead people in Storage suits whom it posed into larger and larger scenes, until eventually it was able to tackle whole battlefields and lay them out in the sixteen square kilometres of territory it possessed in each of its General Bays.

Amorphia completed its sweeping gaze across the bright, silent stillness of the vast killing ground. As an avatar it possessed no real thoughts of its own, but the Mind that was the *Sleeper Service* liked to run the creature off a small sub-routine that was only a little more intelligent than the average human being – while both retaining the option of stepping in, full force, if it needed to and making the avatar behave in a confused, distracted state that the ship believed somehow reflected, on the nearly infinitely smaller human scale, its own philosophical perplexities.

So it was that the semi-human sub-routine looked out across that great tableau, and felt a kind of sadness that it might all have to be dismantled. There was an extra, perhaps deeper melancholy at the thought that it would no longer be able to play host to the living things aboard; the creatures of the sea and the air and the gas-giant atmosphere, and the woman.

Its thoughts turned to that woman; Dajeil Gelian, who in one sense had been the cause, the seed for all of this, and the one person it had wanted to find, the one soul – asleep or awake – it had been determined to offer sanctuary to when it had first renounced the Culture's normality. Now that sanctuary was compromised, and she too would have to be offloaded with all the rest of its waifs and strays and teeming undead. A promise being fulfilled leading to a promise to her being broken, as though she had not experienced enough of that in her life. Still, it would make amends, and for that reason there were a lot of other promises being made and – so far, it would seem – kept. That would have to do.

Movement on the motionless tableau; Amorphia turned its attention there and saw the black bird Gravious flapping away across the field. More movement. Amorphia walked towards it, around and over the poised, charging cavalry and the fallen soldiers, between a pair of convincing-looking hanging fountains of earth where two cannon balls were slamming into the ground and over a small, blood-swollen stream to another part of the battlefield, where a team of three revival drones were floating above a revivee.

This was unusual; people normally wanted to be woken back in their home and in the presence of friends, but over the last couple of decades – as the tableaux had become more impressive – more people had wished to be brought back to life here, in the midst of them.

Amorphia squatted down by the woman, who had been lying posed as a dying soldier, her tunic punctured by bullet holes and stained red. She lay on her back, blinking in the sunlight, attended by machines. The head of the Storage suit had been slipped off and lay like a rubbery mask on the grass beside her; her face looked pale and just a little blotchy; she was an old woman, but her depilated head gave her a curious, baby-like quality of nakedness.

'Hello?' Amorphia said, taking one of the woman's hands in hers and gently detaching that part of the suit too, pulling the hand-covering off inside-out, like a tight glove.

'Whoa,' the woman said, swallowing, her eyes watering.

Sikleyr-Najasa Croepise Ince Stahal da Mapin, Stored thirty-one years ago at the age of three-hundred and eighty-six. Revival criterion: on the acclamation of the next Line Messiah-elect on the planet Ischeis. She had been a scholar of the planet's major religion and had wanted to be present at the Elevation of its next Saviour, an event which had not been anticipated for another two hundred years or so.

Her mouth twisted, and she coughed. 'How—?' she began, then coughed again.

'Just thirty-one standard years,' Amorphia told her.

The woman's eyes widened, then she smiled. 'That was quick,' she said.

She recovered rapidly for one of her age; in a few minutes she was able to be helped to her feet and – taking Amorphia's arm, and trailed by the three drones – they walked across the battlefield towards the nearest edge of the tableau.

They stood on the small hill, Hill 4, that Amorphia had stood on a little earlier. Amorphia was distantly, naggingly aware of the gap the woman's revival had left in the scene. Normally she would have been replaced within the day with another Storee, posed in the same position, but there were none left; the gap she had left

would remain unless the ship plundered another tableau to repair
the hole in this one. The woman gazed around her for some time,
then shook her head.

Amorphia guessed what she was thinking. 'It is a terrible sight,'
it said. 'But it was the last great land battle on Xlephier Prime. To
have one's final significant battle at such an early technological
stage is actually a great achievement for a humanoid species.'

The woman turned to Amorphia. 'I know,' she said. 'I was just
thinking how impressive all this was. You must be proud.'

II

The Explorer Ship *Peace Makes Plenty*, a vessel of the Stargazer
Clan, part of the Fifth Fleet of the Zetetic Elench, had been investigating a little-explored part of the Upper Leaf Swirl on a standard
random search pattern. It had left Tier habitat on n4.28.725.500
along with the seven other Stargazer vessels; they had scattered like
seeds into the depths of the Swirl, bidding each other farewell and
knowing they might never see each other again.

One month in, and the ship had turned up nothing special; just
a few bits of uncharted interstellar debris, duly logged, and that
was all. There was a hint – a probably false-signal resonation in
the skein of space-time behind them – that there might be a craft
following them, but then it was not unusual for other civilisations
to follow ships of the Zetetic Elench.

The Elench had once been part of the Culture proper; they had split
off fifteen hundred years ago, the few habitats and the many Rocks,
ships, drones and humans concerned preferring to take a slightly
different line from the mainstream Culture. The Culture aimed to
stay roughly as it was and change at least a proportion of those
lesser civilisations it discovered, while acting as an honest broker
between the Involved – the more developed societies who made up
the current players in the great galactic civilisational game.

The Elench wanted to alter themselves, not others; they sought
out the undiscovered not to change it but to be changed by it.
The Elencher ideal was that somebody from a more stable society

– the Culture itself was the perfect example – could meet the same Elencher – Rock, ship, drone or human – on successive occasions and never encounter the same entity twice. They would have changed between meetings just because in the interim they had encountered some other civilisation and incorporated some different technology into their bodies or information into their minds. It was a search for the sort of pan-relevant truth that the Culture's monosophical approach was unlikely ever to throw up; it was a vocation, a mission, a calling.

The results of this attitude were as various as might be imagined; entire Elencher fleets had either never come back from expeditions, and remained lost, or had eventually been found, the vessels and their crews completely, if willingly, subsumed by another civilisation.

At its most extreme, in the old days, some craft had been discovered turned entirely into Aggressive Hegemonising Swarm Objects; selfishly auto-replicating organisms determined to turn every piece of matter they found into copies of themselves. There were techniques – beyond simple outright destruction, which was always an option – for dealing with this sort of eventuality which normally resulted in the Objects concerned becoming Evangelical Hegemonising Swarm Objects rather than Aggressive Hegemonising Swarm Objects, but if the Objects concerned had been particularly single-minded, it still meant that people had died to contribute to its greedily ungracious self-regard.

These days, the Elench very rarely ran into anything like that sort of trouble, but they did still change all the time. In a way, the Elench, even more than the Culture, was an attitude rather than an easily definable grouping of ships or people. Because parts of Elench were constantly being subsumed and assimilated, or just disappearing, while at the same time other individuals and small groups were joining it (both from the Culture and from other societies, human and otherwise), there was anyway a turn-over of personnel and secondary ideas that made it one of the most rapidly evolving in-play civilisations. Somehow, though, despite it all, and perhaps because it was more an attitude, a meme, than anything else, the Elench had developed an ability that it had arguably inherited from its parent civilisation; the ability to remain roughly the same in the midst of constant change.

It also had a knack of turning up intriguing things – ancient artifacts, new civilisations, the mysterious remnants of Sublimed species, unguessably old depositories of antique knowledge – not all of which were of ultimate interest to the Elench itself, but many of which might excite the curiosity, further the purposes and benefit the informational or monetary funds of others, especially if they could get to them before anybody else. Such opportunities arose but rarely, but they had occurred sufficiently often in the past for certain societies of an opportunistic bent to consider it worth the expense or the bother of dedicating a ship to follow an Elencher craft, for a while at least, and so the *Peace Makes Plenty* had not been unduly alarmed by the discovery that it might be being tailed.

Two months in. And still nothing exciting; just gas clouds, dust clouds, brown dwarfs and a couple of lifeless star systems. All well enough charted from afar and displaying no sign of ever having been touched by anything intelligent.

Even the hint of the following ship had disappeared; if it ever had been real, the vessel concerned had probably decided the *Peace Makes Plenty* was not going to strike lucky this trip. Nevertheless, everything the Elencher ship came within range of was scanned; passive sensors filtered the natural spectrum for signs of meaning, beams and pulses were sent out into the vacuum and across the skein of space-time, searching and probing, while the ship consumed whatever echoes came back, analysing, considering, evaluating . . .

Seventy-eight days after leaving Tier, approaching a red giant star named Esperi from a direction which according to its records nobody had ever taken before, the *Peace Makes Plenty* had discovered an artifact, fourteen light months distant from the sun itself.

The artifact was a little over fifty kilometres in diameter. It was black-body; an ambient anomaly, indistinguishable from a distance from any given volume of almost empty interstellar space. The *Peace Makes Plenty* only noticed it at all because it occluded part of a distant galaxy and the Elencher ship, knowing that bits of galaxies did not just wink off and back on again of their own accord, had turned to investigate.

The artifact appeared to be either almost completely massless, or – perhaps – some sort of projection; it seemed to make no impression on the skein, the fabric of space-time which any accumulation of matter effectively dents with its mass, like a boulder lying on a trampoline. The artifact/projection gave the impression that it was floating on the skein, making no impression on it whatsoever. This was unusual; this was certainly worth investigating. Even more intriguingly, there was also a possible anomaly in the lower energy grid, which underlay the fabric of real space. There was a region directly underneath the three-dimensional form of the artifact that, intermittently, seemed to lack the otherwise universally chaotic nature of the Grid; there was a vaguest-of-vague hint of order there, almost as if the artifact was casting some sort of bizarre – indeed, impossible – shadow. Even more curious.

The *Peace Makes Plenty* hove to, sitting in front of the artifact – in as much as it could be said to have a front – and trying both to analyse it and communicate with it.

Nothing; the black-body sphere appeared to be massless and inviolable, almost as though it was a blister on the skein itself, as though the signals the ship was sending towards it could never connect with a *thing* there because all they did was slide flickering over that blister almost as though it wasn't there and pass on undisturbed into space beyond; as though, trying to pick up a stone that appeared to be resting on the surface of a trampoline, one discovered that the trampoline surface itself was bulged up to cover the stone.

The ship decided to attempt to contact the artifact in a more direct manner; it would send a drone-probe underneath the object in hyperspace, below the surface of space-time; effectively making a tear, a rent in the fabric of the skein – the sort of opening it would normally create to fashion a way into HS through which it could travel. The drone-probe would attempt, as it were, to surface inside the artifact; if there was nothing there but a projection, it would find out; if there was something there, it would presumably either be prevented from entering it, or accepted within. The ship readied its emissary.

The situation was so unusual the *Peace Makes Plenty* even considered breaking with Elench precedent by informing Tier habitat or one of its peers what was going on; the nearest other Stargazer craft was a month's travel away, but might be able to help if the *Peace Makes Plenty* got itself into trouble. In the end, however, it stuck with tradition and kept quiet. There was a kind of stealthy pragmatism in this; an encounter of the sort the ship was embarking upon might only be successful if the Elencher craft could fairly claim to be acting on its own, without having made what might, to a suspicious contactee, look like a request for reinforcements.

Plus, there was simple pride involved; an Elencher ship would not be an Elencher ship if it started acting like part of a committee; why, it might as well then be a Culture ship!

The drone-probe was dispatched with the *Peace Makes Plenty* keeping in close contact. The instant the probe passed within the horizon of the artifact, it—

The records the drone Sisela Ytheleus 1/2 had access to ended there.

Something, obviously, had happened.

The next thing it personally knew, the *Peace Makes Plenty* had been under attack. The assault had been almost unbelievably swift and ferocious; the drone-probe must have been taken over almost instantaneously, the ship's subsystems surrendered milliseconds later and the integrity of the ship's Mind shattered within – at a guess – less than a second after the drone-probe had infringed the space beneath the artifact.

A few more seconds later and Sisela Ytheleus 1/2 itself had been involved in a last desperate attempt to get word of the ship's plight to the outside galaxy while the vessel's usurped systems did their damnedest to prevent it; by destroying it if necessary. The long-agreed, carefully worked-out ruse using itself and its twin and the preprogrammed independent Displacer unit had worked, though only just, and even so, with considerable damage to the drone that had been Sisela Ytheleus 2/2 and was now Sisela Ytheleus 1/2, with a kind of twisted remnant of Sisela Ytheleus 2/2 lodged within it.

The drone had carried out the equivalent of pressing an ear to the wall of the core with its twin's mind in it, carefully accessing a meaning-free abstract of the activity inside the closed-off core to find out what was happening in there. It was like listening to a furious argument going on in an adjoining room; a chilling, frightening sound; the sort of bawling match that made you expect the sound of screams and things breaking, any moment.

Its original self had probably died in the process of escape; instead of its own body it now inhabited that of its twin, whose violated, defected mind-state now raged helplessly within the core labelled 2/2.

The drone, still tumbling through interstellar space at two hundred and eighty kilometres a second, felt a kind of revulsion at the very idea of having a treacherous, perverted version of its twin locked inside its own mind. Its first reaction was to expunge it; it thought about just dumping the core into the vacuum and wasting it with its laser, the one weapon which still seemed to be working at close to normal capacity; or it could just shut off power to the core, letting whatever was in it die for want of energy.

And yet it mustn't; like the two higher mind components, the ravaged version of its twin's mind-state might contain clues to the nature of the artifact's own mind-type. It, the AI core and the photonic nucleus all had to be kept as evidence; retained, perhaps, as samples from which a kind of antidote to the artifact's poisonous infectivity might be drawn. There was even a chance that something of its twin's true personality might be retained in the rapacious mind-state the two upper minds and the core contained.

Equally, there was a possibility that the ship's Mind had lost control but not integrity; perhaps – like a small garrison quitting the undefendable curtain wall of a great fortress to take refuge in an all-but-invulnerable central keep – the Mind had been forced to dissociate itself from all its subsystems and given up command to the invader, but succeeded in retaining its own personality in a Mind core as invulnerable to infiltration as the electronic core within the drone's mind (where what was left of its twin now seethed) was proof against escape.

Elencher Minds had been in such dire situations before and survived; certainly such a core could be destroyed (they could not have their power turned off, as the drone's core could; Mind cores had their own internal energy sources) but even the most brutal aggressor would far rather lay siege to that keep-core in the knowledge that the information contained within must surely fall to it eventually, than just destroy it.

There was always hope, the drone told itself; it must not give up hope. According to the specifications it had, the Displacer which had catapulted it out of the ill-fated ship had a range – with something the volume of Sisela Ytheleus 1/2 – of nearly a light second. Surely that was far enough to put it beyond range of detection? Certainly the *Peace Makes Plenty*'s sensors wouldn't have had a hope of spotting something so small so far away; it just had to hope that neither could the artifact.

Excession; that was what the Culture called such things. It had become a pejorative term and so the Elench didn't use it normally, except sometimes informally, amongst themselves. Excession; something excessive. Excessively aggressive, excessively powerful, excessively expansionist; whatever. Such things turned up or were created now and again. Encountering an example was one of the risks you ran when you went a-wandering.

So, now it knew what had happened to it and what the core 2/2 contained, the question was; what was to be done?

It had to get word to outside; that was the task it had been entrusted with by the ship, that was what its whole life-mission had become the instant the ship came under such intensive attack.

But how? Its tiny warp unit had been destroyed, its bom-com unit likewise, its HS laser too. It had nothing that worked at translight speeds, no way of unsticking itself or even a signal from the glutinous slowness that trapped anything unable to step outside the skein of space-time. The drone felt as if it was some quick, graceful flying insect, knocked down to a stagnant pond and trapped there by surface tension, all grace abandoned in its bedraggled, doomed struggle with a strange, cloyingly foreign medium.

It considered again the sub-core where its self-repair mechanisms waited. But not its own repair systems; those of its turncoat twin. It was beyond belief that those too had not been subverted by the invader. Worse than useless; a temptation. Because there was a vanishingly small chance that in all the excitement they had not been taken over.

Temptation . . . But no; it couldn't risk it. It would be folly.

It would have to make its own self-repair units. It was possible, but it would take forever; a month. For a human a month was not that long; for a drone – even one thinking at the shamefully slow speed of light on the skein – it was like a sequence of life sentences. A month was not a long time to *wait*; drones were very good at waiting and had a whole suite of techniques to pass the time pleasantly or just side-step it, but it was an abominably long time to have to *concentrate* on anything, to have to *work* at a single task.

Even at the end of that month, it would just be the start. At the very least there would be a lot of fine tuning to be done; the self-repair mechanisms would need direction, amendment, tinkering with; some would doubtless dismantle where they were supposed to build, others would duplicate what they were meant to scour. It would be like releasing millions of potential cancer cells into an already damaged animal body and trying to keep track of each one. It could quite easily kill itself by mistake, or accidentally breach the containment around the core of its corrupted twin or the original self-repair mechanisms. Even if all went well, the whole process could take years.

Despair!

It set the initial routines under way all the same – what else could it do? – and thought on.

It had a few million particles of anti-matter stored, it had some maniple-field capability left (somewhere between finger- and arm-strength, but down-scalable to the point of being able to work at the micrometer scale, and capable of slicing molecular bonds; it would need both capabilities when it came to building the prototype self-repairer constructs), it possessed two hundred and forty one-millimetre-long nanomissiles, also AM tipped, it could still put up a small mirror field about it, and it had its laser, which was not far off maximum potential. Plus it still had the thimbleful of mush that had been the final-resort back-up biochemical brain.

. . . Which might no longer be able to support thought, but could still inspire it . . .

Well, it was one way to use the nasty gooey mess. Sisela Ytheleus 1/2 started to fashion a shielded reaction chamber and began working out both how best to bring the anti-matter and the cellular gunge together to provide itself with the most reaction mass and maximum thrust and how to direct the resulting exhaust plume so as to minimise the chances of attracting attention.

Accelerating into the stars using a wasted brain; it had its amusing side, it supposed. It set those routines in motion too and – with the equivalent of a long sigh and the taking off of a jacket and the rolling up of sleeves – returned its attention to the self-repairer-building problem.

At that instant a skein wave passed around and through it; a sharp, purposeful ripple in space-time.

It stopped thinking for a nanosecond.

A few things produced such waves. Several were natural; collapsing stellar cores, for example. But this wave was compressed, tightly folded; not the massive, swell-long surge created when a star contracted into a black hole.

This wave was not natural; it had been made. It was a signal. Or it was part of a *sense*.

The drone Sisela Ytheleus 1/2 was helplessly aware of its body, the few kilos of mass it represented, resonating; producing an echoing signal that would transmit back along the radius of that expanding circular disturbance in the skein to whatever instrument had produced the pulse in the first place.

It felt . . . not despair. It felt sick.

It waited.

The reaction was not long in coming; a delicate, fanning, probing cluster of maser filaments, rods of energy seeming to converge almost at infinity, some distance off to one side from where it had guessed the artifact was, three hundred thousand or so kilometres away . . .

The drone tried to shield itself from the signals, but they overcame it. It started to shut down certain systems which might conceivably be corrupted by an attack through the maser signal itself, though the characteristics of the beam had not looked particularly sophisticated. Then suddenly the beam shut off.

The drone looked around. Nothing to be seen, but even as it scanned the cold, empty depths of the space around it, it felt the surface of space-time itself tremble again, all around it, ever so slightly. Something was coming.

The distant vibration increased slowly.

. . . The insect trapped in the surface tension of the pond would have gone still now, while the water quivered and whatever was advancing upon it – skating across the water's surface or angling up from underneath – approached its helpless prey.

III

The car zipped along, slung under one of the monorails that ran amongst the superconducting coils beneath the ceiling of the habitat. Genar-Hofoen looked down through the angled windows of the car at the clouded framescape below.

God'shole habitat (it was much too small to be called an Orbital according to the Culture's definitive nomenclature, plus it was enclosed) was – at nearly a thousand years old – one of the Affront's older outposts in a region of space most civilisations had long since agreed to call the Fernblade. The small world was in the shape of a hollow ring; a tube ten kilometres in diameter and two thousand two hundred long which had been joined into a circle; the superconducting coils and EM wave guides formed the inner rim of the enormous wheel. The tiny, rapidly spinning black hole which provided the structure's power sat where the wheel's hub would have been. The circular-sectioned living space was like a highly pressurised tyre bulging from the inner rim, and where its tread would have been hung the gantries and docks where the ships of the Affront and a dozen other species came and went.

The whole lot was in a slow, distant orbit about an otherwise satellite-less brown dwarf mass just too small to be a proper star but which had long had the honour of being in exactly the right place to further the continuing expansion and consolidation of the Affront sphere of influence.

The monorail car rushed towards a huge wall spread entirely across the view ahead. The rails disappeared into a small, circular door, which opened like a sphincter as the car approached, then closed again behind it. It was dim in the car for a while as it traversed a short tunnel, then another door ahead of it dilated and it shot out into a huge open, mist-filled space where the view just disappeared amongst clouds and haze.

The interior of God'shole habitat was sectioned off into about forty individually isolable compartments, most of them criss-crossed by a web-work of frames, girders and tubular members, partly to provide additional strength for the structure but partly because these created a multitude of places for the Affront to anchor the nest spaces that were the basic cellular building-block of their architecture. There were more open compartments every few sections along the habitat, filled with little more than layers of cloud, a few floating nest space bundles and a selection of flora and fauna. These were the sections which more closely mirrored conditions on the sort of mainly methane-atmosphered planets and moons the Affront preferred, and it was in these the Affront indulged their greatest passion, by going hunting. It was one of these immense game reserves that the car was now crossing. Genar-Hofoen looked downwards again, but he couldn't see a hunt in progress.

As much as a fifth of the whole habitat was devoted to hunting space, and even that represented a huge concession to practicality by the Affront; they'd probably have preferred the proportions to be about half-and-half hunting space and everything else, and even then have thought they were being highly responsible and self-sacrificing.

Genar-Hofoen found himself wondering again about the trade-off between skill-honing and distraction that took place in the development of any species likely to end up as one of those in play in the great galactic civilisation game. The Culture's standard assessment held that the Affront spent far too much time hunting and not nearly enough time getting on with the business of being a responsible space-faring species (though of course the Culture was sophisticated enough to know that this was just its, admittedly subjective, way of looking at things; and besides, the more time the Affront spent dallying in their hunting parks and regaling each other with hunting tales in their carousing halls, the less they had for rampaging across their bit of the galaxy being horrible to people).

But if the Affront didn't love hunting as much as they did, would they still be the Affront? Hunting, especially the highly cooperative form of hunting in three dimensions which the Affront had evolved, required and encouraged intelligence, and it was generally – though not exclusively – intelligence that took a species into space. The required mix of common sense, inventiveness, compassion and aggression required was different for each; perhaps if you tried to make the Affront just a little less enraptured by hunting you would only be able to do so by making them much less intelligent and inquisitive. It was like play; it was fun at the time, when you were a child, but it was also training for when you became an adult. Fun was serious.

Still no sign of a hunt in progress, or even of any herds of prey animals. Just a few filmy mats and hanging verticals of floating plant life. Doubtless some of the smaller animals which a few species of the prey-creatures themselves predated would be hanging munching away on the membranes and gas sacs of the flora, but they were invisible from this distance with the haze preventing closer inspection.

Genar-Hofoen sat back. There was no seat to sit back on because the monorail car wasn't built for humans, but the gelfield suit was imitating the effects of a seat. He wore his usual gilet and holster. At his feet was his gelfield hold-all. He looked at it, then prodded it with a foot. It didn't look much to be taking on a round trip of six thousand light years.

~ *Bastards*, the module said inside his head.

~ What? he asked it.

~ *They seem to enjoy leaving everything to the last moment*, the module said, sounding annoyed. ~ *You know, we only just finished negotiating for the hire of the ships? I mean, you're due to leave in about ten minutes; how late can these maniacs leave things?*

~ Ships plural? he asked.

~ *Ships plural*, the module said. ~ *They insist we hire three of their ridiculous tubs. Any one of which could easily accommodate me, I might add; that's another point at issue. But three! Can you believe? That's practically a fleet by their standards!*

~ Must need the money.

~ *Genar-Hofoen, I know you think it amusing to be the cause of the transfer of funds to the Affront, but might I point out to you that where it is not to all intents and purposes irrelevant, money is power, money is influence, money is effect.*

~ 'Money is effect', Genar-Hofoen mused. ~ That one of your own, Scopell-Afranqui?

~ *The point is that every time we donate the Affront extra means of exchange we effectively become part of their expansionist drive. It is not moral.*

~ Shit, we gave them Orbital-building technology; how does that compare with a few gambling debts?

~ *That was different; we only gave them that so they'd stop taking over so many planets and because they didn't trust the Orbitals we made for them. And I'm not talking about your gambling debts, however outrageous, or your bizarre habit of bidding-up the price of bribes. I'm talking about the cost of hiring three Affronter Nova Class Battle-Cruisers and their crews for two months.*

Genar-Hofoen almost laughed out loud. ~ SC isn't putting that on *your* tab, is it?

~ *Of course not. I was thinking of the wider picture.*

~ What the fuck am I supposed to do? he protested. ~ This is the fastest way of getting me where SC wants me to be. Not my fault.

~ *You could have said No.*

~ Could have. And you'd have spent the next year or so biting my ear about not doing my duty to the Culture when I was asked.

~ *Your only motive, I'm sure,* Scopell-Afranqui said sniffily as the monorail car slowed. The module went off-line with an ostentatious click.

Prick, Genar-Hofoen thought, unheard.

The monorail car passed through another couple of habitat section walls, exiting into a crowded-looking industrial section where the keel skeletons of newly begun Affronter ships rose out of the haze like oddly inappropriate collections of spines and ribs, ornate elaborations within the greater framework of buttresses and columns supporting the habitat itself. The monorail car continued to slow until it drew to a stop within a web-tube attached to one of the structural members. The car started to drop, almost in free-fall.

The car vibrated. In fact, it was rattling. Genar-Hofoen had grown up on a Culture Orbital where only sporting vehicles and things you built yourself for a laugh ever vibrated; normal transport systems rarely ever even made a noise unless it was to ask which floor you wanted or whether you'd like the on-board scent changed.

The monorail car flashed through a floor and into another gigantic hangar space where the towering shapes of half-finished craft rose like barbed pinnacles out of the mist-shrouded framework of slender girders below. The bladed hulls of the ships blurred past to one side.

~ *Wee-hee!* said the gelfield suit, which thought Affronter free-fall was just a total hoot.

~ Glad you're amused, Genar-Hofoen thought.

~ *I hope you realise that if this thing crashes now, even I won't be able to stop you breaking most of your major bones*, the suit informed him.

~ If you can't say something helpful, shut the fuck up, he told it.

Another floor rushed up to meet the car; it plummeted through to a vast, misty hall where almost-finished Affronter ships rose like jagged sky-scrapers. The car came juddering and screeching to a halt near the floor of the huge space – the suit clamped around him in support, but Genar-Hofoen could feel his insides doing uncomfortable things under the effects of the additional apparent gravity – then the car cycled through a pair of airlocks and rumbled down a dark tunnel.

It came out on to the edge of the underside of the habitat where a succession of docks shaped like giant rib-cages disappeared away along the lazy curve of the little world; there was a lot of glare but a few bright stars shone in the darkness. About half the docks were occupied, some with Affronter ships, some with craft from a handful of other species. Dwarfing all the others were three huge dark craft, each of which looked vaguely as though it had been modelled by taking a free-fall aerial bomb from one age and welding onto it a profusion of broad swords, scimitars and daggers from an even earlier time and then magnifying the result until each was a couple of kilometres in length. They hung cradled in docks a few kilometres off; the car swung round and headed towards them.

~ *The good ships* SacSlicer II, FrightSpear *and* Kiss The Blade, the suit announced as the car slowed again and the bulbous black bulks of the craft blotted out the stars.

~ Charmed, I'm sure, thought Genar-Hofoen, picking up his hold-all. He studied the hulls of the three warships, looking for the signs of damage that would indicate the craft were veterans. The signs were there; a delicate tracery of curved lines, light grey on dark grey and black, spread out across the spines, blades and curtain hull of the middle ship indicated a probably glancing blow from a plasma blast (which even Genar-Hofoen, who found weapons boring, could recognise); blurred grey roundels like concentric bruises on that middle ship and the nearest vessel were the marks of another weapon system, and sharp, straight lines etched across the various surfaces of the third craft looked like the effects of yet another.

Of course, the Affront's ships were as self-repairing as any other reasonably advanced civilisation's, and the marks that had been left on the vessels were just that; they would be no thicker than a coat of paint and have negligible effect on the ships' operational capability. However, the Affront thought that it was only right that their ships should – like themselves – bear the scars of honour that battle brings, and so allowed their warships' self-repair mechanisms to stop just short of perfection, the better to display the provenance of their war fleets' glorious reputations.

The car stopped directly underneath the middle warcraft in the midst of a forest of giant pipes and tubes which disappeared into the belly of the ship. Crunches, thumps and hisses from outside the car announced all was being made safe. A wisp of vapour burst from a seal, and the car's door swung out and up. There was a corridor beyond. An honour guard of Affronters jerked to attention; not for him, of course, but for Fivetide and the Affronter at his side dressed in the uniform of a Navy Commander. Both of them were half floating, half walking along towards him, paddles rowing and dangling limbs pushing.

'And here's our guest!' Fivetide shouted. 'Genar-Hofoen; allow me to present Commander Kindrummer VI of both the Blades-corner tribe and the Battle-Cruiser *Kiss The Blade*. So, human; ready for our little jaunt?'

'Yup,' he said, and stepped out into the corridor.

IV

Ulver Seich, barely twenty-two, famed scholastic overachiever since the age of three, voted Most Luscious Student by her last five University years and breaker of more hearts on Phage Rock than anybody since her legendary great-great-great grandmother, had been summarily dragged away from her graduation ball by the drone Churt Lyne.

'Churt!' she said, balling her fists in her long black gloves and nodding her head forward; her high heels clicked along the inlaid wood of the vestibule floor. 'How *dare* you; that was a *deeply* lovely young man I was dancing with! He was utterly, utterly *gorgeous*; how could you just drag me *away* like that?'

The drone, hurrying at her back, dived round in front of her and opened the ancient, manually operated double doors leading from the ballroom vestibule, its suitcase-sized body rustling against the bustle of her gown as it did so. 'I'm sorry beyond words, Ulver,' it told her. 'Now, please let's not delay.'

'Mind my bustle,' she said.

'Sorry.'

'He was *gorgeous*,' Ulver Seich said vehemently as she strode down a stone-flagged hallway lined with paintings and urn plants, following the floating drone as it headed for the traveltube doors.

'I'll take your word for it,' it said.

'And he liked my *legs*,' she said, looking down at the slashed front of the gown. Her long, exposed legs were sheathed in sheer blackness. Violet shoes matched her deep-cut gown; its short train hurried after her in quick, sinuous flicks.

'They're beautiful legs,' the drone agreed, signalling ahead to the traveltube controls to hurry things up.

'Damn right they are,' she said. She shook her head. 'He was gorgeous.'

'I'm sure.'

She stopped abruptly. 'I'm going back.' She turned on her heel, just a little unsteadily.

'What?' yelped Churt Lyne. The drone darted round in front of her; she almost bumped into it. 'Ulver!' the machine said, sounding angry. Its aura field flashed white. 'Really!'

'Get out the way. He was gorgeous. He's mine. He deserves me. Come on; shift.'

It wouldn't get out of the way. She balled her fists again and beat at its snout, stamping her feet. She hiccuped.

'Ulver, Ulver,' the drone said, gently taking her hands in its fields. She stuck her head forward and frowned as hard as she could at the machine's front sensory band. 'Ulver,' it said again. 'Please. Please listen; this is—'

'What is it, anyway?' she cried.

'I told you; something you have to see; a signal.'

'Well, why can't you show it to me *here*?' She looked round the hallway, at the softly lit portraits and the variegated fronds, creepers and parasols of the urn plants. 'There isn't even anybody else around!'

'Because it just doesn't *work* that way,' Churt Lyne said, sounding exasperated. 'Ulver, *please*; this is important. You still want to join Contact?'

She sighed. 'I suppose so,' she said, rolling her eyes. 'Join Contact and go exploring . . .'

'Well, this is your invitation.' It let go of her hands.

She stuck her head forward at it again. Her hair was an artful tangle of massed black curls studded with tiny helium-filled globes of gold, platinum and emerald. It brushed against the drone's snout like a particularly decorative thundercloud.

'Will it let me go exploring on that young man?' she asked, trying to keep her face straight.

'Ulver, if you will just do as I ask there is every chance Contact will happily provide you with entire *ships* full of gorgeous young men. Now, please turn round.'

She snorted derisively and went on tip-toes to look wobblingly over the machine's casing in the direction of the ballroom. She could still hear the music of the dance she'd left. 'Yeah, but it was that one I was interested in . . .'

The drone took her hands again in fields coloured yellow green with calm friendliness, bringing her down off her toes. 'Young lady,' it said. 'I shall never say anything more truthful to you than these two things. One; there will be *plenty* more gorgeous young men in your life. Two; you will never have a better chance of getting into Contact, even Special Circumstances, and with *them* owing *you* a favour; or two. Do you understand? This is your big chance, girl.'

'Don't you "girl" me,' she told it sniffily. The drone Churt Lyne had been a family friend for nearly a millennium and parts of its personality were supposed to date back to when they'd been programs in a house-systems computer nine thousand years earlier. It wasn't in the habit of pulling age on her like this and reminding her that she was a mere day-fly to its creakingly venerable antiquity, but it wasn't above doing so when it thought the situation demanded it, either. She closed one eye and looked closely at the machine. 'Did you say "Special Circumstances" just there?'

'Yes.'

She drew back. 'Hmm,' she said, her eyes narrowing.

Behind her, the traveltube chimed and the door rolled open. She turned and started walking towards it. 'Well, come on, then!' she said over her shoulder.

Phage Rock had been wandering the galaxy for nearly nine thousand years. That made it one of the Culture's oldest elements. It had started out as a three-kilometre-long asteroid in a solar system which was one of the first explored by a species that would later form part of the Culture; it had been mined for metals, minerals and precious stones, then its great internal voids had been sealed against the vacuum and flooded with air, it had been spun to provide artificial gravity and it had become a habitat orbiting its parent sun.

Later, when the technology made it possible and the political conditions prevailing at the time made it advisable to quit that system, it had been fitted with fusion-powered steam rockets and ion engines to help propel it into interstellar space. Again due to those political conditions, it armed itself with up-rated signal lasers and a number of at least partially targetable mass launchers which doubled as rail guns. Some years later, scarred but intact, and finally accepted as personally sentient by its human inhabitants, it had been one of the first space-based entities to declare for the new pan-civilisational, pan-species grouping which was calling itself the Culture.

Over the years, decades, centuries and millennia that had followed, Phage had journeyed through the galaxy, wandering from system to system, concentrating on trading and manufacturing at first and then on a gradually more cultural, educatory role as the advances in technology the Culture was cultivating began to distribute the society's productive capacity so evenly throughout its fabric that the ability to manufacture almost anything developed almost everywhere, and trade became relatively rare.

And Phage Rock – by now recognised as one of a distinct category of Culture artifacts which were neither ships nor worlds but something in between – had grown, accruing new bits of systemic or interstellar debris about it as its needs required and its population increased, securing the chunks of metal, rock, ice and compacted dust to its still gnarled outer surface in a slow process of acquisition, consumption and evolution, so that within just a millennium of its transition from mine to habitat its earlier, original self wouldn't have recognised it; it was thirty kilometres long by then, not three, and only the front half of that initial body still peeped out from the prow of the knobbly collection of equipment-scattered mountains and expanded, balloon-like hangar and accommodation rotundae that now formed its roughly conical body.

Phage Rock's rate of accretion had slowed after that, and it was now just over seventy kilometres long and home to one hundred and fifty million people. It looked like a collection of craggy rocks, smooth stones and still smoother shells brought from a beach and cemented into a rough cairn, all dotted with what looked like a museum collection of Culture Equipment Through the Ages: launch pads, radar pits, aerial frames, sensory arrays, telescope dishes, rail-gun pylons, crater-like rocket nozzles, clamshell hangar doors, iris apertures and a bewildering variety of domes large and small, intact and part-dismantled or just ruined.

As its size and its population had grown, so had the speeds Phage Rock was capable of. It had been successively fitted with ever-more efficient and powerful drives and engines, until eventually it was able to maintain a perfectly respectable velocity either warping along the fabric of space-time or creating its own induced-singularity pathway through hyperspace beneath or above it.

Ulver Seich's had been one of the Rock's Founding Families; she could trace her ancestry back through fifty-four generations on Phage itself and numbered amongst her ancestors at least two forebears who were inevitably mentioned in even one-volume Histories of the Culture, as well as being descended from – as the fashions of the intervening times had ordained – people who had resembled birds, fish, dirigible balloons, snakes, small clouds of cohesive smoke and animated bushes.

The tenor of the time had generally turned against such outlandishness and people had mostly returned to looking more like people over the last millennium, albeit assuredly pretty good-looking people, but still, some part of one's appearance was initially at least left to luck and the random nature of genetic inheritance, and it was a matter of some pride to Ulver that she had never had any form of physical alteration carried out (well, apart from the neural lace of course, but that didn't count). It would have been a brave or deranged human or machine who told Ulver Seich to her face that the give-or-take-a-bit human-basic form was not almost unimprovably graceful and alluring, especially in its female state, and even more especially when it was called Ulver Seich.

She looked round the room the drone had brought her to. It was semicircular and moderately big, shaped like an auditorium or a shallowly sloped lecture hall, but most of the steps or seats seemed to be filled with complicated-looking desks and pieces of equipment. A huge screen filled the far wall.

They'd entered the room through a long tunnel which she'd never seen before and which was blocked by a series of thick, mirror-coated doors which had rolled silently back into recesses as they'd approached, and revolved back into place behind them once they'd passed. Ulver had admired her reflection in every one of them, and drawn herself up even straighter in her spectacular violet gown.

The lights had come on in the semicircular room as the last door had rolled back into place. The place was bright, but dusty. The drone whooshed off to one side and hovered over one of the desks.

Ulver stood looking round the space, wondering. She sneezed.

'Bless you.'

'Thank you. What is this place, Churt?' she asked.

'Emergency Centre Command Space,' the drone told her, as the desk beneath it lit up in places and various panes and panels of light leapt up to waver in the air above its surface.

Ulver Seich wandered over to look at the pretty displays.

'Didn't even know this place existed,' she said, drawing one black-gloved finger along the desk's surface. The displays altered and the desk made a chirping noise; Churt Lyne slapped her hand away, going 'tssk' while its aura field flashed white. She glowered at the machine, inspected the grey rim of dust on her finger tip, and smeared it on the casing of the drone.

Normally Churt Lyne would have slicked that part of its body with a field and the dust would just have fallen off, having literally nothing to cling to, but this time it ignored her and just kept on hovering over the desk and its rapidly changing displays, obviously controlling both it and them. Ulver crossed her black-gloved arms in annoyance.

The sliding panels of lights hanging in the air changed and rotated; figures and letters slid across their surfaces. Then they all disappeared.

'Right,' the drone said. A maniple field coloured formal blue extended from the machine's casing and dragged a small sculpted metal seat over, placing it behind her and then shoving it quickly forward; she had no choice but to plonk down into it.

'Ow,' she said, pointedly. She adjusted her bustle and glared at the drone but it still wasn't paying attention.

'Here we go,' it said.

What looked like a pane of brown smoked glass suddenly leapt into existence above the desk. She studied it, attempting to see her reflection.

'Ready?' the drone asked her.

'Mm-hmm,' she said.

'Ulver, child,' the drone said, in a voice she knew it had spent centuries investing with gravitas. It swivelled through the air until it was directly in front of her.

She rolled her eyes. 'Yes? What?'

'Ulver, I know you're a little—'

'I'm drunk, drone, I know,' she told it. 'But I haven't lost my wits.'

'Well, good, but I need to know you're fit to make this decision. What you're about to see might change your life.'

She sighed and put her gloved elbow on the surface of the desk, resting her chin on her hand. 'I've had a few young fellows tell me that before,' she drawled. 'It always turns out to be a disappointment, or a joke of the grossest nature.'

'This is neither. But you must understand that just seeing what I'm about to show you might give Special Circumstances an interest in you that will not pass; even if you decide you don't want to join Contact, or even if you do but you're still refused, it is possible they might watch you for the rest of your life, just because of what you're about to see. I'm sorry to sound so melodramatic, but I don't want you to enter into anything you don't understand the full implications of.'

'Me neither.' She yawned. 'Can we get on with this?'

'You're sure you've understood what I've said?'

'Hell yes!' she exclaimed, waving her arms around. 'Just get on with it.'

'Oh; just one other thing—'

'*What*?' she yelled.

'Will you travel to a distant location in the guise of somebody else and – probably – help kidnap somebody, another Culture citizen?'

'Will I *what*?' she said, wrinkling her nose and snorting with laughter and disbelief.

'Sounds like a "No" to me,' the drone said. 'Didn't think you would. Had to ask though. That means I have no choice but to show you this.' It sounded relieved.

She put both her black-gloved arms on the desk, rested her chin on them and looked as soberly as she could at the drone. 'Churt,' she said. '*What* is going on here?'

'You'll see,' it told her, getting out of the way of the screen. 'You ready?'

'If I get any more ready I'll be asleep.'

'Good. Pay attention.'

'Oh yes, *sir*,' she said, glancing narrow-eyed at the machine.

'Watch!' it said.

She sat back in the seat with her arms folded.

Words appeared on the screen:

("TextTrans" Obscure Term/Acronym Explanation function running, instances flagged thus: {}.)
(Signal sequence received at Phage Rock:)
∞

1) [skein broadcast, Mclear {standard nonary Marain}, received @ n4.28.855.0065+]:

'What's "nonary" mean?'

'Based on nine. Ordinary Marain; the stuff you learned in kindergarten, for goodness' sake; the three-by-three dot grid.'

'Oh.'

The text scrolled on:

!c11505. {trans.: ("*" = broadcast) ("!" = warning) Galaxy sector

number; whole comprises standard-format High-Compression Factor Emergency Warning Signal}
∞

2) [swept beam M1 {Basic Culture Intragalactic Ship Language}, received
@ n4.28.855.0079-]:
   SDA {trans.: Significant Developmental Anomaly}.
   c2314992+52 {trans.: 4th-level-of-accuracy galactic location}
   x {from} **FATC** {trans.: (General Contact Unit) Fate Amenable To Change} @ **n4.28.855.***.

'Could we lose all these strings of figures?' she asked the drone. 'They're not really telling me anything I need to know, are they?'
'I suppose not. There.'

(Command: "TextTrans" Long-Numeral Stripping function enabled, set at five numerals or more, instances flagged thus: •)
∞

3) [swept beam, M2 {Standard Contact Section Idiom}, relay, received
@n•]
   xGCU *Fate Amenable To Change*
     o {to} GSV *Ethics Gradient*
     & as requested:
   Significant developmental anomaly.
   c • {trans.: 8th-level-of-accuracy galactic location}
(@n•).
∞

4) [tight beam, M16 {Special Circumstances Section High Level Code Sequence}, relay, received @n•
   xGCU *Fate Amenable To Change*
     oGSV *Ethics Gradient*
     & only as required:
   Developmental anomaly provisionally rated EqT {trans.: Equivalent-Technology}, **potentially jeopardising, found here c•.**
   My Status: L5 secure, moving to L6ˆ {trans.: Contact Mind prophylactic system security levels}.
   Instigating all other Extreme precautions.
∞

5) [broadcast Mclear, received @n•]:
   *xGCU *Fate Amenable To Change*
     oGSV *Ethics Gradient*
     & *broadcast*:
   Ref. 3 previous compacs {trans.: communication-packages}
[ref 1-3 above].

Panic over.
I misinterpreted.
It's a Scapsile Vault Craft.
Ho hum.
Sorry.
Full Internal Report to follow immediately in High Embarrassment Factor code.

BSTS. H&H. BTB. {trans. "BSTS. H&H. BTB." = "Better Safe Than Sorry. Hale & Hearty. Back To Business." (pre-agreed OK signal between Escarpment Class General Contact Unit *Fate Amenable To Change* and General Systems Vehicle *Ethics Gradient*, confirmed.)}

∞

End Signal Sequence.

'Is that *it*?' she cried, staring at the drone. 'That's the most boring—!'

'No it *isn't*; look!'

She looked back; the text scrolled on.

∞

[Pre-refereed security clearance granted – Ref. Phage Rock.]

[Signal Sequence log unlocked, re-enabled.]

∞

("TextTrans" Record Event function disabled.)

∞

Signal Sequence resuming:

∞

. . .6) [stuttered tight point, M32 SCantk {trans.: Special Circumstances absolute-need-to-know Level Maximum Encryption Code Process}, relay, Tracked Copy 4, received @n•, check to read: [x].

Being read @n• in ECent Command Space on Phage Rock by:

"Text-Trans" (recognised Archaic, v891.4, non sentient. NB: "Text-Trans" Record Event function will remain disabled to document End-Read-point).

(so cleared)

&

Phage-Kwins-Broatsa Ulver Halse Seich dam Iphetra

(so cleared)

&

Escaruze Churt Lyne Bi-Handrahen Xatile Treheberiss

(so cleared).

Sentient sight of the following document will be recorded.
Each check to proceed:
[x]
[x].
Thank you. Proceeding:]
NB: **Attention:** The following is a screen-written text-only dynamically scrolled discrete-assimilation-opportunity document which may not be vocalised, glyphed, diaglyphed, copied, stored or media-transferred in any conventionally accessible form. Any attempt to do so will be noted.
Please adjust reading speed:
[default/human].
NB: **IMPORTANT:** Established SC secrecy methodology applies at M32 level – see following schedule re. definitions, precedents, warnings, likely sanctions and punishments. **You are strongly advised to study this schedule carefully if you are not already fully familiar—**
[override]
[Schedule read-out aborted.]

'You weren't supposed to do that!' Churt Lyne yelped.

Ulver had spotted the part of the text panel that overrode the read-out, and pressed it. She snorted. 'Shh!' she said, nodding at the screen. 'You're missing it!'

Begin-Read point of Tracked Copy document #SC•.c4: +
    xGCU *Fate Amenable To Change*
        oGSV *Ethics Gradient*
        & strictly as SC cleared:
Excession notice @•.
Constitutes formal All-ships Warning Level 0 [(in temporary sequestration) – textual note added by GSV *Wisdom Like Silence* @•].
Excession.
Confirmed precedent-breach. Type K7ˆ. True class non-estimal. Its status: Active. Aware. Contactiphile. Uninvasive sf {trans.:   so far}.
LocStatre {trans.: Locally Static with reference to}: **Esperi (star).**
    First ComAtt {trans.: CommunicationAttempt} **(its, following shear-by contact via my primary scanner @•)** @• **in M1-a16 & Galin II by tight beam, type 2A. PTA** {trans.: Permission To Approach} **& Handshake burst as appended, x@ 0.7Y** {trans.: (light) Year}. **Suspect signal gleaned from Z-E** {trans.: Zetetic Elench}/**Ialsaer ComBeam** {trans.: CommunicationBeam} **spread, 2nd Era. xContact callsigned "I". No other signals registered.**

My subsequent actions: maintained course and speed, skim-declutched {?} primary scanner to mimic 50% closer approach, began directed full passive HS {trans.: HyperSpacial} scan (sync./start of signal sequence, as above), sent buffered Galin II pro-forma message-reception confirmation signal to contact location, dedicated track scanner @ 19% power and 300% beamspread to contact @ -25% primary scanner roll-off point, instigated ^{2}exponential {?} slow-to-stop line manoeuvre synchronised to skein-local stop-point @ 12% of track scanner range limit, ran full systems check as detailed, executed slow/4 {?} swing-around then retraced course to previous closest approach point and stop @ standard ^{2}ex curve {?}. Holding there.

Excession's physical characteristics: (¡am!) {trans.: anti-matter} sphere rad. 53.34km, mass (non-estimal by space-time fabric influence – locality ambiently planar – estimated by pan-polarity material density norms at) $1.45x8^{13}$t. Layered fractal matter-type-intricate structure, self supporting, open to (field-filtered) vacuum, anomalous field presence inferred from 8^{21} kHz leakage. Affirm K7^ category by HS topology & eG {trans.: (hyperspatial) energy Grid} links (inf. & ult.) {trans.: (the hyperspatial directions) infra and ultra}. eG link details non-estimal. DiaGlyph files attached.

Associated anomalous materials presence: several highly dispersed detritus clouds all within 28 minutes, three consistent with staged destruction of $>.1m^3$ near-equiv-tech entity, another ditto approx 3^8 partially exhausted M-DAWS .1cal rounds {trans.: Miniaturised-Drone Advanced Weapon System nanomissiles}, another consisting of general hi-soph level (O_2-atmosphered) ship-internal combat debris. Latter drifting directly away from excession's current position. Retracks of debris clouds' expansion profiles indicate mutual age of 52.5 days. Combat debris cloud implicitly originating @ point 948 milliseconds from excession's current position. DiaGlyph files attached.

No other presences apparent to within 30 years.

My status: H&H, unTouched. L8 secure post system-scour (100%). ATDPSs {trans.: Auto Total Destruct Protocol Suites} engaged. CRTTDPSs {trans.: Coded Remote-Triggered Total Destruct Protocol Suites} engaged.

Repeat:

Excession eGrid (inf. & ult.) linked, confirmed.

eGrid link details non-estimal.

True class non-estimal.

Awaiting.

@n•...

.

...PS:

Gulp.

.

(Document binary choice menu, [1 = Yes or 0 = No]:)
.

Repeat?   [.]
Inspect Reading history?   [.]
Read previous comments?   [.]
Attach comments?   [.]
Read appendices?   [.]
All the above (0 = leave doc): [.]

'We'll dip out here for now,' the drone said.

All the above (0 = leave doc):[0]
End-Read point Tracked Copy document #SC•.c4: +
.

NB: The preceding Tracked Copy document is not readable/copyable/
transmissible without its embedded security program.
NB: **IMPORTANT:** Communicating any part, detail, property, interpretation or attribute of the preceding document, **INCLUDING ITS
EXISTENCE—**
[override]
[Post-document warning read-out aborted.]

  'I wish you'd stop doing that,' the drone muttered.
  'Sorry,' she said. Ulver Seich shook her head slowly at the text
hanging in the air in front of her and the drone Churt Lyne. She
took a deep breath. Suddenly, she felt quite entirely sober. 'Is this
as important as I think it is?'
  'Almost certainly much more so.'
  'Oh,' she said, 'fuck.'
  'Indeed,' the drone replied. 'Any other questions so far?'
  She looked at the last word of the GCU's main signal:

Gulp.

  Gulp. Well, she could relate to that all right.
  'Questions . . .' Ulver Seich said, staring at the holo screen and
blowing her cheeks out. She turned to the drone, her violet ball
gown rustling. 'Lots. First, what are we really . . .? No; hold on.
Just take me through the signal. Never mind all the translations
or whatever; what's it actually *saying*?'

'The General Contact Unit issues an excession notice through its home General Systems Vehicle,' the drone told her, 'but it's prevented from being broadcast by another GSV which the first one obviously contacted before doing anything. The GCU tells us that its sensors clipped this artifact, which then hailed the GCU using an old Elench greeting and an even older Galactic Common Language; then the GCU spends a great deal of the signal detailing how clever it was pretending that it's slower, not as manoeuvrable and less well equipped in the sensor department than actually it is. It describes the object and a few surrounding bits and pieces of debris which imply there was some sort of small-scale military action there fifty-three days earlier, then it assures it's well and unviolated but it's ready to blow itself up, or let somebody else blow it up if its integrity is threatened . . . not a step a GCU takes lightly.

'However, entirely the most important aspect of the signal is that the object it has discovered is linked to the energy grid in both hyperspatial directions; that alone puts it well outside all known parameters and precedents. We have no previous experience whatsoever with something like this; it's unique; beyond our ken. I'm not surprised the GCU is scared.'

'Okay, okay, that's kind of what I thought; shit.' She belched delicately. 'Excuse me.'

'Of course.'

'Now, like I was going to say; what are we really dealing with here; an excession, or something else?'

'Well, if you take the definition of an excession as anything external to the Culture that we should be worried about, this is an excession all right. On the other hand, if you compare it to the average – or even an exceptional – Hegemonising Swarm, it's small, localised, non-invasive, unaggressive, unshielded, immobile . . . and almost chatty, using Galin II to communicate.' The drone paused. 'The crucial characteristic then remains the fact that the thing's linked to the energy grid, both up and down. *That's* interesting, to put it mildly, because as far as we know, nobody knows how to do that. Well, nobody apart from the Elder civilisations . . . probably; they won't say and we can't tell.'

'So this *thing* can do something the Culture can't?'

'Looks like it.'

'And I take it the Culture would like to be able to do what it can do.'

'Oh, yes. Yes, very much so. Or, even if it couldn't partake of the technology, at least it would like to use the implied opportunity the excession may represent.'

'To do what?'

'Wehhll,' Churt Lyne said, drawing the word out while its aura-field coloured with embarrassment and its body wobbled in the air, 'technically – maybe – the ability to travel – easily – to other universes.' The machine paused again, looking at the human and waiting for her sarcastic reply. When she didn't say anything, it continued. 'It should be possible to step outside the time-strand of our universe as easily as a ship steps outside the space-time fabric. It might then become feasible to travel through superior hyperspace upwards to universes older than ours, or through inferior hyperspace downwards to universes younger than our own.'

'*Time* travel?'

'No, but affording the opportunity to become time proof. Age proof. In theory, one might become able to step down consecutively through earlier universes . . . well, forever.'

'Forever?'

'Real forever, as far as we understand it. You could choose the size and therefore age of the universe you wanted to remain within, and/or visit as many as you wanted. You could, for example, head on up through older universes and attempt to access technologies perhaps beyond even this one. But just as interesting is the point that because you wouldn't be tied to one universe, one time stream, you need be involved in no heat death when the time came in your original universe; or no evaporation, or no big crunch, depending.

'It's like being on an escalator. At the moment, confined to this universe, we're stuck to this stair, this level; the possibility this artifact appears to offer is that of being able to step from one stair to another, so that before your stair on the escalator comes to the end of its travel – heat-death, big crunch, whatever – you just step off one level down to another. You could, in effect, live for ever . . . well, unless it's discovered that cosmic fireball engines themselves have a life-cycle; as I understand it the metamath on that implies but does not guarantee perpetuity.'

Seich looked at the drone for a while, her brows furrowed. 'Haven't we *ever* found anything like this before?'

'Not really. There are ambiguous reports of vaguely similar entities turning up in the past – though they tend to disappear before anybody can fully investigate – but as far as we know, *nobody* has ever found anything quite like this before.'

The human was silent for a while. Then she said, 'If you could access any universe, and go back to one universe at a very early, pre-sentience stage with an already highly developed civilisation . . .'

'You could take over the whole thing,' the drone confirmed. 'An entire universe would be yours alone. In fact, go back far enough – that is, to a small enough, early enough, just-post-singularity universe – and you could, conceivably, customise it; mould it, shape it, influence its primary characteristics. Admittedly, that sort of control may well remain in the realm of the fantastic, but it *might* be possible.'

Ulver Seich drew a deep breath, and, looking at the floor, nodded slowly. '. . . And of course,' she said, 'if this thing is what it appears to be, it could be an exit, as well as an entrance.'

'Entirely so; it is almost certainly both at once. As you imply; never mind us getting *into* it, we don't know what might come *out* of it.'

Ulver Seich nodded slowly. '. . . Holy shit,' she said.

'Let's call up the comments,' Churt Lyne suggested.

'Can we miss out the preparatory junk at the start?'

'Allow me. There.'

Read previous comments?   [1]

'. . . And skip all the detailology crap, too. Just who said what.'

'As you wish.'

(Comments section:)

x *Wisdom Like Silence* (GSV, Continent class):
1.0 As agreed within the informal SC Extraordinary Events Core Group (Crisis Preparatory Foresight Sub-Committee, Occasional), we (in multiple mode) have assumed the management of this situation as of n•.
1.1 The following constitute our introductory remarks.
2.0 Might we first beg to record that it goes without saying that we are not only extremely flattered but also deeply humbled to be placed in a

position of such importance on the occasion of this grave, profound and indeed one might even say momentous circumstance.

'Po-faced bastard. Are all Continents this *up* themselves?'
'Want me to ask somebody?'
'Yeah, I'm sure we'd get a straight answer to that one.'
'Just so.'
'Hmm. Meanwhile the bullshit rolls on.'

3.0 Clearly, this is a matter of the utmost consequence. It follows that the manner in which it is presented beyond ourselves must be considered with regard to all the possible ramifications and repercussions such a pan-developmentally crucial subject might reasonably be expected to entail.

'Sit on it, in other words,' Seich said tartly. 'What exactly is a Continent class's multiple mode, anyway?'
'Three-Mind grouping, usually.'
'That's why it's saying everything in triplicate . . .'

3.1 The Excession under consideration is without precedent, but it is also – it would appear – static, and (presently, and again apparently) to all intents and purposes inactive. Thus, caution (born of import, situational stability and imprecedence) would appear to be the order of the moment. We have – as a temporary measure, and with the approval of those comprising the above Group and Sub-Committee who are within reasonable consultative range – deemed the matter to be secrecy-rated such that all discussions and communications regarding it are carried out according to M32 standard.
3.2 Under the terms of the Temporary Emergencies (Allowed Subterfuges) Post-Debacle Steering Committee report following the Azadian Matter, the maximum length of the M32 secrecy interval has been set at 128 days standard from n•, with a Mean Envisaged Duration of 96 days and a full-sub-committee review period of 32 hours.
3.3 The nearest star to this Excession is called Esperi (under Standard Adopted Nomenclature); however, in accordance with M32 procedure we propose the code-term Taussig (from the Primary Random Event-Naming List) be used regarding this matter henceforth.
3.4 This concludes our introductory remarks.
4.0 The following comments will be arranged in sorted-relevance order; actual receive-times and context-schedules are available in the usual appendices.
4.1 We hereby open the discussion on the Taussig Matter.

∞

x *Anticipation Of A New Lover's Arrival, The* (GSV, Plate class):
Right. First, this should not be kept secret, even for a limited time. I object
in the strongest possible terms to the fact that the instant we stumble over
possibly the most important thing anybody's ever found anywhere ever,
the first thing SC does is snap into Full-Scale Raving Paranoia mode and
apply this M32 total-secrecy-or-we'll-pull-your-plugs-out-baby shit. I've
given my word and I'm not going to leak this, but for the record, I believe
we should be telling everybody. (Let's face it, we'll probably have to well
before this unrealistic time-limit of 128 days, anyway.)
.

That said, if we are going to keep this to ourselves for the time being,
might I anticipate SC's all-too-predictable reaction and draw everyone's
attention to a study by the *Added Value* [text and details attached] which
basically says if you surround something like this with a mega-fleet and
it isn't quite omnipotent, just staggeringly powerful and fully invasive,
you're basically giving it an immense, ready-made war-fleet to play with,
if it is hostile. Just a thought.

∞

x *Tactical Grace* (GCU, Escarpment Class):
I agree absolutely with the above and endorse the *Added Value* study.
Let us not thoughtlessly get cannoned up on this one.

∞

x *Woetra* (Orbital Hub, Schiparse-Oevyli system, [solo]):
Some sadness reigns. We may approach the end of our knowing Naïvety.
Draw round (the fire, growing dim, draws too, drawing in its breath for
one fine final burst of flame). Potentially an end of innocence, we face
this, glancing backwards. Within the horizon of our mutual import, an
end and start to Meaning (finally beginning). Ancients (knowing so little)
would have half expected, partly welcomed what we all fear this might
be. We (knowing all too much) would rather deny its untold implications.
Ephemera, they were half happy with and wholly used to the possibility
of an End. By their knowing Immortal, we tremble before the same. My
friends, if we have ever worshipped anything, it has been the great god
Chaos. (What else shields Intelligence from the awful implications of
utter Omniscience?) Might we be looking at our god's Deiclast?

∞

x *Steely Glint* (GCV, Plains Class):
Remarkable. One hears nothing for years then suddenly ... well,
anyway. *Pace* the *Added Value* study mentioned above, I propose the
immediate and complete remilitarisation of all viable units to within
– say – sixty-four days' rush-in distance. Not so much because we
might need to fight the Taussig Matter itself but because this Event

will undoubtedly not stay secret for very long and will – with equal certitude – attract an entire cast of terminological Civiliseds of the distinctly Undesirable persuasion. Serious up-cannoning on our part, for all its intrinsic vulgarity and first-principle undesirability, may be the only way to prevent scalar inter-civilisation conflicts which, at worst, might overshadow the entail of the Matter itself.

∞

x *Serious Callers Only* (LSV, Tundra Class):
Here, in the bare dark face of night
A calm unhurried eye draws sight
- We see in what we think we fear
The cloudings of our thought made clear.

∞

x *Wisdom Like Silence* (GSV, Continent class):
A most interesting contribution, we're sure, but can we keep this just a little more focused?

∞

x *Shoot Them Later* (Eccentric, Culture Ulterior, AhForgetIt tendency [t. rated Integration Factor 73%, vessel rated 99%]):
Illuminating. Unhappy as I am to agree with the *Steely Glint*, I suspect it might be right. There, I said it.

∞

x *Wisdom Like Silence* (GSV, Continent class):
I was not aware that the *Shoot Them Later* was part of this Core Group! No entity with an IF of less than 100% is supposed even to be considered for inclusion in this Group! No Eccentric or Ulterior craft are eligible! LSV *Serious Callers Only*; said message was relayed through you; provide an explanation immediately!

∞

x *Serious Callers Only* (LSV, Tundra Class):
No.

∞

{x *Ethics Gradient* (GSV, Range Class):
With the Group's permission: Hint of warp wake – inadvertent soliton resonation signature – Kraszille system (62 std years xTM), curved V towards TM region. DGs attached. Probably nothing . . .}

∞

x *Limivorous* (GSV, Ocean Class):
This TM, this latest E, this I, this strange new object of concern: telic?

∞

x *Wisdom Like Silence* (GSV, Continent class):
With immense respect to our highly esteemed colleague *Limivorous* and with full cognizance of its most illustrious career and near-legendary

reputation, we have to say we were also not aware that our humble group was graced with its exalted regard! GSV *Anticipation Of A New Lover's Arrival, The*; as relayer, you should have informed us you were in contact with the *Limivorous*!

∞

x *Not Invented Here* (MSV, Desert Class):
Read. Also henotic?

∞

x *Wisdom Like Silence* (GSV, Continent class):
But the *Not Invented Here* was reported destroyed in 2.31! Identify yourself, you liar! Security breach! What is going on here?

∞

x *Shoot Them Later* (Eccentric, Culture Ulterior, AhForgetIt tendency [t. rated Integration Factor 73%, vessel rated 99%]):
Tee hee.

∞

x *Full Refund* (Homomdan 'Empire' Class Main Battle Unit [original name *MBU 604*] Convertcraft [vessel rated Integration Factor 80% {nb; self-assessed}]):
Add delitescent.

∞

x *Wisdom Like Silence* (GSV, Continent class):
What! We can't have a self-assessed ex-enemy craft privy to M32-level matters! What is going on here? Security breach! I invoke my authority as convener of this Group to suspend all M32 level discussion immediately and until further notice while a full security review is carried out.

∞

x *Different Tan* (GCU, Mountain Class):
Indeed so, perhaps. Even – whisper it – an outrance?

∞

x *Wisdom Like Silence* (GSV, Continent class):
The *Different Tan* is also not an accredited member of this Core Group! This has gone far enough! We hereby—

∞

Switching document/comments track.]
[New M32-level Core Group formed.
Name: Interesting Times Gang (Act IV).
Group initially comprises all previously mentioned craft except *Wisdom Like Silence* (GSV, Continent class).]

∞

x *Star Turn* (Rock, First Era):
Filing name change.
From: *Star Turn*

To: *End In Tears.*
∞

x *No Fixed Abode* (GSV, Sabbaticaler, ex Equator Class):
I suggest firstly that we rid ourselves of this ridiculous 'Taussig' nonsense and call the matter after Esperi, the nearest star; I also propose that between eight and sixteen days from now – depending on the availability of more noteworthy news from elsewhere – we move to an information release at M16-level, simply saying that we have discovered an excession of an ambiguous nature, which we are investigating and which we are asking others to stay away from. Assuming that they will not, we should request the *Steely Glint* to instigate a measured and localised military mobilisation, immediately. Beyond that, the normal democratic processes will doubtless apply.
∞

x *Tactical Grace* (GCU, Escarpment Class):
A subtle cannon up, then.
∞

x *Steely Glint* (GCV, Plains Class):
Indeed. An honour; I accept.
∞

x *Serious Callers Only* (LSV, Tundra Class):
And let the *Wisdom Like Silence* be the agent of information release?
∞

x *Shoot Them Later* (Eccentric, Culture Ulterior, AhForgetIt tendency [t. rated Integration Factor 73%, vessel rated 99%]):
Oh, witty. Well, if it isn't in the huff . . .
∞

x *Anticipation Of A New Lover's Arrival, The* (GSV, Plate class):
I think we ought to release immediately.
∞

x *No Fixed Abode* (GSV, Sabbaticaler, ex Equator Class):
Abhorrent as I'm sure we all find such ploys, I suspect that the extra week or two's additional start on everybody else this delay ought to give us will prove significant in preparing for the fray which may result from this becoming public.
∞

x *Different Tan* (GCU, Mountain Class):
As the *Not Invented Here* is the closest major unit to the matter I suggest it makes all speed for the location of the Excession and acts as incident coordinator. I myself am not too far away from the Esperi system; I shall make my way there and rendezvous with the *Not Invented Here.*
∞

x *Not Invented Here* (MSV, Desert Class):

My pleasure.

∞

x *Different Tan* (GCU, Mountain Class):
I also submit that the GSV *Ethics Gradient* and the GCU *Fate Amenable To Change* ought to be invited into the Interesting Times Gang (Act IV) for the duration of the crisis, and both craft instructed to hold back from full investigation of the Excession until further notice. Relayed character assessments of the two craft attached; they look reliable.

∞

x *Woetra* (Orbital Hub, Schiparse-Oevyli system, [solo]):
And call our mutual friend.

∞

x *No Fixed Abode* (GSV, Sabbaticaler, ex Equator Class):
Of course. So, are we all agreed on all the above?

∞

x *Anticipation Of A New Lover's Arrival, The* (GSV, Plate class):
Agreed.

∞

x *Tactical Grace* (GCU, Escarpment Class):
Agreed.

∞

x *Woetra* (Orbital Hub, Schiparse-Oevyli system, [solo]):
Agreed.

∞

x *Steely Glint* (GCV, Plains Class):
Agreed.

∞

x *Serious Callers Only* (LSV, Tundra Class):
Objection!
. . . Na, just kidding:
Agreed.

∞

x *Shoot Them Later* (Eccentric, Culture Ulterior, AhForgetIt tendency [t. rated Integration Factor 73%, vessel rated 99%]):
Agreed.

∞

x *Limivorous* (GSV, Ocean Class):
Agreed.

∞

x *Not Invented Here* (MSV, Desert Class):
Agreed.

∞

x *Full Refund* (Homomdan 'Empire' Class Main Battle Unit [original

name *MBU 604*] Convertcraft vessel rated Integration Factor 80% {nb; self-assessed}):
Agreed.
∞

x *Different Tan* (GCU, Mountain Class):
Agreed.
∞

x *End In Tears* (Rock, First Era, previously *Star Turn*):
Agreed. Doing my bit. Done.
∞

x *No Fixed Abode* (GSV, Sabbaticaler, ex Equator Class):
Agreed.
∞

x *Limivorous* (GSV, Ocean Class):
Good talking to you all again, by the way. So; now we wait.
∞

x *Serious Callers Only* (LSV, Tundra Class):
And see...
·

(End of comments.)
·

(Document binary choice menu, [1 = Yes or 0 = No]:)
·

Repeat?   [·]
Inspect Reading history?   [·]
Read previous comments?   [·]
Attach comments?   [·]
Read appendices?   [·]
All the above (0 = leave doc):   [0]
·

End-Read point Tracked Copy document SC•: +
·

NB: The preceding Tracked Copy document is not readable/copyable/ transmissible without its embedded security program.
NB: **IMPORTANT:** Communicating any part, detail, property, interpretation or attribute of the preceding document, **INCLUDING ITS EXISTENCE—** [override]
[Post-document warning read-out aborted.]

The holo screen disappeared. 'So what does all *that* mean?' she asked.
    '. . . Good grief, Ulver,' the drone said, giving a fair impression of spluttering. 'It's the Heavy Crew! It's the Ghosts!'

'What? The who?' She swivelled in the seat to face the drone.

'Child, there were names appearing there I hadn't seen for *five centuries*. Some of those Minds are *legends*!'

'This is the Interesting Times Gang we're talking about, I take it?'

'That's obviously what they call themselves.'

'Well, good for them, but I still want to know what all that was about.'

'Well, a normal enough but pretty high-power Mind Incident Group gets together to discuss what's going on, then – allowing for signal travel duration – within real-time seconds it's taken over by probably the most respected not to mention enigmatic group of Minds ever assembled together in the same signal sequence since the end of the Idiran War.'

'You don't say,' Ulver said, yawning a little and putting one black-gloved hand over her mouth.

'Yes; in the case of the *Not Invented Here*, everybody I know thought the thing had been lost half a millennium ago! Then they dump the boring, pedantic GSV that happened to be on the Incident Coordinating Rota, agree to wait-and-see with the Excession itself while sending investigatory reinforcements, start a localised mobilisation – mobilisation! – and release a half-truth about the Excession when there's some more exciting news breaking.'

Ulver frowned. 'When did all this happen?'

'Well, if you hadn't turned off the date/time function . . .' muttered the drone, colouring frosty blue. Ulver rolled her eyes again. 'The Excession was discovered and that signal sequence plus comments dates from twelve days ago. The Excession's discovery was announced through the standard channels the day before yesterday.'

The human shrugged. 'I missed it.'

'The headlines concerned the resolution of the Blitteringueh situation.'

'Ah-hah. That would do it, I suppose.'

Most of the developed galaxy had been following that story for the past hundred days, as the aftermath of the short but bitter Blitteringueh–Deluger War played itself out on the CAM-bomb-mined Blitteringueh home planets and the Deluger fleets fleeing with their precious holy relics and Grand House captives. It had ended with relatively little loss of life, but in high drama, and with continuing, developing repercussions; little wonder anything else announced that day had slipped by almost unnoticed and stayed that way.

'And what was that thing towards the end there, about "Calling our mutual friend"?'

'That'll probably turn out to be something to do with inviting some other Mind onto the group.' The drone was silent for a moment. 'Though of course it could be some pre-agreed form of words, a secret signal amongst the group.'

Seich stared at the drone. 'A secret *signal*?' she said. 'In an M32-level transmission?'

'It's possible; no more.'

Seich continued to stare at the machine for a moment. 'You're saying that these Minds are discussing something . . . *agreeing* to something that's so sensitive, so secret they won't even talk about it in Special Circumstances' top-end code, the fucking holy of holies, the unbreakable, inviolable, totally secure M32?'

'No I'm *not*. I'm just saying it's . . . semi-possible.' The drone's aura field flickered grey with frustration. 'In that event, though, I don't think it would be breakability they'd be worried about.'

'What then?' Seich's eyes narrowed. 'Deniability?'

'If we're thinking in such paranoid terms in the first place, yes, that'd be my guess,' the drone said, dipping its front once in a nod and making a noise like a sigh.

'So they're up to something.'

'Well, they're up to a lot, by the sound of it. But it's just possible that some part of what they're up to might be, well, risky.'

Ulver Seich sat back, staring at the empty square of the projected screen, hanging in the air in front of her and the drone Churt Lyne like a pane of slightly opaque smoked glass. 'Risky,' she said. She shook her head and felt a strange urge to shiver, which she suppressed. 'Shit, don't you hate it when the Gods come out to play?'

'In a word,' said the drone, 'yes.'

'So what am I supposed to do? And why?'

'You're supposed to look like this woman,' the drone said, as a bright, still picture flashed on to the smoky screen in front of her.

Ulver studied the face, chin in her hand again. 'Hmm,' she said. 'She's older than me.'

'True.'

'And not as pretty.'

'Fair enough.'

'Why do I have to look like her?'

'To draw the attention of a certain man.'

She narrowed her eyes. 'Wait a minute; I'm not expected to *fuck* this guy, am I?'

'Oh good grief, *no*,' the drone said, its aura field briefly grey again. 'All you have to do is look like an old flame of his.'

She laughed. 'I bet I *am* expected to fuck him!' She rocked back in the little metal seat. 'How quaint! Is this *really* what SC gets up to?'

'No you're *not*,' hissed the drone, aura fields going deep grey. 'You just have to *be* there.'

'I'll bet,' she guffawed, and sat back, crossing her arms. 'So who is he, anyway?'

'Him,' the drone said. Another still face appeared on the screen.

Ulver Seich sat forward again, raising one hand. 'Hold on. I take it all back; actually he's pretty *enticing* . . .'

The drone made a sighing noise. 'Ulver, if you will please try to hold your hormones in check for just a second . . .'

'*What?*' she shouted, spreading her arms.

'Will you do this or not?' it asked her.

She closed one eye and wobbled her head from side to side. 'Maybe,' she slurred.

'It means a trip,' the drone said. 'Leaving tonight—'

'Pah!' She sat back, crossing her arms and looking up at the ceiling. 'Out of the question. Forget it.'

'All right; tomorrow.'

She turned to the drone. 'After lunch.'

'Breakfast.'

'Late breakfast.'

'Oh,' the machine said, aura field briefly grey with frustration. 'All right. Late breakfast. But before noon, in any event.'

Ulver opened her mouth to protest, then gave a tiny shrug and settled for scowling. 'Okay. How long for?'

'You'll be back in a month, if all goes well.'

She tipped her head back, narrowed her eyes again and said quite soberly and precisely, 'Where?'

The drone said, 'Tier.'

'Huh,' she said, tossing her head.

A sore point; Phage had been heading to Tier specifically for that year's Festival but had been diverted off course to help build an Orbital after the part-evacuation of some stupid planet; it had taken forever. The Festival only lasted a month and was now almost over; the Rock was still heading that way but wouldn't arrive for two hundred days or so.

She frowned. 'But that's a couple of months away even on a fast ship.'

'Special Circumstances has its own ships and they're faster; ten days to get there on the one they're giving you.'

'My *own* ship?' Ulver asked, eyes flashing.

'All yours; not even any human crew.'

'Wow!' she said, sitting back and looking pleased with herself. '*Aloof*!'

4
Dependency Principle

[tight beam, M16.4, rec. @n4.28.856.4903]
xGSV *Anticipation Of A New Lover's Arrival, The*
  oEccentric *Shoot Them Later*
Is it just me, or does something smell suspicious about all this?
∞

[tight beam, M16.4, tra. @n4.28.856.6883]
  xEccentric *Shoot Them Later*
    oGSV *Anticipation Of A New Lover's Arrival, The*
  Oh good, an easy one; it's you.
∞

I'm serious. This feels . . . strange.
∞

  How dare you imply I'm not serious.
  Anyway; what's the problem?
  This *is* the most important thing ever, by our understanding.
  Naturally everything and everybody will seem a little odd after such a realisation.
  We cannot help but be affected.
∞

You're right, I'm sure, but I just have this niggling feeling.
No; the more I think about it the more I'm convinced you are right and I am worrying over nothing.
I'll do a little checking for my own peace of mind, but I'm sure it will only help lay my fears to rest.
∞

  You should spend more time in Infinite Fun Space, you know.
∞

You're probably right. Oh well.
∞

  Still, keep in touch.
  Just in case anything does turn up.
Of course.
Take care.

∞
**Good checking, my friend.
You take care, too.**

II

The drone Sisela Ytheleus 1/2 drifted, waiting. Several seconds had passed since the skein pulse had resonated around it and it was still trying to decide what to do. It had passed the time by throwing together the anti-matter reaction chamber as best it could in the short time available, instead of painstakingly putting it together bit by delicate bit. As an after-thought, it released all but one of its nanomissiles and stuck two hundred of them around its heat-scarred rear panel in two groups on either side of the reaction chamber; fortuitously, the panel's damaged surface made it easy for it to embed the tiny missiles so that only the last third of their millimetre-long bodies protruded from the panel. It kept the other thirty-nine missiles ready to fire, for all the good that would do against whatever it was stalking it.

The gentle, buzzing vibrations in the skein had taken on a distinctive signature; something was coming towards it in hyperspace, with a sensory keel in real space, trawling slowly, well below lightspeed. Whatever it was, it was not the *Peace Makes Plenty*; the timbral characteristics were all wrong.

A wash of wide-band radiation, like a sourceless light, a final pulse of maser energies, in real space this time, and then something shimmering away to one side; a ship surfacing into the three-dimensional void, image flickering once then snapping steady.

Ten kilometres away; one klick long. Matched velocity. A fat, grey-black ellipsoid shape, covered with sharp spines, barbs and blades . . .

An Affronter ship!

The drone hesitated. Could this have been the ship that had been following the *Peace Makes Plenty*? Probably. Had it been taken over by the artifact/excession? Possibly. Not that it mattered in the end. *Shit.*

The Affront; no friends of the Elench. Or anybody else, for that matter. *I've failed. They'll reel me in, gobble me up.*

The drone tried desperately to work out what it could do. Did the fact it was an Affronter ship make any real difference? Doubtful. Should it signal it, try to get it to help? It could try; the Affront were signatories to the standard conventions on ships and individuals in distress and in theory they ought to take the drone aboard, help repair it and broadcast a warning about the artifact to the rest of the galaxy.

In practice they would take the drone to bits to find out how it worked, drain it of all its information, ransom it if they hadn't destroyed it in the process of investigation and inquisition, probably try to put a spy-program into it so that it would report back to them once it was back amongst the Elench, and meanwhile try to work out how they could use the artifact/excession, perhaps being foolhardy enough to attempt investigating it in the same final, fatal way the *Peace Makes Plenty* had, or perhaps keeping it secret for now and bringing more ships and technology to bear upon it. Almost certainly the one thing they wouldn't do was play the situation by the book.

EM effector; communicating. Sisela Ytheleus 1/2 readied its shields, for as much as that was worth; probably delay proceedings by, oh, a good nanosecond if the Affronter ship decided to attack it . . .

~ Machine! What are you?

(Well, that was spoken like an Affronter, certainly; it'd bet they hadn't tangled with the artifact/excession yet. Oh well. Play it by the conventions:)

~ *I am Sisela Ytheleus 1/2, drone of the Explorer Ship* Peace Makes Plenty, *a vessel of the Stargazer Clan, part of the Fifth Fleet of the Zetetic Elench, and in distress,* it communicated. ~ *And you?*

~ You are ours now. Surrender or take flight!

(Definitely still 100% Affront.)

~ *Sorry, I missed that. What did you say your name was again?*

~ Surrender at once or take flight, wretch!

~ *Let me think about that.*

(And thinking was exactly what it was doing; thinking hard, thinking feverishly. Stalling for time, but thinking.)

~ No!

The effector signal strength started to soar exponentially. It had plenty of time to slam down its shields.

Bastards, it thought. *Of course; they like a chase . . .*

The drone fired the missiles embedded in its rear panel; the two hundred tiny engines brought unequal amounts of matter and anti-matter together and threw the resulting blast of plasma boiling into the vacuum, careening the machine away across space directly away from the Affronter craft. The acceleration was relatively mild. The drone had no time to test the anti-matter reaction chamber it had constructed; it threw a few particles of each sort into the chamber and hoped. The chamber blew up. *Shit; back to the drawing board.*

Not much damage – not much extra damage, anyway – but not much extra impetus either, and it wouldn't be using the chamber again. The acceleration went on, building slowly. *What else? Think!*

The Affronter ship didn't bother to set off in pursuit of the drone; Sisela Ytheleus 1/2 dropped its plan of leaving a few nanomissiles scattered like mines behind it. (*Who am I trying to kid, anyway? Think; think!*)

Space seemed to buckle and twist in front of it, and suddenly it was no longer heading straight away from the Affronter ship; it was parallel to it again. *Those animal pus-bags are playing with me!*

A flicker from near the Affronter ship's nose. A centimetre-diameter circle of laser light blinked onto the drone's casing and wavered there. The drone instructed the nanomissile engines to shut off and flicked on its mirror shields; the laser beam tracked it unsteadily and narrowed until it was a millimetre in diameter, then its power suddenly leapt by seven orders of magnitude. The drone coned its protesting mirrorfield and turned rear-on to the ship again, presenting the smallest possible target. The laser modulated, stepping up to the ultraviolet. It started strobing.

Playing with me, just fucking playing with me . . . (Think! Think!)

Well, first . . .

It popped the clamps around its two upper-level minds and raised the bit of its casing that would let the two components – AI core and photonic nucleus – free. The casing shuddered and grated, but it moved. Once it was clear of the main casing, the drone nudged the two mind components with its maniple field. Nothing happened. They were stuck.

Panic! If they remained intact and the Affronters captured them and weren't a great deal more careful than they were notorious for being . . . It pushed harder; the components duly drifted out, losing power the instant contact lapsed with the drone's body. Whatever was inside them should be dead or dying now. It blasted them with its laser anyway, turning them into hot dust, then vented the powder behind it round the edge of the mirrorshield, where it might interfere with the laser a little. A very little.

It readied the core inside its present substrate; that would have to be dumped and lasered too.

Then the drone had an idea.

It thought about it. If it had been a human, its mouth would have gone dry.

It turned round inside the tight confines of its pummelled shield and fired all two hundred of the nanomissile engines. It shook off the remaining loose nanomissiles and fired thirty of them straight at the Affronter ship. The other nine it left tumbling behind it like a handful of tiny black-body needle-tips, with their own instructions and the small amount of spare capacity in their microscopic brains packed with coded nonsense.

The nanomissiles fired at the Affronter ship accelerated towards it in a cloud of sparkling light ahead of the drone; they were picked off, one by one, over the course of a millisecond, in a dizzy flaring scatter of light-blossoms, their tiny warheads and the remains of their anti-matter fuel erupting together; the last one to be targeted by the Affronter's effector and forced to self-destruct had closed the range to the ship by less than a kilometre.

Behind, all nine of the tumbling nanomissiles must have been picked out by the effector as well, because they detonated too.

And with any luck you'll think those were my messages in bottles and that *was my neat idea*, Sisela Ytheleus 1/2 thought, decoupling the core with its twin's mind-state in it. The core de-powered. Whatever was in there died. It had no time to mourn; it rearranged its internal state to shunt the core to the outside, then let its body settle back to normal. It pushed the core back down over its blistered, cracked casing, to the top of the rear panel, near where the wreckage of the cobbled-together and blown-apart reaction chamber hung, then it let the core fall into the livid plasma and sleeting radiation of the nanomissiles' exhausts; it flared and disintegrated, falling astern in a bright trail of fire.

The laser targeted on the drone was heading into the X-ray part of the spectrum; it would break through the mirror shield in a second and a half. It would take the drone four and a half seconds to get within range of the ship.

Shit. It waited until the mirrorshield was a couple of tenths of a second from failing, then signalled: ~ *I surrender!*, and hoped that it was talking to another machine; if it was relying on Affronter reactions it'd be fried before the message got through to their stupid animal brains.

The laser flicked off. The drone kept its EM shields up.

It was heading towards the Affronter vessel at about half a klick a second; the ship's be-bladed, swollen-looking bulk drifted closer.

~ Turn off your shields!

~ *I can't!* It put expression into the signal, so that it came across as a wail.

~ Now!

~ *I'm trying! I'm trying! You damaged me! Damaged me even more! Such weaponry! What chance have I, a mere drone, something smaller than an Affronter's beak, against such power?*

Nearly in range. Not far. Not far now. Another two seconds.

~ Drop your shields instantly and allow yourself to be taken over or suffer instant destruction.

Still nearly two seconds. It would never keep them talking long enough . . .

~ *Please don't! I'm attempting to shut off the shield projector, but it's in fail-safe mode; it won't let itself be shut off. It's arguing; can you believe that? But, honestly; I am doing my best. Please believe me. Please don't kill me. I'm the only survivor, you know; our ship was attacked! I was lucky to get away. I've never seen anything like it. Never heard of anything like it either.*

A pause. A pause of animal dimensions. Time for animal thoughts. Loads of time.

~ Final chance; turn off—

~ *There; turning shields off now. I'm all yours.*

The drone Sisela Ytheleus 1/2 turned off its electromagnetic mirrorshield. In the same instant, it fired its laser straight at the Affronter ship.

An instant later it released the containment around its remaining stock of anti-matter, detonated its in-built self-destruct charge and instructed the single nanomissile it still carried within its body to explode too.

~ *Fuck you!* were its final words.

Its last emotion was a mixture of sorrow, elation, and a kind of desperate pride that its plan might have worked . . . Then it died, instantly and forever, in its own small fireball of heat and light.

To the Affronter ship, the effect of the tiny drone's laser was rather less than a tickle; it flickered across its hull and barely singed it.

The cloud of glowing wreckage the drone's self-destruction had caused passed over the Affronter ship, and was duly swept by analysing sensors. Plasma. Atoms. Nothing as big as a molecule. Likewise the slowly expanding debris from the two groups of nanomissiles.

Disappointment, then; that had been a particularly sophisticated model of Elencher drone, not far behind the leading-edge of Culture drone technology. Capturing one would have been a good prize. Still, it had put up a reasonable fight considering, and provided a morsel of unexpected sport.

The Affront light cruiser *Furious Purpose* came about and headed slowly away from the scene of its miniature battle, carefully scanning for more nanomissiles. They posed no threat to the cruiser, of course, but the small drone appeared to have tried to use some of the tiny weapons to place information in, and it might have left others behind which were not inclined to self-destruct when effector-targeted. None showed up. The cruiser back-tracked along the course the drifting drone appeared to have taken. It discovered a small cooling cloud of matter at one point, the remnants of some sort of explosion apparently, but that was all. Beyond that; nothing. Nothing everywhere one looked. Most dissatisfying.

The *Furious Purpose*'s restless officers debated how much more time they should spend looking for this lost Elencher ship. Had something happened to it? Had the small drone been lying? Might there be a more interesting opponent floating around out here somewhere?

Or might it all be a ruse, a decoy? The Culture – the real Culture, the wily ones, not these semi-mystical Elenchers with their miserable hankering to be somebody else – had been known to give whole Affronter fleets the run-around for several months with not dissimilar enticements and subterfuges, keeping them occupied, seemingly on the track of some wildly promising prey which turned out to be nothing at all, or a Culture ship with some ridiculous but earnestly argued excuse, while the Culture or one of its snivelling client species got on – or away – with something else somewhere else, spoiling rightful Affronter fun.

How were they to know this was not one of those occasions? Perhaps the Elencher ship was under contract to the Culture proper. Perhaps they had lost the Explorer craft and a GCU – trailing them as they had been trailing the Elench craft – had slipped in to take its place. Might this not be true?

No, argued some of the officers, because the Culture would never sacrifice a drone it considered sentient.

The rest thought about this, considered the Culture's bizarrely sentimental attitude to life, and were forced to concede the point.

The cruiser spent another two days around the Esperi system and then broke away. It returned to the habitat called Tier with a trivial but niggling engine fault.

III

Technically, it was a branch of metamathematics, usually called metamathics. Metamathics; the investigation of the properties of Realities (more correctly, Reality-fields) intrinsically unknowable by and from our own, but whose general principles could be hazarded at.

Metamathics led to everything else, it led to the places that nobody else had ever seen or heard of or previously imagined.

It was like living half your life in a tiny, stuffy, warm grey box, and being moderately happy in there because you knew no better . . . and then discovering a little hole in one corner of the box, a tiny opening which you could get a finger into, and tease and pull at, so that eventually you created a tear, which led to a greater tear, which led to the box falling apart around you . . . so that you stepped out of the tiny box's confines into startlingly cool, clear fresh air and found yourself on top of a mountain, surrounded by deep valleys, sighing forests, soaring peaks, glittering lakes, sparkling snowfields and a stunning, breathtakingly blue sky. And that, of course, wasn't even the start of the real story, that was more like the breath that is drawn in before the first syllable of the first word of the first paragraph of the first chapter of the first book of the first volume of the story.

Metamathics led to the Mind equivalent of that experience, repeated a million times, magnified a billion times, and then beyond, to configurations of wonder and bliss even the simplest abstract of which the human-basic brain had no conceivable way of comprehending. It was like a drug; an ultimately liberating, utterly enhancing, unadulterably beneficial, overpoweringly glorious drug for the intellect of machines as far beyond the sagacity of the human mind as they were beyond its understanding.

This was the way the Minds spent their time. They imagined entirely new universes with altered physical laws, and played with them, lived in them and tinkered with them, sometimes setting up the conditions for life, sometimes just letting things run to see if it would arise spontaneously, sometimes arranging things so that life was impossible but other kinds and types of bizarrely fabulous complication were enabled.

Some of the universes possessed just one tiny but significant alteration, leading to some subtle twist in the way things worked, while others were so wildly, aberrantly different it could take a perfectly first-rate Mind the human equivalent of years of intense thought even to find the one tenuously familiar strand of recognisable reality that would allow it to translate the rest into comprehensibility. Between those extremes lay an infinitude of universes of unutterable fascination, consummate joy and absolute enlightenment. All that humanity knew and could understand, every single aspect, known, guessed at and hoped for in and of the universe was like a mean and base mud hut compared to the vast, glittering cloud-high palace of monumentally exquisite proportions and prodigious riches that was the metamathical realm. Within the infinities raised to the power of infinities that those metamathical rules provided, the Minds built their immense pleasure-domes of rhapsodic philosophical ecstasy.

That was where they lived. That was their home. When they

weren't running ships, meddling with alien civilisations or planning the future course of the Culture itself, the Minds existed in those fantastic virtual realities, sojourning beyondward into the multi-dimensioned geographies of their unleashed imaginations, vanishingly far away from the single limited point that was reality.

The Minds had long ago come up with a proper name for it; they called it the Irreal, but they thought of it as Infinite Fun. That was what they really knew it as. The Land of Infinite Fun.

It did the experience pathetically little justice.

. . . The *Sleeper Service* promenaded metaphysically amongst the lush creates of its splendid disposition, an expanding shell of awareness in a dreamscape of staggering extent and complexity, like a gravity-free sun built by a jeweller of infinite patience and skill. *It is absolutely the case*, it said to itself, *it is absolutely the case* . . .

There was only one problem with the Land of Infinite Fun, and that was that if you ever did lose yourself in it completely – as Minds occasionally did, just as humans sometimes surrendered utterly to some AI environment – you could forget that there was a base reality at all. In a way, this didn't really matter, as long as there was somebody back where you came from minding the hearth. The problem came when there was nobody left or inclined to tend the fire, mind the store, look after the housekeeping (or however you wanted to express it), or if somebody or something else – somebody or something from outside, the sort of entity that came under the general heading of an Outside Context Problem, for example – decided they wanted to meddle with the fire in that hearth, the stock in the store, the contents and running of the house; if you'd spent all your time having Fun, with no way back to reality, or just no idea what to do to protect yourself when you did get back there, then you were vulnerable. In fact, you were probably dead, or enslaved.

It didn't matter that base reality was petty and grey and mean and demeaning and quite empty of meaning compared to the glorious majesty of the multi-hued life you'd been living through metamathics; it didn't matter that base reality was of no conse-quence aesthetically, hedonistically, metamathically, intellectually and philosophically; if that was the single foundation-stone that all your higher-level comfort and joy rested upon, and it was kicked away from underneath you, you fell, and your limitless pleasure realms fell with you.

It was just like some ancient electricity-powered computer; it didn't matter how fast, error-free and tireless it was, it didn't matter how great a labour-saving boon it was, it didn't matter what it could do or how many different ways it could amaze; if you pulled its plug out, or just hit the Off button, all it became was a lump of matter; all its programs became just settings, dead instructions, and all its computations vanished as quickly as they'd moved.

It was, also, like the dependency of the human-basic brain on the human-basic body; no matter how intelligent, perceptive and gifted you were, no matter how entirely you lived for the ascetic rewards of the intellect and eschewed the material world and the ignobility of the flesh, if your heart just gave out . . .

That was the Dependency Principle; that you could never forget where your Off switches were located, even if it was somewhere tiresome. It was the problem that Subliming dispensed with, of course, and it was one of the (usually more minor) reasons that civilisations chose Elderhood; if your course was set in that direction in the first place then eventually that reliance on the material universe came to seem vestigial, untidy, pointless, and even embarrassing.

It wasn't the course the Culture had fully embarked upon, at least not yet, but as a society it was well aware of both the difficulties presented by remaining in base reality and the attractions of the Sublime. In the meantime, it compromised, busying itself in the macrocosmic clumsiness and petty, messy profanity of the real galaxy while at the same time exploring the transcendental possibilities of the sacred Irreal.

It is absolutely the—

A single signal flicked the great ship's attention entirely back to base reality:

xRock *End In Tears*
    oGSV *Sleeper Service.*
Done.

The ship contemplated the one-word message for what was, for it, a very long time, and wondered at the mixture of emotions it felt. It set its newly manufactured drone-fleet to work in the external environments and re-checked the evacuation schedule.

Then it located Amorphia – the avatar was wandering bemused through kilometres of tableaux exhibition space that had once been accommodation sections – and instructed it to re-visit the woman Dajeil Gelian.

IV

Genar-Hofoen was distinctly unimpressed with his quarters aboard the Battle-Cruiser *Kiss The Blade*. For one thing, they smelled.

~ What is that? he asked, his nose wrinkling. ~ Methane?

~ *Methane is odourless, Genar-Hofoen*, the suit said. ~ *I believe the smell you find objectionable may be a mixture of methanal and methylamine.*

~ Fucking horrible smell, whatever it is.

~ *I'm sure your mucous membrane receptors will cease to react to it before long.*

~ I certainly hope so.

He was standing in what was supposed to be his bedroom. It was cold. It was very big; a ten-metre square – plenty of headroom – but it was cold; he could see his breath. He still wore most of the gelfield suit but he'd detached all but the nape-part of the neck and let the head of the suit flop down over his back so that he could get a fresher impression of his quarters, which consisted of a vestibule, a lounge, a frighteningly industrial-looking kitchen-diner, an equally intimidatingly mechanical bathroom and this so-called bedroom. He was starting to wish he hadn't bothered. The walls, floor and ceiling of the room were some sort of white plastic; the floor bulged up to create a sort of platform on which a huge white thing lay spread, like a cloud made solid.

~ What, he asked, pointing at the bed, ~ is that?

~ *I think it is your bed.*

~ I'd guessed. But what is that . . . thing lying on it?

~ *Quilt? Duvet? Bed-covering.*

~ What do you want to cover it for? he asked, genuinely confused.

~ *Well, it's more to cover you, I think, when you're asleep*, the suit said, sounding uncertain.

The man dropped his hold-all onto the shiny plastic floor and went forward to heft the white cloudy thing. It felt quite light. Possibly a little damp, unless the suit's tactiles were getting confused. He pulled a glove-section back and touched the bed-cover thing with his bare skin. Cold. Maybe damp. ~ Module? Genar-Hofoen said. He'd get its opinion on all this.

~ *You can't talk to Scopell-Afranqui directly, remember?* the suit said politely.

~ Shit, Genar-Hofoen said. He rubbed the material of the bed-cover between his fingers. ~ This feel damp to you, suit?

~ *A little. Do you want me to ask the ship to patch you through to the module?*

~ Eh? Oh, no; don't bother. We moving yet?

~ *No.*

The man shook his head. ~ Horrible smell, he said. He prodded the bed-cover thing again. He wished now he'd insisted that the module be accommodated on board the ship so that he could live inside it, but the Affronters had said this wasn't possible; hangar space was at a premium on all three ships. The module had protested, and he'd made supportive noises, but he had been rather entertained by the idea that Scopell-Afranqui would have to stay here while he went zapping off to far-off parts of the galaxy on an important mission. Seemed like a good idea at the time. Now he wasn't so sure.

There was a distant growling noise and a tremor underfoot; then there came a jerk that almost threw the human off his feet. He staggered to one side and had to sit down on the bed.

It made a squelching sound. He stared at it, aghast.

~ Now *we're moving,* said the suit.

V

Singing softly to himself, the man tended the little fire he had started on the floor of the hall, beneath and between the stored ships, arrayed in the blackness like the trunks of enormous trees in a silent, petrified forest. Gestra Ishmethit was surveying his charges in the deep-buried darkness that was Pittance.

Pittance was a huge irregular lump of matter, two hundred kilometres across at its narrowest point and ninety-eight per cent iron by volume. It was the remnant of a catastrophe which had occurred over four billion years earlier, when the planet of whose core it had been part had been struck by another large body. Expelled from its own solar system by that cataclysm, it had wandered between the stars for a quarter of the life of the universe, uncaptured by any other gravity well but subtly affected by all it passed anywhere near. It had been discovered drifting in deep space a millennium ago by a GCU taking an eccentrically trajectorial course between two stellar systems, it had been given the brief examination its simple and homogeneous composition deserved and then had been left to glide, noted, effectively tagged, untouched, but given the name Pittance.

When the time came, five hundred years later, to dismantle the colossal war machine the Culture had created in order to destroy that of the Idirans, Pittance had suddenly been found a role.

Most of the Culture's warships had been decommissioned and dismantled. A few were retained, demilitarised, to act as express delivery systems for small packages of matter – humans, for example – on the rare occasions when the transmission of information alone was not sufficient to deal with a problem, and an even smaller number were kept intact and operational; two hundred years after the war ended, the number of fully active warcraft was actually smaller than it had been before the conflict began (though, as the Culture's critics never tired of pointing out, the average – and avowedly completely peaceful – General Contact Unit was more than a match for the vast majority of alien craft it was likely to bump into over the course of its career).

Never a civilisation to take too many risks, however, and priding itself on the assiduity of its bet-hedging, the Culture had not disposed of all the remaining craft; a few thousand – representing less than a per cent of the original total – were kept in reserve, fully armed save for their usual complement of Displacer-dispatched explosive warheads (a relatively minor weapon system anyway), which they and other craft would manufacture in the event of mobilisation. Most of the mothballed ships were retained within a scattering of Culture Orbitals, chosen so that if there ever was an emergency which the craft would be required to deal with, no part of the greater galaxy would be more than a month or so's flight away.

Still guarding against threats and possibilities even it found difficult to specify, some of the Culture's stored warvessels were harboured not in or around highly populated Orbitals full of life and the comings and goings of cruise ships and visiting GSVs, but in places as far out of the way as it was possible to find amongst the cavernously cold and empty spaces of the great lens; quiet, secret, hidden places; places off the beaten track, places possibly nobody else even knew existed.

Pittance had been chosen as one of those places.

The General Systems Vehicle *Uninvited Guest* and a fleet of accompanying warcraft had been dispatched to rendezvous with the cold, dark, wandering mass. It was found exactly where it had been predicted it ought to be, and work began. Firstly, a series of enormous halls had been hollowed out of its interior, then a precisely weighed and shaped piece of the matter mined from one of those giant hangars had been aimed with millimetric accuracy and fired at Pittance by the GSV, leaving a small new crater on the surface of the world, exactly as though it had been struck by another, smaller, piece of interstellar debris.

This was done because Pittance wasn't spinning quite quickly enough or heading in exactly the right direction for the Culture's purposes; the exquisitely engineered collision made both alterations at once. So Pittance spun a little quicker to provide a more powerful hint of artificial gravity inside and its course was altered just a fraction to deflect it from a star system it would otherwise have drifted through in five and a half thousand years or so.

A number of giant Displacer units were set within the fabric of Pittance and the warships were safely Displaced, one at a time, into the giant spaces the GSV had created. Lastly, a frightening variety and number of sensory and weapon systems had been emplaced, camouflaged on the surface of Pittance and buried deep underneath it, while a cloud of tiny, dark, almost invisible but apocalyptically powerful devices were placed in orbit about the slowly tumbling mass, also to watch for unwelcome guests, and – if necessary – welcome them with destruction.

Its work finished, the *Uninvited Guest* had departed, taking with it most of the iron mined from Pittance's interior. It left behind a world that – save for that plausible-looking extra crater – seemed untouched; even its overall mass was almost exactly as it had been before, again, minus a little to allow for the collision it had suffered, the debris of which was allowed to drift as the laws of gravity dictated, most of it sailing like lazy shrapnel spinning into space but a little of it – captured by the tiny world's weak gravitational field – drifting along with it, and so incidentally providing perfect cover for the cloud of black-body sentry devices.

Watching over Pittance from near its centre was its own quiet Mind, carefully designed to enjoy the quiet life and to take a subdued, passive pride in the feeling of containing, and jealously guarding, an almost incalculable amount of stored, latent, preferably never-to-be-used power.

The rarefied, specialist Minds in the warships themselves had been consulted like the rest on their fate those five hundred years ago; those in Storage at Pittance had been of the persuasion that preferred to sleep until they might be needed, and been prepared to accept that their sleep might be very long indeed, before quite probably ending in battle and death. What they had all agreed they would prefer would be to be woken only as a prelude to joining the Culture's ultimate Sublimation, if and when that became the society's choice. Until then they would be content to slumber in their dark halls, the war gods of past wrath implicitly guarding the peace of the present and the security of the future.

Meanwhile the Mind of Pittance watched over them, and looked out into the resounding silence and the sun-freckled darkness of the spaces between the stars, forever content and ineffably satisfied with the absence of anything remotely interesting happening.

Pittance was a very safe place, then, and Gestra Ishmethit liked safe places. It was a very lonely place, and Gestra Ishmethit had always craved loneliness. It was at once a very important place and a place that almost nobody knew or cared about or indeed probably ever would, and that also suited Gestra Ishmethit quite perfectly, because he was a strange creature, and accepted that he was.

Tall, adolescently gawky and awkward despite his two hundred years, Gestra felt he had been an outsider all his life. He'd tried physical alteration (he'd been quite handsome, for a while), he'd tried being female (she'd been quite pretty, she'd been told), he'd tried moving away from where he'd been brought up (he'd moved half the galaxy away to an Orbital quite different but every bit as pleasant as his home) and he'd tried a life lived adream (he'd been a merman prince in a water-filled space ship fighting an evil machine-hive mind, and according to the scenario was supposed to woo the warrior princess of another clan) but in all the things he'd tried he had never felt anything else than awkward: being handsome was worse than being gangly and bumbling because his body felt like a lie he was wearing; being a woman was the same, and somehow embarrassing, as well, as though it was somebody else's body he had kidnapped from inside; moving away just left him terrified of having to explain to people why he'd wanted to leave home in the first place, and living in a dream scenario all day and night just felt wrong; he had a horror of immersing himself in that virtual world as completely as his merman did in his watery realm and thus losing hold of what he felt was a tenuous grip on reality at the best of times, and so he'd lived the scenario with the nagging sensation that he was just a pet fish in somebody else's fish tank, swimming in circles through the prettified ruins of sunken castles. In the end, to his mortification, the princess had defected to the machine hive-mind.

The plain fact was that he didn't like talking to people, he didn't like mixing with them and he didn't even like thinking about them individually. The best he could manage was when he was well away from people; then he could feel a not unpleasant craving for their company as a whole, a craving that quite vanished – to be replaced by stomach-churning dread – the instant it looked like being satisfied.

Gestra Ishmethit was a freak; despite being born to the most ordinary and healthy of mothers (and an equally ordinary father), in the most ordinary of families on the most ordinary of Orbitals and having the most ordinary of upbringings, an accident of birth, or some all-but-impossible conjunction of disposition and upbringing, had left him the sort of person the Culture's carefully meddled-with genes virtually never threw up; a genuine misfit, something even rarer in the Culture than a baby born physically deformed.

But whereas it was perfectly simple to replace or regrow a stunted limb or a misshapen face, it was a different matter when the oddness lay inside, a fact Gestra had always accepted with an equanimity he sometimes suspected people regarded as even more freakish than his original almost pathological shyness. Why didn't he just have the condition treated? his relations and few acquaintances asked. Why didn't he ask to remain as much himself as possible, yet with this strange aberrancy removed, expunged? It might not be easy, but it would be painless; probably it could be done in his sleep; he'd remember nothing about it and when he woke up he could live a normal life.

He came to the attention of AIs, drones, humans and Minds that took an interest in that sort of thing; soon they were queuing up to treat him; he was a challenge! He became so frightened by their – by turns – kind, cheery, cajoling, brusque or just plain plaintive entreaties to talk to him, counsel him, explain the merits of their various treatments and courses to him that he stopped answering his terminal and practically became a hermit in a summer house in his family's estate, unable to explain that despite it all – indeed, exactly because of all his previous attempts to integrate with the rest of society and what he had learned about himself through them – he wanted to be who he was, not the person he would become if he lost the one trait that distinguished him from everybody else, no matter how perverse that decision seemed to others.

In the end it had taken the intervention of the Hub Mind of his home Orbital to come up with a solution. A drone from Contact had come to speak to him one day.

He'd always found it easier talking to drones rather than humans, and this drone had been somehow particularly business-like but unconcernedly charming as well, and after probably the longest conversation with anybody Gestra had ever had, it had offered him a variety of posts where he could be alone. He had chosen the position where he could be most alone and most lonely, where he could happily yearn for the human contact he knew was the one thing he was incapable of appreciating.

It was, in the end, a sinecure; it had been explained from the beginning that he would not really have anything to *do* on Pittance; he would simply *be* there; a symbolic human presence amongst the mass of quiescent weapons, a witness to the Mind's silent sentinelship over the sleeping machines. Gestra Ishmethit had been perfectly happy with that lack of responsibility, too, and had now been resident on Pittance for one and a half centuries, had not once left to go anywhere else, had not received a single visitor in all that time and had never felt anything less than content. Some days, he even felt happy.

The ships were arranged in lines and rows sixty-four at a time in the series of huge dark spaces. Those great halls were kept cold and in vacuum, but Gestra had discovered that if he found some rubbish from his quarters and kept it warm in a gelfield sack, and then set it down on the chill floor of one of the hangars and blew oxygen over it from a pressurised tank, it could be made to burn. Quite a satisfactory little fire could be got going, flaring white and yellow in the breath of gas and producing a quickly dispersing cloud of smoke and soot. He had found that by adjusting the flow of oxygen and directing it through a nozzle he had designed and made himself, he could produce a fierce blaze, a dull red glow or any state of conflagration in between.

He knew the Mind didn't like him doing this, but it amused him, and it was almost the only thing he did which annoyed it. Besides, the Mind had grudgingly admitted both that the amount of heat produced was too small ever to leak through the eighty kilometres of iron to show up on the surface of Pittance and that ultimately the waste products of the combustion would be recovered and recycled, so Gestra felt free to indulge himself with a clear conscience, every few months or so.

Today's fire was composed of some old wall hangings he'd grown tired of, some vegetable scraps from past meals, and tiny bits and pieces of wood. The wooden scraps were produced by his hobby, which was constructing one-in-one-twenty-eighth scale models of ancient sailing ships.

He had drained the swimming pool in his quarters and turned it into a miniature forestry plantation and farm using some of the biomass the Mind and he had been provided with; tiny trees grew there which he cut down and sliced into little planks and turned on lathes to produce all the masts, spars, decks and other wooden parts the sea ships required. Other bonsai plants in the forest provided long fibres which he teased and twisted and coiled into thread- and string-thin ropes to make halyards and sheets. Different plants let him create still thinner fibres which he wove into sails on infinitesimal looms he had also constructed himself. The iron and steel parts were made from material scraped from the iron walls of Pittance itself. He smelted the metal in a miniature furnace to rid it of the last traces of impurities and either flattened it in a tiny hand-turned rolling mill, cast it using wax and talc-like fines, or turned it on microscopic lathes. Another furnace fused sand – taken from the beach which had been part of the swimming pool – to make wafer-thin sheets of glass for portholes and skylights. Yet more of the life-support system's biomass was used to produce pitch and oils, which caulked the hull and greased the little winches, derricks and other pieces of machinery. His most precious commodity was brass, which he had to pare from an antique telescope his mother had given him (with some ironic comment he had long chosen to forget) when he'd announced his decision to leave for Pittance. (His mother was herself Stored now; one of his great grand-nieces had sent him a letter.)

It had taken him ten years to make the tiny machines to make the ships, and then making each ship occupied another twenty years of his time. He had constructed six vessels so far, each slightly larger and better made than the one before. He had almost completed a seventh, with just the sails to finish and sew; the scraps of wood he was burning were the last of its off-cuts and compacted sawdust.

The little fire burned well enough. He let it blaze and looked around. His breath sounded loud in his suit as he lifted his head to gaze around the dark space. The sixty-four ships stored in this hall were Gangster Class Rapid Offensive Units; slim segmented cylinders over two hundred metres tall and fifty in diameter. The tiny glow from the fire was lost to normal sight amongst the spire-like heights of the ships; he had to press the control surfaces on the forearm of the ancient space suit to intensify the image displayed on the visor-screen in front of him.

The ships looked like they'd been tattooed. Their hulls were covered in a bewildering swirl of patterns upon patterns upon patterns, a fractal welter of colours, designs and textures that saturated their every square millimetre. He had seen this a hundred times before but it never failed to fascinate and amaze him.

On a few occasions he had floated up to some of the ships and touched their skins, and even through the thickness of the gloves on the millennium-old suit he had felt the roughened surface, whorled and raised and encrusted beneath. He had looked closely, then more closely still, using the suit's lights and the magnification on the visor-screen to peer into the gaudy display in front of him, and found himself becoming lost within concentric layers of complexity and design. Finally the suit was using electrons to scan the surface and imposing false colours on the surfaces displayed and still the complexity went on, down and down to the atomic level. He had pulled back out through the layers and levels of motifs, figures, mandalas and fronds, his head buzzing with the extravagant, numbing complexity of it all.

Gestra Ishmethit remembered seeing screen-shots of warships; they had been whatever colour they wanted to be – usually perfectly black or perfectly reflecting when they were not hidden by a hologram of the view straight through them – but he could not recall ever having seen such odd designs upon them. He had consulted the Mind's archives. Sure enough, the ships had been ordinary, plain-hulled craft when they had flown here. He asked the Mind why the ships had become decorated so, writing to it on the display of his terminal as he always did when he wanted to communicate: *Why ships tattooed look?*

The Mind had replied: *Think of it as a form of armour, Gestra.*

And that was all he could get out of it.

He decided he would have to be content to remain puzzled.

The little fire sent quivering veins of dim light into the hollow shadows around the enigmatic towers of the dazzlingly patterned ships. The only sound was his breathing. He felt wonderfully alone here; even the Mind couldn't communicate with him here as long as he kept the suit's communicator turned off. Here was perfect; here was total and complete loneliness, here was peace, and quiet, and a fire in the vacuum. He lowered his gaze again, towards the embers.

Something glinted near the floor of the hall, a couple of kilometres away.

His heart seemed to freeze. The thing glinted again. Whatever it was, it was coming closer.

He turned the suit communicator on with a shaking hand.

Before his quivering fingers could tap in a question to the Mind, the display on his visor-screen, lit up: *Gestra, we are to be visited. Please return to your quarters.*

He stared at the text, his eyes wide, his heart thudding in his chest, his mind reeling. The glowing letters stayed where they were, they added up to the same thing; they would not go away. He inspected each one in turn, looking for mistakes, desperately trying to make some different kind of sense from them, but they kept repeating the same sentence, they kept meaning the same thing.

Visited, he thought. *Visited? Visited? Visited?*

He felt terror for the first time in one and a half centuries.

The drone which had glinted in the shadows, which the Mind had sent to summon him because his suit communicator had been turned off, had to carry the man back to his quarters, he was shaking so much. It had picked up the oxygen cylinder too, turning it off.

Behind it, the fire went on glowing faintly for a few seconds in the darkness, then even that baleful glimmer succumbed to the empty coldness, and it winked out.

5
Kiss The Blade

I

The Explorer Ship *Break Even* of the Stargazer Clan's Fifth fleet, part of the Zetetic Elench, looped slowly around the outer limit of the comet cloud of the star system Tremesia I/II, scanning beams briefly touching on as many of the dark, frozen bodies as it could, searching for its lost sister vessel.

The double-sun system was relatively poor in comets; there were only a hundred billion of them. However, many of them had orbits well outside the ecliptic and that helped to make the search every bit as difficult as it would have been with a greater number of comet nuclei but in a more planar cloud. Even so, it was impossible to check all of them; ten thousand ships would have been required to thoroughly check every single sensor trace in the comet cloud to make sure that one of them was not a stricken ship, and the best the *Break Even* could do was briefly fasten its gaze on the most likely looking candidates.

Just doing that bare minimum would take a full day for this system alone, and it had another nine stars allocated to it as prime possibilities, plus another eighty less likely solar systems. The other six vessels of the Fifth fleet had similar schedules, similar allocations of stellar systems to attempt to search.

Elencher ships sent routine location and status reports back to a responsible and reliable habitat, facility or course-scheduled craft every sixteen standard days. The *Peace Makes Plenty* had signalled safely back to the Elench embassy on Tier along with the other seven ships of the fleet sixty-four days after they'd all left the habitat.

Day eighty had come, and only seven had reported in. The others immediately stopped heading any further away if that was the course they'd been set on; four days later, still with no word, and with no sign of anybody else having heard anything, the seven remaining ships of the Fifth fleet set their courses to converge on the last known position of the missing ship and accelerated to their maximum speed. The first of them had arrived in the general volume where the *Peace Makes Plenty* ought to be five days later; the last one appeared another twelve days after that.

They had to assume that the ship they were looking for had not travelled at that sort of speed since it had last signalled, they had to assume that it had been cruising, even loitering amongst the systems it had been investigating, they had to assume that it was somewhere within a stellar system, small nebula or gas cloud in the first place, and they had to assume that it was not deliberately trying to hide from them, or that somebody else was not deliberately trying to hide it from them.

The stars themselves were relatively easy to check; microscopic as it might be compared to the average sun, a half-million tonne ship containing a few tonnes of anti-matter and a variety of highly exotic materials falling into a star left a tiny but distinct and unmistakable flash behind it, and usually a mark on the stellar surface that lasted for days at least; one loop round the star could tell you if that kind of disaster had befallen a missing craft. Small solid planets were easy too, unless a ship was deliberately hiding or being hidden, which of course was perfectly possible in such situations and considerably more likely than a ship suffering some natural disaster or terminal technical fault. Large gaseous planets presented a bigger challenge. Asteroid belts, where they existed, could pose real problems, and comet clouds were a nightmare.

In the vast majority of solar systems the spaces between the inner system and the comet cloud were easy to search for big, obvious things and pointless to search for small things or anything trying to hide. Interstellar space was the same, but much worse; unless something was trying to signal you from out there, you could more or less forget about finding anything smaller than a planet.

The *Break Even* and its crew, like the rest of the fleet, the Clan and the Elench, had no illusions about the likelihood of success their search offered. They were doing it because you had to do something, because there was always just a chance, no matter how remote, that their sister ship was somewhere findable and obvious – orbiting a planet, sitting in a 1/6 Stabile round a big planet's orbit – and you wouldn't be able to live with yourself if you took the cold statistical view that there was next to zero hope of finding the ship intact, and then later discovered it had been there all along, savable at the time but later lost because nobody could be bothered to hope – and act – against the odds. Still, the statistics did not make optimistic reading, indicating that the whole task was as close to being impossible as made little difference, and there was a morbid, depressing quality about such searches, almost as though they were more a kind of vigil for the dead, part of a funeral ceremony, than a practical attempt to look for the missing.

The days went by; the ships, aware that whatever had befallen the *Peace Makes Plenty* might as easily happen to them, signalled their locations to each other every few hours.

Sixteen days after the first ship had started searching and hundreds of investigated star systems later, the quest began to be wound down. Over the next few days, five of the ships returned to the other parts of the Upper Leaf Spiral they had been exploring while two remained behind in the volume the *Peace Makes Plenty* ought still to be in, somewhere, carrying out more thorough explorations of the star systems as part of their normal mission profile, but always hoping that their missing sister ship might turn up, or at the very least that they might uncover some fragment of evidence, some hint of what had happened to their missing sibling.

The fact that the ship had disappeared would not be reported outside the fleet for another sixteen days; the Stargazer clan would pass the sad news on to the rest of the Elench eight days subsequently, and the outside galaxy would be informed, if it cared, another month after that. The Elench looked after their own, and kept themselves to themselves, as well.

The *Break Even* powered away from the last stellar system it had investigated, leaving the red giant astern with a kind of dismal relief. It was not one of the two craft who'd stay to continue the scaled-down search; it was heading back to the volume where it had been before the *Peace Makes Plenty* had gone missing. It kept all its sensors sweeping on full scan as it moved away from the giant sun, through the orbits of two small, cold planets and, further out, the dark, gelid bodies of the comet nuclei. Its course took it directly towards the next nearest star; on the way it swept interstellar space with its sensors too, still hoping, still half dreading ... but nothing turned up. Esperi's single, dim-red globe fell away astern, like an ember cooling to ash in the freezing night.

A few hours later the ship was out of the volume altogether, heading out-down-spinward back to its allotted crop of distant, anonymous stars.

II

[tight beam, M32, tra. @n4.28.860.0446]
xGSV *Anticipation Of A New Lover's Arrival, The*
    oEccentric *Shoot Them Later*
I think I have discovered something. Attached are course schedules for the Steely Glint and No Fixed Abode. (DiaGlyphs attached.) (The movements of the Not Invented Here can only be guessed at.) Note that both alter within hours of each other for no given reason, nineteen days ago. The GCU Fate Amenable To Change which discovered the Excession also made a sudden and acute course-change nineteen days ago; a new heading which took it almost straight to the Excession. Then there is a report from the GCU Reasonable Excuse – charged with oversight of our semidetached friend the GCU Grey Area – that the ship left its most recent place of interest two days ago and was last detected heading in the direction of the Lower Leaf Swirl; possibly Tier.
∞
[tight beam, M32, tra. @n4.28.860.2426]
    xEccentric *Shoot Them Later*
        oGSV *Anticipation Of A New Lover's Arrival, The*
Yes?
∞
Do not be obtuse.
∞
I am not being obtuse.
You are being paranoid.
A lot of course schedules have been altered recently thanks to this thing.
I'm thinking about finding an excuse to edge in that direction myself.
And as you point out yourself, the Meatfucker is heading towards the Lower Swirl, not the Upper.

∞

There is a certain potential rendezvous implied in that direction; do I have to spell it out? And the point remains; these are the only three schedules which change at the same point.

∞

They alter over the course of five hours; hardly a 'point'. And even so; what if they do? And what's so special about nineteen or even nineteen/two days ago?

∞

[stuttered tight point, M32]
It does not worry you that there might be a conspiracy in the highest levels of a Contact/SC committee? I am suggesting that there may be prior knowledge here; that some tip or clue was received by one of our colleagues which was not passed on to anybody else. That is what is so special about nineteen days ago; it is less than fifty-seven days ago, when whatever took place in the vicinity of the excession appears to have occurred.

∞

Yes yes yes. But: SO WHAT? My dear ship, which of us has not taken part in some scheme, some ruse or secret plan, some stratagem or diversion, sometimes of quite a sizable and labyrinthine nature and involving matters of considerable import? They're what makes ordinary life worth living! So some of our chums in the Core Group may have had a sniff of something interesting in that region. Good for them, I say! Have you never had some clue, some lead, a hint of some potential sport, amusement, jape or focus of contemplation that was certainly worth acting upon but equally decidedly did not merit advertising due to some reservation concerning potential embarrassment, the wish not to seem vain or simply a desire for privacy?
Really, I think there is no conspiracy here whatsoever, and that even if there is, it is a benign one. Apart from anything else, there is one question you have not, I believe, addressed: What is the conspiracy *for*? If it was merely a couple of Minds getting wind of something odd in the Upper Leaf Spiral and finessing a search there, are they not simply to be congratulated?

∞

But there has been nothing this important before! This is perhaps our first real OCP and we may not be up to the challenge it represents. *Meat* it makes me ashamed! I just find this all so distressing! For millennia we have congratulated ourselves on our wisdom and maturity and revelled in our freedom from baser drives and from the ignobility of thought and action that desperation born of indigence produces. My fear – my terror! – is that our freedom from material concern has blinded us to our true, underlying nature; we have been good because we have never needed to make the choice between that and anything else. Altruism has been imposed upon us!

Now suddenly we are presented with something we cannot manufacture or simulate, something which is to us as precious metals or stones or just other lands were to ancient monarchs, and we may find that we are prepared to cheat and lie and scheme and plot like any bloody tyrant and contemplate adopting any behaviour however reprehensible so that we may grab this prize. It is as if we have been children until this point, playing without care and dressing in but not filling adult clothes, blithely assuming that when we are grown we shall behave as we have done in the headlong, heedless innocence that has been our life so far.

∞

But, my dear friend, none of this has *happened* yet!

∞

Have you not carried out the projections? I took your advice to spend more time in metamathical pursuits, modelling the likely course of events, divining the shape of the future. The results worry me. What I feel myself worries me. I wonder what we may stop at, what we may *not* stop at to attain the prize this Excession may offer.

∞

I meant spend more time enjoying yourself, as you well know. Besides: simulations, abstractions, projections; these are only themselves, not the reality of what they claim to represent. Attend to the actuality of events. We have a fascinating phenomenon before us and we are taking all reasonable precautions as we deal, or prepare to deal, with it. Some of our colleagues show laudable enterprise and initiative while others – ourselves – exhibit caution just as commendable as – and in sum complementary to – their ambition. What is there to fear but the wild imaginings which may well be the result of looking too far beyond the scale of relevance?

∞

I suppose so. Perhaps it is me. Certainly I see worrying signs everywhere. I dare say it must be me. I may still make some further inquiries, but I take your point.
∞

Make your inquiries if you must, but frankly I think it is this constant urge to inquire that causes you such pain; when one is able to scrutinise a subject as closely as we are – and to do so with the cross-referential capacity we possess, then the closer one looks into *anything* the more coincidences one finds, perfectly innocent though they may be.
What is the point of inquiring at such depth that one loses sight of the sunlit surface?
Lay up that magnifying glass and take up thy drink glass, my friend.
Slip off the academic gown and on with the antic pants!
∞

I thank you for your advice. I am reassured somewhat. I shall consider what you say. Do keep in touch. Farewell for now.

[stuttered tight point, M32, tra. @n4.28.862.3465]
xEccentric *Shoot Them Later*
    oLSV *Serious Callers Only*
The *Anticipation Of A New Lover's Arrival* was in touch again (signal file attached). I still think it could be one of them.
∞

[stuttered tight point, M32, tra. @n4.28.862.3980]
    xLSV *Serious Callers Only*
        oEccentric *Shoot Them Later*
And I still think you should let it in with us. It almost certainly now suspects you are part of the conspiracy.
∞

I have an image to maintain! And I would point out that we are still very much in the dark; we are not yet sure there *is* a conspiracy beyond the kind of normal outsmarting, outcliqueing nonsense in which all of us indulge from time to time. What purpose would formally extending the circumference of our concern serve, for now? Our sleuth is still behaving as though it is one of us but it knows nothing of our scepticism; we have naught to gain by bringing it aboard at present. If it is genuine it will apply itself to our purpose and if discovered the shadow of its guilt will not fall across us; if it is a test then it – they – may decide to bait us with more information of genuine interest, delivered at no cost to our virtue. Are we agreed? Have I convinced you? Anyway, enough of that; have we yet a plan? What was the result of your own investigations?

∞

Frustratingly vague. An exhaustive search has thrown up one remote possibility . . . but it remains an improbability predicated upon an uncertainty.

∞

Pray tell.

∞

Well . . . Let me ask you a question. What do *you* understand results by our communicating with our mutual friend?

∞

Why, that we are allowed to share in its inimitable objectivity. What else?

∞

That is the general volume of my concern. I'll say no more.

∞

What? Don't be ridiculous. Elaborate.

∞

No. You know what you said to our unwitting fellow in suspicion about not advertising lines of inquiry which might end in embarrassment . . .

∞

Unfair! After all I've shared with you!

∞

Yes, including the exciting opportunity to get involved with this in the first place. Thanks a lot.

∞

Cast *that* up to me again would you? I've *said* I'm *sorry*. Wish I'd never said anything now.

∞

Yes, but if the *Anticipation Of A New Lover's Arrival* finds out who passed on the information which led to the *Fate Amenable To Change's* search in the first place . . .

∞

I know, I know. Look; I'm doing all I can. I have requested a sympathetic ship to divert itself to Pittance, just in case. That's

where *my* prognostications indicate a site for possible future mischief.

∞

Death! If it comes to that ...

III

The twittering batball bounced off the centre of the high-scoring wall and flew straight towards Genar-Hofoen. The creature's tiny, clipped wings paddled frantically at the atmosphere as it tried to right itself and flee. One of its stumpy wings was ragged, perhaps even broken. It started to curve away as it approached the human. He took a good back-swing with his bat and slammed it into the little creature, sending it yelping and spinning away. He'd intended it to head for the high-scoring wall, but the stroke had been slightly off-target, resulting in the spin he'd given the thing and its course towards the corner between the high-scoring wall and the right-side forfeit baffle. Shit, he thought; the batball thrashed at the atmosphere and curved further towards the forfeit baffle.

Fivetide darted forward and with a flip of the bat strapped to one of his front limbs – and a resounding, 'Ha!' – snapped the batball into the centre of the high-scoring wall again; it thudded against the roundel and ricocheted off at an angle Genar-Hofoen knew he wasn't going to be able to intercept. He lunged at it anyway, but the creature sailed slackly past, half a metre away from his outstretched bat. He fell to the floor and rolled, feeling the gelfield suit tensing and squeezing him as it absorbed the shock. He picked himself up to a sitting position and looked around. He was breathing hard and his heart was hammering; playing this sort of game against another human would have been no joke in Affronter gravity. Playing it against an Affronter, even one with half his tentacles sportingly tied round its back, was even harder work.

'Hopeless!' Fivetide roared, crossing towards where the batball lay motionless near the back of the court. As he passed the human he flicked a tentacle under Genar-Hofoen's chin and levered him up. The gesture was almost certainly meant to be helpful, but it would have broken the average unprotected human neck. Genar-Hofoen merely found himself propelled off the floor like a rock out of a catapult and sent sailing towards the ceiling of the court, arms flailing.

~ *Idiot!* the suit said, as Genar-Hofoen reached the top of his trajectory. He assumed the suit was talking about Fivetide.

A tentacle wrapped itself round his waist like a whip. 'Oops!' Fivetide said, and lowered him safely to the floor with surprising gentleness. 'Sorry about that, Genar-Hofoen,' he yelled. 'You know what they say; "It's a wise lad knows his own strength when he's having fun," eh!' He patted the human relatively gently on the head, then continued over to the motionless body of the batball. He prodded it with the bat.

'Don't breed them like they used to,' he said, then made a noise Genar-Hofoen had learned to interpret as a sigh.

~ *Tentacled scumbag fuckwit*, said the suit.

~ Suit, really! he thought, amused.

~ *Well . . .*

The suit was not in the best of moods. He and it were spending a lot more time together; the suit didn't trust the containment around Genar-Hofoen's quarters in the ship and had insisted that the human keep it on, even when he was asleep. Genar-Hofoen had grumbled, but not over-much; there were too many funny smells in his quarters for him to have complete faith in the Affront's attempt at a human life-support system. The most the gelfield suit would let him do at night was peel aside its head section so that he could sleep with his face exposed; that way, even if his environment collapsed suddenly and totally, the suit would be able to protect him.

Fivetide flicked the batball up with the end of his bat and flicked it over the transparent wall of the court, into the spectators' seats. Then he banged on the wall, waking the snoozing form of the gelding on the far side.

'Wake up, you dozy *pellet*!' Fivetide bellowed. 'Another batball, dolt!'

The neutered Affronter adolescent jumped to its tentacle tips, its eye stalks waving around wildly, then it reached into a small cage by its side with one limb while another tentacle opened the door in the court wall. It picked one batball out of the dozen or so tied up in the cage and handed the squirming creature to the adult Affronter, who accepted it then jerked forward and hissed at the adolescent, making it flinch. It closed the door quickly.

'Ha!' Fivetide shouted, putting the trussed, wriggling batball to his forebeak and tearing the cord that had held it immobile. 'Another game, Genar-Hofoen?' Fivetide spat the short length of cord away and patted the batball up and down in one of his limbs while the little animal flexed its abbreviated wings.

'Why not?' Genar-Hofoen said coolly. He was exhausted, but he wasn't going to let Fivetide know.

'Nine–nil to me, I believe,' the Affronter said, holding the batball up to his eyes. 'I know,' he said. 'Let's make it more interesting.' He put the struggling batball into the tip of his forebeak, his eye stalks bent forward and down to look at what he was doing. There was a delicate movement around Fivetide's beak-fronds and a tiny screech, accompanied by a faint pop.

Fivetide withdrew the creature from his beak and inspected it, apparently satisfied. 'There,' he said. 'Always good for a change, playing with a blinded one.' He threw the writhing, mewling creature to Genar-Hofoen. 'Your serve, I believe.'

The Culture had a problem with the Affront. The Affront had a problem with the Culture, too, for that matter, but it was a pretty plain thing in comparison; the Affront's problem with the Culture was simply that the older civilisation stopped it doing all the things it wanted to do. The Culture's problem with the Affront was like an itch they couldn't scratch; the Culture's problem with the Affront was that the Affront existed at all and the Culture couldn't in all conscience do anything about it.

The problem stemmed from an accident of galactic topography and a combination of bad luck and bad timing.

The fuzzily specified region which had given rise to the various species that had eventually made up the Culture had been on the far side of the galaxy from the Affront home planet, and contacts between the Culture and the Affront had been unusually sparse for a long time for a variety of frankly banal reasons. By the time the Culture came to know the Affront better – shortly after the long distraction of the Idiran war – the Affront were a rapidly developing and swiftly maturing species, and short of another war there was no practical way of quickly changing either their nature or behaviour.

Some Culture Minds had argued at the time that a quick war against the Affront was exactly the right course of action, but even as they'd started setting out their case they'd known it was already lost; for all that the Culture was just then at a peak of military power it had never expected to attain at the start of that long and terrible conflict, just so there was a corresponding determination at all levels that – the task of stopping the Idirans' relentless expansion having been accomplished – the Culture would neither need nor seek to achieve such a martial zenith again. Even while the Minds concerned had been contending that a single abrupt and crushing blow would benefit all concerned – including the Affront, not just ultimately, but soon – the Culture's warships were being stood down, deactivated, componented, stored and demilitarised by the tens of thousands, while its trillions of citizens were congratulating themselves on a job well done and returning with the relish of the truly peace-loving to the uninhibited enjoyment of all the recreational wonders the resolutely hedonism-focused society of the Culture had to offer.

There had probably never been a less propitious time for arguing that more fighting was a good idea, and the argument duly foundered, though the problem remained.

Part of the problem was that the Affront had the disturbing habit of treating every other species they encountered with either total suspicion or amused contempt, depending almost entirely on whether that civilisation was ahead of or behind them in technological development. There had been one developed species – the Padressahl – in that same volume of the galaxy which had been sufficiently like the Affront in terms of evolutionary background and physical appearance to be treated almost as friends by the Affront and which yet had a moral outlook similar enough to the Culture's to consider it worth the effort of chaperoning the Affront with the other local species, and, to their eternal credit, the Padressahl had been doggedly endeavouring to nudge the Affront into something remotely resembling decent behaviour for more centuries than they cared to remember or admit.

It was the Padressahl who had given the Affront their name; originally the Affront had called themselves after their home world, Issorile. Calling them the Affront – following an episode involving a Padressahl trade mission to Issorile which the recipients had treated more as a food parcel – had been most decidedly intended as an insult, but the Issorilians, as they then were, thought that 'Affront' sounded much better and had steadfastly refused to drop their new name even after they had formed their loose patron/protégé alliance with the Padressahl.

However, a century or so after the end of the Idiran War, the Padressahl had had what the Culture regarded as the gross bad manners to suddenly sublime off into Advanced Elderhood at just the wrong time, leaving their less mature charges joyfully off the leash and both snapping at the heels of the local members of the Culture's great long straggling civilisational caravan wending its way towards progress (whether they went wittingly or not), and positively savaging several of the even less well-developed neighbouring species which for their own good nobody else had yet thought fit to contact.

Suggestions by a few of the more cynical Culture Minds that the Padressahl decision to hit the hyperspace button and go for full don't-give-a-damn-anymore god-head had been caused partially if not principally by their frustration and revulsion at the incorrigible ghastliness of Affront nature had never been either fully accepted or convincingly refuted.

Whatever; in the end, with a deal of arm and tentacle twisting, some deftly managed suitable-technology donation (through what the Affront Intelligence Regiment still gleefully but naïvely thought was some really neat high-tech theft on their part), the occasional instance of knocking heads together (or whatever anatomical feature was considered appropriate) and a hefty amount of naked bribery (woefully inelegant to the refined intellect of the average Culture Mind – their tastes generally ran to far more rarefied forms of chicanery – but undeniably effective) the Affront had – kicking and screaming at times, admittedly – finally been more or less persuaded to join the great commonality of the galactic meta-civilisation; they had agreed to abide by its rules almost all the time and had grudgingly accepted that other beings beside themselves might have rights, or at least tolerably excusable desires (such as those concerning life, liberty, self-determination and so on), which occasionally might even override the self-evidently perfectly natural, demonstrably just and indeed arguably even sacred Affronter prerogative to go wherever they wanted and do whatever they damn well pleased, preferably while having a bit of fun with the locals at the same time.

All that, however, represented only a partial solution to the least vexing part of the problem. If the Affront had been simply one more expansionist species of callously immature but technologically localised adventurers with bad contact manners, the problem they represented to the Culture would have subsided to the sort of level that would have gone more or less unnoticed; they would have become just another part of the general clutter of inventively obdurate species struggling to express themselves in the vast emptiness that was the galaxy.

The problem was rooted deeper, however; it went back further, it was more intrinsic. The problem was that the Affront had spent uncounted millennia long before they'd even got off their own fog-bound moon-planet tinkering with and carefully altering the flora and, especially, the fauna of that environment. They had discovered at a relatively early point in their development how to change the genetic make-up of both their own inheritance – which almost by definition needed little further amendment, given their manifest superiority – and that of the creatures with whom they shared their home world.

Those creatures had all, accordingly, been amended as the Affront saw fit, for their own amusement and delight. The result was what one Culture Mind had described as a kind of self-perpetuating, never-ending holocaust of pain and fear.

Affronter society rested on a huge base of ruthlessly exploited juvenile geldings and a sub-class of oppressed females who unless born to the highest families – and not always even then – could count themselves lucky if they were only raped by the males from their own tribe. It was generally regarded as significant – within the Culture if nowhere else – that one of the few aspects of their own genetic inheritance with which the Affront had deemed it desirable to meddle had been in the matter of making the act of sex a somewhat less pleasurable and considerably more painful act for their females than their basic genetic legacy required; the better, it was claimed, to further the considered good of the species rather than the impetuously selfish pleasure of the individual.

When an Affronter went hunting for the artificially fattened treehurdlers, limbcroppers, paralice or skinstrippers that were their favoured prey, it was in a soar-chariot pushed by the animals called swiftwings which lived in a state of perpetual dread, their nervous systems and pheromone receptors painstakingly tuned to react with ever increasing levels of dread and the urge to escape as their masters became more and more excited and so exuded more of the relevant odours.

The hunted animals themselves were artificially terrified as well, just by the very appearance of the Affronters, and so driven to ever more desperate manoeuvres in their frantic urge to escape.

When an Affronters' skin was cleaned it was by the small animals called xysters, whose diligence had been vastly improved by giving them such a frenetic hunger for an Affronter's dead skin cells that unless they were overcome by exhaustion they were prone to bloating themselves literally to the point of bursting.

Even the Affront's standard domesticated food animals had long since been declared as tasting much more interesting when they betrayed the signs of having been severely stressed, and so had also been altered to such a pitch of highly strung anxiety – and husbanded in conditions diligently contrived to intensify the effect – that they inevitably produced what any Affronter worth his methylacetylene would agree was the most inspiringly tasty meat this side of an event horizon.

The examples went on; in fact, reviewing their society, it was more or less impossible to avoid manifestations of the Affronters' deliberate, even artistic use of genetic manipulation to produce through a kind of ebulliently misplaced selfishness – which to them was indistinguishable from genuine altruism – the sort of result it took most societies paroxysms of self-destructive wretchedness to generate.

Hearty but horrible; that was the Affront. 'Progress through pain!' It was an Affronter saying. Genar-Hofoen had even heard Fivetide say it. He couldn't recall exactly, but it had probably been followed by a bellowed, 'Ho ho ho!'

The Affront appalled the Culture; they appeared so unamendable, their attitude and their abominable morality seemed so secured against remedy. The Culture had offered to provide machines to do the kind of jobs the juvenile castrati did, but the Affront just laughed; why, they could quite easily build machines of their own, but where was the honour in being served by a mere *machine*?

Similarly, the Culture's attempts to persuade the Affront that there were other ways to control fertility and familial inheritance besides those which relied on the virtual imprisonment, genetic mutilation and organised violation of their females, or to consume vat-grown meat – better, if anything, than the real thing – or to offer non-sentient versions of their hunting animals all met with equally derisive if brusquely good-humoured dismissals.

Still, Genar-Hofoen liked them, and had come even to admire them for their vivacity and enthusiasm; he had never really sub-scribed to the standard Culture belief that any form of suffering was intrinsically bad, he accepted that a degree of exploitation was inevitable in a developing culture, and leant towards the school of thought which held that evolution, or at least evolutionary pressures, ought to continue within and around a civilised species, rather than – as the Culture had done – choosing to replace evolution with a kind of democratically agreed physiological stasis-plus-option-list while handing over the real control of one's society to machines.

It was not that Genar-Hofoen hated the Culture, or particularly wished it ill in its present form; he was deeply satisfied that he had been born into it and not some other humanoid species where you suffered, procreated and died and that was about it; he just didn't feel at home in the Culture all the time. It was a motherland he wanted to leave and yet know he could always return to if he wanted. He wanted to experience life as an Affronter, and not just in some simulation, however accurate. Plus, he wanted to go somewhere the Culture had never been, and well, explore.

Neither ambition seemed to him *all* that much to ask, but he'd been thwarted in both desires until now. He'd thought he'd detected movement on the Affronter side of things before this *Sleeper* business had come up, but now, if all concerned were to be believed, he could more or less have whatever he wanted, no strings attached.

He found this suspicious in itself. Special Circumstances was not notorious for its desire to issue blank cheques to anyone. He wondered if he was being paranoid, or had just been living with the Affront for too long (none of his predecessors had lasted longer than a hundred days and he'd been here nearly two years already).

Either way, he was being cautious; he had asked around. He still had some replies to receive – they should be waiting for him when he arrived at Tier – but so far everything seemed to tally. He had also asked to speak to a representation of the Desert Class MSV *Not Invented Here*, the ship acting as incident coordinator for all this – again, this ought to happen on Tier – and he'd looked up the craft's own history in the module's archives and transferred the results to the suit's own AI.

The Desert Class had been the first type of General Systems Vehicle the Culture had constructed, providing the original template for the Very Large Fast Self-Sufficient Ship concept. At three-and-a-bit klicks in length it was tiny by today's standards – ships twice its length and eight times its volume were routinely constructed inside GSVs the size of the *Sleeper Service* and the whole class had been demoted to Medium Systems Vehicle status – but it certainly had the distinction of age; the *Not Invented Here* had been around for nearly two millennia and boasted a long and interesting career, coming as close as the Culture's distributed and democratic military command structure had allowed to being in advisory control of several fleets in the course of the Idiran War. It was now in that equivalent of serenely glorious senescence that affected some ancient Minds; no longer producing many smaller ships, taking relatively little to do with Contact's normal business, and keeping itself relatively sparsely populated.

It remained, nevertheless, a full Culture ship; it hadn't taken a sabbatical, gone into a retreat or become an Eccentric, nor had it joined the Culture Ulterior – the fairly recently fashionable name for the bits of the Culture that had split away and weren't really fully paid-up members any more. All the same, and despite the fact that the archive entry on the old ship was huge (as well as all the naked factual stuff, it contained one hundred and three different full-length biographies of the craft which it would have taken him a couple of years to read), Genar-Hofoen couldn't help feeling that there was a slight air of mystery about the old ship.

It also occurred to him that Minds wrote voluminous biographies of each other in order to cover the odd potentially valuable or embarrassing nugget of truth under a mountain of bullshit.

Also included in the archive entries were some fairly wild claims by a few of the smaller, more eccentric news and analyses journals and reviews – some of them one-person outfits – to the effect that the MSV was a member of some shadowy cabal, that it was part of a conspiracy of mostly very old craft which stepped in to take control of situations which might threaten the Culture's cozy proto-imperialist meta-hegemony; situations which proved beyond all doubt that the so-called normal democratic process of general policy-making was a complete and utter ultra-statist sham and the humans – and indeed their cousins and fellow dupes in this Mind-controlled plot, the drones – had even less power than they thought they had in the Culture. . . . There was quite a lot of stuff like that. Genar-Hofoen read it until his head felt as if it was spinning, then he stopped; there came a point when if a conspiracy was *that* powerful and subtle it became pointless to worry about it.

Whatever; doubtless the old MSV was not itself in total command of the situation he was allowing himself to be dragged into, but just the tip of the iceberg, representing a collection, if not a cabal, of other interested and experienced Minds who'd all be having a say in the immediate reaction to the discovery of this artifact near Esperi.

As well as his request for a talk with a personality-state of the *Not Invented Here*, Genar-Hofoen had sent messages to ships, drones and people he knew with SC connections, asking them if what he'd been told was all true. A few of the nearer ones had got replies to him before he'd left God'shole habitat, each confirming that what they had been told of what he was asking about – which admittedly varied according to how much whatever collection of Minds the *Not Invented Here* was representing had chosen to tell the individuals concerned. The information he'd received looked genuine and the deal he'd been offered sounded good. At any rate, by the time he'd got to Tier and received all his replies he reckoned so many other people and Minds not irretrievably complicit with SC would have heard about what he'd been offered it would become impossible for SC to wriggle out of its deal with him without losing an unthinkable amount of face.

He still suspected there was a lot more to this than he was being told, and he had no doubt he was and would continue to be both manipulated and used, but providing the price they were paying him was right, that didn't bother him, and at least the job itself sounded simple enough.

He'd taken the precaution of checking up on the story his uncle had told him about the disappearing trillion-year-old sun and the orbiting artifact. Sure enough, there it was; a semi-mythological story set way back in the archives, one of any number of weird-sounding tales with frustratingly little evidence to back them up. Certainly nobody seemed able to explain what had happened in this case. And of course there was nobody around to ask anymore. Except for the lady he was travelling to talk to.

The captain of the good ship *Problem Child* had indeed been a woman; Zreyn Tramow. Honorary Contact Fleet Captain Gart-Kepilesa Zreyn Enhoff Tramow Afayaf dam Niskat-west, to give her her official title and Full Name. The archives held her picture. She'd looked proud and capable; a pale, narrow face, with close-set eyes, centimetre-short blonde hair and thin lips, but smiling, and with what appeared to him at least to be an intelligent brightness to those eyes. He liked the look of her.

He'd wondered what it would be like to have been Stored for two-and-a-bit millennia and then be woken up with no body to return to and a man you'd never seen before talking to you. And trying to steal your soul.

He'd stared at the photograph for a while, trying to see behind those clear blue mocking eyes.

They played another two games of batball; Fivetide won those as well. Genar-Hofoen was quivering with fatigue by the end. Then it was time to freshen up and head for the officers' mess, where there was a full-dress uniform celebration dinner that evening because it was Commander Kindrummer VI's birthday. The carousing went on long into the night; Fivetide taught the human some obscene songs, Genar-Hofoen responded in kind, two Atmosphere Force Wing Captains had an only semi-serious duel with grater muffs – much blood, no limbs lost, honour satisfied – and Genar-Hofoen did a tightrope walk over the commander's table pit while the scratchounds howled beneath. The suit swore it hadn't contributed to the feat, though he was sure it had steadied him a couple of times. However, he didn't say anything.

Around them, the *Kiss The Blade* and its two escorts powered their way through the spaces between the stars, heading for Tier habitat.

IV

Ulver Seich woke up in the best possible way. She surfaced with a languorous slowness through fuzzy layers of luxurious half-dreams and memories of sweetness, sensuality and sheer carnal bliss . . . to find it all merging rather splendidly into reality, and what was happening right now.

She toyed with the idea of pretending she was still asleep, but then he must just have touched exactly the right spot and she couldn't help making a noise and moving and clenching and so she rolled over and took his face in her hands and kissed it.

'Oh no,' she croaked, laughing. 'Don't stop; that's a *fine* way to say good morning.'

'Nearly afternoon,' the young man breathed. He was called Otiel. He was tall and very dark-skinned and he had fabulously blond hair and a voice that could raise bumps on your skin at a hundred metres, or, better still, millimetres. Metaphysics student. Swam a lot and free-climbed. The one she'd set her heart on the previous evening. The leg-liker. Long, sensitive fingers.

'Hmm . . . Really? Well . . . you know . . . maybe you can say that later, but meantime you just keep right on – WHAT?'

Ulver Seich jerked to a sitting position, eyes wide open. She slapped the young man's hand away and stared wildly around. She was in what she thought of as her Romantic bed. It was more of a chamber, really; a ruched, pavilion-ceilinged five-metre crimson hemisphere filled with billowy bolsters and slinky sheets which blended into puffy paddings forming the single wall of the chamber and which swelled out in places to form various projections, shelves, straps and little seat-like things. She had other beds; her childhood bed, still stuffed with toys; her Just Sleep bed, comfy and surrounded by nocturne plants; a huge grandly formal and terribly old-fashioned canopied Reception bed, for when she wanted to receive friends, and an oil bed, which was basically a four-metre sphere of warm oils; you had to put little nose-plug things in and the air was Displaced into you. Not to everybody's taste, sadly, but *very* erotic.

Her neural lace had woken up already with the adrenaline rush. It told her it was half an hour to noon. Shit. She'd thought she'd set an alarm to wake her an hour ago. She'd meant to. Must have slipped her mind due to the fun; hormonal re-prioritisation. Well, it happened.

'What . . . ?' Otiel said, smiling. He was looking at her oddly. Like he was wondering whether this was part of some game. Twinkle in the eye. He reached out for her.

Damn, the gravity was still on. She commanded the bed controls to switch to one-tenth G. 'Sorry!' she said, blowing him a kiss as the apparent gravity cut by ninety per cent. The padding beneath their bodies suddenly had a lot less weight to support; the effect was to produce a very gentle, padded pat on the bottom which was enough to send them both floating fractionally upwards. He looked surprised; it was such a sweet, boyish, innocent expression she almost stayed.

But she didn't; she jumped out of the bed, kicking up through the air and raising her arms above her head to dive through the loose gatherings of the chamber's tented ceiling and out into the bedroom beyond, arcing out over the padded platform around the bed chamber and falling gently back into the clutches of its standard gravity. She ran down the curved steps to the bedroom floor and almost bumped into the drone Churt Lyne.

'I know!' she yelled, flapping one hand at it.

It lifted out of her way, then turned smoothly and followed her across the floor of the bedroom towards the bathroom, its fields formal blue but tinged with a rosy humour.

Ulver broke into a run. She'd always liked big rooms; the bedroom one was twenty metres square and five high. One wall was window. It looked out onto a tightly curved landscape of fields and wooded hills dotted with towers and ziggurats. This was Interior Space One, the central and longest cylinder of a cluster of independently revolving five-kilometre diameter tubes which formed the main living areas in the Rock.

'Anything I can do?' the drone asked as Ulver ran into the bathroom. Behind it, there was a shout and then a series of curses as the young man tried to exit the bed chamber in the same way Ulver had and got the gravity-transition wrong. The drone turned briefly towards the disturbance, then swivelled back as Ulver's voice floated out through the noise of rushing fluids. 'Well, you could throw *him* out . . . Nicely, mind.'

'*What?*' Ulver screamed. 'You get me to ditch a luscious new guy after one night, you make me scrap *all* my engagements for a *month* and then you won't even let me take a few pets? Or a couple of *pals?*'

'Ulver, can I talk to you alone?' Churt Lyne said calmly, rotating to point at a room off the main gallery.

'No you *can't!*' she yelled, throwing down the cloak she'd been carrying. 'Anything you have to say to me you can damn well say in front of my friends.'

They were in the outer gallery of Iphetra, a long reception area lined with windows and old paintings; it looked out to the formal gardens and Interior Space One beyond. A couple of traveltubes waited beyond doors set into the wall full of portraits. She'd told everybody to rendezvous here. She'd missed the noon deadline by over an hour, but there were certain things about one's toilet that simply couldn't be rushed, and – as she'd told a briefly but fetchingly incandescently furious Churt Lyne from her milk-bath – if she was really that important to all these top-secret plans, SC had no choice but to wait. As a concession to the urgency of the situation she had left her face unadorned, tied her hair back into a simple bun and slipped into a conservatively patterned loose pants and jacket combination; even choosing her jewellery for the day had taken no more than five minutes.

The gallery had got quite busy; her mother was here, tall and tousled in a jellaba, three cousins, seven aunts and uncles, about a dozen friends – all house-guests and a little bleary-eyed after the Graduation party – and a couple of house-slaved drones attempting to control the animals; a brace of tawny speytlid hunters looking about at everybody and snuffling and slavering with excitement and her three hooded but still restless alseyns which kept stretching their wings and giving their piercing, plangent cry. Another drone waited outside the nearest window with Brave, her favourite mount, saddled up and pawing the ground, while the three drones she'd decided were the minimum she could manage with were taking care of her luggage trunks, which were still appearing from the house lift. A tray floated at her side with breakfast; she'd just started munching on a chislen segment when the drone had told her she had to make this journey alone.

Churt Lyne didn't reply in speech. Instead – astonishingly – it spoke through her neural lace:

~ Ulver, for pity's sake, this is a secret mission for Special Circumstances, not a social outing with your girlfriends.

'And don't secret-talk me!' Ulver hissed through clenched teeth. 'Grief, that's so *rude*!'

'Quite right, dear,' muttered her mother, yawning.

A couple of her friends laughed lightly.

Churt Lyne came right up to her until it was almost touching her, and then the next thing she knew there was a sort of grey cylinder around her and the machine; it stretched from wooden floor to stone-carved ceiling and it was about a metre and a half in diameter, neatly enclosing her, Churt and the tray carrying breakfast. She stared at the drone, her mouth open, eyes wide. It had never done anything like this before! Its aura field had disappeared. It hadn't even had the decency to square the field and put the field on a mirror finish; at least she could have checked her appearance.

'Sorry about this, Ulver,' the machine said. Its voice sounded flat in the narrow cylinder. Ulver closed her mouth and prodded the field the drone had slung around them. It was like touching warm stone. 'Ulver,' the drone said again, taking one of her hands in a maniple field, 'I apologise; I ought to have made the point earlier. I just assumed . . . Well, never mind. I'm supposed to come with you to Tier, but not anybody else. Your friends have to stay here.'

'But Peis and I always go deep space together! And Klatsli is my new protégé; I promised her she could stick around me; I can't just abandon her! Do you have any idea what that could do to her development? To her social life? People might think I've dumped her. Besides, she's got an utterly *exquisite* older brother. If I—'

'You can't take them,' the drone said loudly. 'They're not included in the invitation.'

'I heard what you said yesterday, you know,' Ulver said, shaking her head and leaning forward at the drone. '"Keep it secret"; I haven't told them where we're going.'

'That's not the point. When I said don't tell a soul I meant don't tell a soul you're going, not don't tell a soul exactly *where* you're going.'

She laughed, throwing her head back. 'Churt; real space here! My diary is a public document, hadn't you noticed? There are at least three channels devoted to me – all run by rather desperate young men, admittedly, but nevertheless. I can't change my *eye* colour without anybody on the Rock who follows fashion knowing about it within the hour. I can't just disappear! Are you *mad*?'

'And I don't think the animals can come either,' Churt Lyne said smoothly, ignoring her question. 'The protira certainly can't. There isn't room on the ship.'

'Isn't *room*?' she roared. 'What size *is* this thing? Are you sure it's *safe*?'

'Warships don't have stables, Ulver.'

'It's an *ex*-warship!' she exclaimed, waving her arms around. 'Ow!' She sucked at the knuckle she'd hit against the field cylinder.

'Sorry. But still.'

'What about my clothes?'

'A cabin full of clothes is perfectly all right, though I don't know for whose benefit you're going to be wearing them.'

'What about when I get to Tier?' she cried. 'What about this guy I'm not supposed to fuck? Am I supposed to just wander past him *naked*?'

'Take two roomsful; three. Clothes are not a problem, and you can pick up more when you get there – no, wait a minute, I know how long it takes you to choose new clothes; just take what you want. Four cabins; there.'

'But my *friends*!'

'Tell you what; I'll show you the space you've got to work with. Okay?'

'Oh, okay,' she said, shaking her head and sighing heavily.

The drone fed convincing-looking pictures of the ex-warship's interior into Ulver's brain through the neural lace.

She caught her breath. Her eyes were wide when the display stopped. She stared at the drone. 'The rooms!' she exclaimed. 'The cabins; they're so small!'

'Quite. Still think you want to take your friends?'

She thought for a second. 'Yes!' she yelled, thumping a fist on the little tray floating at her side. It wobbled, trying not to spill the fruit juice. 'It'd be cozy!'

'What if you fall out?'

That stopped her for a moment. She tapped her lips with one finger, frowning into space. She shrugged. 'I can cut people dead in a traveltube, Churt. I can ostracise people in the same *bed*.' She leant towards the machine again then glanced round at the grey walls of the field cylinder. 'I can ostracise people in something *this* big,' she said pointedly, her hands on her hips. She put her head back, narrowed her eyes and lowered her voice. 'I could just refuse to go, you know.'

'You could,' the machine said with a pronounced sigh. 'But you'd never get into Contact, and SC would be forced to try and get a double – a synthetic entity – to impersonate this woman on Tier. The authorities there wouldn't be amused if they found out.'

She gazed levelly at the machine for a moment. She sighed and shook her head. 'Bugger,' she breathed, snatching the glass of fruit juice from the floating tray and looking in distaste at where the juice had run down the outside of the glass. 'I hate this acting adult shit.' She knocked the juice back, set the glass back down and licked her lips. 'Okay; let's go, let's go!'

The goodbyes took a while. Churt Lyne glowed greyer and greyer with frustration until it turned into a sort of off-black sphere; then it dropped its aura field altogether and sped out of the nearest opened window. It raced around in the air outside for a while; a couple of sonic booms nearly had the mounts bolting.

Eventually, though, Ulver had said her farewells, decided to leave all her animals and two trunks of clothes behind and then – having remained serene in the midst of much hullabaloo and some tears from Klatsli – entered a traveltube with a frostily blue Churt Lyne and was taken to the Forward Docks and a big, brightly lit hangar, where the Psychopath Class ex-Rapid Offensive Unit *Frank Exchange of Views* was waiting for her.

Ulver laughed. 'It looks,' she snorted, 'like a dildo!'

'That's appropriate,' Churt Lyne said. 'Armed, it can fuck solar systems.'

She remembered when she was a little girl and had stood on a bridge over a gorge in one of the other Interior Spaces; she had a stone in her hand and her mother had held her up to the bridge parapet so that she could look over the edge and drop the stone into the water below. She'd held the stone – it was about the same size as her little fist – right up to one eye and closed her other eye so that the dark stone had blotted out everything else she could see. Then she'd let it go.

She and Churt Lyne stood in the ship's tiny hangar area, surrounded by her cases, bags and trunks as well as a deal of plain but somehow menacing-looking bits and pieces of military equipment. The way that stone had fallen towards the dark water then, shrinking and shrinking, was very like the way Phage Rock fell silently away from the old warship now.

This time, of course, there was no splash.

When Phage had entirely disappeared, she switched out of the view her neural lace had imported into her head and turned to the drone, thinking a thought that would have occurred to her a lot earlier, she hoped, if she'd been sober and unimpassioned over the last day.

'When was this ship sent to Phage, Churt, and from where?'

'Why don't you ask it yourself?' it said, turning to indicate a small drone approaching over the jumble of equipment.

~ Churt? she asked via the neural lace.

~ Yes?

~ Damn; I was hoping the ship's rep might be a dazzling handsome young man. Instead it's something that looks like a—

Churt Lyne interrupted:

~ Ulver; you are aware that the ship itself acts as exchange hub for these communications?

~ Oh dear, she thought, and felt herself colour as the little drone approached. She smiled broadly at it.

'No offence,' she said.

'None taken,' said the little machine as it came to a halt in front of her. It had a reedy but reasonably melodious voice.

'For the record,' she said, still smiling, and still blushing, 'I thought you looked a bit like a jewellery box.'

'Could have been worse,' chipped in Churt Lyne. 'You should hear what she calls me sometimes.'

The little drone's snout dipped once in a sort of bow. 'That's quite all right, Ms Seich,' it said. 'Delighted to meet you. Allow me to welcome you aboard the Very Fast Picket *Frank Exchange of Views*.'

'Thank you,' she said, also nodding slowly. 'I was just asking my friend where you'd come from, and when you'd been dispatched.'

'I didn't come from anywhere except Phage,' the ship told her. She felt her eyes widen. 'Really?'

'Really,' it said laconically. 'And the answer to your next three questions, I'd guess, are: because I was very well hidden and that's actually quite easy in a conglomeration of matter the size of Phage; getting on for five hundred years; and there are another fifteen like me back home. I trust you are reassured rather than shocked and that we may rely on your discretion in the future.'

'Oh, golly, absolutely,' she said, nodding, and felt half inclined to click her heels and salute.

V

Dajeil had been spending a lot more time with the beasts. She swam with the great fish and the sea-evolved mammals and reptiles, she donned a flyer suit and cruised high above the sea with her wide wings extended alongside the dirigible creatures in the calm currents of air and the cloud layers, and she donned a full gelfield suit with a secondary AG unit and carved her way amongst the poison gases, the acid clouds and the storm bands of the upper atmosphere, surrounded by noxiousness and the ferocious beauty of the ecosystem there.

She even spent some time walking in the ship's top-side parks, the nature reserves which the *Sleeper Service* had possessed even when it had been a regular, well-behaved GSV and diligent member of the Contact section; the parks – complete landscapes with hills, forests, plains, river and lake systems and the remains of small resort villages and hotels – covered all the great ship's flat top surfaces and together measured over eight hundred square kilometres. With the humans gone from the ship there were fairly large populations of land animals in the park lands, including grazers, predators and scavengers.

She'd never really paid any of them much attention – her interests had always been with the larger, buoyant animals of the fluid environments – but now that they were all likely to suffer the same exile or unconsciousness as the rest, she had started to take a belated, almost guilty interest in them (as though, she thought ruefully, her attention bestowed some special significance on the behaviour she witnessed, or meant anything at all to the creatures concerned).

Amorphia did not come for its regular visit; another couple of days passed.

When the avatar came to her again, she had been swimming with the purple-winged triangular rays in the shallow part of the sea extending beyond the sheer, three-kilometre cliff which was the rear of the craft. Returning, she had taken the flyer which the ship habitually put at her disposal, but asked it to drop her at the top of the scree slope beneath the cliff facing the tower.

It was a bright, cold day and the air tasted sharp; this part of the ship's environment was cycling towards winter; all the trees save for a few everblues had lost their leaves, and soon the snows would come.

The air was very clear and from the top of the scree slope she could see the Edge islands, thirty kilometres away, out close to where the inner containment field of the ship came down like a wall across the sea.

She had scrambled down the scree in small rattles of stones like dry, fanning rivers of pebbles and dust. She had long ago learned how to use her altered centre of gravity to her advantage in this sort of adventure, and had never yet fallen badly. She got to the bottom, her heart beating hard, her leg muscles warm with the effort expended and her skin bright with sweat. She walked quickly back through the salt marsh, along the paths the ship had fashioned for her.

The sun-line was near setting when she returned to the tower, breathless and still perspiring. She took a shower and was sitting by the log fire the tower had lit for her, letting her hair dry naturally, when Gravious the black bird rapped once on the window and then disappeared again.

She pulled her robe tighter about her as the tall, dark-dressed figure of Amorphia climbed the stairs and entered the room.

'Amorphia,' she said, tucking her wet hair into the hood of the robe. 'Hello. Can I get you anything?'

'No. No, thank you,' the avatar said, looking nervously around the circular living room.

Dajeil indicated a chair while she sat on a couch by the fire.

'Please.' She pulled her legs up underneath her. 'So, what brings you here today?'

'I—' the avatar began, then stopped, and pulled at its lower lip with its fingers. 'Well, it seems,' it started again, then hesitated once more. It took a breath. 'The time,' it said, then stopped, looking confused.

'The time?' Dajeil Gelian said.

'It's . . . it's come,' Amorphia said, and looked ashamed.

'For the changes you talked about?'

'Yes,' the avatar said, sounding relieved. 'Yes. For the changes. They have to start now. In fact, they have already begun. The rounding-up of the creatures comes first, and the . . .' It looked unsure again, and frowned deeply. 'The . . . the de-landscaping,' it gulped. It tripped up on the next words in its rush to say them. 'The un-geometri— . . . The un-geomorphologising. The . . . the pristinisation!' it said, almost shouting.

Dajeil smiled, trying not to show the alarm she felt. 'I see,' she said slowly. 'So it is all definitely going to happen?'

'Yes,' Amorphia said, breathing heavily. 'Yes, it is.'

'And I will have to leave the ship?'

'Yes. You'll have to leave the ship. I . . . I'm sorry.' The avatar looked suddenly crestfallen.

'Where am I to go?'

'Where?' Confused.

'Where are you going to stop, or where will I be taken? Is it another ship, or a habitat, or an O or a planet, a rock? What?'

'I . . .' The avatar frowned again. 'The ship does not know yet,' it said. 'Things are being worked out.'

Dajeil looked at Amorphia for a while, her hands absently stroking the bulge of her belly under her robe. 'What is happening, Amorphia?' she asked, keeping her voice soft. 'Why is all this taking place?'

'I can't . . . there is no need . . . no need for you to know,' the avatar said hesitantly. It looked exasperated, and shook its head as though angry, gaze flicking up and around the room, as though seeking something.

Finally it looked back at her. 'I might be able to tell you more, later, if you will agree to stay on board until . . . until a time comes when I can only evacuate you by another vessel.'

She smiled. 'That sounds like no great hardship. Does that mean I can stay here longer?'

'Not here; the tower and everything else will have gone; it will mean living inside. Inside the GSV.'

Dajeil shrugged. 'All right. I suppose I can suffer that. When will that have to happen?'

'In a day or two,' Amorphia said. Then the avatar looked concerned, and sat forward on the seat. 'There . . . it's possible . . . it's possible there . . . might be a slightly increased risk to you, staying aboard until then. The ship will do all it can to minimise that, of course, but the possibility exists. And it might be . . .' Amorphia's head shook suddenly. 'I – the ship, would like you to remain on board, if possible, until then. It might be . . . important. Good.' The avatar looked as though it had startled itself. Dajeil suddenly recalled having held a tiny baby when it had farted loudly; the look of utter, blinking surprise on its face was not dissimilar to that on Amorphia's face now. Dajeil choked back an urge to laugh, and it disappeared anyway when, as though prompted by the thought, her child kicked within her. She clamped a hand to her belly. 'Yes,' Amorphia said, nodding vigorously. 'It would be *good* if you stayed on board. . . . Good might come of it altogether.' It sat staring at her, panting as though from exertion.

'Then I had better stay, hadn't I?' Dajeil said, again keeping her voice steady and calm.

'Yes,' said the avatar. 'Yes; I'd appreciate that. Thank you.' It stood up suddenly from the seat, as though released by a spring within. Dajeil was startled; she almost jumped. 'I must go now,' Amorphia said.

Dajeil swung her legs out and stood too, more slowly. 'Very well,' she said as the avatar made its way to the staircase set onto the wall of the tower. 'I hope you'll tell me more later.'

'Of course,' the avatar mumbled, then it turned and bowed quickly and was gone, bootsteps clattering down the stairs.

The door slammed some moments later.

Dajeil Gelian climbed the steps to the parapet of the tower. A breeze caught her robe's hood and spilled her heavy, still-wet hair out and down. The sun-line had set, throwing highlights of gold and ruby light across the sky and turning the starboard horizon into a fuzzy violet border. The wind stiffened. It felt cold.

Amorphia was not walking back this evening; after the creature had hurried up the narrow path through the tower's walled garden and out of the land-gate, it just rose up into the air, without any obvious AG pack or flying suit, and then accelerated through the air in a dark, thin blur, curving through the air to disappear a few seconds later over the edge of the cliff beyond.

Dajeil looked up. There were tears in her eyes, which annoyed her. She sniffed them back angrily and wiped her cheeks. A few blinks, and the view of the sky was steady and unobscured again.

It had indeed already begun.

A flight of the dirigible creatures were dropping down from the red-speckled clouds above her, heading for the cliffs. Looking closely, she could see the accompanying drones that were their herders. Doubtless the same scene was being repeated at this moment both beneath the grey surface of the sea on the far side of the tower as well as above, in the region of furious heat and crushing pressure that was the gas-giant environment.

The dirigible creatures hesitated in the skies above; in front of them, a whole area of the cliff, perhaps a kilometre across and half that in height, simply folded in on itself in four parcel-neat sections and disappeared backwards into four huge, long glowing halls. The reassured dirigible creatures were shepherded towards one of the opened bays. Elsewhere, other parts of the cliffs were performing similar tricks; lights sparkled in the spaces revealed. The entire swathe of grey-brown scree – easily twenty kilometres across and a hundred metres in both depth and height – was folding and tipping in eight gigantic Vs and channelling several billion tonnes of real-enough rock into eight presumably reinforced ship bays, doubtless to undergo whatever transformational process was in store for the sea and the gas-giant atmosphere.

A titanic, bone-resounding tremor shook the ground and rumbled over the tower while huge clouds of dust leapt billowing into the chilly air as the rock disappeared. Dajeil shook her head – her wet hair flapping on the sodden shoulders of her robe – then walked towards the doorway which led to the rest of the tower, intending to retreat there before the clouds of stone dust arrived.

The black bird Gravious made to settle on her shoulder; she shooed it off and it landed flapping uproariously on the edge of the opened trap door.

'My tree!' it screamed, hopping from leg to leg. 'My tree! They've – I – my – it's *gone*!'

'Too bad,' she said. The sound of another great tumble of falling rock split the skies. 'Stay wherever it puts me,' she told the bird. 'If it'll let you. Now get out of my way.'

'But my food for the winter! It's gone!'

'*Winter* has gone, you stupid bird,' she told it. The black bird stopped moving and just perched there, head thrown forward and to one side, right eye staring at her, as though trying to catch some more meaningful echo of what she had just told it. 'Oh, don't worry,' she said. 'I'm sure you'll be accommodated.' She waved it off its perch and it flapped noisily away.

A last earthquake of sound rolled under and over the tower. The woman Dajeil Gelian looked round at the twilight-lit rolling grey dust clouds to see the light from opened bays beyond shine through, as the pretence at natural form was dispensed with and the overall shape of the craft's fabric began to reveal itself.

The Culture General Systems Vehicle *Sleeper Service*. No longer just her gallant protector and a grossly over-specified mobile game reserve . . . It seemed that the great ship had finally found something to become involved with which was more in keeping with the extent of its powers. She wished it well, though with trepidation.

The sea like stone, she thought. She turned and stepped down into the warmth of the tower, patting the bulge that was her sleeping, undreaming child. *A stern winter indeed; harder than any of us had anticipated.*

VI

Leffid Ispanteli was trying desperately to remember the name of the lass he was with. Geltry? Usper? Stemli?

'Oh, yes, yes, ffffuck! Gods, *yes*! More, more; now, yes! There! There! Yes! That's oohhh . . . !'

Soli? Getrin? Ayscoe?

'Oh, fuck! There! More! Harder! Right . . . right . . . now! . . .*Aah*!'

Selas? Serayer? (Grief; how ungallant of him!)

'Oh, sweet providence! Oh FUCK!'

No wonder he couldn't think of her name; the girl was kicking up such a racket he was surprised he could think at all. Still, a chap shouldn't grumble, he supposed; always nice to be appreciated. Even if it was the yacht that was doing most of the work.

The diminutive hire yacht continued to shudder and buck beneath them, spiralling and curving through space a few hundred kilometres away from the huge stepped world that was Tier.

Leffid had used these little yachts for this sort of thing before; if you fed a nicely jagged course into their computers they'd do most of the bumping and grinding for you while leaving just enough apparent gravity to brace oneself without leaving one feeling terribly *heavy*. Programming in the odd power-off interval gave moments of delicious free-fall, and drew the small craft further away from the great world, so that gradually the view beyond the viewing ports increased in majesty as more and more of the conical habitat was revealed, turning slowly and glittering in the light of the system's sun. Altogether a wonderful way of having sex, really, providing one found a suitable and willing partner.

'Aw! Aw! *Aaawww*! Force! Push, push, push; *yes*!'

She held his thrusting hips, smoothed his feathered scalp and used her other hand turned out to stroke his lower belly. Her huge dark eyes glittered, myriad tiny lights sparkling somewhere inside them in pulsing vortexes of colour and intensity that varied charmingly with the intensity of her pleasure.

'Come on! Yes! Come on up; further! Further! Aaarrrhh.'

Dammit all; what *was* her name?

Geldri? Shokas? Esiel?

Grief; what if it wasn't even a Culture name? He'd been certain it was but now he was starting to think maybe it wasn't after all. That made it even more difficult. More excusable, maybe, too, but certainly more difficult too.

They'd met at the Homomdan Ambassador's party to celebrate the start of the six-hundred and forty-fifth Festival of Tier. He'd resolved to have his neural lace removed for the month of the Festival, deciding that as this year's theme was Primitivism he ought to give up some aspect of his amendments. The neural lace had been his choice because although there was no physical alteration and he looked just the same to everybody else, he'd reckoned he'd *feel* more different.

Which he did. It was oddly liberating to have to ask things or people for information and not know precisely what the time was and where he was located in the habitat. But it also meant that he was forced to rely on his own memory for things like people's names. And how imperfect was the unassisted human memory (he'd forgotten)!

He'd even thought of having his wings removed too, at least partly to *show* that he was taking part in the spirit of the Festival, but in the end he'd stuck with them. Probably just as well; this girl had made a big thing about the wings; headed straight for him, masked, body glittering. She was nearly as tall as he was, perfectly proportioned, and she had four arms! A drink in each hand, too. His kind of female, he'd decided instantly, even as she was looking admiringly at his folded, snow-white wings. She wore some sort of gelsuit; basically deep blue but covered with a pattern like gold wire wrapped all over it and dotted with little diamonds of contrasting, subtly glowing red. Her whiskered mask was porcelain-bone studded with rubies and finished with iridescent badra feathers. Stunning perfume.

She handed him a glass and took off her mask to reveal eyes the size of opened mouths; eyes softly, blackly featureless in the lustrous lights of the vibrantly decorated dome until he'd looked carefully and seen the tiny hints of lights within their curved surfaces. The gelfield suit covered her everywhere except those heavily altered eyes and a small hole at the back of her head where a plait of long, shiningly auburn hair spilled out. Wrapped in gold wire, it ended at the small of her back and was tethered to the suit there.

She'd said her first name; the gelsuit's lips had parted to show white teeth and a pink tongue.

'Leffid,' he'd replied, bowing deeply but watching her face as best he could while he did so. She'd looked up at his wings as they'd risen up and towards her over the plain black robe he'd worn. He'd seen her take a deep breath. The lights in her eyes had sparkled brightly.

Ah-ha! he'd thought.

The Homomdan ambassador had turned the riotously deco-rated, stadium-sized bowl that was her residential quarters into an old-fashioned fun-fair for the party. They had wandered through the acts, tents and rides, he and she, talking small talk, passing comment on other people they passed, celebrating the refreshing absence of drones at the party, discussing the merits of whirligigs, shubblebubs, helter-skelters, ice-flumes, quittletraps, slicicles, boing-braces, airblows, tramplescups and bodyflaggers, and bemoaning the sheer pointlessness of inter-species funny-face competitions.

She was on an improving tour from her home Orbital, cruising and learning with a party of friends on a semi-Eccentric ship that would be here as long as the Festival lasted. One of her aunts had some Contact contacts and had swung an invitation to the ambassador's celebration; her friends were *so* jealous. He guessed she was still in her teens, though she moved with the easy grace of somebody older and her conversation was more intelligent and even shrewder than he'd have expected. He was used to being able to almost switch off talking to most teenagers but he was having to race after her meanings and allusions at time. Were teenagers getting even smarter? Maybe he was just getting old! No matter; she obviously liked the wings. She asked to stroke them.

He told her he was a resident of Tier, Culture or ex-Culture depending how you wanted to look at it; it wasn't something he bothered about, though he supposed if forced he felt more loyalty to Tier, where he'd lived for twenty years, than to the Culture, where he'd lived for the rest of his life. In the AhForgetIt Tendency, that was, not the Culture proper, which the Tendency regarded as being far too serious and not nearly as dedicated to hedonistic pursuits as it ought to be. He'd first come here as part of a Tendency cultural mission, but stayed when the rest returned back to their home Orbital. (He'd thought about saying, Well, actually I was in the Tendency's equivalent of Special Circumstances, kind of a spy, really, and I know lots of secret codes and stuff . . . but that probably wasn't the sort of line that would work with a sophisticated girl like this.)

Oh, much older than her; quite middle-aged, at one hundred and forty. Well, that was kind of her to say so. Yes, the wings worked, in anything less than 50% standard gravity. Had them since he was thirty. He lived on an air level here with 30% gravity. *Huge* web-trees up there. Some people lived in their hollowed-out fruit husks, though he preferred a sort of wispy house-thing made from sheets of chaltressor silk stretched over hi-pressure thinbooms. Oh yes, she'd be very welcome to see it.

Had she seen much of Tier? Arrived yesterday? Such good timing for the Festival! He'd love to be her guide. Why not now? Why not. They could hire a yacht. First though they would go and make their apologies to the Ambassador. Of course; he and she were old pals. Something to tell that aunt of hers. And they'd call by the cruise ship; bring the others? Oh, just a little camera drone? Well why not? Yes, Tier's rules could be tiresome at times, couldn't they?

'Yes! Yes! Yeeehhhsss . . .'

That was him; she'd given one final, ear-splitting shriek and then gone limp, with just a huge grin on her gelsuited face (she'd kept it on, another aperture had obligingly opened). Time to bring this bout to a climax . . .

The yacht had served him before; it heard what he said and took that as a signal to cut engines and go into free-fall. He loved technology.

The neural lace would have handled his orgasm sequence better, controlling the flow of secretions from his drug glands so that they more precisely matched and enhanced the extended human-basic physiological process taking place, but it was still pretty damn good all the same; his didn't last quite as long as hers obviously had, but he'd put it at over a minute, easily.

He floated, still joined to her, watching the smile on her face and the tiny, dim lights in the huge dark eyes. Her fabulous chest heaved now and again; her four arms waved round with a graceful, under-sea motion. After a while, one of her hands went to the nape of her neck. She took the gelsuit's head off and let it float free.

The deep dark eyes stayed; the rest of her face was brown flushed with red, and quite beautiful. He smiled at her. She smiled back.

With the gelsuit's head removed, a little sweat beaded on her forehead and top lip. He gently fanned her face with his wings, bringing them sweeping softly from behind his shoulders and then back. The huge eyes regarded him for a while, then she put her head back, stretching and sighing. A couple of pink cushions floated past, bumping into her floating arms and ricocheting slowly away.

The yacht's hire-limit warning chimed; it wasn't allowed to stray too far from Tier. He'd already told it to cruise back in when it hit the limit; it duly fired its engines and they were pressed back into the slickly warm surfaces of the couches and cushions in a delicious tangle of limbs for a while. The girl wriggled with a succulent slowness, eyes quite dark now.

He looked over to one side and saw the little camera drone she'd brought, sitting on the ledge under one of the diamond view ports, its one beady eye still fastened on the two of them. He winked at it.

Something moved outside, in the darkness, amongst the slow wheeling turn of stars. He watched it for a while. The yacht murmured, engine firing quietly; some apparent gravity stuck him and the girl to the ceiling for a second or two, then weightlessness returned. The girl made a couple of small noises that might have indicated she was asleep, and seemed to relax inside, letting go of him. He pulled her closer with his arms while his wings beat once, twice, bringing them both closer to the view port.

Outside, close, by, a ship was passing by, heading inbound on its final approach for Tier. They must have been almost directly in its path; the yacht's engine-burn had been avoidance action. Leffid looked down at the sleeping girl, wondering if he ought to wake her so that she could watch; there was something magical about seeing this great craft going sliding silently by, its dark, spectacularly embellished hull slicing space just a hundred metres away.

He had an idea, and grinned to himself and stretched out his hand to take the little camera drone – currently getting a fine view of the lass's backside and his balls – and turn it round, point it out the view port at the passing ship, so that she would have a surprise when she watched her recording, but then something else caught his attention, and his hand never did touch the camera drone.

Instead he stared out of the port, his eyes fastened on a section of the vessel's hull.

The ship passed on by. He kept staring out into space.

The girl sighed and moved; two of her arms went out and drew his face towards hers; she squeezed him from inside.

'Wooooo,' she breathed, and kissed him. Their first real kiss, without the gelsuit over her face. Eyes still enchanting, oceanically deep and enchanting . . .

Estray. Her name was Estray. Of course. Common enough name for an uncommonly attractive girl. Here for a month, eh? Leffid congratulated himself. This could end up being a *good* Festival.

They started caressing each other again.

It was just as good as the first time, but no better because he *still* wasn't able to give the proceedings his full attention; now, instead of trying to remember what the girl's name was, he couldn't stop wondering why there was an Elencher emergency message spattered minutely across the scar-hull of an Affronter light cruiser.

6
Pittance

I

Ulver Seich sobbed into her pillow. She had felt bad before; her mother had refused her something, some lad had – unbelievably – preferred somebody else to her (admittedly very rare), she had felt terribly alone, exposed and vulnerable the first time she had camped out under the stars on a planet, and various pets had died . . . but nothing as terrible as this.

She raised her tear-marked face up from the sodden pillow and looked again at her reflection in the reverser field on the walk-in across the horribly small cabin. She saw her face again and howled with anguish, burying her head in the pillow once again and bashing her feet up and down on the under-cover, which wobbled like a jelly in the AG field, trying to compensate.

Her face had been altered. While she'd slept, during the night, one day out from Phage. Her face, her beautiful, heart-shaped, heart-winning, heart-melting, heart-breaking face, the face which she had sat and gazed at in a mirror or a reverser field for hours at a time on occasion when she'd been old enough for her drug glands to come on line and young enough to experiment with them, the face she had gazed at and gazed at not because she was stoned but because she was just so damned *lovely* . . . her face had been made to look like somebody else's. And there was worse.

It might be hurting a little now if she wasn't keeping the pain turned off, but that wasn't what mattered; what mattered was that her face was: a) puffy, swollen and discoloured after the nanotechs had done their work, b) not her own any longer, and, c) older! The woman she was supposed to look like was older than she! Much older! Sixty years older!

People claimed that nobody in the Culture really changed much in appearance between about twenty-five and two hundred and fifty (then there was a slow but sure ageing to the three-fifty, four hundred mark, by which time your hair would be white (or gone!) your skin would be wrinkled like some basic's scrotum and your tits swinging round your belly-button – ugh!) but she had *always* been able to tell how old people were; she was rarely more than five or ten years out – never more than twenty, at any rate – and she could *see* how old she was now, even beneath the puffiness and shadowy bruising; she was seeing how she would look when she was older, and it didn't matter that it wasn't her own face, it didn't matter that she would probably look much better than this by the time she was in her mid-eighties (she had pictures of 99.9 per cent certain projections prepared for her by the house AI which showed *exactly* how she'd look at every decade for two centuries ahead, and they looked great); what mattered was that she looked old and dowdy and that would make her feel old and dowdy and therefore that would make her behave old and dowdy, and that feeling and that way of behaving and therefore that look might not go away when she was returned to her normal, her natural, her *own* appearance.

This wasn't turning out as she'd hoped at all; no friends, no pets, no fun, and the more she thought about it, the riskier it all might be, the less certain she was what she was getting into. This whole thing was supposed to be an adventure, but this part on the ship was just boring and so would the return journey be as well, and in the middle lay who-knew-what? Everybody knew how devious SC was; what were they really up to, what did they really want her to do? Even if it did turn out to be somehow exciting and even fun, she wouldn't be allowed to tell anybody about it, and where was the point in fun if you couldn't talk about it later?

Of course, she could tell other people, but then she wouldn't be able to stay in Contact. Hell, Churt was being ambiguous about whether she was in it *now* or not. Well was she or wasn't she? Was this a real Contact and even SC mission she was engaged in – as she'd dreamed of, fantasised about since early childhood – or some extracurricular wheeze, even a test of some sort?

She bit the pillow, and the particular texture of the fabric in her mouth and between her teeth, and the sensation of her face being puffed-up while her eyes stung with tears, took her back to childhood again.

She raised her head, licking her top lip clear of the salty fluid, and then snorted and sniffed back both the tears and the snot that was filling her nose. She thought about glanding some *calm*, but decided not to. She did some deep breathing, then swivelled round on the bed and sat up and looked at herself in the reverser, raising her chin at the hideous image it showed and sniffing again and wiping her face with her hands and swallowing hard and fluffing out her hair (at least it could stay as it was), sniffing again, and stared herself in the eyes and forbade herself to cry or look away.

After a few minutes, her cheeks had dried and her eyes were coming clear again, losing their red puffiness. She was still abhorrently ugly and even disfigured by her own high standards, but she was not a child and she *was* still the same person inside. Ah well. She supposed a little suffering might do her some good.

She had always been pampered; all her hardships had been self-inflicted and recreational in the past. She had gone hungry and unwashed when hiking somewhere primitive, but there had always been food at the end of the day, and a shower or at the very least a peelspray to remove the grime and sweat.

Even the pain of what had felt on occasion like an irretrievably broken heart had consistently proved less lasting than she'd initially imagined and expected; the revelation that a boy's taste was so grotesquely deficient he could prefer somebody else to her always reduced both the intensity and the duration of the anguish her heart demanded be endured to mark such a loss of regard.

She had always known there were too few real challenges in her life, too few genuine risks; it had all been too easy, even by Culture standards. While her life-style and material circumstances in Phage had been no different from that of any other person her age, it was true that just because the Culture was so determinedly egalitarian, what little hierarchic instinct remained in the population of the Rock manifested itself in the ascription of a certain cachet to belonging to one of the Founder Families.

In a society in which it was possible to look however one wanted to look, acquire any talent one wished to acquire and have access to as much property as one might desire, it was generally accepted that the only attributes which possessed that particular quality of interest which derives solely from their being difficult to attain were entry into Contact and Special Circumstances, or having some familial link with the Culture's early days.

Even the most famous and gifted of artists – whether their talents were congenital or acquired – were not regarded in quite the same hallowed light as Contact members (and, somewhere really old, like Phage, direct descendants of Founders). Being a famous artist in the Culture meant at best it was accepted you must possess a certain gritty determination; at worst it was generally seen as pointing to a pitiably archaic form of insecurity and a rather childish desire to show off.

When there were almost no distinctions to be drawn between people's social standing, the tiny differences that did exist became all the more important, to those who cared.

Ulver's feelings about her family's ancient name were mostly negative. Admittedly, possessing an old name meant some people were prepared to make an advance on any respect they might come to feel was rightly your due, but on the other hand Ulver wanted to be admired, worshipped and lusted after for herself, just her, just this current collection of cells, right here, with no reference to the inheritance those cells carried.

And what was the point of having what was sometimes insultingly referred to as an advantage in life if it couldn't even smooth your way into Contact? If anything, it had been hinted, it was a *dis*advantage; she would have to do *better* than the average person, she would have to be so completely, utterly, demonstrably perfect for the Contact Section that there could be no question of anybody ever thinking she'd got in because the people and machines on the admissions board knew the name Seich from their history lessons.

Well, Churt had been right; this was her big chance. She had been and would be unamendedly beautiful, she was intelligent, charming and attractive and she had common sense by the bucket-load, but she couldn't expect to breeze this the way she had breezed everything else in her life so far; she'd work at it, she'd study, she'd be diligent, assiduous and industrious and all the other things she'd worked so hard at not being while ensuring that her university results had sparkled as brilliantly as her social life.

Maybe she had been a spoiled brat; maybe she still was a spoiled brat, but she was a ruthlessly determined spoiled brat, and if that ruthless determination dictated ditching spoiled brathood, then out it would go, faster than you could say 'Bye.

Ulver dried her eyes, collected herself – still without the help of any glandular secretions – then got up and left the cabin. She would sit in the lounge where there was more space, and there she would find out all she could about Tier, this man Genar-Hofoen, and anything else that might be relevant to what they wanted her to do.

II

Leffid Ispanteli eased himself into the seat beside the vice-consul for the AhForgetIt Tendency, carefully hooking his wings over the seat back and smiling at the vice-consul, who regarded him with that particular kind of vacant look people tend to assume when they're communicating by neural lace.

Leffid held up his hand. 'Words, I'm afraid, Lellius,' he said. 'Had my lace removed for the Festival.'

'Very primitive,' vice-consul Lellius said approvingly, nodding gravely and returning his attention to the race.

They were sitting in a carousel suspended beneath a vast carbon-tubed structure sculpted in the image of a web tree; the thousands of viewing carousels dangled like fruit from the canopy and were multifariously connected by a secondary web of delicate, swaying cable bridges. The view beneath and to either side was of a series of great steps of stone dotted with vegetation and moving figures; it was very like looking at an ancient amphitheatre which had been lifted from the horizontal to the vertical and each of whose seat levels was able to rotate independently. The moving figures were ysner-mistretl combinations; the ysners were the huge two-legged flightless (and almost brainless) birds doing the running while their thinking was done by the mistretl jockey each carried on its back. Mistretls were tiny and almost helpless but brainy simians and the combination of one of them per ysner was a naturally occurring one from a planet in the Lower Leaf Spiral.

Ysner-mistretl races had been a part of life on Tier for millennia, and running them on a giant mandala two kilometres across composed of steps or levels all rotating at different speeds had been traditional for most of that time. The huge slowly turning race-course looked a little like Tier itself, which took its name from its shape.

Tier was a stepped habitat; its nine levels all revolved at the same speed, but that meant that the outer tiers possessed greater apparent gravity than those nearer the centre. The levels themselves were sectioned into compartments up to hundreds of kilometres long and filled with atmospheres of different types and held at different temperatures, while a stunningly complicated and dazzlingly beautiful array of mirrors and mirrorfields situated within the staggered cone of the world's axis provided amounts of sunlight precisely timed, attenuated and where necessary altered in wavelength to mimic the conditions on a hundred different worlds for a hundred different intelligent species.

This environmental diversity and the civilisational co-dependence it implied and intermingling it encouraged had been Tier's *raison d'être*, the very foundation of its purpose and fame for the seven thousand years it had existed. Its original builders were, perhaps, unknown; they were believed to have Sublimed shortly after building it, leaving behind a species – or model, depending how you defined these things – of biomechanical sintricate which ran and maintained the place, were individually dull but collectively highly intelligent, took the shape of a small sphere covered with long articulated spines, were between half a metre and two metres in size and had seemed to have an intense suspicion of anything possessing less of a biological basis than they did themselves. Drones and other AIs were tolerated on Tier but very closely watched, followed everywhere and their every communication and even thought monitored. Minds were immune to this sort of treatment of course, but their avatars tended to attract a degree of intense physical observation which bordered on harassment, and so they rarely bothered entering the world itself, sticking to the outer docks where they were made perfectly welcome and afforded every hospitality. Tier, after all, was a statement, a treasure, a symbol, and as such any small discriminatory foibles it chose to display were considered perfectly tolerable.

The ysner-mistretl race track was one level up from the tier where the Homomdan mission was housed and three levels down from Leffid's home circumference.

'Leffid,' the vice consul said. He was a rotund, massy male of apparently indeterminate species, vaguely human in shape but with a triangular head and an eye at each corner. His skin was bright red; the flowing robes he wore were a vivid but gradually shifting shade of blue. He turned his head slightly so that two of his eyes regarded Leffid while the third continued to watch the race. 'Did I see you at the Homomdan do last night? I can't remember.'

'Briefly,' Leffid said. 'I waved Hello but you were busy with the Ashpartzi delegate.'

Vice-consul Lellius wheezed with laughter. 'Trying to hold the blighter down. It was having buoyancy problems inside its new suit; automatics weren't really up to the job with the AI removed. Terrible thing when one of these gas-giant floater beasties suffers from flatulence, you know.'

Leffid recalled that Lellius had rather looked as though he'd been wrestling with the bow-rope for what appeared to be a small airship at the Homomdan ambassador's party. 'Not as terrible as it must be for the inhabitant of the suit, I'd guess.'

'Ha, indeed,' Lellius chuckled, nodding and wheezing. 'May I order you some refreshment?'

'No, thank you.'

'Good; I have given up emoter-keyed foods and drinks for the duration of the Festival and would only be jealous.' He shook his head. 'I thought primitives were supposed to have more fun, but everything I could think of changing the better to partake in the Festival's spirit seemed to make life less fun,' he said, then made a tutting noise at something on the race course.

Leffid looked to see one of the ysner-mistretl pairs failing to make a jump, hitting the ramp just behind and falling down to another level. They picked themselves up and ran on, but they'd need to be very lucky to win now. Lellius shook his head and used the flat end of a stylo to smooth a number off the wood-bordered wax tablet he held in his broad red hand.

'You winning?' Leffid asked him.

Lellius shook his head and looked sad.

Leffid smiled, then made a show of inspecting the race track and the contending ysner-mistretl pairs. 'They don't look very festive to me,' he said. 'I expected something more . . . well, festive,' he concluded, lamely.

'I believe the race authorities regard the Festival with the same misanthropic dubiety as I,' Lellius said. 'The festival is – what? – two days old?'

Leffid nodded.

'And already I am tired of it,' Lellius said, scratching behind one of his three ears with the wax tablet stylo. 'I thought of taking a holiday while it was occurring, but I am expected to be here, of course. A month of challenging, ground-breaking art and ruthlessly enforced fun.' Lellius shook his head heavily. 'What a prospect.'

Leffid put his chin in his cupped hand. 'You've never really been a natural for the AhForgetIt Tendency, have you, Lellius?'

'I joined hoping it would make me more . . .' Lellius looked up contemplatively at the broad spread of the tree sculpture hanging above them. '. . . cavort-prone,' he said, and nodded. 'I wished to be more prone to cavorting and so I joined the Tendency hoping that the natural hedonism of people like your good self would somehow infect my own more deliberate, phlegmatic soul.' He sighed. 'I still live in hope.'

Leffid laughed lightly, then looked slowly around. 'You here alone, Lellius?'

Lellius looked thoughtful. 'My incomparably efficient Clerical Assistant Number Three visits the latrines, I believe,' he wheezed. 'My wastrel son is probably trying to invent new ways of embarrassing me, my mate is half a galaxy away – very nearly enough – and my current darling stays at home, indisposed. Or rather, disposed not to come to what she terms a boring bird-and-monkey race.' He nodded slowly. 'I could reasonably be said to be alone, I suppose. Why do you ask?'

Leffid sat a little closer, arms on the carousel's small table. 'Saw something strange last night,' he said.

'That young thing with the four arms?' Lellius asked, at least one eye twinkling. 'I did wonder if any other of her anatomical features were also doubled-up.'

'Your prurience flatters me,' Leffid said. 'Ask her nicely and she will probably furnish you with a copy of a recording which proves both our relevant bits were quite singular.'

Lellius chuckled and drank from a strawed flask. 'Not that, then. What?'

'*Are* we alone?' Leffid asked quietly.

Lellius stared blankly at him for a moment. 'Yes; my lace is now turned off. There is nothing else I know of watching or listening. What is this thing you saw?'

'I'll show you.' Leffid took a napkin from the table's slot and from a pocket in his shirt extracted the terminal he was using instead of the neural lace. He looked at the markings on the instrument as though trying to remember something, then shrugged and said, 'Umm, terminal; become a pen, please.'

Leffid wrote on the napkin, producing a sequence of seven pendant rhombi each composed of eight dots or tiny circles. When he'd finished he turned the napkin towards Lellius, who looked carefully down at it and then equally deliberately up at Leffid.

'Very pretty,' he wheezed. 'What is it?'

Leffid smiled. He tapped the rightmost symbol. 'First, it's an Elench signal because it's base eight and arranged in that pattern. This first symbol is an emergency distress mark. The other six are probably – almost certainly, by convention – a location.'

'Really?' Lellius did not sound especially impressed. 'And the location of this location?'

'About seventy-three years into the Upper Swirl from here.'

'Oh,' Lellius said with a sort of rumbling noise that probably meant he was surprised. 'Just six digits to define such a precise point?'

'Base two-five-six; easy,' Leffid said, shrugging his wings. 'But what's interesting is where I *saw* this signal.'

'Mm-hmm?' Lellius said, momentarily distracted by something happening on the race track. He took another drink then returned his attention to the other man.

'It was on an Affronter light cruiser,' Leffid said quietly. 'Burned into its scar-hull. Very lightly, very shallowly; at an angle across the blades—'

'Blades?' Lellius asked.

Leffid waved one hand. 'Decoration. But it was there. If I hadn't been very close to the ship – in a yacht – as it was approaching Tier I'd never have seen it. And the intriguing possibility exists, of course, that the ship doesn't know it bears this message.'

Lellius stared at the napkin for a moment. He sat back. 'Hmm,' he said. 'Mind if I turn on my lace?'

'Not at all,' Leffid said. 'I already know the ship's called the *Furious Purpose* and it's back here unscheduled, in Dock 807b. If it's a mechanical problem it's got, I can't imagine it's anything to do directly with the scarring. As for the location in the signal; it's about half way between the stars Cromphalet I/II and Esperi . . . slightly closer to Esperi. And there's nothing there. Nothing that anybody knows about, anyway.'

Leffid tapped at the pocket terminal and after some experimentation got the beam to brighten until it ignited the napkin he'd written on. He let it burn and was about to sweep the ashes into the table's disposal slot when Lellius – who was slumped back in the seat, looking blank – reached out one red hand and absently ground the ashes under his palm before scattering them to the breeze; they fell floating away from the carousel in an insubstantial cloud, towards the seats and private boxes stacked below.

'Some minor running-gear problem,' Lellius said. 'The Affronter ship.' He was silent a moment longer. 'The Elench may have had a problem,' he said, nodding slowly. 'A clan-fleet – eight ships – left here a hundred days ago to investigate the Swirl.'

'I remember,' Leffid said.

'There have been,' Lellius paused, '. . . indications – barely even rumours – that not all has been right with them.'

'Well,' Leffid said, placing his palms flat on the table and making to rise from his seat, 'it may be nothing, but I just thought I'd mention it.'

'Kind,' Lellius wheezed, nodding. 'Not sure what the Tendency can do with it; last ship we had coming here went Sabbatical on us, ungrateful cur, but we might be able to trade it to the Mainland.'

'Yes, the dear old Mainland,' Leffid said. It was the term the AhForgetIt Tendency usually employed to refer to the Culture proper. He smiled. 'Whatever.' He held his wings away from the seat-back as he stood.

'Sure you won't stay?' Lellius said, blinking. 'We could have a betting competition. Bet you'd win.'

'No thanks; this evening I'm playing host to a lady who needs two place settings at a time and I have to go polish my cutlery and make sure my flight feathers are fettled for ruffling.'

'Ah. Have armfuls of fun.'

'I suspect I shall.'

'Oh, damn,' Lellius said sadly, as a great shout went up from below and to most sides; the race was over.

Lellius leant over and scratched out another couple of numbers on the wax tablet.

'Never mind,' Leffid said, patting the vice-consul on his ample shoulder as he headed for the swaying cable bridge that would take him back to the main trunk of the huge artificial tree.

'Yes,' Lellius sighed, looking at the smudge of ash on his hand. 'I'm sure there'll be another race starting in a while.'

III

The black bird Gravious flew slowly across the re-creation of the great sea battle of Octovelein, its shadow falling over the wreckage-dotted water, the sails and decks of the long wooden ships, the soldiers who stood massed on the decks of the larger vessels, the sailors who hauled at ropes and sheets, the rocketeers who struggled to rig and fire their charges, and the bodies floating in the water.

A brilliant, blue-white sun glared from a violet sky. The air was crisscrossed by the smoky trails of the primitive rockets and the sky seemed supported by the great columns of smoke rising from stricken warships and transports. The water was dark blue, ruffled with waves, spattered with the tall feathery plumes of crashing rockets, creased white at the stem of each ship, and covered in flames where oils had been poured between ships in desperate attempts to prevent boarding.

The bird flew over the edge of the sea scene, where the water ended like a still, liquid cliff and the unadorned floor of the general bay resumed, just five metres below, its surface also covered with what looked like wreckage – as though the tide had somehow gone out in this part of the bay but not the other – but which on closer inspection proved to be objects – parts of ships, parts of people – which had been in the process of construction. The incomplete sea battle filled less than half of the bay's sixteen square kilometres. This would have been the *Sleeper Service*'s master-work, its definitive statement. Now it might never be finished.

The black bird flew on, passing a few of the ship's drones on the surface of the bay, gathering the construction debris and loading it onto an insubstantial conveyor belt which appeared to consist of a thin line of shady air. It kept beating. Its goal lay on the far end of the doubled general bay, between this internal section and the bay that opened to the rear of the ship. Damn the woman for choosing to stay at the bows, nearest to where the tower had been. Bad luck the place it had to be was so close to the stern.

It had already flown through twenty-five kilometres of interior space, down the gigantic, dark internal corridor in the centre of the ship, between closed bay doors where a few dim lights glowed and utter silence reigned, a kilometre of air below its gently flapping wings, another above and one to each side.

The bird had looked about it, taking in the huge, gloomy volumes and supposing it ought to feel privileged; the ship had kept it out of these places for the last forty years, restricting it to the upper kilometre of its hull which housed the old accommodation areas and the majority of its Storees. Gravious had senses beyond those normally available to an ordinary animal, and it had employed a couple of them in an attempt to probe the bay doors and find out what lay behind them, if anything. As far as it could tell, the thousands of bays were empty.

That had only taken it as far as the general bay engineering space, the biggest single volume in the ship with the divisions down; nine thousand metres deep, nearly twice that across and filled with noise and flickering lights and blurringly fast motion as the ship created thousands of new machines to do . . . who-knew-what.

Most of the engineering space wasn't even filled with air; the material, components and machines could move faster that way. Gravious was flying down a transparent traveltube set into the ceiling. Nine kilometres of that took it to a wall which led into the relative serenity – or at least, stillness – of the sea battle tableau. It was half way across that now; just another four thousand metres to go. Its wing muscles ached.

It landed on the parapet of a balcony which looked out into the rear of this set of general bays. Beyond were thirty-two cubic kilometres of empty air; a perfectly empty general bay, the sort of place where a normal GSV of this size would be building a smaller GSV, playing host to one which was visiting, housing an alien environment like a gigantic guests' room, turning over to some sports venue, or sub-dividing into smaller storage or manufacturing spaces.

Gravious looked back at the modest tableau on the balcony, which in its previous existence, before the GSV had decided to go Eccentric, had been part of a café with a fine view of the bay. Here were posed seven humans, all with their backs to the view of the empty bay and facing the hologram of a calm, empty swimming pool. The humans wore trunks; they sat in deck chairs around a couple of low tables full of drinks and snacks. They had been caught in the acts of laughing, talking, blinking, scratching their chin, drinking.

Some famous painting, apparently. It didn't look very artistic to Gravious. It supposed you had to see it from the right angle.

It lifted one leg up from the parapet, and slipped, falling into the air of the general bay. It hit something between it and the bay and fell, bouncing off the bay's rear wall, then off the invisible wall, then found its bearings, flapped close and parallel to the wall, twisted in the air when it got back to the level of the balcony, and returned to it.

Uh-huh, it thought. It risked using again the senses it was not supposed to have. Solidity in the bay. What it had hit was not glass, and not a field between it and the empty bay; the bay was not empty, and what it had hit was the field-edge of a projection. On the far side, for at least two kilometres, there was solid matter. Dense, solid matter. Partially exotic dense solid matter.

Well, there you were. The bird shook itself and preened a little, combing its feathers smooth with its beak. Then it looked around and half hopped, half flew over to one of the posed figures. It inspected each one briefly, staring into an eye here, seemingly looking for a juicy parasite in an ear here, peering at a stray hair here and carefully studying a nostril here.

It often did this, studying the next ones to go, the ones who would next be revived and taken away. As though there was something to be learned from their carefully artificial postures.

It pecked, in a desultory, barely interested sort of way at a stray hair in one man's armpit, then hopped away, studying the group from a variety of nearby tables and angles, trying to find the correct perspective from which to view the scene. Soon to be gone, of course. In fact, they were all going. This lot with the rest, but this lot to re-awakening whereas most of them would just be Stored somewhere else. But this lot, when they were woken in a few hours, would be coming back to life, somewhere. Funny to think of it.

Finally, the bird shook its head, stretched its wings, and hopped through the hologram and into the deserted café beyond, ready to begin the first leg of its journey back to its mistress.

*   *   *

A few moments later, the avatar Amorphia stepped out of another part of the hologram, turned once to glance back at where the bird had hopped through the projection, then went and squatted before the figure of the man at whose armpit Gravious had pecked.

IV

[tight beam, M32, tra. @n4.28.864.0001]
xEccentric *Shoot Them Later*
    oGSV *Anticipation Of A New Lover's Arrival, The*
It was me.
∞

[tight beam, M32, tra. @n4.28.864.1971]
    xGSV *Anticipation Of A New Lover's Arrival, The*
        oEccentric *Shoot Them Later*
    What was you?
∞

I was the go-between for the information transmitted from the AhForgetIt Tendency to SC. One of our people on Tier saw the Affront light cruiser *Furious Purpose* as it arrived back there; it had a location in Elench code burned onto its scar-hull. The information was transmitted from the Tendency mission on Tier to me; I passed it on to the *Different Tan* and the *Steely Glint*, my usual contacts in the Group/Gang. I would guess the signal was then relayed to the GSV *Ethics Gradient*, home ship of the GCU *Fate Amenable To Change*, which subsequently discovered the Excession.
So in a sense, this is all my fault. I apologise.
I had hoped this confession would never be necessary, but having turned this over in my mind I have concluded that – as was the case concerning the passing-on of the original information regarding the scar-hull signal in the first place – I had no choice. Had you guessed? Had you started to? Do you still trust me?
∞

    It had occurred to me, but I had no access to Tendency transmission records and was unwilling to ask the other Gang

members directly. I trust you no less for what you say. Why are you telling me now?

∞

I would like to retain that trust. Have you discovered anything else?

∞

   Yes. I think there is a link to a man called Genar-Hofoen, a Contact representative with the Affront on a habitat called God'shole, in the Fernblade. He left there the day after the Excession was discovered; SC has hired three Affronter battle cruisers to take him to Tier. They are due there in fourteen days. His biography: (files attached). You see the connection? That ship again.

∞

You think it involved beyond what we believe we have agreed to already?

∞

   Yes. And the *Grey Area.*

∞

The times look a little unlikely; if it really pushed itself the *GA* can reach Tier in, what? . . . three days or so after this human gets there? But that still leaves our other concern two months or more out of touch.

∞

   I know. Still, I think there is something going on. I am following up all the avenues of investigation I can. I'm making further inquiries through the more likely contacts mentioned in his file, but it's all going terribly slowly. Thank you for your candour. I shall remain in touch.

∞

You're welcome. Do keep me informed.

[stuttered tight point, M32, tra. @n4.28.865.2203]
xEccentric *Shoot Them Later*
   oLSV *Serious Callers Only*
Got fed up waiting; I called it (signal file attached).

∞

[stuttered tight point, M32, tra. @n4.28.865.2690]
   xLSV *Serious Callers Only*
      oEccentric *Shoot Them Later*

And now it 'trusts you no less'. Ha!

∞

I remain convinced it was the right thing to do.

∞

Whatever; it is done. What of the ship you asked to head for Pittance?

∞

On its way.

∞

And why Pittance?

∞

Is it not obvious? Perhaps not. Mayhap the paranoia of *The Anticipation Of A New Lover's Arrival* is contagious . . . However that may be, let me make my argument: Pittance houses a veritable cornucopia of weaponry; indeed, the weapons deployed there just to protect the main cache of munitions – that is, the ships – alone represents a vast stockpile of potential destruction. Certainly the store's course takes it nowhere near the Excession, but it *has* taken it into the general volume within which the Affront have some interest. Now, while it has almost certainly gone unnoticed and even if it is spotted and tracked it can be of no interest to the Affront (and, of course, it is anyway well able to defend itself), and it is not part of the subtle mobilisation being organised by the *Steely Glint*, it nevertheless represents the greatest concentration of matériel in the vicinity.

I start to wonder; when, roughly, did the Culture start to have doubts – serious doubts – about the Affront? And when was Pittance chosen as one of the ship stores? Around the same time. Indeed, Pittance was chosen, fitted out and stocked entirely within the time-scale of the debate which took place at the end of the Idiran War regarding military intervention against the Affront. There are billions of bodies like Pittance; the galaxy is littered with such pieces of wreckage wandering between the stars. Yet Pittance was chosen as one of only eleven such stores; a rock whose slow progress would take it into Affronter space within five or six centuries – depending on how fast the Affront expanded their sphere of influence – and which might well remain within that sphere for the foreseeable future, given that Affronter influence could easily push its borders out at a greater rate than that of a slowly tumbling rock moving at much less than a per cent of light speed. How fortuitous to have such a wealth of weaponry embedded in Affront space!

Might not this all, in fact, be a set-up?

Think about this; is this not just the sort of thing *you* would be proud to have thought up? Such foresight, such patience, such attention to the long game, such plausible protestations of innocence should the coincidence be remarked upon or revealed! I know *I'd* be pleased with myself had I been part of such a plan.

Lastly, on the committee of Minds which oversaw the choice of these stores, the names *Woetra*, *Different Tan* and *Not Invented Here* all sound rather familiar, think ye not?

Taken all together, and even recognising that this is almost certainly a blind alley, I thought it irresponsible not to have a sharp eye attached to a sympathetic mind in the vicinity of that precious little rock.

∞

All right. Point taken.

∞

And what of whatever you were working on?

∞

My original idea was to attempt to find someone acceptable on Tier who might be persuaded to our purpose; however, this proved impractical; there is considerable Contact and SC presence on the habitat but nobody I think we could risk sharing our apprehensions with. Instead, I have the tentative agreement of an old ally to support our cause should the occasion arise. It is a month or more from Tier, and the Excession lies beyond there on its orientation, but it has access to a number of warships. The tricky part is that some of them may be called up in the mobilisation, but a few may be put at our disposal. Not *as warships*, I hasten to add, certainly not against other Culture ships, but as counters, as it were, or delivery systems, if and when we find a vulnerable point in the conspiracy we believe might exist.

This Genar-Hofoen person; I may make my own inquiries in that direction, if I can avoid stepping on the metaphorical toes of our co-concernee.

The Affront angle is the one that worries me. So aggressive! Such drive! For all our oft-repeated horror at their effects on others, there exists, I think, a kind of grudging admiration in many Culture folk for the Affront's energy, not to mention their apparent freedom from the effects of moral conscience. Such an easy threat to see, and yet so difficult a problem to deal with. I dread to think what awful plan might be hatched with a thoroughly clear conscience by perfectly estimable Minds to deal with such a perceived menace.

Equally, given the qualitative scale of the opportunity which may be presented by the Excession, the Affront are just the sort of species – and at precisely the most likely stage in their development – to attempt some sort of mad undertaking which, however likely to fail, if it did succeed might offer rewards justifying the risk. And who is to say they would be wrong in making such a judgement?

∞

Look, the damned Excession hasn't *done* anything yet. All this nuisance has been caused by everybody's reaction to it. Serve us all right if it turned out it is a projection of some sort, some God's jest. I'm growing impatient, I don't mind telling you. The *Fate Amenable To Change* stands off, watching the Excession doing nothing and reporting on it every now and again, various low-level Involveds are puffing themselves up and girding their scrawny loins with a view to taking a sight-seeing trip to the latest show in town and in the vague hope that if there is some sort of action they'll be able to pick up some of it, and all that the rest of us are doing is sitting around waiting for the big guns to arrive. I wish something would *happen*!

V

'Good travelling with you, Genar-Hofoen,' Fivetide boomed. They slapped limbs; the man had already braced one leg and the gelfield suit absorbed the actual impact, so he didn't fall over. They were in the Entity Control area of the Level Eight docks, Affronter section, surrounded by Affronters, their slaved drones and other machines, a few members of other species who could tolerate the same conditions as the Affront, as well as numerous Tier sintricates – floating around like little dark balls of spines – all coming and going, leaving or joining travelators, spin cars, lifts and inter-section transport carriages.

'Not staying for some rest and recreation?' Genar-Hofoen asked the Affronter. Tier boasted a notoriously excellent Affront hunting reserve section.

'Ha! On the way back, perhaps,' Fivetide said. 'Duty calls elsewhere in the meantime.' He chuckled.

Genar-Hofoen got the impression he was missing a joke here. He wondered about this, then shrugged and laughed. 'Well, I'll see you back on God'shole, no doubt.'

'Indeed!' Fivetide said. 'Enjoy yourself, human!' The Affronter turned on his tentacle tips and swept away, back to the battle-cruiser *Kiss The Blade*. Genar-Hofoen watched him go, and watched the lock doors close on the transit tunnel, with a frown on his face.

~ What's worrying you? asked the suit.

The man shook his head. ~ Ah, nothing, he said. He stooped and picked up his hold-all.

'Human male Byr Genar-Hofoen plus gelfield suit?' said a sintricate, floating up to him. It looked, Genar-Hofoen thought, like an explosion in a sphere of black ink, frozen an instant after it began.

He bowed briefly. 'Correct.'

'I am to escort you to the Entity Control, human section. Please follow me.'

'Certainly.'

They found a spin car, little more than a platform dotted with seats, stanchions and webbing. Genar-Hofoen hopped on, followed by the sintricate, and the car accelerated smoothly into a transparent tunnel which ran out along the underside of the habitat's outer skin. They were heading spinward, so that as the car gained speed they seemed to lose weight. A field shimmered over the car, seeming to mould itself to the curved roof of the tunnel. Gases hissed. They went underneath the huge hanging bulk of one of the other Affronter ships, all blades and darkness. He watched as it detached itself from the habitat, falling massively, silently away into space and the circling stars. Another ship, then another and another dropped away after it. They disappeared.

~ What was the fourth ship? the man asked.

~ The Comet class light cruiser *Furious Purpose*, the suit said.

~ Hmm. Wonder where they're off to.

The suit didn't reply.

It was getting misty in the car. Genar Hofoen listened to gases hiss around him. The temperature was rising, the atmosphere in the field-shrouded car changing from an Affronter atmosphere to a human atmosphere. The car zoomed upwards for lower, less gravity intense levels, and Genar-Hofoen, used to Affronter gravity for these last two years, felt as though he was floating.

~ How long before we rendezvous with the *Meatfucker*? he asked.

~ Three days, the suit told him.

~ Of course, they won't let you into the world proper, will they? the man said, as though realising this for the first time.

~ No, said the suit.

~ What'll you do while I'm off having fun?

~ The same; I've already inquired ahead and come to an arrangement with a visiting Contact ship GP drone. So I shall be in Thrall.

It was Genar-Hofoen's turn not to say anything. He found the whole idea of drone sex – even if it was entirely of the mind, with no physical component whatsoever – quite entirely bizarre. Ah well, each to his own, he thought.

'Mr Genar-Hofoen?' said a stunningly, heart-stoppingly beautiful woman in the post-Entity Reception Area, Human. She was tall, perfectly proportioned, her hair was long and red and extravagantly curled and her eyes were a luminous green just the right side of natural. Her loose, plain tabard exposed smoothly muscled, glossily tanned skin. 'Welcome to Tier; my name's Verlioef Schung.' She held out a hand and shook his, firmly.

Skin on skin; no suit, at last. It was a good feeling. He was dressed in a semi-formal outfit of loose pantaloons and long shirt, and enjoying the lushly sensual sensation of the glidingly smooth materials on his body.

'Contact sent me to look after you,' Verlioef Schung said with a hint of ruefulness. 'I'm sure you don't need it, but I'm here if you do. I, ah . . . I hope you don't mind.' Her voice . . . her voice was something to immerse yourself in.

He smiled broadly and bowed. 'How could I?' he said.

She laughed, putting one hand over her mouth – and, of course, her perfect teeth – as she did so. 'You're very kind.' She held out a hand. 'May I take your bag?'

'No, that's all right.'

She raised her shoulders and let them drop. 'Well,' she said, 'you've missed the Festival, of course, but there's a whole gang of us who did, too, and we've sort of decided to have our own over the next few days and, well, frankly we need all the help we can get. All I can promise you is luxurious accommodation, great company and more delectable preparations than you can shake a principle at, but if you care to make the sacrifice, I promise we'll all try to make it up to you.' She flexed her eyebrows and then made a mock-frightened expression, pulling down the corners of her succulently perfect mouth.

He let her hold the look for a moment, then patted her on the upper arm. 'No, thank you,' he said sincerely.

Her expression became one of hurt sadness. 'Oh . . . are you sure?' she said in a small, softly vulnerable voice.

''Fraid so. Made my own arrangements,' he said, with genuine but determined regret. 'But if there was anyone who was likely to tempt me away from them, it would be you.' He winked at her. 'I'm flattered by your generous offer, and do tell SC I appreciate the trouble they've gone to, but this is my chance to cut loose for a few days, you know?' He laughed. 'Don't worry; I'll have some fun and then I'll be ready to ship on out when the time comes.' He fished a small pen terminal out of one pocket and waved it in front of her face. 'And I'll keep my terminal with me at all times. Promise.' He put the terminal back in his pocket.

She gazed intently into his eyes for a few moments, then lowered her eyes and then her head and gave a small shrug. She looked back up, expression ironic. When she spoke, her voice had changed as well, modulating into something deeper and more considered, almost regretful. 'Well,' she sighed, 'I hope you enjoy yourself, Byr.' She grinned. 'Our offer stands, if you wish to reconsider.' Brave smile. 'My colleagues and I wish you well.' She looked furtively round the busy concourse and bit her bottom lip, frowning slightly. 'Don't suppose you fancy a drink or something anyway, do you?' she said, almost plaintively.

He laughed, shook his head, and bowed as he backed off, hoisting his hold-all over his shoulder.

*   *   *

Genar-Hofoen had arrived a few days after the end of Tier's annual Festival. There was an air of autumnal desuetude mixed with high-summer torpor about the place when he arrived; people were cleaning up, calming down, getting back to normal and generally behaving themselves. He'd signalled ahead and succeeded in booking the services of an erotroupe as well as reserving a garden penthouse in the View, the best hotel on Level Three.

All in all, entirely worth passing up the rather too obvious advances of his perfect woman for (well, no it wasn't . . . except it was when your perfect woman was almost certainly a Special Circumstances agent altered to look like the creature of your fantasies and sent to look after you, keep you happy and safe, when what you actually wanted was a bit of variety, some excitement and some un-Culture-like danger; his perfect partner certainly *looked* like the very splendid Verlioef Schung, but she was even more positively not SC, not Contact, and probably not even Culture either. It was that desire for strangeness, for apartness, for alienness they probably couldn't understand).

He lay in bed, pleasantly exhausted, the odd muscle quivering now and again of its own accord, surrounded by sleeping pulchritude, his head buzzing with the after-effects of some serious glanding and watched the Tier news (Culture bias) channel on a screen hanging in the air in front of the nearest tree. An ear-pip relayed the sound.

Still leading with the Blitteringueh–Deluger saga. Then came a feature on the increase in Fleeting in Culture ships. Fleeting was when two or more ship Minds decided they were fed up being all by themselves and only being able to exchange the equivalent of letters; instead they got together, keeping physically close to each other so that they could converse. Operationally most inefficient. Some older Minds were worried it represented their more recently built comrades going soft and wanted the premise-states of Minds which would be constructed in the future to be altered to deal with this weak, overly chummy decadence.

Local news; there was a brief follow-up report basically saying that the mysterious explosion which had happened in dock 807b on the third day of the Festival was still a mystery; the Affronter cruiser *Furious Purpose* had been lightly damaged by a small, pure energy detonation which had done nothing more than locally burn off a layer of its scar-hull. An over-enthusiastic Festival prank was suspected.

Not quite so locally, the arguments were still going on about the creation of a new Hintersphere a few kiloyears anti-spinward. A Hintersphere was a volume of space in which FTL flights were banned except in the direst of emergencies, and life generally moved at a slower pace than elsewhere in the Culture. Genar-Hofoen shook his head at that one. Pretentious rusticism.

Nearer home again, back-up craft were only a day away from the location of the possible anomaly near Esperi. The discovering GCU was still reporting no change in the artifact. Despite requests from Contact section, various other Involved civilisations had sent or were sending ships to the general volume, but Tier itself had forgone dispatching a craft. To the surprise of most observers, the Affront had criticised the reaction of those who had decided to be nosy and had stayed severely away from the anomaly, though there were unconfirmed reports of increased Affront activity in the Upper Leaf Swirl, and just today four ships—

'Off,' Genar-Hofoen said quietly, and the screen duly vanished. One of the erotroupe stirred against him. He looked at her.

The girl's face was the very image of that belonging to Zreyn Tramow, one-time captain of the good ship *Problem Child*. Her body was different from the original, altered in the direction of Genar-Hofoen's tastes, but subtly. There were two like her and three who looked exactly like famous personalities – an actress, a musician and a lifestyler. Zreyn and Enhoff, Shpel, Py and Gidinley. They had all been perfectly charming as well as being quite plausible impersonators, but Genar-Hofoen thought you had to wonder at the mentality of people who actually chose to alter their appearance and behaviour every few days just to suit the tastes – usually though not always sexual – of others. But maybe he was just being a bit fuddy-duddyish. Perhaps they were slightly boring people otherwise, or perhaps they just liked a deal more variety in such matters than other people.

Whatever their motivations, all five had fallen politely asleep on the AG bed after the fun, which had been preceded by a meal and a party. The troupe's Exemplary Couple, Gakic and Leleeril were asleep too, lying in each other's arms on the carpet-like lawn between the bed platform and the stream which threaded its way from the tinkling waterfall and the pool. Detumesced, the man's prick was almost normal looking. Genar-Hofoen felt slightly sleepy himself, but he was determined to stay awake for the whole holiday; he brushed the sleepiness back under the edges of his mind with a glandular release of *gain*. Doing this for three days solid would leave him needing lots of sleep, but there would be a week on the *Grey Area/Meatfucker*; plenty of time to recover. The buzz of *gain* coursed through him, clearing his head and ridding his body of the effects of fatigue. Gradually a feeling of rested, ready peacefulness washed over and through him.

He clasped his hands behind his neck and gazed happily upwards past the fronds of a couple of overhanging trees at the blue, cloud-strewn sky. Just that movement, performed in the gravity of Tier's standard-G level, gave him a good, light, almost childishly enjoyable sensation. Affronter standard gravity was more than twice the Culture-promoted human norm, and he supposed it was a sign of how well and how easily his body had adapted to conditions on God'shole habitat that he had quickly and long since stopped noticing how much heavier he had felt from day to day.

A thought occurred to him. He closed his eyes briefly, going quickly into the semi-trance that the average Culture adult employed, when they needed to and could be bothered, to check on their physiological settings. He dug around inside various images of his body until he saw himself standing on a small sphere. The sphere was set at one standard gravity; his subconscious had registered the fact that he had been in a steady, reduced gravity field for longer than a few hours and had re-set itself. Left to its own devices, his body would now start to lose bone and muscle mass, thin the walls of his blood vessels and perform a hundred other tiny but consequential alterations the better to suit his frame, tissues and organs to that reduced severity of weight. Well, his subconscious was only doing its job, and it didn't know he would be back in Affronter gravity again in a month or so. He increased the size of the sphere his image stood upon until it was back to the two point one gravities his body would have to readjust itself to once he returned to God'shole. There, that should do it. He cast a quick look round his internal states while he was here, not that there ought to be anything amiss; warning signs made themselves obvious automatically. Sure enough, all was well; fatigue being dealt with, presence of *gain* noted, blood sugar returning to normal, hormones generally being gathered back to optimum levels.

He came out of the semi-trance, opened his eyes and looked over at where the pen terminal lay on a sculpted, smoothly varnished tree stump at the bedside. So far he had mostly used it to check up on the replies from his Contact contacts, confirming what they could concerning this – so far – pleasantly undemanding mission. The terminal was supposed to blink a little light if it had a message stored for him. He was still waiting to hear from the GSV *Not Invented Here*, the Incident Coordinator for the Excession. The terminal lay where he'd left it, dull. No new messages. Oh well.

He looked away and watched the clouds move in the sky for a while, then wondered what it looked like turned off.

'Sky, off,' he said, keeping his voice low.

The sky disappeared and the true ceiling of the penthouse suite was revealed; a slickly black surface studded with projectors, lights and miscellaneous bumps and indentations. The few gentle animal sounds faded away. In the View Hotel, every suite was a penthouse corner suite; there were four per floor, and the only floor which didn't have four penthouse suites was the very top one, which, so that nobody in the lower floors would feel they were missing out on the real thing when it was available, was restricted to housing some of the hotel's machinery and equipment. Genar-Hofoen's was called a jungle suite, though it was entirely the most manicured, pest-free and temperately, temperature-controlled and generally civilised jungle he had ever heard of.

'Night sky, on,' he said quietly. The slick black ceiling was replaced by blackness scattered with sharply bright stars. Some animal noises resumed, sounding different compared to those heard in the daylight. They were real animals, not recordings; every now and again a bird would fly across the clearing where the bed was situated, or a fish would splash in the bathing pool or a chattering simian would swing across the forest canopy or a huge, glittering insect would burr delicately through the air.

It was all terribly tasteful and immaculate, and Genar-Hofoen was already starting to look forward to the evening, when he intended to dress in his best clothes and hit the town, which in this case was Night City, located one level almost straight down, where, traditionally, anything on Tier that could breathe a nitrogen-oxygen atmosphere and tolerate one standard gravity

– and had any sort of taste for diversion and excitement – tended to congregate.

A night in Night City would be just the thing to complete this first mad rush of fun at the onset of his short holiday. Calling ahead and ordering up a fabulously expensive erotroupe to act out his every sexual fantasy was one thing – one extremely wonderful and deeply satisfying thing, beyond all doubt, he told himself with all due solemnity – but the idea of a chance meeting with somebody else, another free, independent soul with their own desires and demands, their own reservations and requirements; that, just because it was all up to chance and up to negotiation, just because it all might end in nothing, in rejection, in the failure to impress and connect, in being found wanting rather than being wanted, that was a more valuable thing, that was an enterprise well worthy of the risk of rebuff.

He glanded *charge*. That ought to do it.

Seconds later, filled to bursting with the love of action, movement and the blessed need to be *doing something*, he was bouncing out of bed, laughing to himself and apologising to the sleepily grumbling but still palatably comely cast of the erotroupe.

He skipped to the warm waterfall and stood under it. As he showered he told a blue-furred, wise-looking little creature dressed in a dapper waistcoat and sitting on a nearby tree what clothes he wished prepared for the evening. It nodded and swung off through the branches.

VI

'It's nothing to worry about, Gestra,' the drone told him as he stepped out of the bulky suit in the vestibule beyond the airlocks. Gestra Ishmethit leant against a maniple field which the drone extended for him. He looked down the corridor to the main part of the accommodation unit, but there was no sign of anybody yet. 'The ship has come with new codes and updated security procedures,' the drone continued. 'It's some years before these were due to be altered, but there has been some unusual activity in a nearby volume – nothing threatening as such, but it's always best to be careful – so it's been decided to move things along a bit and perform the update now rather than later.' The drone hung the man's suit up near the airlock doors, its surface sparkling with frost.

Gestra rubbed his hands together and accepted the trousers and jacket the drone handed him. He kept glancing down the corridor.

'The ship has been verified and authenticated by the necessary outside referees,' the drone told him, 'so it's all above-board, you see?' The machine helped him button up the jacket and smoothed his thin, fair hair. 'The crew have asked to come inside; just curious, really.'

Gestra stared at the drone, obviously distressed, but the machine patted him on the shoulder with a rosy field and said, 'It'll be all right, Gestra. I thought it only polite to grant their request, but you can stay out of their way if you like. Saying hello to them at first would probably go down well, but it isn't compulsory.' The Mind had its drone study the man for a moment, checking his breathing, heart rate, pupil dilation, skin response, pheromone output and brain-waves. 'I know what,' it said soothingly, 'we'll tell them you've taken a vow of silence, how's that? You can greet them formally, nod, or whatever, and I'll do the talking. Would that be all right?'

Gestra gulped and said, 'Y-y-yes! Yes,' he said, nodding vigorously. 'That ... that would be good ... good idea. Tha-thank you!'

'Right,' the machine said floating at the man's side as they headed down the corridor for the main reception area. 'They'll Displace over in a few minutes. Like I say; just nod to them and let me say whatever has to be said. I'll make your excuses and you can go off to your suite if you like; I'm sure they won't mind being shown round by this drone. Meanwhile I'll be receiving the new ciphers and routines. There's a lot of multiple-checking and bureaucratic book-keeping sort of stuff to be done, but even so it should only take an hour or so. We won't offer them a meal or anything; with any luck they'll take the hint and head off again, leave us in peace, eh?'

After a moment, Gestra nodded at this, vigorously. The drone swivelled in the air at the man's side to show him it was looking at him. 'Does all this sound acceptable? I mean, I could put them off completely; tell them they're just not welcome, but it would be terribly rude, don't you think?'

'Y-yes,' Gestra said, frowning and looking distinctly uncertain. 'Rude. Suppose so. Rude. Mustn't be rude. Probably come a long way, should think?' A smile flickered around his lips, like a small flame in a high wind.

'I think we can be pretty sure of that,' the drone said with a laugh in its voice. It clapped him gently on the back with a field.

Gestra was smiling a little more confidently as he walked into the accommodation unit's main reception area.

The reception area was a large round room full of couches and chairs. Gestra usually paid it no attention; it was just a largish space he had to walk through on his way to and back from the airlocks which led to the warship hangars. Now he looked at each of the plumply comfortable-looking seats and sofas as though they represented some terrible threat. He felt his nervousness return. He wiped his brow as the drone stopped by a couch and indicated he might like to sit.

'Let's have a look, shall we?' the drone said as Gestra sat. A screen appeared in the air on the far side of the room, starting as a bright dot, quickly widening to a line eight metres long then seeming to unroll so that it filled the four-metre space between floor and ceiling.

Blackness; little lights. Space. Gestra realised suddenly how long it had been since he'd seen such a view. Then, sweeping slowly into view came a long, dark grey shape, sleek, symmetrical, double-ended, reminding Gestra of the axle and hubs of a ship's windlass.

'The Killer class Limited Offensive Unit *Attitude Adjuster*,' the drone said in a matter-of-fact, almost bored-sounding voice. 'Not a type we have here.'

Gestra nodded. 'No,' he said, then stopped to clear his throat a few times. 'No pattern . . . patterns on it . . . its hull.'

'That's right,' the drone said.

The ship was stopped now, almost filling the screen. The stars wheeled slowly behind it.

'Well, I—' the drone said, then stopped. The screen on the far side of the room flickered.

The drone's aura field flicked off. It fell out of the air, bouncing off the seat beside Gestra and toppling heavily, lifelessly, to the floor.

Gestra stared at it. A voice like a sigh said, '. . . sssave yoursssselfff . . .' then the lights dimmed, there was a buzzing noise from all around Gestra, and a tiny tendril of smoke leaked out of the top of the drone's casing.

Gestra leapt up out of the seat, staring wildly around, then jumped up on the seat, crouching there and staring at the drone. The little wisp of smoke was dissipating. The buzzing noise faded slowly. Gestra squatted, hugging his knees with both arms and looking all about. The buzzing noise stopped; the screen collapsed to a line hanging in the air, then shrank to a dot, then winked out. After a moment, Gestra reached forward with one hand and prodded the drone's casing with one hand. It felt warm and solid. It didn't move.

A sequence of thuds from the far side of the room shook the air. Beyond where the screen had hung in the air, four tiny mirror spheres bloated suddenly, growing almost instantly to over three metres in diameter and hovering just above the floor. Gestra jumped off the seat and started back away from the spheres. He rubbed his hands together and glanced back at the corridor to the airlock. The mirror spheres vanished like exploding balloons to reveal complicated things like tiny space-ships, not much smaller than the mirror spheres themselves.

One of them rushed towards Gestra, who turned and ran.

He pelted down the corridor, running as fast as he could, his eyes wide, his face distorted with fear, his fists pumping.

Something rushed up behind him, crashed into him and knocked him over, sending him sprawling and tumbling along the carpeted floor. He came to a stop. His face hurt where it had grazed along the carpet. He looked up, his heart twitching madly in his chest, his whole body shaking. Two of the miniature ship things had followed him into the corridor; each floated a couple of metres away, one on either side of him. There was a strange smell in the air. Frost had formed on various parts of the ship things. The nearer one extended a thing like a long hose and went to take him by the neck. Gestra ducked down and doubled himself up, lying on his side on the carpet, face tucked into his knees, arms hugging his shins.

Something prodded him about the shoulders and rump. He

could hear muffled noises coming from the two machines. He whimpered.

Then something very hard slammed into his side; he heard a cracking noise and his arm burned with pain. He screamed, still trying to bury his face in his knees. He felt his bowels relax. Warmth flooded his pants. He was aware of something inside his head turning off the searing pain in his arm, but nothing could turn off the heat of shame and embarrassment. Tears filled his eyes.

There was a noise like, 'Ka!' then a whooshing noise, and a breeze touched his face and hands. After a moment he looked up and saw that the two machines had gone down to the airlock doors. There was movement in the reception area, and then another one of the machines came down the corridor; it slowed down as it approached him. He ducked his head down again. Another whoosh and another breeze.

He looked up again. The three machines were moving around near the airlock doors. Gestra sniffed back his tears. The three machines drew back from the doors, then settled down onto the ground. Gestra waited to see what would happen next.

There was a flash, and an explosion. The middle set of doors blew out in a burst of smoke that rolled up the corridor and then collapsed backwards, seemingly sucking the whole explosion back into where the doors had been. The doors had gone, leaving a dark hole.

A breeze tugged at Gestra, then the breeze turned to a wind and the wind became a storm that howled and then screamed past him and then started moving him bodily along the floor. He shouted in fear, trying to grab hold of the carpet with his one good arm; he slid down the corridor in the roar of air, his fingers scrabbling for a grip. His nails dug in, found purchase, and his fingers closed around the fibres, pulling him to a stop.

He heard thuds and looked up, gasping, towards the reception area, eyes streaming with tears as the wind whipped by him. Something moved, bouncing in the lighted doorway of the circular lounge. He saw the vague, rounded shape of a couch thudding into the floor twenty metres away and flying towards him on the howling stream of air. He heard himself shout something. The couch thudded into the floor ten metres away, tumbling end over end.

He thought it was going to miss him, but one end of it smashed into his dangling feet, tearing him away; the storm of air picked him up bodily and he screamed as he fell with it past the shapes of the three watching machines. One of his legs hit the jagged edges of the breach in the airlock doors and was torn off at the knee. He flew out into the huge space beyond, the air pulled from his mouth first by his scream and then by the vacuum of the hangar itself.

He skidded to a stop on the cold hard floor of the hangar fifty metres from the wrecked doors, blood oozing then freezing around his wounds. The cold and the utter silence closed in; he felt his lungs collapse and something bubbled in his throat; his head ached as if his brain were about to burst out of his nose, eyes and ears, and his every tissue and bone seemed to ring with brief, stunning pain before going numb.

He looked into the enveloping darkness and up at the towering, heedless heights of the bizarrely patterned ships.

Then the ice crystals forming in his eyes fractured the view and made it splinter and multiply as though seen through a prism, before it all went dim and then black. He was trying to shout, to cry out, but there was only a terrible choking coldness in his throat. In a moment, he couldn't even move, frozen there on the floor of the vast space, immobile in his fear and confusion.

The cold killed him, finally, shutting off his brain in concentric stages, freezing the higher functions first, then the lower mammal brain, then finally the primitive, near-reptilian centre. His last thoughts were that he would never see his model sea ships again, nor know why the warships in the cold, dark halls were patterned so.

Victory! Commander Risingmoon Parchseason IV of the Farsight tribe nudged the suit forward, floating out through the torn doors of the airlock and into the hangar space. The ships were there. Gangster class. His gaze swept their ranks. Sixty-four of them. He had, privately, thought it might all be a hoax, some Culture trick.

At his side, his weapons officer steered his suit across the floor – over the body of the human – and up towards the nearest of the ships. The other suited figure, the Affronter Commander's personal guard, rotated, watching.

'If you'd waited another minute,' the voice of the Culture ship said tiredly through the suit's communicator, 'I could have opened the airlock doors for you.'

'I'm sure you could,' the Commander said. 'Is the Mind quite under your control?'

'Entirely. Touchingly naïve, in the end.'

'And the ships?'

'Quiescent; undisturbed; asleep. They will believe whatever they are told.'

'Good,' the Commander said. 'Begin the process of waking them.'

'It is already under way.'

'Nobody else here,' his security officer said over the communicator. He had gone on into the rest of the human accommodation section when they had made their way to the airlock doors.

'Anything of interest?' the Commander asked, following his weapons officer towards the nearest warship. He had to try to keep the excitement out of his voice. They had them! They *had* them! He had to brake the suit hard; in his enthusiasm he almost collided with his weapons officer.

In the ruined suite that had been the place where the human had lived, the security officer swivelled in the vacuum, surveying the wreckage the evacuating whirlwind of air had left. Human coverings; clothes, items of furniture, some complicated structures; models of some sort. 'No,' he said. 'Nothing of interest.'

'Hmm,' the ship said. Something about the tone communicated unease to the Commander. At the same moment, his weapons officer turned his suit to him. 'Sir,' he said. A light flicked on, picking out a metre-diameter circle of the ship's hull. Its surface was riotously embellished and marked, covered in strange, sweeping designs. The weapons officer swept the light over nearby sections of the vessel's curved hull. It was all the same, all of it covered with these curious, whorled patterns and motifs.

'What?' the Commander said, concerned now.

'This . . . complexity,' the weapons officer said, sounding perplexed.

'Internal, too,' the Culture ship broke in.

'It . . .' the weapons officer said, spluttering. His suit moved closer to the warship's hull, until it was almost touching. 'This will take for ever to scan!' he said. 'It goes down to the atomic level!'

'*What* does?' the Commander said sharply.

'The ships have been baroqued, to use the technical term,' the Culture ship said urbanely. 'It was always a possibility.' It made a sighing noise. 'The vessels have been fractally inscribed with partially random, non-predictable designs using up a little less than one per cent of the mass of each craft. There is a chance that hidden in amongst that complexity will be independent security nano-devices which will activate at the same time as each ship's main systems and which will require some additional coded reassurance that all is well, otherwise they will attempt to disable or even destroy the ship. These will have to be looked for. As your weapons officer says, the craft will each have to be scanned at least down to the level of individual atoms. I shall begin this task the instant I have completed the reprogramming of the base's Mind. This will delay us, that's all; the ships would have required scanning in any event, and in the meantime, nobody knows we're here. You will have your war fleet in a matter of days rather than hours, Commander, but you will have it.'

The weapons officer's space suit turned to face the Commander's. The light illuminating the outlandish designs switched off. Somehow, from the way he performed these actions, the weapons officer conveyed a mood of scepticism and perhaps even disgust to the Commander.

'Ka!' the Commander said contemptuously, whirling away and heading back towards the airlock doors. He needed to wreck something. The accommodation section ought to provide articles which would be satisfying but unimportant. His personal guard swept after him, weapons ready.

Passing over the still, frozen body of the human – even *that* hadn't provided any sport – Commander Risingmoon Parchseason IV of the Farsight tribe and the battleship *Xenoclast* – on secondment to the alien ship *Attitude Adjuster* – unholstered one of the external weapons on his own suit and blasted the small figure into a thousand pieces, scattering fragments of frosty pink and white across the cold floor of the hangar like a small, delicate fall of snow.

7

Tier

Such investigations took time. There was the time that even hyperspacially transmitted information took to traverse the significant percentages of the galaxy involved, there were complicated routes to arrange, other Minds to talk to, sometimes after setting up appointments because they were absent in Infinite Fun space for a while. Then the Minds had to be casualed up to, or gossip or jokes or thoughts on a mutual interest had to be exchanged before a request or a suggestion was put which re-routed and disguised an information search; sometimes these re-routes took on extra loops, detours and shuntings as the Minds concerned thought to play down their own involvement or involve somebody else on a whim, so that often wildly indirect paths resulted, branching and re-branching and doubling back on themselves until eventually the relevant question was asked and the answer, assuming it was forthcoming, started the equally tortuous route back to the original requester. Frequently simple seeker-agent programs or entire mind-state abstracts were sent off on even more complicated missions with detailed instructions on what to look for, where to find it, who to ask and how to keep their tracks covered.

Mostly it was done like that; through Minds, AI core memories and innumerable public storage systems, information reservoirs and databases containing schedules, itineraries, lists, plans, catalogues, registers, rosters and agenda.

Sometimes, though, when that way – the relatively easy, quick and simple way – was closed to the inquirer for some reason, usually to do with keeping the inquiry secret, things had to be done the slow way, the messy way, the physical way. Sometimes there was no alternative.

The vacuum dirigible approached the floating island under a brilliantly clear night sky awash with moon and star light. The main body of the airship was a giant fat disk half a kilometre across with a finish like brushed aluminium; it glinted in the blue-grey light as if frosted, though the night was warm, balmy and scented with the heady perfume of wineplant and sierra creeper. The craft's two gondolas – one on top, one suspended underneath – were smaller, thinner disks only three storeys in height, each slowly revolving in different directions, their edges glowing with lights.

The sea beneath the airship was mostly black-dark, but in places it glowed dimly in giant, slowly fading Vs as giant sea creatures surfaced to breathe or to sieve new levels of the waters for their tiny prey, and so disturbed the light-emitting plankton near the surface.

The island floated high in the breeze-ruffled waters, its base a steeply fluted pillar that extended a kilometre down into the sea's salty depths, its thin, spire-like mountains thrusting a similar distance into the cloudless air. It too was scattered with lights; of small towns, villages, individual houses, lanterns on beaches and smaller aircraft, most of them come out to welcome the vacuum dirigible.

The two slowly revolving gondola sections slid gradually to a halt, preparatory to docking. People in both segments congregated on the sides nearest the island, for the view. The airship's system registered the imbalance building up and pumped bubblecarbon spheres full of vacuum from one lot of tanks to another, so maintaining a suitably even keel.

The island's main town drifted slowly closer, the docking tower bright with lights. Lasers, fireworks and searchlights all fought for attention.

'I really should go, Tish,' the drone Gruda Aplam said. 'I didn't promise, but I did kind of say I'd probably stop by . . .'

'Ah, stop by on the way back,' Tishlin said, waving his glass. 'Let them wait.'

He stood on the balcony outside one of the lower gondola's mid-level bars. The drone – a very old thing, like two grey-brown rounded cubes one on top of the other and three-quarters the size of a human – floated beside him. They'd only met that day, four days into the cruise over the Orbital's floating islands and they'd got on famously, quite as though they'd been friends for a century or more. The drone was much older than the man but they found they had the same attitudes, the same beliefs and the same sense of humour. They both liked telling stories, too. Tishlin had the impression he hadn't yet scratched the veneer off the old machine's tales of when it had been in Contact – a millennium before he had, and goodness knew he was considered an old codger these days.

He liked the ancient machine; he'd really come on this cruise looking for romance, and he still hoped to find it, but in the meantime finding such a perfect companion and raconteur had already made him glad he'd come. The trouble was the drone was supposed to get off here and go to visit some old drone pals who lived on the island, before resuming its cruise on the next dirigible, due in a few days' time. A month from now, it would be leaving on the GSV that had brought it here.

'But I feel I'd be letting them down.'

'Look, just stay another day,' the man suggested. 'You never did finish telling me about – what was it, Bhughredi?'

'Yes, Bhughredi.' The old drone chuckled.

'Exactly. Bhughredi; the sea nukes and the interference effect thing or whatever it was.'

'Damnedest way to launch a ship,' the old drone agreed, and made a sighing noise.

'So what did happen?'

'Like I said, it's a long story.'

'So stay tomorrow; tell me it. You're a drone for goodness' sake; you can float back by yourself . . .'

'But I said I'd visit them when the airship got here, Tish. Anyway; my AG units are due a service; they'd probably fail and I'd end up at the bottom of the sea having to be rescued; very embarrassing.'

'Take a flyer back!' the man said, watching the island's shore slide underneath. People gathered round fires on the beach waved up at the craft. He could hear music drifting on the warm breeze.

'Oh, I don't know . . . They'd probably be upset.'

Tishlin drank from his glass and frowned down at the waves breaking on the beach which led towards the lights of the town. A particularly large and vivid firework detonated in the air directly above the bright docking tower. *Oos* and *Aahs* duly sounded round the crowded balcony.

The man snapped his fingers. 'I know,' he said. 'Send a mind-state abstract.'

The big drone hesitated, then said, 'Oh, one of those. Hmm. Well; still not really the same thing, I think. Anyway, I've never done one. Not sure I really approve. I mean, it's you but it's not you, you know?'

Tishlin nodded. 'Certainly do know. Can't say I think they're as, you know, benign as they're cracked up to be either; I mean, it's supposed to *act* sentient without *being* sentient, so isn't it *actually* sentient? What happens to it when it's just turned off? I'm not convinced there isn't some sort of iffy morality here, either. But I've done it myself. Talked into it. Reservations, like you say, but . . .' He looked round, then leant closer to the machine's dull brown casing. 'Bit of a Contact thing, actually.'

'Really?' the old machine said, tipping its whole body away from him for a moment, then tipping it back so that it leant towards him. It extended a field round the two of them; the exterior sounds faded. When it spoke again, it was with a slight echo that indicated the field was keeping whatever they said between the two of them. 'What was that . . . Well, wait a moment, if you aren't supposed to tell anybody . . .'

Tishlin weaved his hand. 'Well, not officially,' he said, brushing white hair over one ear, 'but you're a Contact veteran, and you know how SC always dramatises things.'

'SC!' the drone said its voice rising. 'You didn't say it was them! I'm not sure I want to hear this,' it said, through a chuckle.

'Well, they asked . . . a favour,' the man said, quietly pleased that he seemed finally to have impressed the old drone. 'Sort of a family thing. Had to record one of these damn things so it could go and convince a nephew of mine he should do his bit for the great and good cause. Last I heard the boy had done the decent thing and taken ship for some Eccentric GSV.' He watched the outskirts of the town slide underneath. A flower-garlanded terrace held groups of people pattern-dancing; he could imagine the whoops and wild, whirling music. The scent of roasting meat came curling over the balcony parapet and made it through the hushfield.

'They asked if I wanted it to be reincorporated after it had done its job,' he told the drone. 'They said it could be sent back and sort of put back inside my head, but I said no. Gave me a creepy feeling just thinking about it. What if it had changed a lot while it was away? Why, I might end up wanting to join some retreatist order or autoeuthenise or something!' He shook his head and drained his glass. 'No; I said no. Hope the damn thing never was really alive, but if it was, or is, then it's not getting back into my head, no thank you, I'm sorry.'

'Well, if what they told you was true, it's yours to do with as you wish, isn't it?'

'Exactly.'

'Well, I don't think I'll take the same step,' the drone said, sounding thoughtful. It swivelled as though to face him. The field around them collapsed. The sound of the fireworks returned. 'Tell you what,' the old drone said. 'I will get off here and see the guys, but I'll catch up with you in a couple of days, all right? We'll probably fall out in a day or two anyway; they're cantankerous old buggers, frankly. I'll take a flyer or try floating myself if I feel adventurous. Deal?' It extended a field.

'Deal,' Tishlin said, slapping the field with his hand.

The drone Gruda Aplam had already contacted its old friend the GCU *It's Character Forming*, currently housed in the GSV *Zero Gravitas* which was at that point docked under a distant plate of Seddun Orbital. The GCU communicated with the Orbital Hub Tsikiliepre, which in turn contacted the Ulterior Entity *Highpoint*, which signalled the LSV *Misophist*, which passed the message on to the University Mind at Oara, on Khasli plate in the Juboal system, which duly relayed the signal, along with an interesting series of rhyme-scheme glyphs, ordinary poems and word games all based on the original signal, to its favoured protégé, the LSV *Serious Callers Only* . . .

[stuttered tight point, M32, tra. @n4.28.866.2083]
  xLSV *Serious Callers Only*
    oEccentric *Shoot Them Later*
It is Genar-Hofoen. I am now convinced. I am not certain why he may be important to the conspiracy, but he surely is. I have drawn up a plan to intercept him, on Tier. The plan involves Phage Rock; will you back me up if I request its aid?
∞

[stuttered tight point, M32, tra. @n4.28.866.2568]
  xEccentric *Shoot Them Later*
    oLSV *Serious Callers Only*
My dear old friend, of course.
∞

Thank you. I shall make the request immediately. We shall be reduced to dealing with amateurs, I'm afraid. However, I hope to

find a high-profile amateur; a degree of fame may protect where SC
training is not available. What of our fellow counter-conspirator?
∞

No word. Perhaps it's spending more time in The Land of IF.
∞

And the ship and Pittance?
∞

Arriving in eleven and a half days' time.
∞

Hmm. Four days after the time it will take for us to get somebody to Tier.
It is within the bounds of possibility this ship will be heading into
a threatening situation. Is it able to take care of itself?
∞

Oh, I think it capable of giving a good account of itself.
Just because I'm Eccentric doesn't mean I don't know some
big hitters.
∞

Let us hope such throw-weight is not required.
∞

Absolutely.

II

A Plate class General Systems Vehicle was quite a simple thing, in
at least one way. It was four kilometres thick; the lowest kilometre
was almost all engine, the middle two klicks were ship space – an
entire enclosed system of sophisticated dockyards and quays, in
effect – and the topmost thousand metres was accommodation,
most of it for humans. There was, of course, a great deal more to
it than that, but this covered the essentials.

Using these broad-brush figures, it was a simple matter for
anybody to work out the craft's approximate maximum speed
from the cubic kilometrage of its engines, the number of ships of
any given size it could contain according to the volume given over
to the various sizes of bays and engineering space, and the total

number of humans it could accommodate by simply adding up how many cubic kilometres were given over to their living-space.

The *Sleeper Service* had retained an almost pristine original specification internally, which was a rare thing in an Eccentric vessel; usually the first thing they did was drastically reconfigure their physical shape and internal lay-out according to the dictates of some private aesthetic, driving obsession or just plain whim, but the fact the *Sleeper Service* had stuck to its initial design and merely added its own private ocean and gas-giant environment on the outside made it relatively easy to measure its actual behaviour against what it ought to be capable of, and so ensure that it wasn't up to any extra mischief besides being Eccentric in the first place.

In addition to such simple, arithmetical estimates of a ship's capability, it was, of course, always a good idea when dealing with an Eccentric craft to have just that little extra bit of an edge. Intelligence, to be specific; an inside view; a spy.

As it approached the Dreve system, the Plate class GSV *Sleeper Service* was travelling at its usual cruising speed of about forty kilolights. It had already announced its desire to stop off in the inner system, and so duly started braking as it passed through the orbit of the system's outer-most planet, a light week distant from the sun itself.

The *Yawning Angel*, the GSV which was shadowing the larger craft, decelerated at the same rate, a few billion kilometres behind. The *Yawning Angel* was the latest in a long line of GSVs which had agreed to take a shift as the *Sleeper Service*'s escort. It wasn't a particularly demanding task (indeed, no sensible GSV would wish it to be), though there was a small amount of vicarious glamour associated with it; guarding the weirdo, letting it roam wherever it wanted, but maintaining the fraternal vigilance that such an enormously powerful craft espousing such an eccentric credo patently merited. The only qualifications for being a *Sleeper Service* shadow were that one was regarded as being reliable, and that one was capable of staying with the SS if it ever decided to make a dash for it; in other words, one had to be quicker than it.

The *Yawning Angel* had done the job for the best part of a year and found it undemanding. Naturally, it was somewhat annoying not to be able to draw up one's own course schedule, but providing one took the right attitude and dispensed with the standard Mind conviction that held efficiency to the absolute bottom line of everything, it could be an oddly enhancing, even liberating experience. GSVs were always wanted in many more places at the same time than it was possible to be, and it was something of a relief to be able to blame somebody else when one had to frustrate people's and other ships' wishes and requests.

This stop at Dreve had not been anticipated, for example – the *SS*'s course had seemed set on a reasonably predictable path which would take it through the next month – but now it was here, the *Yawning Angel* would be able to drop off a few ships, take another couple on, and swap some personnel. There should be time; the *SS* had never acknowledged the presence of any of the vessels tailing it, and it hadn't posted a course schedule since it had turned Eccentric forty years earlier, but it had certain obligations in terms of setting re-awakened people back in the land of the living again, and it always announced how long it would be staying in the systems it visited.

It would be here in Dreve for a week. An unusually long time; it had never stayed anywhere for longer than three days before. The implication, according to the group of ships considered experts on the behaviour of the *Sleeper Service*, and given what the GSV itself had been saying in its increasingly rare communications, was that it was about to off-load all its charges; all the Storees and all the big sea, air and gas-giant-dwelling creatures it had collected over the decades would be moved – physically, presumably, rather than Displaced – to compatible habitats.

Dreve would be an ideal system to do this in; it had been a Culture system for four thousand years, comprising nine more or less wilderness worlds and three Orbitals – hoops, giant bracelets of living-space only a few thousand kilometres across but ten million kilometres in diameter – calmly gyrating in their own carefully aligned orbits and housing nearly seventy billion souls. Some of those souls were far from human; one third of each of the system's Orbitals was given over to ecosystems designed for quite different creatures; gas-giant dwellers on one, methane atmospherians on another and high temperature silicon creatures on another. The fauna the *SS* had picked up from other gas-giant planets would all fit comfortably into a sub-section of the Orbital designed with such animals in mind, and the sea and air creatures ought to be able to find homes on that or either of the other worlds.

A week to hang around; the *Yawning Angel* thought that would go down particularly well with its human crew; one of the many tiny but significant and painful ways a GSV could lose face amongst its peers was through a higher than average crew turn-over rate, and, while it had been expecting it, the *Yawning Angel* had found the experience most distressing when people had announced they were fed up not being able to have any reliable advance notice of where they were going from week to week and month to month and so had decided to live elsewhere; all its protestations had been to no avail. What would in effect be a week's leave in such a cosmopolitan, sophisticated and welcoming system really should convince a whole load of those currently wavering between loyalty and ship-jumping that it was worth staying on with the good old *Yawning Angel*, it was sure.

The *Sleeper Service* came to an orbit-relative stop a quarter-turn in advance along the path of the middle Orbital, the most efficient position to assume to distribute its cargo of people and animals evenly amongst all three worlds. Permission to do so was finally received from the last of the Orbitals' Hub Minds, and the *Sleeper Service* duly began getting ready to unload.

The *Yawning Angel* watched from afar as the larger craft detached its traction fields from the energy grid beneath real space, closed down its primary and ahead scan fields, dropped its curtain shields and generally made the many great and small adjustments a ship normally made when one was intending to stick around somewhere for a while. The *Sleeper Service*'s external appearance remained the same as ever; a silvery ellipsoid ninety kilometres long, sixty across the beam and twenty in height. After a few minutes, however, smaller craft began to appear from that reflective barrier, speeding towards the three Orbitals with their cargoes of Stored people and sedated animals.

All this matched with the intelligence the *Yawning Angel* had already received regarding the set-up and intentions of the Eccentric GSV. So far so good, then.

Content that all was well, the *Yawning Angel* drifted in to match velocities with Teriocre, the middle Orbital and the one with the gas-giant environments. It docked underneath the Orbital's most populous section and drew up a variety of travel and leave arrangements for its own inhabitants while setting up a schedule of visits, events and parties aboard to thank its hosts for their hospitality.

Everything went swimmingly until the second day.

Then, without warning, just after dawn had broken over the part of the Orbital the *Yawning Angel* had docked beneath, Stored bodies and giant animals started popping into existence all over Teriocre.

Posed people, some still in the clothes or uniforms of the tableaux they had been part of on board the *Sleeper Service*, suddenly appeared inside sports halls, on beaches, terraces, boardwalks and pavements, in parks, plazas, deserted stadia and every other sort of public space the Orbital had to offer. To the few people who witnessed these events, it was obvious the bodies had been Displaced; the appearance of each was signalled by a tiny point of light blinking into existence just above waist level; this expanded rapidly to a two-metre grey sphere which promptly popped and disappeared, leaving behind the immobile Storee.

Unmoving people were left lying on dewy grass or sitting on park benches or scattered by the hundred across the patterned mosaic of squares and piazzas as though after some terrible disaster or a particularly assertive public sculpture exhibition; dim cleaning machines spiralling methodically within such spaces were left bemused, picking erratic courses amongst the rash of new and unexpected obstructions.

In the seas, the surface swelled and bulged in hundreds of different places as whole globes of water were carefully Displaced just beneath the surface; the sea creatures contained within were still gently sedated and moved sluggishly in their giant fish bowls, each of which retained its separation from the surrounding water for a few hours, osmosing fields gradually adjusting the conditions within to those in the sea outside.

In the air, similar gauzy fields surrounded whole flocks of buoyant atmosphere fauna, bobbing groggily in the breeze.

Further along the vast shallow sweep of the Orbital, the gas-giant environments were witness to equivalent scenes of near-instant immigration followed by gradual integration.

The *Yawning Angel*'s own drones – its ambassadors on the Orbital – were witness to a handful of these sudden manifestations. After a nanosecond's delay to ask permission, the GSV clicked into the Orbital's own monitoring systems, and so watched with growing horror as hundreds, thousands, tens of thousands more Stored bodies and animals came thumping into existence all over the surface and all through the air, water and gas-ecologies of Teriocre.

The *Yawning Angel* flash-woke all its systems and switched its attention to the *Sleeper Service*.

The big GSV was already moving, rolling and twisting to point directly upwards out of the system. Its engine fields reconnected with the energy grid, its scanners were all already back on line and the rest of its multi-layered field complex was rapidly configuring itself for sustained deep-space travel.

It moved off, not especially quickly. Its Displacers had switched to *pick* rather than *put* now; in a matter of seconds they had snapped almost its entire fleet of smaller ships out of the system, their genuine yet deceptive delivery missions completed. Only the furthest, most massive vessels were left behind.

The *Yawning Angel* was already frantically making its own preparations to depart in pursuit, closing off most of its transit corridors, snap-Displacing drones from the Orbital, hurrying through a permission-to-depart request to the world's Hub and drawing up schedules for ferrying people back to the Orbital on smaller craft once it had got under way while at the same time bringing other personnel back before its own velocity grew too great.

It knew it was wasting its energy, but it signalled the *Sleeper Service* anyway. Meanwhile, it watched intently as the departing ship accelerated away.

The *Yawning Angel* was gauging, judging, calibrating.

It was looking for a figure, comparing an aspect of the reality that was the absconding craft with the abstraction that was a simple but crucial equation. If the *Sleeper Service*'s velocity could at any point over time be described by a value greater than $.54 \times ns^2$, the *Yawning Angel* might be in trouble.

It might be in trouble anyway, but if the larger vessel was accelerating significantly quicker than its normal design parameters implied – allowing for the extra mass of the craft's extraneous environments – then that trouble started right now.

As it was, the *Yawning Angel* was relieved to see, the *Sleeper Service* was moving away at exactly that rate; the ship was still perfectly apprehendable, and even if the *Yawning Angel* waited for another day without doing anything it would still be able to track the larger craft with ease and catch up with it within two days. Still suspecting some sort of trick, the *Yawning Angel* started an observation routine throughout the system for unexpected Displacings of gigatonnes of water and gas-giant atmosphere; suddenly dumping all that extra volume and mass now would be one way the *Sleeper Service* could put on an extra burst of speed, even if it would still be significantly slower than the *Yawning Angel*.

The smaller GSV retransmitted its polite but insistent signal. Still no reply from the *Sleeper Service*. No surprise there then.

The *Yawning Angel* signalled to tell other Contact craft what was happening and sent one of its fastest ships – a Cliff class superlifter stationed in space outside the GSV's own fields for exactly this sort of eventuality – in pursuit of the escaping GSV, just so it would know this precocious, irksome action was being taken seriously.

Probably the *Sleeper Service* was simply being awkward rather than up to something more momentous, but the *Yawning Angel* couldn't ignore the fact the larger craft was abandoning a significant proportion of its smaller ships, and had resorted to Displacing people and animals. Displacing was – especially at such speed – inherently and unfinessably dangerous; the risk of something going horribly, terminally wrong was only about one in eighty million for any single Displacement event, but that was still enough to put the average, fussily perfectionist ship Mind off using the process for anything alive except in the direst of emergencies, and the *Sleeper Service* – assuming it had rid itself of its entire complement of souls – must have carried out thirty-thousand plus Displacements in a minute or less, nudging the odds up well into the sort of likelihood-of-fuck-up range any sane Mind would normally recoil from in utter horror. Even allowing for the *Sleeper Service*'s Eccentricity, that did tend to indicate that there was something more than usually urgent or significant about its current actions.

The *Yawning Angel* looked up what was in effect an annoyance chart; it could leave right now – within a hundred seconds – and aggravate lots of people because they were on board itself instead of the Orbital, or vice-versa . . . or it could depart within twenty hours and leave everybody back where they ought to be, even if they were irritated at their plans being upset.

Compromise; it set an eight-hour departure time. Terminals in the shape of rings, pens, earrings, brooches, articles of clothing

– and the in-built versions, neural laces – woke startled Culture personnel all over the Orbital and the wider system, insisting on relaying their urgent message. So much for keeping everybody happy with a week's leave . . .

The *Sleeper Service* accelerated smoothly away into the darkness, already well clear of the system. It began to Induct, flittering between inferior and superior hyperspace. Its apparent real-space velocity jumped almost instantly by a factor of exactly twenty-three. Again, the *Yawning Angel* was comforted to see, spot on. No unpleasant surprises. The superlifter *Charitable View* raced after the fleeing craft, its engines unstressed, energy expenditure throttled well back, also threading its way between the layers of four-dimensional space. The process had been compared to a flying fish zipping from water to air and back again, except that every second air-jump was into a layer of air beneath the water, not above it, which was where the analogy did rather break down.

The *Yawning Angel* was quickly customising thousands of carefully composed, exquisitely phrased apologies to its personnel and hosts. Its schedule of ship returns, varied to reflect the different courses the *Sleeper Service* might take if it didn't remain on its present heading, didn't look too problematic; it had delayed letting people venture far away until the *Sleeper Service* had sent most of its own fleet out, an action even it had thought over-cautious at the time but which now seemed almost prescient. It delegated part of its intellectual resources to drawing up a list of treats and blandishments with which to mollify its own people when they returned, and planned for a *two*-week return to Dreve, packed with festivities and celebrations, to say sorry when it was free of the obligation to follow this accursed machine and was able to draw up its own course schedule again.

The *Charitable View* reported that the *Sleeper Service* was still proceeding as could be expected.

The situation, it appeared, was in hand.

The *Yawning Angel* reviewed its own actions so far, and found them exemplary. This was all very vexing, but it was responding well, playing it by the book where possible and extemporising sensibly but with all due urgency where it had to. Good, good. It could well come out of this shining.

Three hours, twenty-six minutes and seventeen seconds after setting off, the General Systems Vehicle *Sleeper Service* reached its nominal Terminal Acceleration Point. This was where it ought to stop gaining speed, plump for one of the two hyperspatial volumes and just cruise along at a nice steady velocity.

It didn't. Instead it accelerated harder; that .54 figure zoomed quickly to .72, the Plate class's normal design maximum.

The *Charitable View* communicated this turn of events back to the *Yawning Angel*, which went into shock for about a millisecond. It rechecked all its in-system ships, drones, sensors and external reports. There was no sign that the *Sleeper Service* had dumped its extra mass anywhere within range of the *Yawning Angel*'s sensors. Yet it was behaving as though it had. Where had it done it? Could it have secretly built longer-range Displacers? (No; half its mass would have been required to construct a Displacer capable of dumping so much volume beyond the range of the *Yawning Angel*'s sensors, and that included all the extra mass it had taken on board over the years in the form of the extraneous environments in the first place . . . though – now that it was thinking in such outrageous terms – there was another, associated possibility that just might . . . but no; that couldn't be. There had been no intelligence, no hint . . . no, it didn't even want to think about that . . .)

The *Yawning Angel* rescheduled everything it had already arranged in a flurry of re-drafted apologies, pleas for understand-ing and truncated journeys. It halved the departure warning time it had given. Thirty-three minutes to departure, now. The situation, it tried to explain to everybody, was becoming more urgent.

The *Sleeper Service*'s acceleration figures remained steady at their design maxima for another twenty minutes, though the *Charitable View* – keeping a careful watch on every aspect of the GSV's performance from its station a few real-space light days behind – reported some odd events at the junctions of the *Sleeper Service*'s traction fields with the energy grid.

By now the *Yawning Angel* was existing in a state of quiveringly ghastly tension; it was thinking at maximum capacity, worrying at full speed, suddenly and appallingly aware *how long things took to happen*; a human in the same state would have been clutching a churning stomach, tearing their hair out and gibbering incoherently.

Look at these humans! How could such glacial slowness even be called *life*? An age could pass, virtual empires rise and fall in the time they took to open their mouths to utter some new inanity!

Ships, even ships; they were restricted to speeds below the speed of sound in the bubble of air around the ship and the docks it was joined to. It reviewed how practicable it would be to just let the air go and move everything in vacuum. It made sense. Thankfully, it had already shifted all vulnerable pleasure craft out of the way and sealed and secured its unconnected hull apertures. It told the Hub what it was doing; the Hub objected because it was losing some of *its* air. The GSV dumped the air anyway. Everything started moving a little faster. The Hub screamed in protest but it ignored it.

Calm; calm; it had to remain calm. Stay focused, keep the most important objectives in mind.

A wave of what would have been nausea in a human swept through the *Yawning Angel*'s Mind as a signal came in from the *Charitable View*. Now what?

Whatever it might have feared, this was worse.

The *Sleeper Service*'s acceleration factor had started to increase. Almost at the same time, it had exceeded its normal maximum sustainable velocity.

Fascinated, appalled, terrified, the *Yawning Angel* listened to a running commentary on the other GSV's progress from its increasingly distant child, even as it started the sequence of actions and commands that would lead to its own near-instant departure. Twelve minutes early, but that couldn't be helped, and if people were pissed off, too bad.

Still increasing. Time to go. Disconnect. There.

The *Charitable View* signalled that the *Sleeper Service*'s outer-most field extent had shrunk to within a kilometre of naked-hull minima.

The *Yawning Angel* dropped away from the orbital, twisting and aiming and punching away into hyperspace only a few kilometres away from the world's undersurface, ignoring incandescent howls of protest from the Hub over such impolite and feasibly dangerous behaviour and the astonished – but slow, so *slow* – yelps from people who an instant earlier had been walking down a transit corridor towards a welcoming foyer in the GSV and now found themselves bumping into emergency seal-fields and staring at nothing but blackness and stars.

The superlifter's continuous report went on: the *Sleeper Service*'s acceleration kept on increasing slowly but steadily, then it paused, dropping to zero; the craft's velocity remained constant.

Could that be it? It was still catchable. Panic over?

Then the fleeing ship's velocity increased again; as did its rate of acceleration. *Impossible!*

The horrific thought which had briefly crossed the *Yawning Angel*'s mind moments earlier settled down to stay with all the gruesome deliberation of a self-invited house guest.

It did the arithmetic.

Take a Plate class GSV's locomotive power output per cubic kilometre of engine. Add on sixteen cubic klicks of extra drive at that push-per-cube value . . . make that thirty-two at a time . . . and it matched the step in the *Sleeper Service*'s acceleration it had just witnessed. General bays. Great grief, it had filled its General bays with engine.

The *Charitable View* reported another smooth increase in the *Sleeper Service*'s rate of progress leading to another step, another pause. It was increasing its own acceleration to match.

The *Yawning Angel* sped after the two of them, already fearing the worst. Do the sums, do the sums. The *Sleeper Service* had filled at least four of its General bays with extra engine, bringing them on line two at a time, balancing the additional impetus . . .

Another increase.

Six. Probably all eight, then. What about the engineering space behind? Had that gone too?

Sums, sums. How much mass had there been aboard the damn thing? Water; gas-giant atmosphere, highly pressurised. About four thousand cubic kilometres of water alone; four gigatonnes. Compress it, alter it, transmute it, convert it into the ultra dense exotic materials that comprised an engine capable of reaching out and down to the energy grid that underlay the universe and pushing against it . . . ample, ample, more than enough. It would take months, even years to build that sort of extra engine capacity . . . or only days, if you'd spent, say, the last few decades preparing the ground.

Dear holy shit, if it was all engine even the superlifter wouldn't be able to keep up with it. The average Plate class could sustain about one hundred and four kilolights more or less indefinitely; a good Range class, which was what the *Yawning Angel* had always been proud to count itself as, could easily beat that by forty kilolights. A

Cliff class superlifter was ninety per cent engine; faster even than a Rapid Offensive Unit in short bursts. The *Charitable View* could hit two-twenty-one flat out, but that was only supposed to be for an hour or two at a time; that was chase speed, catch-up speed, not something it could maintain for long.

The figure the *Yawning Angel* was looking at was the thick end of two-thirty-three, if the *Sleeper Service*'s engineering space had been packed with engine too.

The *Charitable View*'s tone had already turned from one of amusement to amazement, then bewilderment. Now it was plain peevish. The *Sleeper Service* was topping the two-fifteen mark and showing no signs of slowing down. The superlifter would have to break away within minutes if it didn't top-out soon. It asked for instructions.

The *Yawning Angel*, still accelerating for all its worth, determined to track and follow for as long as it could or until it was asked to give up the chase, told its offspring craft not to exceed its design parameters, not to risk damage.

The *Sleeper Service* went on accelerating. The superlifter *Charitable View* gave up the chase at two-twenty. It settled back to a less frenetic two hundred, dropping back all the time; even so it was still not a speed it could maintain for more than a few hours.

The *Yawning Angel* topped out at one forty-six.

The *Sleeper Service* finally hit cruise at around two-thirty-three and a half, disappearing ahead into the depths of galactic space. The superlifter reported this but sounded like it couldn't believe it.

The *Yawning Angel* watched the other GSV race away into the everlasting night between the stars, a sense of hopelessness, of defeat, settled over it.

Now it knew it had shaken off its pursuers the *Sleeper Service*'s course was starting to curve gently, no doubt the first of many ducks and weaves it would carry out, if it was trying to conceal its eventual goal, and assuming that it had a goal other than simply giving the slip to its minders . . . Somehow, the *Yawning Angel* suspected its Eccentric charge – or ex-charge – did have a definite goal; a place, a location it was headed for.

Two hundred and thirty-three thousand times the speed of light. Dear holy fucking shit. The *Yawning Angel* thought there was something almost vulgar about such a velocity. Where the hell was it *heading* for? *Andromeda*?

The *Yawning Angel* drew a course-probability cone through the galactic model it kept in its mind.

It supposed it all depended how devious the *Sleeper Service* was being, but it looked like it might be headed for the Upper Leaf Swirl. If it was, it would be there within three weeks.

The *Yawning Angel* signalled ahead. Look on the bright side; at least the problem was out of its fields now.

The avatar Amorphia stood – arms crossed, thin, black-gloved hands grasping at bony elbows – gaze fastened intently upon the screen on the far side of the lounge. It showed a compensated view of hyperspace, vastly magnified.

Looking into the screen was like peering into some vast planetary airscape. Far below was a layer of glowing mist representing the energy grid; above was an identical layer of bright cloud. The skein of real space lay in between both of these; a two-dimensional layer, a simple transparent plane which the GSV went flickering through like a weaving shuttle across an infinite loom. Far, far behind it, the tiny dot that was the superlifter shrank still further. It too had been bobbing up and down through the skein on a sine wave whose length was measured in light minutes, but now it had stopped oscillating, settling into the lower level of hyperspace.

The magnification jumped; the superlifter was a larger dot now, but still dropping back all the time. A light-point tracing its own once wavy now straight course even further behind was the pursuing GSV. The star of the Dreve system was a bright spot back beyond that, stationary in the skein.

The *Sleeper Service* reached its maximum velocity and also ceased to oscillate between the two regions of hyperspace, settling into the larger of the two infinities that was ultraspace. The two following ships did the same, increasing their speed fractionally but briefly. A purist would call the place where they now existed ultraspace one positive, though as nobody had ever had access to ultraspace one negative – or infraspace one positive, for that matter – it was a redundant, even pedantic distinction. Or it had been until now. That might be about to change, if the Excession could deliver what it appeared to promise . . .

Amorphia took a deep breath and then let it go.

The view clicked off and the screen disappeared.

The avatar turned to look at the woman Dajeil Gelian and the black bird Gravious. They were in a recreation area on the Ridge class GCU *Jaundiced Outlook*, housed in a bay in one of the *Sleeper Service*'s mid-top strakes. The lounge was pretty well standard Contact issue; deceptively spacious, stylishly comfortable, punctuated by plants and subdued lighting.

This ship was to be the woman's home for the rest of the journey; a life boat ready to quit the larger craft at a moment's notice and take her to safety if anything went wrong. She sat on a white recliner chair, dressed in a long red dress, calm but wide-eyed, one hand cupped upon her swollen belly, the black bird perched on one arm of the seat near her hand.

The avatar smiled down at the woman. 'There,' it said. It made a show of looking around. 'Alone at last.' It laughed lightly, then looked down at the black bird, its smile disappearing. 'Whereas you,' it said, 'will not be again.'

Gravious jerked upright, neck stretching. '*What?*' it asked. Gelian looked surprised, then concerned.

Amorphia glanced to one side. A small device like a stubby pen floated out of the shadows cast by a small tree. It coasted up to the bird, which shrank back and back from the small, silent missile until it almost fell off the arm of the chair, its blue-black beak centimetres from the nose cone of the tiny, intricate machine.

'This is a scout missile, bird,' Amorphia told it. 'Do not be deceived by its innocent title. If you so much as think of committing another act of treachery, it will happily reduce you to hot gas. It is going to follow you everywhere. Don't do as I have done; do as I say and don't try to shake it off; there is a tracer nanotech on you – in you – which will make it a simple matter to follow you. It should be correctly embedded by now, replacing the original tissue.'

'*What?*' the bird screeched again, head jerking up and back.

'If you want to remove it,' Amorphia continued smoothly, 'you may, of course. You'll find it in your heart; primary aortic valve.'

The bird made a screaming noise and thrashed vertically into the air. Dajeil flinched, covering her face with her hands. Gravious wheeled in the air and beat hard for the nearest corridor. Amorphia watched it go from beneath cold, lid-hooded eyes. Dajeil put both her hands on her abdomen. She swallowed. Something black drifted down past her face and she picked it out of the air. A feather.

'Sorry about that,' Amorphia said.

'What . . . what was all that about?' Gelian asked.

Amorphia shrugged. 'The bird is a spy,' it said flatly. 'Has been from the first. It got its reports to the outside by encoding them on a bacterium and depositing them on the bodies of people about to be returned for re-awakening. I knew about it twenty years ago but let it pass after checking each signal; it was never allowed to know anything the disclosure of which could pose a threat. Its last message was the only one I ever altered. It helped facilitate our escape from the attentions of the *Yawning Angel*.' Amorphia grinned, almost childishly. 'There's nothing further it can do; I set the scout missile on it to punish it, really. If it distresses you, I'll call it off.'

Dajeil Gelian looked up into the steady grey eyes of the cadaverous, dark-clad creature for some time, quite as if she hadn't even heard the question.

'Amorphia,' she said. 'Please; what is going on? What is really going on?'

The ship's avatar looked pained for a moment. It looked away, towards the plant the scout missile had been hiding underneath. 'Whatever else,' it said awkwardly, formally, 'always remember that you are free to leave me at any time; this GCU is entirely at your disposal and no order or request of mine will affect its actions.' It looked back at her. It shook its head, but its voice sounded kinder when it spoke again; 'I'm sorry, Gelian; I still can't tell you very much. We are going to a place near a star called Esperi.' The creature hesitated, as though unsure, gaze roaming the floor and the nearby seats. 'Because I want to,' it said eventually, as though only realising this itself for the first time. 'Because there may be something I can do there.' It raised its arms out from its body, let them fall again. 'And in the meantime, we await a guest. Or at any rate, *I* await a guest. You may not care to.'

'Who?' the woman asked.

'Haven't you guessed?' the avatar said softly. 'Byr Genar-Hofoen.'

The woman looked down then, and her brows slowly creased, and the dark feather she had caught fell from her fingers.

III

[stuttered tight point, M32, tra. @n4.28.867.4406]
xLSV *Serious Callers Only*
    oEccentric *Shoot Them Later*
Have you heard? Was I not right about Genar-Hofoen? Do the times not now start to tally?
∞

[stuttered tight point, M32, tra. @n4.28.868.4886]
    xEccentric *Shoot Them Later*
        oLSV *Serious Callers Only*
Yes. Two three three. What's it doing – going for some kind of record? Yes yes yes all right you were correct about the human. But why didn't *you* have any warning of this?
∞

I don't know. Two decades of reliable but totally boring reports and then just when it might have been handy to know what the big bugger was really up to, the intelligence conduit caves in. All I can think of is that our mutual friend . . . oh, hell, might as well call it by its real name now I suppose . . . is that the *Sleeper Service* discovered the link – we don't know when – and waited until it had something to hide before it started messing with our intelligence.
∞

Yes, but what's it *doing*? We thought it was just being invited to join the Group out of politeness, didn't we? Suddenly it's acting like a fucking missile. What is it *up* to?
∞

This may seem rather obvious, but we could always just *ask* it.
∞

Tried that. Still waiting.
∞

Well you could have *said* . . .
∞

I beg your pardon. So now what?

∞

Now I get a load of bullshit from the *Steely Glint*. Excuse me.

∞

[tight beam, M32, tra. @n4.28.868.8243]
xLSV *Serious Callers Only*
  oGCV *Steely Glint*

Our mutual friend with the velocity obsession. This wouldn't be what we really expected, would it? Some private deal, by any chance?

∞

[tight beam, M32, tra. @n4.28.868.8499]
  xGCV *Steely Glint*
    oLSV *Serious Callers Only*

No it *isn't*! I'm getting fed up repeating this; I should have posted a general notice. No; we wanted the damn thing's views, some sort of entirely outside viewpoint, not it tearing off to anywhere near the Excession itself.

It was part of the Gang before, you know. We owed it that, no matter that it is now Eccentric.

Would that we had known how much . . .

Now we've got another horrendous variable screwing up our plans.

If you have any helpful suggestions I'd be pleased to hear them. If all you can do is make snide insinuations then it would probably benefit all concerned if you bestowed the fruits of your prodigious wit on someone with the spare time to give them the consideration they doubtless deserve.

∞

[stuttered tight point, M32, tra. @n4.28.868.8978]
xLSV *Serious Callers Only*
  oEccentric *Shoot Them Later*

(signal file attached) What did I tell you? I don't know about this. Looks suspicious to me.

∞

Hmm. And I don't know, either. I hate to say it, but it sounds genuine. Of course, if I prove to be wrong you will never confront me with this, ever, all right?

∞

If, after all this is over, we are both still in a position for me to

confer and you to benefit from such leniency, I shall be infinitely glad to extend such forbearance.

∞

Well, it could have been expressed more graciously, but I accept this moral blank cheque with all the deference it merits.

∞

I'm going to call the *Sleeper Service*. It won't take any notice of me but I'm going to call the meatworm anyway.

IV

Genar-Hofoen didn't take his pen terminal with him when he went out that evening, and the first place he visited in Night City was a Tier-Sintricate/Ishlorsinami Tech. store.

The woman was small for an Ishy, thought Genar-Hofoen. Still, she towered over him. She wore the usual long black robes and she smelled . . . musty. They sat on plain, narrow seats in a bubble of blackness. The woman was bent over a tiny fold-away screen balanced on her knees. She nodded and craned her body over towards him. Her hand extended, close to his left ear. A sequence of shining, telescoping rods extended from her fingers. She closed her eyes. In the dimness, Genar-Hofoen could see tiny lights flickering on the inside of her eyelids.

Her hand touched his ear, tickling slightly. He felt his face twitch. 'Don't move,' she said.

He tried to stay still. The woman withdrew her hand. She opened her eyes and peered at the point where the tips of three of the delicate rods met. She nodded and said, 'Hmm.'

Genar-Hofoen bent forward and looked too. He couldn't see anything. The woman closed her eyes again; her lid screens glowed again.

'Very sophisticated,' she said. 'Could have missed it.'

Genar-Hofoen looked at his right palm. 'Sure there's nothing on this hand?' he asked, recalling Verlioef Schung's firm handshake.

'As sure as I can be,' the woman said, withdrawing a small transparent container from her robe and dropping whatever she

had taken out of his ear into it. He still couldn't see anything there.

'And the suit?' he asked, fingering one lapel of his jacket.

'Clean,' the woman said.

'So that's it?' he asked.

'That is all,' she told him. The black bubble disappeared and
they were sitting in a small room whose walls were lined with
shelves overflowing with impenetrably technical-looking gear.

'Well, thanks.'

'That will be eight hundred Tier-sintricate-hour equivalents.'

'Oh, call it a round thousand.'

He walked along Street Six, in the heart of Night City Tier. There
were Night Cities throughout the developed galaxy; it was a kind
of condominium franchise, though nobody seemed to know to
whom the franchise belonged. Night Cities varied a lot from place
to place. The only certain things about them was that it would
always be night when you got there, and you'd have no excuse
for not having fun.

Night City Tier was situated on the middle level of the world, on
a small island in a shallow sea. The island was entirely covered by
a shallow dome ten kilometres across and two in height. Internally,
the City tended to take its cue from each year's Festival. The last
time Genar-Hofoen had been here the place had taken on the
appearance of a magnified oceanscape, all its buildings turned
into waves between one and two hundred metres tall. The theme
that year had been the Sea; Street Six had existed in the long
trough between two exponentially swept surges. Ripples on the
towering curves of the waves' surfaces had been balconies, burning
with lights. Luminous foam at each wave's looming, overhanging
crest had cast a pallid, sepulchral light over the winding street
beneath. At either end of the Street the broadway had risen to
meet crisscrossing wave fronts and connect – through oceanically
inauthentic tunnels – with other highways.

The theme this year was the Primitive and the City had
chosen to interpret this as a gigantic early electronic circuit
board; the network of silvery streets formed an almost perfectly
flat cityscape studded with enormous resistors, dense-looking,
centipedally legged flat-topped chips, spindly diodes and huge
semi-transparent valves with complicated internal structures, each

standing on groups of shining metal legs embedded in the network of the printed circuit. Those were the bits that Genar-Hofoen sort of half recognised from his History of Technical Stuff course or whatever it had been called when he'd been a student; there were lots of other jagged, knobbly, smooth, brightly coloured, matt black, shiny, vaned, crinkled bits he didn't know the purpose or the name of.

Street Six this year was a fifteen-metre wide stream of quickly flowing mercury covered with etched diamond sheeting; every now and again large coherent blobs of sparkling blue-gold went speeding along the mercury stream underfoot. Apparently these were symbolised electrons or something. The original idea had been to incorporate the mercury channels into the City transport system, but this had proved impractical and so they were there just for effect; the City tube system ran deep underground as usual. Genar-Hofoen had jumped on and off a few of the underground cars on his way to the City and on and off a couple more once he'd arrived, hoping to give the slip to anybody following. Having done this and had the tracer in his ear removed, he was happy he'd done the best he could to ensure that his evening's fun would take place unobserved by SC, though he wasn't particularly bothered if they were still watching him; it was more the principle of the thing. No point getting obsessive about it.

Street Six itself was packed with people, walking, talking, staggering, strolling, rolling along within bubblespheres, riding on exotically accoutred animals, riding in small carriages drawn by ysner-mistretl pairs and floating along under small vacuum balloons or in force field harnesses. Above, in the eternal night sky beneath the City's vast dome, this part of the evening's entertainment was being provided by a city-wide hologram of an ancient bomber raid.

The sky was filled with hundreds and hundreds of winged aircraft with four or six piston engines each, many of them picked out by searchlights. Spasms of light leaving black-on-black clouds and blossoming spheres of dimming red sparks were supposed to be anti-aircraft fire, while in amongst the bombers smaller single and twin-engined aircraft whizzed; the two sorts of aircraft were shooting at each other, the large planes from turrets and the smaller ones from their wings and noses. Gently curving lines of white, yellow and red tracer moved slowly across the sky and every now and again an aircraft seemed to catch fire and start to fall out of the sky; occasionally one would explode in mid air. All the time, the dark shapes of bombs could be glimpsed, falling to explode with bright flashes and vivid gouts of flame on parts of the City seemingly always just a little way off. Genar-Hofoen thought it all looked a little contrived, and he doubted there'd ever been such a concentrated air battle, or one in which the ground fire kept up while interceptor planes did their intercepting, but as a show it was undeniably impressive.

Explosions, gunfire and sirens sounded above the chatter of people filling the street and was sporadically submerged by the music spilling from the hundreds of bars and multifarious entertainment venues lining the Street. The air was full of half-strange, half-familiar, entirely enticing smells and wild pheremonic effects understandably banned everywhere else on Tier.

Genar-Hofoen strolled down the middle of the Street, a large glass of Tier 9050 in one hand, a cloud cane in the other and a small puff-creant nestling on one shoulder of his immaculately presented ownskin jacket. The 9050 was a cocktail which notoriously involved about three hundred separate processes to make, many of them involving unlikely and even unpleasant combinations of plants, animals and substances. The end result was an acceptable if strong-tasting drink composed largely of alcohol, no more, but you didn't really drink it for the internal effect, you drank it to show you could afford to; they put it in a special crystal field-goblet so you could show that you could. The name was meant to imply that after sinking a few you were ninety per cent certain to get laid and fifty per cent assured of ending up in legal trouble (or it may have been the other way round – Genar-Hofoen could never remember).

The cloud cane was a walking stick burning compressed pellets of a mildly and brief-acting psychotropic mixture; taking a suck on its pierced top cap was like sliding two distorting lenses in front of your eyes, sticking your head underwater and shoving a chemical factory up your nose while standing in a shifting gravity field.

The puff-creant was a small symbiont, half animal half vegetable, which you paid to squat on your shoulder and cough up your nose every time you turned your face towards it. The cough contained spores that could do any one of about thirty different and interesting things to your perceptions and moods.

Genar-Hofoen was particularly pleased with his new suit. It was made of his own skin, genetically altered in various subtle ways, specially vat-grown and carefully tailored to his exact specifications. He'd donated a few skin cells to – and left the order and payment with – a gene-tailor here on Tier two and a half years earlier when he was on his way to God'shole habitat. It had been a whim after a drinking session (as had an animated obscene tattoo he'd removed a month later). He hadn't really expected to pick the suit up for a while. Fortunately long-term fashions hadn't changed too much in the interim. The suit and its accompanying cloak looked terrific. He felt great.

SPADASSINS DIGLADIATE!   ZIFFIDAE AND XEBECS CONTEND!   GOLIARD DUNKING!

Slogans, signs, announcements, odours and personal greeters vied for attention, advertising emporia and venues. Stunning 'scapes and scenes played out in sensorium bubbles bulging out into the centre of the street, putting you instantly into bedrooms, feast-halls, arenae, harems, seaships, fair rides, space battles, states of temporary ecstasy; tempting, prompting, suggesting, offering, providing entrance, stimulating appetites, prompting desires; suggesting, propositioning, pandering.

RHYPAROGRAPHY! KELOIDAL ANAMNESIS! IVRESSE!

Genar-Hofoen walked through it all, soaking it all in, refusing all the offers and suggestions, politely turning down the overtures and come-ons, the recommendations and invitations.

ZUFULOS! ORPHARIONS! RASTRAE! NAUMACHIA HOURLY!

For now, he was content just to be here, walking, promenading, watching and being watched, sizing up and – with any luck – being sized up. It was evening – real evening – in this level of Tier, the time when Night City started to become busy; everywhere was open, nowhere was full, everybody wanted your custom, but nobody was really settling on a venue yet; just cruising, grazing, petting. Genar-Hofoen was happy to be part of that general drift; he loved this, he gloried in it. This was where he felt most himself. For now, there was simply no better place to be, and he believed in entering into the experience with all due and respectful intensity; these were his sort of people, here was where his sort of thing happened and this was his sort of place.

PILIOUS OMADHAUNS INVITE RASURE! LAGOPHTHALMISCITY GUAR-
ANTEED WHEN YOU SEE THE JEISTIECORS AND LORICAS OF OUR
MARTICHORASTIC MINIKINS!

He saw her outside a Sublimer sekos set under the rotundly
swollen bulk of a building shaped like a giant resistor. The
entrance to the cult's sacred place was a brightly shining loop,
like a thick but tiny rainbow layered in different shades of white.
Young Sublimers stood outside the enclosure, clad in glowing
white robes. The Sublimers – each tall and thin – glowed, too;
their skin glowed gently, pallid to the point of unhealthy-looking
bloodlessness. Their eyes shone, soft light spilling from the wide,
open whites, while the same half-silvery light was projected from
their teeth when they smiled. They smiled all the time, even when
they were talking. The woman was standing looking at the pair
of enthusiastically gesticulating Sublimers with an expression of
amused disdain.

She was tall, tawny-skinned. Her face was broad, her nose thin
and almost parallel with the planes of her cheeks; her arms were
crossed, her body tilted back from the two young people, her
weight taken on one black-booted heel as she looked down
that long nose at the shining Sublimers. Her eyes and her hair
looked as dark as the featureless shadowrobe which hid the rest
of her frame.

He stopped in the middle of the street and watched her arguing
with the two Sublimers for a few moments. Her gestures and the
way she held her body were different but the face was very similar
to the way he remembered her looking, forty years ago; just a
little older, perhaps. He had always wondered how much she'd
changed.

But it couldn't be her. Tishlin had said she was still on board
the *Sleeper*. They'd have mentioned if she'd left, wouldn't they?

He let a group of squatly chortling Bystlians pass him, then saun-
tered a little way back up the street, studying the architecture of the
giant valve bulging over it from the opposite pavement and sniffing
from his cloud cane in a vague, bored manner while watching a line
of dark bombs flit out of the darkness above to fall and detonate
somewhere beyond the line of barrel-like resistors that formed the
other side of the street; bright yellow-orange explosions lit up the
sky and debris rose slowly and fell. Further up the avenue, some
sort of commotion surrounded a large animal.

He turned and looked back down the crowded street. At that moment a giant blue-gold shape slid under his feet, rushing silently along within the mercury stream beneath the diamond plate. The girl arguing with the Sublimers turned, glancing at the street as the blob went gliding past. As she looked back to the two young glowing people she caught sight of him watching her. Her gaze settled on him for a moment and the flicker of an expression – a glimmer of recognition? – passed briefly over her face before she started talking to the Sublimers again. He hadn't had time to look away even if he'd wanted to.

He was wondering whether he ought to go over to her now, wait and see if she stepped back into the thoroughfare and maybe approach her then, or just walk away, when a tall girl in a glowing gown stepped up to him and said, 'May I help you, sir? You seem taken with our place of exaltation. Do you have any questions you'd like to ask? Is there anything I can do to enlighten you?'

He turned to the Sublimer. She was almost as tall as he; her face was pretty but somehow vacuous, though he knew that might have been prejudice on his part.

Sublimers had turned what was a normal but generally optional part of a species' choice of fate into a religion. Sublimers believed that everybody ought to Sublime, that every human, every animal, every machine and Mind ought to head straight for ultimate transcendence, leaving the mundane life behind and setting as direct a course as possible for nirvana.

People who joined the cult spent a year trying to persuade others of this before they Sublimed themselves, joining one of the sect's group-minds to contemplate irreality. The few drones, other AIs and Minds that became persuaded of the merit of this course of action through the arguments of the Sublimers tended to do what any other machine did on such occasions and disappear in the direction of the nearest Sublimed Entity, though one or two stuck around in a pre-Sublimed state long enough to help the cause. In general, though, the cult was regarded as rather a pointless one. Subliming was seen as something that usually happened to entire societies, and more as a practical lifestyle alteration than a religious commitment; more like moving house than entering a sacred order.

'Well, I don't know,' Genar-Hofoen said, sounding wary. 'What exactly do you people believe in again?'

The Sublimer looked up the street behind him. 'Oh, we believe in the power of the Sublime,' she said. 'Let me tell you more.' She glanced up the avenue again. 'Oh; perhaps we ought to get off the street, don't you think?' She held out her hand and took a step back towards the pavement.

Genar-Hofoen looked back, to where things were getting noisy. The giant animal he'd noticed earlier – a sexipedal pondrosaur – was advancing slowly down the avenue in the midst of a retinue and a crowd of spectators. The shaggy, brown-furred animal was six metres tall, splendidly liveried with long, gaudy banners and ribbons and commanded by a garishly uniformed mahout brandishing a fiery mace. The beast was surmounted by a glitteringly black and silver cupola whose bulbously filigreed windows gave no hint of who or what might be inside; similarly ornamented bowls covered the great animal's eyes. It was attended by five loping kliestrithrals, each black tusked creature pawing at the street surface and snorting and held on a tight lead by a burly hire guard. A knot of people held the procession up; the pondrosaur paused and put its long head back to let out a surprisingly soft, subdued roar, then it adjusted its eye-cups with its two leg-thick fore-limbs and bobbed its head to either side. The gaggle of promenaders began to disperse and the great beast and its escorts moved forward again.

'Hmm, yes,' Genar-Hofoen said. 'Perhaps we'd better move out the way.' He finished the 9050 and looked round for a place to deposit the empty container.

'Please; allow me.' The Sublimer girl took the field-goblet from him as though it was some sort of holy object. Genar-Hofoen followed her onto the sidewalk; she put an arm through his and they proceeded slowly towards the entrance to the sekos, where the woman was still standing talking to the other two Sublimers with her look of ironic curiosity.

'Have you heard of Sublimers before?' the girl on his arm asked.

'Oh, yes,' he said, watching the other woman's face as they approached. They stopped on the pavement outside the Sublimer building, entering a hushfield in which the only sound was gently tinkling music and a background of waves on a beach. 'You believe everybody should just sort of disappear up their own arses, don't you?' he asked with every appearance of innocence. He was only a few metres from the woman in the shadowrobe, though the compartmented hushfield meant he couldn't hear what she was saying. Her face was much like he remembered it; the eyes and mouth were the same. She had never worn her hair up like that, but even its shade of black-blue was the same.

'Oh, no!' the Sublimer girl said, her expression terribly serious. 'What we believe in takes one completely *away* from such bodily concerns . . .'

Out of the corner of his eye he could see up the street, where the pondrosaur was shuffling forwards through a thick crowd of admirers. He smiled at the Sublimer girl as she talked on. He shifted a little so that he could see the other woman better.

No, it wasn't her. Of course it wasn't. She'd have recognised him, she'd have reacted by now. Even if she'd been trying to pretend she hadn't seen him he'd have been able to tell; she'd never been very good at hiding her feelings from anybody, least of all from him. She glanced at him again, then quickly away. He felt a sudden, unbidden sensation of fearful pleasure, a jolt of excitement which left his skin tingling.

'. . . highest expression of our quintessential urge to be greater than we . . .' He nodded and looked at the Sublimer girl, who was still babbling away. He frowned a little and stroked his chin with his free hand, still nodding. He kept watching the other woman. Out on the street, the pondrosaur and its retinue had come to a stop almost alongside them; a Tier Sintricate was hovering level with the giant animal's mahout, who seemed to be arguing angrily with it.

The woman was smiling at the other two Sublimers with what appeared to be an expression of tolerant ridicule. She kept her eyes on the Sublimer fellow doing the talking at that point, but took a long, deep breath, and – just as she let it out – glanced at Genar-Hofoen again with the briefest of smiles and a flick of her eyebrows before looking back at the Sublimers and tipping her head just a little to one side.

He wondered. Would SC really go this far to keep him under their control, or at least under their eye? How likely was it that he should find somebody who looked so much like her? He supposed there must be hundreds of people who bore a passing resemblance to Dajeil Gelian; perhaps there were even a few who had heard something about her and deliberately assumed her appearance;

that happened all the time with genuinely famous people and just because he'd never heard of anybody taking on Dajeil's looks didn't mean nobody had ever done so. If this person was one of them, it was just possible he would have to be on his guard . . .

'. . . personal ambition or the desire to better oneself or to provide opportunities for one's children is but a pale reflection of, compared to the ultimate transcendence which true Subliming offers; for, as it is written . . .'

Genar-Hofoen leant closer to the girl talking to him and tapped her lightly on the shoulder. 'I'm sure,' he said quietly. 'Would you excuse me for just a moment?'

He took the two steps over to the woman in the shadowrobe. She turned her head from the two Sublimers and smiled politely at him. 'Excuse me,' he asked. 'Don't I know you from somewhere?' He grinned as he said it, acknowledging both the well-worn nature of the line and the fact that neither he nor she was really interested in what the Sublimers had to say.

She nodded her head politely to him. 'I don't think so,' she said. Her voice was higher than Dajeil's; more girlish, and with a quite different accent. 'Though if we had met and you hadn't altered in some way and I'd forgotten, certainly I'd be far too ashamed to admit it.' She smiled. He did the same. She frowned. 'Unless . . . do you live on Tier?'

'Just passing through,' he told her. A bomber, in flames, tore past just overhead and exploded in a burst of light behind the Sublimer building. On the street, the argument around the pondrosaur seemed to be getting more heated; the animal itself was staring intently at the Sintricate and its mahout was standing up on its neck, pointing the flaming mace at the darkly spiny being to emphasise whatever points he was making.

'But I've been this way before,' Genar-Hofoen said. 'Perhaps we bumped into each other then.'

She nodded thoughtfully. 'Perhaps,' she conceded.

'Oh, you two know each other?' said the young Sublimer man she'd been talking to. 'Well, many people find that Subliming in the company of a loved one or just somebody they know is—'

'Do you play Calascenic Crasis?' she asked, cutting across the young Sublimer. 'You may have seen me at a game here.' She put her head back, looking down that long nose at him. 'If so, I'm disappointed you left it till now to say hello.'

'Ah!' the Sublimer lad said. 'Games; an expression of the urge to enter into worlds beyond ourselves! Another—'

'I've never even heard of the game,' he confessed. 'Do you recommend it?'

'Oh yes,' she said, and sounded ironic. 'It benefits all who play.'

'Well, I'm always willing to entertain some new experience. Perhaps you could teach me.'

'Ah, now; the *ultimate* new experience—' began the Sublimer lad.

Genar-Hofoen turned to him and said, 'Oh, shut up!' It had been an instinctive reaction, and for a moment he was worried he might have said the wrong thing, but she didn't seem to be regarding the young Sublimer's hurt look with any great degree of sympathy.

She looked back to him. 'All right,' she said. 'You stand me my stake and I'll teach you Crasis.'

He smiled, wondering if that had been too easy. 'It's a deal,' he said. He waved the cloud cane under his nose and took a deep breath, then bowed. 'My name's Byr.'

'Pleased to meet you.' She nodded again. 'Call me Flin,' she said, and, taking hold of the cane, waved it under her own nose.

'Shall we, Flin?' he said, and indicated the street beyond, where the pondrosaur had sunk to its belly, its four legs doubled up underneath it and both fore-limbs folded beneath its chin, as though bored. Two Sintricates were shouting at the enraged mahout, who was shaking the flaming mace at them. The hire guards were looking nervous and patting the restless kliestrithrals.

'Certainly.'

'Remember where you met!' the Sublimer called after them. 'Subliming is the ultimate meeting of souls, the pinnacle of . . .' They left the hushfield. His voice was drowned out by the thudding of projected anti-aircraft fire as they walked along the pavement.

'So, where are we going?' he asked her.

'Well, you can take me for a drink and then we'll hit a Crasis bar I know. Sound all right?'

'Sounds fine. Shall we take a trap?' he said, pointing a little way up the street to a two-wheeled open vehicle waiting by the kerb. A ysner-mistretl pair were harnessed between the traces, the ysner craning its long neck down to peck at a feed bag in the gutter, the small, smartly uniformed mistretl on its back looking around alertly and tapping its thumbs together.

'Good idea,' she said. They walked up to the trap and climbed aboard. 'The Collyrium Lounge,' the woman said to the mistretl as they sat in the rear of the small vehicle. It saluted and pulled a whip out from its fancy jerkin. The ysner made a sighing noise.

The trap shook suddenly. A great deep burst of noise came from the street behind them. They all looked round. The pondrosaur was rearing up, bellowing; its mahout nearly fell off its neck. His mace tumbled from his grasp and bounced on the street. Two of the kliestrithrals jumped up and leapt into the crowd, snarling and dragging their handlers with them. The two Sintricates who'd been arguing with the mahout rose quickly into the air out of the way; people in float harnesses took avoiding action through the confusion of searchlight beams and anti-aircraft fire. Flin and Genar-Hofoen watched people scatter in all directions as the pondrosaur leapt forward with surprising agility and started charging down the street towards them. The mahout clung desperately to the beast's ears, screeching at it to stop. The stabilised black and silver cupola on the animal's back seemed to float along above it until the animal's increasing speed forced it to oscillate from side to side. At Genar-Hofoen's side, Flin seemed frozen.

Genar-Hofoen glanced round at the mistretl. 'Well,' he said, 'let's get going.' The little mistretl blinked quickly, still staring up the street. Another bellow echoed off the surrounded buildings. Genar-Hofoen looked back again.

The charging pondrosaur reached up with one fore-limb and ripped its eye-cups off to reveal huge, faceted blue eyes like chunks of ancient ice. With its other limb it gripped the mahout by one shoulder and wrenched him off its neck; he wriggled and flailed but it brushed him to one side and onto the pavement; he landed running, fell and rolled. The pondrosaur itself thundered on down the street; people threw themselves out of its way. Somebody in a bubblesphere didn't move fast enough; the giant transparent ball was kicked to the side, smashing into a hot food-stall; flames leapt from the wreckage.

'Shit,' Genar-Hofoen said as the giant bore down upon them. He turned to the mistretl driver again. He could see the face of the ysner, turned back to look up the street behind too, its big face expressing only mild surprise. 'Move!' he shouted.

The mistretl nodded. 'Goo' i'ea,' it chirped. It reached behind to slip a knot on the rear of the ysner and jabbed its bootheels into the animal's lower neck. The startled ysner took off, leaving the trap behind; the vehicle tipped forward as the ysner-mistretl pair disappeared down the rapidly clearing street. Genar-Hofoen and Flin were thrown forward in a tangle of harnesses. He heard her shout, 'Fuck!' then go *oof* as they hit the street.

Something hit him hard on the head. He blacked out for a moment then came to looking up at a huge face, a monstrous face, gazing down at him with huge prismed blue eyes. Then he saw the woman's face. The face of Dajeil Gelian. She had blood on her top lip. She looked groggily at him and then turned to gaze up at the huge animal face looking down at them. There was a sort of buzzing sensation from somewhere; Genar-Hofoen felt his legs go numb. The woman collapsed over his legs. He felt sick. Lines of red dots crossing the sky floated behind his eyelids when they closed. When he forced his eyes open again, she was there again. Somebody looking like Dajeil Gelian who wasn't her. Except it wasn't Flin either. She was dressed differently, she was taller and her expression was . . . not the same. And anyway, Flin was still draped unconscious over his legs.

He really didn't understand what was going on. He shook his head. This hurt.

The girl who wasn't Dajeil or Flin stooped quickly, looked into his eyes, whirled the cloak off her shoulders and onto the street beside him in one movement, then rolled him over onto it, heaving Flin's immobile body out of the way as she did so. He tried waving his arms around but it didn't do much good.

The cloak went rigid underneath him and floated into the air, wrapping round him. He cried out and tried to fight against its enclosing black folds, but the buzzing came again and his vision faded even before the cloak finished wrapping itself round him.

8

Killing Time

I

The usual way to explain it was by analogy; this was how the idea was introduced to you as a child. Imagine you were travelling through space and you came to this planet which was very big and almost perfectly smooth and on which there lived creatures who were composed of one layer of atoms; in effect, two-dimensional. These creatures would be born, live and die like us and they might well possess genuine intelligence. They would, initially, have no idea or grasp of the third dimension, but they would be able to live perfectly well in their two dimensions. To them, a line would be like a wall across their world (or, from the end, it would look like a point). An unbroken circle would be like a locked room.

Perhaps, if they were able to build machines which allowed them to journey at great speed along the surface of their planet – which to them would be their universe – they would go right round the planet and come back to where they had started from. More likely, they would be able to work this out from theory. Either way, they would realise that their universe was both closed, and curved, and that there was, in fact, a third dimension, even if they had no practical access to it. Being familiar with the idea of circles, they would probably christen the shape of their universe a 'hypercircle' rather than inventing a new word. The three-dimensional people would, of course, call it a sphere.

The situation was similar for people living in three dimensions. At some point in any civilisation starting to become advanced it was realised that if you set off into space in what appeared to be a perfectly straight line, eventually you would arrive back at where you started, because your three-dimensional universe was really a four-dimensional shape; being familiar with the idea of spheres, people tended to christen this shape a hypersphere.

Usually around the same point in a society's development it was understood that – unlike the planet where the two-dimensional creatures lived – space was not simply curved into a hypersphere, it was also expanding; gradually increasing in size like a soap-bubble on the end of a straw which somebody was blowing into. To a four-dimensional being looking from far enough away, the three-dimensional galaxies would look like tiny designs imprinted onto the surface of that expanding bubble, each of them, generally, heading away from all the others because of the hypersphere's general expansion, but – like the shifting whorls and loops of colour visible on the skin of a soap bubble – able to slide and move around on that surface.

Of course, the four-dimensional hypersphere had no equivalent of the straw, blowing air in from outside. The hypersphere was expanding all by itself, like a four-dimensional explosion, with the implication that, once, it had been simply a point; a tiny seed which had indeed exploded. That detonation had created – or at least had produced – matter and energy, time and the physical laws themselves. Later – cooling, coalescing and changing over immense amounts of time and expansion – it had given rise to the cool, ordered, three-dimensional universe which people could see around them.

Eventually in the progress of a technologically advanced society, occasionally after some sort of limited access to hyperspace, more usually after theoretical work, it was realised that the soap bubble was not alone. The expanding universe lay inside a larger one, which in turn was entirely enclosed by a bubble of space-time with a still greater diameter. The same applied within the universe you happened to find yourself on/in; there were smaller, younger universes inside it, nested within like layers of paper round a much-wrapped spherical present.

In the very centre of all the concentric, inflating universes lay the place they had each originated from, where every now and again a cosmic fireball blinked into existence, detonating once more to produce another universe, its successive outpourings of creation like the explosions of some vast combustion engine, and the universes its pulsing exhaust.

There was more; complications in seven dimensions and beyond that involved a giant torus on which the 3-D universe could be described as a circle, contained and containing other nested tori, with further implications of whole populations of such meta-Realities ... but the implications of multiple, concentric, sequential universes was generally considered enough to be going on with for the moment.

What everybody wanted to know was whether there was any way of travelling from one universe to another. Between any pair of universes there was more than just empty hyperspace; there was a thing called an energy grid. It was useful – strands of it could help power ships, and it had been used as a weapon – but it was also an obstacle, and – by all accounts so far – one which had proved impenetrable to intelligent investigation. Certain black holes appeared to be linked to the grid and perhaps therefore to the universe beyond, but nobody had ever made it intact into one, or ever reappeared in any recognisable form. There were white holes, too; ferociously violent sources spraying torrents of energy into the universe with the power of a million suns and which also seemed to be linked to the grid . . . but no body, no ship or even information had ever been observed appearing from their tumultuous mouths; no equivalent of an airborne bacteria, no word, no language, just that incoherent scream of cascading energies and super energetic particles.

The dream that every Involved had, which virtually every technologically advanced civilisation clove to with almost religious faith, was that one day it would be possible to travel from one universe to another, to step up or down through those expanding bubbles, so that – apart from anything else – one need never suffer the final fate of one's own universe. To achieve that would surely be to Sublime, truly to Transcend, to consummate the ultimate Surpassing and accomplish the ultimate empowerment.

The River class General Contact Unit *Fate Amenable To Change* lay in space. It was locally stationary, taking its reference from the Excession. The Excession was equally static, taking its reference from the star Esperi. The entity sat there, a few light minutes away, a featureless dot on the skein of real space with a single equally dull-looking strand of twisted, compressed space-time fabric leading down to the lower layer of energy grid . . . and a second leading upwards to the higher layer.

The Excession was doing exactly what it had been doing for the past two weeks; nothing. The *Fate Amenable To Change* had carried out all the standard initial measurements and observations of the entity, but had been very forcefully advised indeed not to do any more; no direct contact was to be attempted, not even by probes, smaller craft or drones. In theory it could disobey; it was its own ship, it could make up its own mind ... but in practice it had to heed the advice of those who knew if not more than it, better than it.

Collective responsibility. Also known as sharing the blame.

So all it had done after the first exciting bit, when it had been the centre of attention and everybody had wanted to know all it could tell them about the thing it had found, had been to hang around here, still at the focus of events in a sense, but also feeling somehow ignored.

Reports. It filed reports. It had long since stopped trying to make them different or original.

The ship was bored. It was also aware of a continuing under-current of fear; a real emotion that it was by turns annoyed at, ashamed of and indifferent to, according to its mood.

It waited. It watched. Beyond it, around it, most of its small fleet of modules and satellites, a few of its most space-capable drones and a variety of specialist devices it had constructed specifically for the purpose also floated, watching and waiting. Inside the vessel its human crew discussed the situation, monitored the data coming in from the ship's own sensors and those coming in from the small cloud of dispersed machines. The ship passed some of the time by making up elaborate games for the humans to play. Meanwhile it kept up its observation of the Excession and scanned the space around, waiting for the first of the other ships to arrive.

Sixteen days after the Culture craft had stumbled upon the Excession and six days after the discovery had been made public, the first ship appeared, its presence noted initially within the *Fate Amenable To Change*'s main sensor array. The GCU moved one state of readiness higher, signalled what was happening to the *Ethics Gradient* and the *Not Invented Here*, fastened its track scanner on the incoming signal, began a tentative reconfiguration of its remote sensor platforms and started to move towards the newcomer round the perimeter of the Excession's safe limit at a speed it hoped was pitched nicely between polite deliberation and alarm-raising urgency. It sent a standard interrogatory signal burst to the approaching craft.

The vessel was the *Sober Counsel*, an Explorer Ship of the Zetetic Elench's Stargazer Clan's Fifth fleet. The *Fate Amenable To Change* felt relief; the Elench were friends.

Identifications completed, the two ships rendezvoused, locally stationary just a few tens of kilometres apart on the outskirts of the safe limit from the Excession the Culture vessel had set.

~ Welcome.

~ Thank you. . . . Dear holy stasis. Is that thing attached to the grid, or is it my sensors?

~ If it's your sensors, it's mine too. Impressive, isn't it? Becomes greatly less so once you've sat looking at it for a week or two, take my word for it. I hope you're just here to observe. That's all I'm doing.

~ Waiting on the big guns?

~ That's right.

~ When do they arrive?

~ That's restricted. Promise this won't go outside the Elench?

~ Promise.

~ A Medium SV gets here in twelve days; the first General SV in fourteen, then one every few days for a week, then one a day, then several a day, by which time I expect a few other Involveds will probably have started to show. Don't ask me what the GSVs will consider a quorum before they act. How about you?

~ Can we talk off the record, just the two of us?

~ All right.

~ We have another ship heading here, two days away still. The rest of the fleet are still undecided, though they have stopped drawing further away. We lost a ship somewhere round here. The *Peace Makes Plenty*.

~ Ah. Did you indeed? About when?

~ Some time between 28.789 and 805.

~ This is still confidential within the Elench, then?

~ Yes. We searched this volume as best we could for two weeks but found nothing. What brought you here?

~ Suggestion by my home GSV, the *Ethics Gradient*. That was in 841. Wanted me to look in the Upper Leaf Swirl Cloud Top. No reason given. Bumped into this on the way there. That's all I know. (And the *Fate Amenable To Change* thought coldly about that suggestion. The Cloud Top volume was a long way from here, but that meant nothing. What mattered was that it had been given a relatively precise location within the Cloud Top to head for, and been given the subtlest of hints to watch out for anything interesting while en route. Given where it had been when it had received the suggestion from its home GSV, its route had inevitably taken it near the Excession. . . . Thirty-six days had elapsed between the date the Elench knew they might have lost a ship and the time when it had been dispatched on what was starting to look a little like a set-up . . . It wondered what had taken place in between. Could some Elench ship have leaked word to the Culture? But then how had such a leak apparently produced such accuracy, given that it, a single ship, had practically run straight into the damn Excession, while the Elench had spent two weeks here with seven-eighths of a full fleet and spotted nothing?) ~ Feel free to ask the *Ethics Gradient* what prompted its suggestion, it added.

~ Thank you.

~ You're welcome.

~ I'd like to try contacting the Excession. This might be where our comrade disappeared. At the least it might have some information. At most, and for all we know, our ship is still in there. I want to talk to it, maybe send a drone-ship in if it doesn't reply.

~ Madness. This thing is welded into the grids, both directions. Know anything that can do that? Me neither. I'm not even going to *start* feeling safe until there's a fleet of GSVs round here. Heck, I was pleased to see you there; Company at last, I thought. Somebody to pass the time with while I sit out my lonely vigil. Now you want to start poking this thing with a stick. Are you crazy?

~ No, but we might have a ship in distress in there. I can't just sit here doing nothing. Have you attempted to contact the entity?

~ No. I sent back a pro forma to its initial Hello, but . . . wait a moment. Look at the signal it sent (signal enclosed).

~ There. You see? I told you! That was probably an Elench-sourced handshake burst.

~ Meatshit. Yes, I see. Well, maybe your pal did find the damn thing first, but if it did, it probably did exactly what you're proposing to do. And it's gone. Disappeared. You seeing where this is leading?

~ I intend to be careful.

~ Uh-huh. Was your comrade vessel notoriously careless?

~ Indeed not.

~ Well then.

~ I appreciate your concern. Was there any sign of contention in the volume when you got here? Emergency or distress signals? Voyage Event Record Ejectiles?

~ There was this, here (material analysis/location enclosed), but if you want to mention any of this stuff on record you'd better make it look like you just stumbled across the debris, all right?

~ Thank you. Yes, of course. ... Looks like one of our little-drones was caught up in something. Hmm. Sort of ... smells subsidiary somehow, don't you think?

~ Possibly. I know what you mean. It's untidy.

~ Back on record?

~ Okay.

~ I hereby give notice I intend to attempt to contact the entity.

~ I beg you not to. Let me make a request that you be allowed to take part in the Culture investigation when it takes place. I'm sure there is every chance you will be welcome to share in the relevant data.

~ I'm sorry, I have my own reasons for considering the matter urgent.

~ Off record again?

~ All right.

~ My records show you to be – to all intents and purposes – identical to the *Peace Makes Plenty.*

~ Yes. Go on?

~ Don't you see? Look, if this thing jeopardised your comrade with no more fuss than an escaped little-drone, what's it going to be able to do now that it's had a chance to pick over the structure and mind-set of your sister craft for at least sixty-six days?

~ I have the benefit of being forewarned. And the entity may not have been able entirely to take over the *Peace Makes Plenty* yet. The ship might be inside there, under siege. Perhaps all the entity's intellectual energies are being absorbed in the maintenance of that blockade. That being the case my intervention may lift the siege and free my comrade.

~ Cousin, this is self-delusion. We have already dealt with the issue of the minimal extra safeguarding provided by you having been alerted to the entity's potential danger; the *Peace Makes Plenty* could hardly have been less prepared. I appreciate your feelings towards your fellow craft and Fleet-mate, but it rends the bounds of possibility to believe that something capable of perpetuating E-grid links in both directions is going to be substantially troubled by craft with the capabilities of ourselves. The Excession has not troubled me but then I did not trouble it;

we exchanged greetings, no more. What you propose might be construed as interference, or even as a hostile act. I have accepted a duty to observe and won't be able to help you if you get into trouble. Please, *please* reconsider.

~ I take your point. I still intend to attempt communication with the entity but I shall not recommend that a drone approach be made. I have to put all this to my humans, of course, but they usually concur.

~ Naturally. I urge you to argue strongly against sending any object towards the Excession, should your human crew suggest this.

~ I'll see which way they jump. This could take a while; they like arguing.

~ Don't be in any rush on my account.

II

The Torturer class Rapid Offensive Unit *Killing Time* swung out of the darkness between the stars and braked hard, scrubbing velocity off in a wild, extravagant flare of energies which briefly left a livid line of disturbance across the surface of the energy grid. It came to a local-relative stop a light month out from the cold, dark, slowly tumbling body that was the ship store Pittance, some way beyond the outside edge of the tiny world's spherical cloud of defence/attack mechanisms. It flashed a Permission-To-Approach signal at the rock.

The reply took longer than it would have expected.

tight beam, M16, tra. @n4.28.882.1398]
   xPittance Store
      oROU *Killing Time*
   (Permission withheld.) What is your business here?
∞

[tight beam, M16, tra. @n4.28.882.1399]
xROU *Killing Time*
   oPittance Store

Just stopping by to make sure you're all right. What's the problem? (PTA burst.)

∞

   (Permission withheld.) Who sent you?

∞

What makes you think I had to be sent? (PTA burst.)

∞

   (Permission withheld.) I am a restricted entity. I have no duty or obligation to permit any other craft to approach my vicinity. Traditionally Stores are only approached on a need-to basis. What is your need?

∞

There is some activity in the volume which includes your current location. People are concerned. A neighbourly check-up seemed timely. (PTA burst.)

∞

   (Permission withheld.) Such concern would be better expressed by leaving me alone. Your visit might even attract attention, all of which I find intrinsically unwelcome. Please leave immediately, and kindly create less of a display on departure than you made on your arrival.

∞

I consider it my duty to assess your current state of integrity. I regret to say I have not been reassured by your recalcitrant attitude. You will do me the minimally polite honour of allowing me to interface with your independent external event-monitoring systems. (PTA burst.)

∞

   (Permission withheld.) No! I shall not! I am perfectly able to take care of myself and there is nothing of interest contained within my associated independent security systems. Any attempt to access them without my permission will be treated as an act of aggression. This is your last chance to quit my jurisdiction before I emit a protest-registering signal concerning your unreasonable and boorish behaviour.

∞

I have already composed my own report detailing your bizarre and uncooperative attitude and copying this signal exchange. I shall release the compac immediately if a satisfactory reply is not received to this message. (PTA burst.)

. . .
Acknowledge signal.
. . .
Acknowledge signal!
I repeat: I have already composed my own report detailing your bizarre and uncooperative attitude. I shall release the compac immediately if a satisfactory reply is not received to this message. I shall not warn you again. (PTA burst.)
∞

(Permission granted.) Purely in the interests of a quiet life, only on condition that my associate security monitoring systems remain untouched, and under protest.
∞

Thank you; of course.
Under way. Heaving to at 2km from your rotational envelope in thirty minutes.

~ Thanks to your delaying tactics, Commander, it probably already suspects something and may well have signalled back to whoever sent it already. Think yourself lucky we have as much as half an hour to prepare; it is being cautious.

They had re-sealed the airlocks from the accommodation section and pumped in some real atmosphere. Commander Risingmoon Parchseason IV of the Farsight tribe had been able to shed his space suit some days earlier. The gravity was still far too mild but it was better than floating. The Commander clicked his beak at the image on the screen presented by the mobile command centre they'd set up in what had been the humans' pool/growing unit. A lieutenant at the Commander's side spoke quietly but urgently to the twenty other Affronters distributed throughout the base's caverns, letting them know what was going on.

The Commander looked back impatiently, waiting for the servant who'd been sent to fetch his suit the instant the Culture warship had appeared on the other craft's sensors. On secondary screens, he could see suited Affronter technicians, their machines and some slaved drones working on the exteriors of the stored ships. They had about half of them ready to get out and go; a decent fleet, but they needed the rest, and preferably all at once, and as a complete surprise to the Culture and everybody else.

'Can't you destroy it?' the Commander asked the traitor Culture vessel. He glanced at the status of the nearest Affront vessels. Far too far away. They had avoided approaching Pittance in case they could be monitored by other Culture craft.

The *Attitude Adjuster* didn't like vocalising; it preferred to print out its side of a conversation:

~ If it gets to within a few minutes, yes, perhaps. It might have been relatively easy, if I could have caught it completely unawares. However, I doubt that was ever very likely given that it must have been suspicious to come here in the first place and is almost certainly completely out of the question now.

'What about the ships we've cleared?'

~ Commander, they haven't been woken up yet. Until I've done that they're useless. And if we wake half of them now they'll have too long to think, too much time to do their own checking around before we need them for the main action. Our project must all happen in a rush, in a state of perceived chaos, panic and urgency, or it cannot happen effectively at all.

There was a pause while the message scrolled along and off the screen, then:

~ Commander, I suspect this will be a formality, but I have to ask; do you wish to admit to what has happened here and turn your command over without a fight to the ROU *Killing Time*? This will probably be our last opportunity to avoid hostilities.

'Don't be ridiculous,' the Commander said sourly.

~ I thought not. Very well. I shall vector away in the skein-shadow of the rock and try to loop round behind the ROU. Let it enter the defence system. Wait until it's a week inside, no more, and then set everything you have upon it. I urge you again, Commander; turn over the tactical command apparatus to me.

'No,' the Commander said. 'Leave and do whatever you think will best jeopardise the Culture vessel. I shall allow it to arrive at a point three weeks in and then attack.'

~ I am on my way. Do *not* let the ship come within a light week of the store itself, Commander. I know how it will think if it is attacked; this is not some genteel Orbital Mind or a nicely timorous General Contact Unit; this is a Culture warship showing every sign of being fully armed and ready to press matters.

'What, creeping in as it is?' the Commander sneered.

~ Commander, you would be amazed and appalled at how few bright sides there are concerning the appearance and behaviour of a warship like this. The fact it's not charging in through the defence screen and metaphorically skidding to a stop is almost certainly a bad sign; it probably means it's one of the wily ones. I repeat; do *not* wait until it is most of the way into the defence system before opening fire. Assaulted so far inside the defensive field it may well figure that it has no chance of escape and so might as well continue towards you and attack, and at that sort of range it would stand a decent chance of being able to obliterate the entire store and all the ships within it.

The Commander felt almost annoyed that the ship hadn't appealed to his own personal sense of self-preservation. 'Very well,' he snapped. 'Half way in; two weeks.'

~ Commander, *no*! That is still too close. If we cannot destroy the ship in the first instant of the engagement it must be presented with a reasonable opportunity to escape, otherwise it may go for glory rather than attempt to extricate itself.

'But if it escapes it can alert the Culture!'

~ If our attack is not immediately successful it will signal elsewhere anyway, assuming it has not already done so. We shall not be able to stop it. In that case, we shall have been discovered ... though with any luck that will only put our plans out by a few days. Believe me, the craft's physical escape will not bring the Culture here any quicker than a signal would. You will be putting this entire mission in jeopardy if you allow the vessel to come within more than three light weeks of the store.

'All right!' the Commander spat. He flicked a tentacle over the glowing board of the command desk. The communication link was cut. The *Attitude Adjuster* did not attempt to re-establish it.

'Your suit, sir,' said a voice from behind. The Commander whirled round to find the gelding midshipman – uniformed but not suited – with his space suit in his limbs.

'Oh, at *last*!' the Commander screamed; he flicked a tentacle at the creature's eye stalks; the blow bounced them back off its casing. The gelding whimpered and fell back, gas sac deflating. The Commander grabbed his suit and pulled himself inside it. The midshipman staggered along the floor, half blinded.

The Commander ordered his lieutenant to reconfigure the command desk. From here they could personally control all the systems that had been entrusted by the Culture to the Mind which the traitor ship had killed. The command desk was like an ultimate instrument of destruction; a giant keyboard to play death tunes on. Some of the keys, admittedly, had to be left to trigger themselves once set, but these controls really did *control*.

The holo screen projected a sphere out towards the Commander. The globe displayed the volume of real space around Pittance, with tiny green, white and gold flecks representing major components of the defence system. A dull blue dot represented the approaching warship, coasting in towards them. Another dot, bright red, on the directly opposite side of the ship store from the blue dot and much closer – though drawing quickly away – was the traitor ship *Attitude Adjuster*.

Another screen alongside showed an abstracted hyperspatial view of the same situation, indicating the two ships on different surfaces of the skein. A third screen showed a transparent abstract of Pittance itself, detailing its ship-filled caverns and surface and internal defence systems.

The Commander finished getting into his space suit and powering it up. He settled back into position. He reviewed the situation. He knew better than to try to conduct matters at a tactical level, but he appreciated the strategic influence he could wield here. He was dreadfully tempted, all the same, to take personal control and fire all the defence systems personally, but he was aware of the enormous responsibility he had been given in this mission and was equally conscious that he had been carefully selected for this task. He had been chosen because he knew when not to – what had the traitor ship called it? Go for glory. He knew when not to go for glory. He knew when to back off, when to take advice, when to retreat and regroup.

He flicked open the communicator channel to the traitor ship. 'Did the warship stop exactly a light month out?' he asked.

~ Yes.

'That's thirty-two standard Culture days.'

~ Correct.

'Thank you.' He closed the channel.

He looked at the lieutenant at his side. 'Set everything within range to open fire on the warship the instant it crosses the eight-point one days' limit.' He sat back as the lieutenant's limbs flickered over the holo displays, putting his command into effect. Only just in time, the Commander noted. He'd been longer getting into his suit than he'd thought.

'Forty seconds, sir,' the lieutenant said.

'. . . Give it just enough time to relax,' the Commander said, more to himself than to anybody else. 'If that is how these things work . . .'

Exactly eight and a tenth light days in from the position the Rapid Offensive Unit *Killing Time* had held while negotiating its permission to approach, space all around the blue dot on the screen scintillated abruptly as a thousand hidden devices of a dozen different types suddenly erupted into life in a precisely ordered sequence of destruction; in the real-space holo sphere it looked like a miniaturised stellar cluster suddenly bursting into existence all around the blue dot. The trace disappeared instantly inside a brilliant sphere of light. In the hyperspace holo sphere, the dot lasted a little longer; slowed down, it could be seen firing some munitions back for a microsecond or so, then it too disappeared in the wash of energies bursting out of the real-space skein and into hyperspace in twin bulging plumes.

The lights in the accommodation space flickered and dimmed as monumental amounts of power suddenly diverted to the rock's own long-range weaponry.

The Commander left the comm channel to the traitor ship open. Its own course had altered the instant the defence weaponry had been unleashed; now its course was hooked, changing colour from red to blue and curving up and round and vectoring in hyperspace too, looping round to the point where the slowly fading and dissipating radiation shells marked the focus of the system's annihilatory power.

A flat screen to the Commander's left wavered, as if some still greater power surge had sucked energy even from its protected circuits. A message flashed up on it:

~ Missed, you fuckers! the legend read.

'What?' the Commander said.

The display flashed once and came clear again.

~ Commander; the *Attitude Adjuster* here again. As you may have gathered, we have failed.

'What? But . . !'

~ Keep all defence and sensory systems at maximum readiness; ramp the sensor arrays up to significant degradation point in a week; we shall not need them beyond then.

'But what happened? We got it!'

~ I shall move to plug the gap the attack left in our defences. Ready all the cleared ships for immediate awakening; I may have to rouse them within a day or two. Complete the tests on the Displacers; use a real ship if you have to. And run a total level-zero systems check of your own equipment; if the ship was able to insert a message into your command desk it may have been able to carry out more pertinent mischief therein.

The Commander slammed a limb end down on the desk. '*What* is going on?' he roared. 'We got the bastard, didn't we?'

~ No, Commander. We 'got' some sort of shuttle or module. Somewhat faster and better equipped than the average example such a ship would normally carry, but possibly constructed en route with such a ruse in mind. Now we know why its approach appeared so politely leisurely.

The Commander peered into the holo spheres, juggling with magnifications and field-depths. 'Then where the hell *is* it?'

~ Give me control of the primary scanner, Commander, just for a moment, will you?

The Commander fumed in his space suit for a moment, then nodded his eye stalks at the lieutenant.

The second holo sphere became a narrow, dark cone and swung so that the wide end was directed towards the ceiling. Pittance glowed at the very point of the other end of the projection, the screen of defence devices reduced to a tiny florette of coloured light, close in to the cone's point. At the far, wide end there was a tiny, fiercely, almost painfully red dot.

~ *There* is the good ship *Killing Time*, Commander. It set off at almost the same time I did. Regrettably, it is both quicker and faster than I. It has already done us the honour of copying to me the signal it sent to the rest of the Culture the moment we opened fire on its emissary. I'll transmit you a copy too, minus the various, venomous unpleasantnesses directed specifically at myself. Thank you for the use of your control desk. You can have it back now.

The cone collapsed to become a sphere again. The traitor ship's last message scrolled off the side of the flat screen. The Commander and the lieutenant looked at each other. The small screen came up with another incoming signal.

~ Oh, and will you contact Affront High Command, or shall I? Somebody had better tell them we're at war with the Culture.

III

Genar-Hofoen woke up with a headache it took *minutes* to calm down; performing the relevant pain-management inside his head took far too much concentration for somebody feeling this bad to perform quickly. He felt like he was a child on a beach, swinging a toy spade and building a sea wall all around him as the tide rushed in; waves kept over-topping and he was constantly shovelling sand up to small breaches in his defences, and the worst of it was the more sand he piled up the deeper he dug and higher he had to throw. Eventually water started seeping in from the bottom of his sea fort, and he gave in; he just blanketed all pain. If somebody started holding flames to his feet or he jammed his fingers in a door that'd just be too bad. He knew better than to shake his head, so he imagined shaking his head; he'd never had a hangover this bad.

He tried opening one eye. It didn't seem too keen on cooperating. Try the other one. No, that one didn't want to face the world either. Very dark. Like being wrapped up inside a big dark cloak or some—

He jerked; both eyes tore open, making both smart and water.

He was looking at some sort of big screen, in-holo'd. Space; stars. He looked down, finding it difficult to move his head. He was held inside a large, very comfortable but very secure chair; it was made of some sort of soft hide, it was half reclined and it smelled very pleasant, but it had big padded hoops that had clamped themselves over his forearms and his lower legs. A similar hide-covered bar looped over his lower abdomen. He tried moving his head again. It was held inside some sort of open-face helmet which felt like it was attached to the headrest of the chair.

He looked to one side. Hide-covered wall; polished wood. A panel or screen showing what looked like an abstract painting. It *was* an abstract painting; a famous one. He recognised it. Ceiling black, light studded. In front just the screen. Floor carpeted. Looked much like the inside of a standard Culture module so far. Very quiet. Not that that meant anything. He looked to his right.

There were two more seats like his across the width of the cabin – it was probably a cabin and this was almost certainly a nine or twelve person module; he couldn't see behind to tell. The seat in the middle, the one nearer him, was occupied by a bulky, rather antique-looking drone, its flat-topped bulk resting on the cushion of the seat. People always said drones looked a bit like suitcases but this one reminded Genar-Hofoen of an old-fashioned sledge. Somehow, it gave the impression that it was staring at the screen. Its aura field was flickering as though it was undergoing rapid mood-changes; mostly it displayed a mixture of grey, brown and white.

Frustration, displeasure and anger. Not an encouraging combination.

The seat on the far side of the cabin held a beautiful young woman who looked just a little like Dajeil Gelian. Her nose was smaller, her eyes were the wrong colour, her hair was quite different. It was hard to tell whether her figure bore any resemblance to the other woman because she was inside what looked like a jewelled space suit; a standard-ish Culture hard suit plated in platinum or silver and liberally plastered in gems that certainly glittered and flashed in the overhead lights as though they were things like rubies, emeralds, diamonds and so on. The suit's helmet, equally encrusted, rested on the arm of her seat. *She* wasn't shackled into place in the seat, he noticed.

The girl bore on her face a frown so deep and severe he imagined it would have made almost anybody else look quite supremely ugly. On her it looked rather fetching. Probably not the desired effect at all. He decided to risk a smile; the open-faced helmet he was wearing ought to let her see it.

'Umm, hello,' he said.

The old drone rose and flicked round as if glancing at him. It thumped back into the seat cushion, its aura fields off. 'It's hopeless,' it announced, as though it hadn't heard what the man had said. 'We're locked out. Nowhere to go.'

The girl in the far seat narrowed her fiercely blue eyes and glared at Genar-Hofoen. When she spoke, her voice was like an ice stiletto. 'This is all your fault, you ghastly piece of shit,' she said.

Genar-Hofoen sighed. He was losing consciousness once more but he didn't care. He had absolutely no idea who this creature was, but he liked her already.

It went dark again.

IV

```
[stuttered tight point, M32, tra. @n4.28.882.4656]
```
xLSV *Serious Callers Only*
   oEccentric *Shoot Them Later*
It's war! Those insane fucks have declared war! They're mad!
∞

```
[stuttered tight point, M32, tra. @4.28.882.4861]
```
   xEccentric *Shoot Them Later*
     oLSV *Serious Callers Only*
I was about to call. I just got the message from the ship I requested attend Pittance. This looks bad.
∞

Bad? It's a fucking catastrophe!
∞

   Did your girl get her man?
∞

Oh, she got him all right, but then a few hours later the Affront High Command announced the birth of a bouncing baby war. The ship Phage sent to Tier was standing a day's module travel away; it decided it had better things to do than hang around on a mission it had never been very happy with even from the beginning. I think the declaration of war came almost as a relief to it. It promptly announced its position to the *Steely Glint* and was immediately asked to ship out at maximum speed on some desperate defence mission. Bastard wouldn't even tell me where. Took me real milliseconds to argue it out of confessing all to the *Steely Glint* and telling it exactly why it was anywhere near Tier in the first place. I was able to persuade it Phage's honour rested on it keeping quiet; I don't think it'll squeal. I let it know I give serious grudge.
∞

   But it was Demilled. Hasn't it just gone back to Phage for munitioning?
∞

Ha! Demilitarised my backup. Fucker left Phage fully tooled. Phage's own idea, sneaky scumbag. Always was over-protective. What comes of being that geriatric I suppose. Anyway, the *Frank Exchange Of Views* is cannoned to the gunwales and itching for a brawl, apparently. Whatever; it has gone. Which leaves our lass and the captive Genar-Hofoen floating in a module nearly a day out of Tier with nowhere to go. Tier is requesting – make that insisting – all Culture and Affront craft and personnel leave it for the duration of the hostilities and nobody's being allowed in. I've tried to find somebody else within range to pick them up but it's hopeless.

A Tier deep-scan inventory has already identagged their module. The *Meatfucker* is skimming in a day away and the module can make, oh, all of two hundred lights . . . Guess what happens next. We've failed.

∞

  So it would appear. Was this the aim and is this now the result of the conspiracy? War with the Affront?

∞

I believe so. The Excession is still the more important matter, but its appearance and the possibilities it may open up have been used by the conspiracy to tempt the Affront into initiating hostilities. Pittance is worse, though.

That Pittance has fallen implies entrapment. It points to treachery. The *Killing Time* believes there was another Culture or ex-Culture ship there; not one of the stored vessels but another craft, something no less old than the stored vessels, but wiser and more experienced; something that's been around as long as they, but awake all that time.

It believes that this ship was taking the part of the Pittance Mind when it communicated with it on its approach. I suspect it will prove to be a warship which apparently went Eccentric or Ulterior at some point in the last five hundred years and was – supposedly, not actually – demilitarised by one of the conspirators. I have a list of suspects.

The *Killing Time* suggests that this ship tricked its way beneath the Pittance Mind's guard and either destroyed it or took it over. The store was then turned over to the Affront. They now have a ready-made instant battle fleet of Culture warcraft tech generations of development beyond their own ships and just nine days' journey from the Excession. Nothing we can put in place in the time available can stop them.

For what it's worth, the *Killing Time* is making all speed for Esperi. Nine days from now we'll have the *Not Invented Here* and the *Different Tan* from the Gang there. The *NIH* has two operational Thug class ROUs it's in the process of cannoning-up, a Hooligan LOU and a Delinquent GOU. Another couple of GSVs should be there too if they aren't diverted because of the war, with a total of five OUs, two of them Torturer class. Eight of Phage's Psychopath ROUs are bound for the Excession but the rest are down for defensive duties elsewhere to cope with likely threats from Affront battle units. Even those eight won't get within punch-throwing range of the Excession until two days after the Affront can be there. Bottom line is there are a total of ten warships of various classes capable of making it to the Excession in time to make a stand against the Affront; enough to hold off the entire Affront navy if that was all we were going to be faced with, but simply not capable of holding back more than an eighth of the ships that could come out of Pittance. If they all go straight to the Excession, it will be theirs.

For the record, *all* the remaining ship stores are breaking themselves open, but the nearest is over five weeks' travel away. A gesture, that's all.

Oh, and a few other Involveds have offered help but they're all either too weak or too far away. A couple of other barbarics are probably going to declare for the Affront once they've stopped scratching their heads and worked out what they might be able to get up to with the Culture's attention diverted, but they're even less relevant.

And if we were expecting some well-disposed Elders to step into the nursery and confiscate all our toys and restore order, it doesn't look very likely so far; no notice taken, as far as anybody can tell.

∞

So. That just leaves our old friend, currently – possibly, probably, almost certainly – also en route. Wild card? Somehow part of the conspiracy? Have we any more thoughts? Come to that, have you had any reply from it?

∞

None, and no. No offence, but the *SS* is one of the more unfathom-able Eccentrics. Perhaps it thinks the Excession requires Storing, perhaps it intends to ram it at that speed, or attempt to plunge into it and access other universes . . . I don't know. There is some private issue being played out in this, I believe, and Genar-Hofoen fits in somewhere. I have almost given up thinking about this aspect of affairs. I shall continue my attempts to contact it but I don't think it's even looking at its signal files. The point is that the war itself takes precedence, with the Excession prioritised beyond that.

∞

   No offence taken. So we are left with the Affront on the cusp of apotheosis or nemesis.

∞

Indeed. Quite how they intend to use these elderly but still potent warships to take control of the Excession one can only hazard at; perhaps they intend surrounding it and charging admission . . . But they have begun a war which – unless they can somehow gain control of the Excession and exploit it – they can only lose. They have a few hundred half-millennium-old warships; capable of inflicting untold damage let loose in a peaceable, un-militarised if relatively un-populated section of the galaxy, certainly, but only for a month or two at most. Then the Culture gathers the force to crush them utterly, and moves on to rip the Affront hegemony to shreds and impose its own peace upon it. There can be no other outcome. Unless the Excession does come into play. Which I doubt.

Maybe it *is* some sort of projection; maybe its appearance was not fortuitous but planned. This looks unlikely, I know, but everything else about this has been so cunningly put together . . .

Whatever; the argument which everybody had thought was lost at the end of the Idiran War is about to be won. The agreement come to then is in the process of being overturned.

I for one am not going to stand for this. We may have failed to frustrate the conspiracy but it will still be possible to work towards the discovery of the guilty parties involved in its planning and implementation, both during and after the hostilities. I intend to copy all my thoughts, theories, evidence, communications and all other relevant documentation to every trusted colleague and contact I possess. If you have any intention of taking part in the course of action I am suggesting, I urge you to do the same and to relay this advice to *The Anticipation Of A New Lover's Arrival.*

I intend to pursue the perpetrators of this unnecessary war for as long as it takes until they are brought to justice, and I am aware both that I will no longer be able to do so without them knowing that I am doing so, and that there is no better circumstance to arrange for the jeopardisation of a fellow Mind than in time of war, when blanket secrecies are imposed, warcraft of every sort are loosed, mistakes can be claimed to have been made, deals done, mercenaries hired and old scores settled.

I do not believe I am being melodramatic in this. I will be under terminal threat and so will anybody else who determines to adopt the same course as I. The conspirators have played exceedingly dirty until this point and I cannot imagine they will do other than continue to do so now that their filthy scheme is on the very brink of success.

What do you say? Will you join in this perilous mission?

∞

How I wish that I could persuade myself, never mind you, that you are being melodramatic.

You risk more than I. My Eccentricity might save me. We have gone this far together. Count me in.

Oh, meat, they never said this would happen when they invited me onto the Group and into the Gang . . .

Hmm. I had forgotten how unpleasant the emotion of fear is. This is hateful! You're right. Let's get these bastards. How *dare* they disturb my peace of mind so just to teach some tentacled bunch of backwoods barbarians a lesson!

V

The battle-cruiser *Kiss The Blade* caught the cruise ship *Just Passing Through* on the outskirts of the Ekro system. The Culture craft – ten-kilometres of sleek beauty host to two hundred thousand holidaying travellers of umpteen different species-types – hove to as soon as the battle-cruiser came within range but the Affronter vessel put a shot across its bows anyway, just on general principles. The more determinedly assiduous revellers hadn't believed the announcement about the war anyway, and thought the missile warhead's detonation which lit up the skies ahead of the ship was just some particularly big but otherwise unimpressive firework.

It had been close. Another hour's warning and the Culture ship's hurried reconfiguring and matter-scavenging engine-rebuild would have ensured its escape. But it wasn't to be.

The two ships joined. In the reception vestibule, a small party of people met a trio of suited Affronters as they emerged from the airlocks in a swirl of cool mists.

'You are the ship's representative?'

'Yes,' the squat figure at the front of the humans said. 'And you?'

'I am Colonel Alien-Befriender (first class) Fivetide Humidyear VII of the Winterhunter tribe and the battle-cruiser *Kiss The Blade*. This ship is claimed as prize in the name of the Affront Republic according to the normal rules of war. If you obey all our instructions promptly, there is every possibility that no harm will come to you, your passengers or crew. In case you have any illusions concerning your status, you are now our hostages. Any questions?'

'None that I either can't guess the answer to or imagine you'd answer truthfully,' the avatar said. 'Your jurisdiction is accepted under force of arms alone. Your actions while this situation persists will be recorded. Nothing less than the total destruction of this vessel atom by atom will wipe out that record, and when in due course—'

'Yes, yes. I'll contact my lawyers now. Now take me to your best suite fitted out for Affront physiology.'

The girl was indignant with a kind of ferocity probably only somebody from the Peace faction could muster in such a situation. 'But we're the *Peace* faction,' she protested for the fifth or sixth time. 'We're ... we're like the true Culture, the way it used to be ...'

'Ah,' Leffid said, grimacing as somebody pushed behind him and forced his chest into the front of the bar. He glanced round, scowling, and ruffled his wings back into shape. The Starboard lounge of the *Xoanon* was crowded – the ship was crowded – and he could see his wings were going to end up in a terrible shape by the time this was over. Mind you, there were compensations; somebody pushed into the bar and squeezed the Peace faction girl closer to him, so that her bare arm touched him and he could feel the warmth of her hip against his. She smelled wonderful. 'Now that could be your problem,' he said, trying to sound sympathetic. 'Calling yourselves the true Culture, you see? To the Tier Sintricates, and even to the Affront, that could sound, well confusing.'

'But everybody knows we won't have anything to do with war. It's just so un*fair*!' She flicked her short black hair and stared into the drug bowl she held. It was fuming too. '*Fucking* war!' She sounded close to tears.

Leffid judged the time right to put his arm round her. She didn't seem to mind. He thought the better of hinting that in his own small way he might have helped start the war. Sort of thing some people might be impressed with, but not all.

Besides, he'd given his word, and the Tendency had been rewarded for its tip-off to the Mainland with this very ship, currently engaged in the highly humanitarian task of helping to evacuate Tier habitat of all Temporarily Undesirable Aliens, not to mention earning the Tendency some much-needed cordiality credit with a whole raft of other Involveds and strands of the Culture. The girl sighed deeply and held the drug bowl to her face, letting some of the heavy grey smoke tip towards her exceedingly pretty little nose. She glanced round at him with a small brave smile, her gaze rising over his shoulder.

'Like your wings,' she said.

He smiled. 'Why, thank you . . .' (Damn!) '. . . ah, my dear.'

The professor blinked. Yes, it really was an Affronter floating at the far end of the room, near the windows. Suit like a small, tubby spacecraft, all gleaming knobbly bits, articulated limbs and glistening prisms. The gauzy white curtains blew in around it, letting bright, high-angled sunlight flow in waves across the carpet. Oh dear, was that her underwear draped over a hassock in the Affronter's shadow?

'I beg your pardon?' she said. She wasn't sure she'd heard right.

'Phoese Cloathel-Beldrunsa Khoriem Iel Poere da'Merire, you have been deemed the senior human representative on the Orbital named Cloathel. You are hereby informed that this Orbital is claimed in the name of the Affront Republic. All Culture personnel are now Affront citizens (third class). All orders from superiors will be obeyed. Any resistance will be treated as treason.'

The professor rubbed her eyes.

'Cloudsheen, is that you?' she asked the Affronter. The destroyer *Wingclipper* had arrived the day before with a cultural exchange group the university had been expecting for some weeks. Cloudsheen was the ship's captain; they'd had a good talk about pan-species semantics at the party just the night before. Intelligent, surprisingly sensitive creature; not remotely as aggressive as she'd expected. This looked like him, but different. She had a disquieting feeling the extra bits on his suit were weapons.

'*Captain* Cloudsheen, if you please, professor,' the Affronter said, floating closer. It was directly above her skirt, lying crumpled on the floor. Heavens, she had been messy last night.

'Are you serious?' she asked. She had a strong urge to fart but she held it in; she was oddly concerned that the Affronter would think she was being insulting.

'I am perfectly serious, professor. The Affront and the Culture are now at war.'

'Oh,' she said. She glanced over at her terminal brooch, lying on an extension of the bed's headboard. Well, the Newsflash light was winking, right enough; practically strobing in fact; must be urgent indeed. She thought. 'Shouldn't you be addressing this to the Hub?'

'It refuses to communicate,' the Affronter officer said. 'We have surrounded it. You have been deemed most senior Culture – ex-Culture, I should say – representative in its place. This is not a joke, professor, I'm sorry to say. The Orbital has been mined with AM warheads. If it proves necessary, your world will be destroyed. The full cooperation of yourself and everybody else on the Orbital will help ensure this does not happen.'

'Well, I don't accept this honour, Cloudsheen. I—'

The Affronter had turned and was floating back towards the windows again. It swivelled in the air as it retreated. 'You don't have to,' it said. 'As I said, you have been deemed.'

'Well then,' she said, 'I deem you to be acting without any authority I care to recognise and—'

The Affronter darted through the air towards her and stopped directly above the bed, making her flinch despite herself. She smelled . . . something cold and toxic. 'Professor,' Cloudsheen said. 'This is not an academic debate or some common room word-game. You are prisoners and hostages and all your lives are forfeit. The sooner you understand the realities of the situation, the better. I know as well as you that you are in no way in charge of the Orbital, but certain formalities have to be observed, regardless of their practical irrelevance. I consider that duty has now been discharged and frankly that's all that matters, because I have the AM warheads; and you don't.' It drew quickly away, sucking a cool breeze behind it. It stopped just before the windows again. 'Lastly,' it said, 'I am sorry to have disturbed you. I thank you personally and on behalf of my crew for the reception party. It was most enjoyable.'

He left. The curtains soughed in and out, slowly golden.

Her heart, she was surprised to discover, was pounding.

The *Attitude Adjuster* woke them one by one, telling each the same story; Excessionary threat near Esperi, Deluger craft mimicking Culture ship configurations, cooperation of Affront, extreme urgency; obey me, or our Affront allies if I should be lost. Some of the vessels were immediately suspicious, or at least puzzled. The confirmatory messages from other craft – the *No Fixed Abode*, the *Different Tan* and the *Not Invented Here* – convinced them in every case.

Part of the *Attitude Adjuster* felt sick. It knew it was doing the right thing, in the end, but at a simple, surface level it felt disgust at the deception it was having to foist upon its fellow ships. It tried to tell itself that it would all end with little or no blood spilled and few or no Mind-deaths, but it knew that there was no guarantee. It had spent years thinking all this through, shortly after the proposition had been put to it seventy years earlier, and had known then, accepted then that it might come to this, but it had always hoped it would not. Now the moment was at hand it was starting to wonder if it had made a mistake, but knew it was too late to turn back now. Better to believe that it had been right then and now it was merely being short-sighted and squeamish.

It could not be wrong. It was not wrong. It had had an open mind and it had become convinced of the rightness of the course which was being suggested and in which it would play such an important part. It had done as it had been asked to do; it had watched the Affront, studied them, immersed itself in their history, culture and beliefs. And in all that time it had achieved a kind of sympathy for them, an empathy, even, and at the start perhaps a degree of admiration for them, but it had also built up a cold and terrible hatred of their ways.

In the end, it thought it understood them because it was just a little like them.

It was a warship, after all. It was built, *designed* to glory in destruction, when it was considered appropriate. It found, as it was rightly and properly supposed to, an awful beauty in both the weaponry of war and the violence and devastation which that weaponry was capable of inflicting, and yet it knew that attractiveness stemmed from a kind of insecurity, a sort of childishness. It could see that – by some criteria – a warship, just by the perfectly articulated purity of its purpose, was the most beautiful single artifact the Culture was capable of producing, and at the same time understand the paucity of moral vision such a judgement implied. To fully appreciate the beauty of a weapon was to admit to a kind of shortsightedness close to blindness, to confess to a sort of stupidity. The weapon was not itself; nothing was solely itself. The weapon, like anything else, could only finally be judged by the effect it had on others, by the consequences it produced in some outside context, by its place in the rest of the universe. By this measure the love, or just the appreciation, of weapons was a kind of tragedy.

The *Attitude Adjuster* thought it could see into the souls of the Affronters. They were not the happy-go-lucky life-and-soul-of-the-party grand fellows with a few bad habits they were commonly thought to be; they were not thoughtlessly cruel in the course of seeking to indulge other more benign and even admirable pleasures; they were not merely terrible rascals.

They gloried, first and foremost, in their cruelty. Their cruelty was the point. They were not thoughtless. They knew they hurt their own kind and others and they revelled in it; it was their purpose. The rest – the robust joviality, the blokish vivacity – was part happy accident, part cunningly exaggerated ploy, the equivalent of an angelic-looking child discovering that a glowing smile will melt the severest adult heart and excuse almost any act, however dreadful.

It had agreed to the plan now coming to fruition with a heavy soul. People would die, Minds be destroyed because of what it was doing. The ghastly danger was gigadeathcrime. Mass destruction. Utter horror. The *Attitude Adjuster* had lied, it had deceived, it had acted – by what it knew would be the consensual opinion of all but a few of its peers – with massive dishonour. It was all too well aware its name might live for millennia hence as that of a traitor, as an abhorrence, an abomination.

Still, it would do what it had become convinced had to be done, because to do otherwise would be to wish an even worse self-hatred upon itself, the ultimate abomination of disgust at oneself.

Perhaps, it told itself as it brought another slumbering warcraft to wakefulness, the Excession would make everything all right. The half-thought was already ironic, but it continued with it anyway. Yes; maybe the Excession was the solution. Maybe it really was worth all that was being risked in its name, and capable of bringing placid resolution. That would be sweet; the excuse takes over, the *casus belli* brings peace . . . *Like fuck*, it thought. The ship sneered at itself, examining the idiotic thought and then discarding it with probably less contempt than it deserved.

It was, anyway, too late to reconsider now. Too much had been done already. The Pittance Mind was already dead, choosing self-destruction rather than compromise; the human who had been the only other conscious sentience in the rock had been killed, and the de-stored ships would speed, utterly deceived, to what could well prove to be their doom; the future alone knew who or what else they would take with them. The war had begun and all the *Attitude Adjuster* could do was play out the part it had agreed to play.

Another warship Mind surfaced to wakefulness.

. . . Excessionary threat near Esperi, the *Attitude Adjuster* told the newly woken ship; Deluger craft mimicking Culture ship configurations, cooperation of Affront, extreme urgency; obey me, or our Affront allies if I should be lost. Confirmatory messages from the GSV *No Fixed Abode*, the GCU *Different Tan* and the MSV *Not Invented Here* attached . . .

*   *   *

The module Scopell-Afranqui left the urgencies of the instant behind for a moment and retreated into a kind of simulation of its plight.

The craft had a romantic, even sentimental streak which Genar-Hofoen had rarely glimpsed in all the two years they had spent together on God'shole habitat (and which, indeed, it had deliberately kept hidden for fear of his ridicule), and it saw itself now as being like the castellan of some small fortified embassy in a teeming barbarian city, far from the civilised lands that were his home; a wise, thoughtful man, technically a warrior, but more of a thinker, one who saw much more of the realities behind the embassy's mission than those in his charge, and who had devoutly hoped that his warrior skills would never be called upon. Well, that time had come; the native soldiers were hammering at the compound's gates right now and it was only a matter of time before the embassy compound fell. There was treasure in the embassy and the barbarians would not rest until they had it.

The castellan left the parapet where he had looked out upon the besieging forces and retreated to his private chamber. His few troops were already putting up the best defence they could; nothing he could do or say would do other than hinder them now. His few spies had been dispatched some time ago through secret passageways into the city, to do what damage they could once the embassy itself was destroyed, as it surely must be. There was nothing else which awaited his attention. Save this one decision.

He had already opened the safe and taken out the sealed orders; the paper was in his hand. He read it again. So it was to be destruction. He had guessed as much, but it was still a shock somehow.

It should not have come to this, but it had. He had known the risks, they had been pointed out at the beginning, when he had taken up this position, but he had not really imagined for a moment that he would really be faced with either utter dishonour and the vicarious treachery of forced collaboration, or death at his own hand.

There was, of course, no real choice. Call it his upbringing. He looked ruefully around the small private chamber that held the memories of home, his library, his clothes and keepsakes. This was him. This was who he was. The same beliefs and principles that had led him here to this lonely outpost required that there was no choice over surrender or death. But there was still one choice to make, and it was a bitter one to be given.

He could destroy the embassy – and himself with it, of course – completely, so that all that would be left to the barbarians would be its stones. Or he could take the entire city with him. It was not just a city; in one sense it was not even principally a city; it was a vast arsenal, a crowded barracks and a busy naval port; altogether an important component of the barbarians' war effort. Its destruction would benefit the side that the castellan was loyal to, the cause that he absolutely believed in; arguably it would save lives in the long run. Yet the city had its civilians too; the out-numbering innocents that were the women and children and the subjugated underclasses, not to mention the blameless others from neutral lands who just happened to find themselves caught up in the war through no fault of their own. Had he a right to snuff them out too by destroying the city?

He put the piece of paper down. He looked at his reflection in a distant looking glass.

Death. In all this choice there was no doubt about his own fate, only about how he would be remembered. As humanitarian, or weakling? As mass-murderer, or hero?

Death. How strange to contemplate it now.

He had always wondered how he would face it. There was a certain continued existence, of course. He had faith in that; the assurances of the priests that his soul was recorded in a great book, somewhere, and capable of resurrection. But the precise *he* he was right now; that would assuredly end, and soon; that was over.

Death, he remembered somebody saying once, was a kind of victory. To have lived a long good life, a life of prodigious pleasure and minimal misery, and then to die; that was to have won. To attempt to hang on for ever risked ending up in some as yet unglimpsed horror-future. What if you lived for ever and all that had gone before, however terrible things had sometimes appeared to be in the past, however badly people had behaved to each other throughout history, was nothing compared to what was yet to come? Suppose in the great book of days that told the story of everything, all the gone, done past was merely a bright, happy introduction compared to the main body of the work, an unending tale of unbearable pain scraped in blood on a parchment of living skin?

Better to die than risk that.

Live well and then die, so that the you that is you now can never be again, and only tricks can re-create something that might think it is you, but is not.

The outer gates fell; he heard them go. The castellan stood up and went to the casement. In the courtyard, the barbarian soldiers flowed through to the last line of defence.

Soon. The choice, the choice. He could spin a coin, but that would be . . . cheap. Unworthy.

He walked to the device that would destroy the embassy compound, and the city too, if he chose.

There was no choice here, either. Not really.

There would be peace again. The only question was when.

He could not know if ultimately more people would suffer and die because he was choosing not to destroy the city, but at least this way the damage and the casualties would be confined to the minimum for the longest possible time. And if in the future he would be judged to have done the wrong thing and to have made the incorrect decision . . . well, death had the other advantage that he would not be present to suffer that knowledge of that judgement.

He double-checked that the device was set so that only the embassy would be destroyed, he waited a moment longer to be sure that he was calm and clear about what he was doing, then as the tears came to his eyes, he activated the device.

The module Scopell-Afranqui self-destructed in a blink of annihilatory energies centred on its AI core, obliterating it entirely; the module itself was blasted into a million pieces. The explosion sent a shiver through the fabric of God'shole habitat that was felt all the way round that great wheel; it took out a significant section of the surrounding inner docks area and caused a rupture in the skin of the engineering compartment beneath; this was quickly repaired.

The destroyer *Riptalon* was damaged and would require a further week in dock, though there were no fatalities or serious injuries on board. The explosion killed five officers and a few dozen soldiers and technicians in the docks and smaller craft alongside the module; a number of semi-aware AI entities were also lost and their cores later found to be corrupted by agent entities the module had succeeded in infiltrating into the habitat's systems shortly before its destruction, despite every precaution. These, or their descendants, continued to significantly reduce the habitat's contribution to the war effort for the duration of hostilities.

~ So what's it like being at war?

~ Scary, when you have every reason to believe you may be sitting next to the real reason it was declared.

The GCU *Fate Amenable To Change* floated in a triangular pattern with the two Elencher vessels *Sober Counsel* and *Appeal To Reason*. The two Elench ships had repeatedly attempted to communicate with the Excession, entirely without success. The *Fate* was getting nervous, just waiting for the pressure building up with the crews of the two Elencher ships for more intrusive action to overcome the reticence of the craft themselves.

The three craft had secretly declared their own little pact over the last few days after the second Elencher ship had appeared on the scene. They had exchanged drone and human avatars, opened up volumes of their mind-sets they would not normally have exposed to craft of another society, and pledged not to act without consulting the others. That agreeable agreement would lapse if the Elenchers chose to try to interfere with the Excession. It would have to lapse to some extent anyway in a couple of days when the MSV *Not Invented Here* arrived and – the *Fate* suspected – started bossing everybody about, but it was trying desperately to dissuade the two Elencher ships from doing anything rash in the meantime.

~ Are there any Affront warships known to be anywhere in this volume? the *Appeal To Reason* asked.

~ No, the *Fate Amenable To Change* replied. ~ In fact they've been staying away and telling everybody else to do so as well. I suppose we should have guessed that was suspicious in itself. That's the trouble with people like them I suppose; whenever you think you're detecting the first signs of them starting to behave responsibly it's just them being even more devious and underhand than usual.

~ You think they want the Excession? the *Sober Counsel* asked.

~ It's possible.

~ Perhaps they're not coming here, suggested the *Appeal To Reason*. ~ Aren't they attacking the whole Culture? There are reports of scores of ships and Orbitals being taken . . .

~ I don't know, the *Fate* admitted. It looks like madness to me; they can't defeat the whole Culture.

~ But they're saying a ship-store at this rock Pittance has fallen, the *Sober Counsel* sent.

~ Well, yes. Officially there's still a blackout on that, but (off record, of course), if they are coming in this direction I wouldn't want to be here in about a week's time.

~ So if we're going to get through to the entity, we'd better do it soon, the *Appeal To Reason* sent.

~ Oh, don't start on about that again; you said yourself they might not be coming . . . the *Fate* began, then broke off. ~ Hold on. Are you getting this?

...(SEMIWIDE BEAM, AFFRONTBASE ALLTRANS, LOOP.)
ATTENTION ALL CRAFT IN ESPERI NEAR SPACE: THE ENTITY LOCATED AT (location sequence enclosed) WAS FIRST DISCOVERED BY THE AFFRONT CRUISER *FURIOUS PURPOSE* ON (trans; n4.28.803.8+) AND IS HEREBY FULLY AND RIGHTFULLY CLAIMED ON THE BEHALF OF THE AFFRONT REPUBLIC AS AN INTEGRAL AND FULLY SOVEREIGN AFFRONT PROPERTY SUBJECT TO AFFRONT LAWS, EDICTS, RIGHTS AND PRIVILEGES.

IN THE LIGHT OF THE CULTURE-PROVOKED HOSTILITIES NOW EXISTING BETWEEN THE AFFRONT AND THE CULTURE, THE FULL CUSTODIAL PROTECTION OF AFFRONT ADMINISTRATION HAS BEEN EXTENDED TO THE FOREMENTIONED VOLUME AND TO THAT END AN ORDINANCE ABSOLUTELY PROHIBITING ALL NON-AFFRONT TRAFFIC WITHIN TEN STANDARD LIGHT YEARS AROUND THE ENTITY HAS BEEN ISSUED WITH IMMEDIATE EFFECT AND HENCE ALL CRAFT INSIDE THIS VOLUME ARE ORDERED TO VACATE SAID VOLUME FORTHWITH.

ALL CRAFT AND MATERIAL FOUND TO BE WITHIN THIS VOLUME WILL BE DEEMED TO BE IN CONTRAVENTION OF AFFRONT LAW AND IN CONTEMPT OF THE AFFRONT SUPREME COMMITTEE THUS SUBJECTING THEMSELVES TO THE FULL PUNITIVE MIGHT OF THE AFFRONT MILITARY.

TO ENFORCE SAID ORDINANCE A HUNDREDS-STRONG

WAR FLEET OF EX-CULTURE CRAFT WHICH HAVE CHO-
SEN TO RENOUNCE THEIR PREVIOUS ALLEGIANCE TO
THE ENEMY HAVE BEEN DISPATCHED TO THE ABOVE-
MENTIONED LOCATION WITH INSTRUCTIONS RUTH-
LESSLY TO ENFORCE THIS ORDER.
GLORY TO THE AFFRONT!

~ So there, the *Sober Counsel* communicated. ~ That's us told.
~ And they can be here in a week, added the *Appeal To
Reason*.
~ Hmm. That location they gave, the *Fate* sent. ~ Look where
it's centred.
~ Ah-hah, replied the *Sober Counsel*.
~ Ah-hah what? asked the *Appeal To Reason*.
~ It's not centred on the entity itself, the other Elench ship
pointed out. ~ It's just off-centre where whatever happened to
that little-drone took place.
~ The *Furious Purpose* is one of a couple of Affronter craft that
left Tier at the same time the fleet did; it could have been following
the *Peace Makes Plenty*, the *Sober Counsel* told the Culture ship.
~ It is certainly the ship that returned to Tier . . . thirty-six days
after whatever happened here.
~ That's a little slow, the *Fate* sent. ~ According to my records
a meteorite-class light cruiser should have been able to do it in . . .
oh, wait a moment; it had an engine fault. And then while it was
on Tier it suffered some sort of . . . hmm. Oh; *look*!
The Excession was doing something.

[stuttered tight point, M32, tra. @4.28.883.1344]
xGSV *Anticipation Of A New Lover's Arrival, The*
  oGSV Sabbaticaler *No Fixed Abode*
**Right. I have thought about this. No, I will not help in trapping
the *Serious Callers Only* or the *Shoot Them Later*. I reported my
previous misgivings and the fact that I had shared them with the
other two craft because in the course of my investigations into
what I perceived as a dangerous conspiracy I became convinced
of the need to deal decisively with the Affront. I still do not
approve of the way this has been done, but by the time your
plans became uncovered it would arguably have caused more
damage attempting to arrest them than letting them go ahead. I**

still find it hard to believe that the rogue ship which tricked the ship store at Pittance was acting alone and that you merely took advantage of the ruse, despite your assurances. However, I have no evidence to the contrary. I have given my word and I will not go public with all this, but I will consider that agreement dependent on the continued well-being and freedom from persecution of both the *Serious Callers Only* and the *Shoot Them Later*, as well, of course, as being contingent upon my own continued integrity. I don't doubt you will think me either paranoid or ridiculous for systematising this arrangement with various other friends and colleagues, particularly given the hostilities which commenced yesterday. I am thinking of taking some sabbatical time myself soon, and going off course-schedule. I shall, in any event, be quitting the Group.

∞

[stuttered tight point, M32, tra. @4.28.883.2182]
    xGSV Sabbaticaler *No Fixed Abode*
      oGSV *Anticipation Of A New Lover's Arrival, The*
I understand completely. There is, you must, must believe, no desire on our part to cause any harm to you or the two craft you mention. We have been concerned purely to expedite the resolution of this unfortunate state of affairs; there will be no recriminations, no witch-hunts, no pogroms or purges on our behalf. With your assurance that this ends here, we are perfectly, quintessentially content. A great relief!

Let me add that it is hard for me to find the words to communicate to you the depth of my – our – gratitude in this matter. You have shown irreproachable moral integrity combined with a truly objective open-mindedness; virtues that all too often are regarded as being as tragically incompatible as they are infinitely desirable. You are an example to all of us. I *beg* you not to leave the Group. We would lose too much. Please; reconsider. No one would deny that you have earned a thousand rests, but please take pity on those who would dare ask you to forgo one, for their own selfish benefit.

∞

Thank you. However, my decision is irrevocable. Should I still be welcome, I may hope for a request to rejoin you at some point in the future should some exceptional situation stimulate the thought that I might again be of service.

∞

My dear, dear ship. If you really must go, please do so with our fondest regards, so long as you swear never to forget that your invitation to restore your wisdom and probity to our small team stands in perpetuity!

VI

Genar-Hofoen spent quite a lot of time on the toilet. Ulver Seich was hell when she was cross and she had been in a state of virtually permanent crossness ever since he'd properly woken up; in fact, since well before. She'd been cross – cross with him – while he'd been unconscious, which seemed unfair somehow.

If he slept too long or day-dozed she got even crosser, so he went to the toilet for fairly long intervals. The toilet in a nine-person module consisted of a sort of thick flap that hinged down from a recess in the back wall of the small craft's single cabin. A semi-cylindrical field popped into being when the flap was in place, isolating the enclosed space from the rest of the cabin, and there was just enough room to make the necessary adjustments to one's clothing and stand or sit in comfort; usually some pleasantly bland music played, but Genar-Hofoen preferred the perfect silence the field enclosure produced. He sat there in the gentle, pleasantly perfumed downward breeze, not, as a rule, actually doing anything, but content to have some time to himself.

Stuck on a tiny but perfectly comfortable module with a beautiful, intelligent young woman. It ought to be a recipe for unbridled bliss; it was practically a fantasy. In fact, it was sheer hell. He'd felt trapped before, but never like this, never so completely, never so helplessly, never with somebody who seemed to find him quite so annoying just to be in the presence of. He couldn't even blame the drone. The drone was, in a sense, in the way, but he didn't mind. Just as well it was, in fact; he didn't know what Ulver Seich might have done to him if it hadn't been in the way. Hell, he quite *liked* the drone. The girl he could easily fall in love with, and in the right circumstances certainly admire and be impressed by and, yes, perfectly possibly like, even be friends with . . . but right now he didn't like her any more than she liked him, and she really didn't like him a lot.

He supposed these just were not the right circumstances. The right circumstances would involve them both being somewhere extremely civilised and cultured with lots of other people around and things happening and stuff to do and opportunities to choose when and where to get to know each other, not cooped up – grief, and it was only for two days so far but it felt more like a month – in a small module in the middle of a war with no apparent idea where they were supposed to go and all their plans seemingly thwarted. It probably didn't help that he was effectively their prisoner, either.

'So who was the first girl?' he asked her. 'The one outside the Sublimers' place?'

'Probably SC,' Ulver Seich told him grumpily. She glared back at the drone. The two humans were in the same seats they'd been in when he'd first woken up. The floor of the cabin area behind them could contort and produce various combinations of seats, couches, tables and so on, but every now and again they just sat in the forward-facing seats, looking at the screen and the stars. The drone Churt Lyne sat oblivious on the floor of the cabin, taking no apparent notice of the girl's glare. The drone seemed to be glare-proof. Somehow it was allowed to get away with being uncommunicative.

Genar-Hofoen sat back in the seat. The stars ahead looked the same as they had a few minutes ago. The module wasn't really heading anywhere purposefully; it was just moving away from Tier, down one of the many corridors approved by Tier traffic control as free from warships and/or volume warnings or restrictions. The girl and the drone hadn't allowed him to contact Tier or anybody else. They had been in touch with what sounded like a ship Mind, communicating by screen-written messages he wasn't allowed to see. Once or twice the girl and the drone had gone quiet and still together, obviously in touch through its communicator and a neural lace.

In theory he might have been able to wrest control of the module from them at such a point, but in practice it would have been futile; the module had its own semi-sentient systems which he had no way of subverting and little chance of arguing round even if he had somehow got the better of the girl and the drone, and anyway, where was he supposed to go? Tier was out, he had no idea where the *Grey Area* or the *Sleeper Service* were and suspected that probably nobody else knew where the two ships were either. He assumed SC would be looking for him. Better to let himself be found.

Besides, when they'd finally released him from the chair he'd been secured to while he'd been unconscious, the drone had shown him an old but shinily mean-looking knife missile it contained within its casing and given him a brief but nasty stinging sensation in his left little finger that it assured him was about a thousandth of the pain its effector was capable of inflicting on him if he tried anything silly. He had assured the machine that he was no warrior and that any martial skills he might have been born with had entirely atrophied at the expense of an overdeveloped sense of self-preservation.

So he was content to let them get on with it when they communicated silently. Made a welcome change, in fact. Anyway, whatever it was they had discovered through all this communicating, they didn't seem terribly happy with it. The girl in particular seemed upset. He got the impression she felt cheated, that she'd discovered she'd been lied to. Perhaps because of that she was telling him things she wouldn't have told him otherwise. He tried to put together what she'd just said about Special Circumstances with what she'd already let him know.

His head ached briefly with the effort. He'd hit it when he'd fallen out of the trap, in Night City. He was still trying to work out what happened there.

'But I thought you said you were with SC?' he said. He couldn't help it; he knew it would just annoy her again, but he was still confused.

'I said,' she hissed, through gritted teeth, 'that I *thought* I was working for SC.' She looked to one side and sighed heavily, then turned back to him. 'Maybe I am, maybe I was, maybe there's different bits of SC, maybe something else entirely, I just *don't know*, don't you understand?'

'So who sent you?' he asked, crossing his arms. The ownskin jacket slid round his torso; the module's bio unit was cleaning his shirt. The suit still looked pretty good, he thought. The girl hadn't changed out of her jewelled space suit (though she had used the module's toilet, rather than whatever built-in units the suit had). She looked less and less like Dajeil Gelian every hour, he thought, her face becoming younger and finer and more beautiful all the time. It was a fascinating transformation to watch and if the circumstances had been different he'd have been aching at least to test the waters with her to see if there was any sort of mutuality of attraction here ... but the circumstances were as they were, and right now the last thing he wanted to do was give her any impression he was ogling her.

'I told you who sent me,' she said, her voice cold. 'A Mind. With the help ... well, it looks more like collusion now, actually,' she said with an insincere smile, 'of my home world's Mind.' She took a deep breath, then set her lips in as tight a line as their fullness would permit. 'I had my own warship for grief's sake,' she said bitterly, addressing the stars on the screen ahead of them. 'Is it any wonder I thought it was all SC-arranged?'

She glanced back at the silent drone, then looked at him again. 'Now we're told our ship's fucked off and we've to keep quiet about where we are. And the sort of trouble we had getting you off Tier ...' She shook her head. 'Looked like SC to me ... not that I know that much, but the machine thinks so too,' she said, jerking her head to indicate the drone again. She looked him down and up. 'Wish we'd left you there now.'

'Well, so do I,' he said, trying to sound reasonable.

She'd got to Tier a few days before him, sent to look for him, in effect given a blank cheque and yet not able to find out where he was the easy way, through just asking; hence the business with the pondrosaur. Which made sense if it wasn't Special Circumstances which had sent her, because it was SC who had been looking after him on Tier, and why would they be trying to kidnap him from themselves? And yet she'd had her own warship, apparently, and been given the intelligence that had led her to Tier to intercept him in the first place; information SC would naturally restrict to a small number of trusted Minds. Mystifying.

'So,' she said. 'What exactly were you supposed to be doing after you left Tier, or was this rather pathetic attempt to reclaim your lost youth by trying to seduce women who looked like an old flame the totality of your mission?'

He smiled as tolerantly as he could. 'Sorry,' he said. 'I can't tell you.'

Her eyes narrowed further. 'You know,' she said, 'they might just ask us to throw you outboard.'

He allowed himself to sit back, looking surprised and hurt. A little shiver of real fear did make itself felt in his guts. 'You wouldn't, would you?' he asked.

She looked forward at the stars again, eyebrows gathered, mouth set in a down-turned line. 'No,' she admitted, 'but I'd enjoy thinking about it.'

There was silence for a while. He was conscious of her breathing, though he looked in vain at the attractively sculpted chest of her suit for any sign of movement. Suddenly, her foot clunked down on the carpet beneath her jewel-encrusted boot. 'What *were* you supposed to be doing?' she demanded angrily, turning to face him. 'Why *did* they want you? Fuck it, I've told you why I was there. Come on; *tell* me.'

'I'm sorry,' he sighed. She was already starting to blush with anger. Oh no, here we go, he thought. Tantrum time again.

Then the drone jerked up into the air behind them and something flashed round the edges of the module's screen.

'Hello in there,' said a large, deep voice, all around them.

VII

[stuttered tight point, M32, tra. @4.28.883.4700]
   xGSV *Anticipation Of A New Lover's Arrival, The*
      oLSV *Serious Callers Only*
I regret to inform you that I have changed my position concerning the so-called conspiracy concerning the Esperi Excession and the Affront. It is now my judgement that while there may have been certain irregularities of jurisdiction and of operational ethics involved, these were of an opportunistic rather than a conspiratorial nature. Further, I am, as I have always been, of the opinion that while the niceties of normal moral constraints should be our guides, they must not be our masters.

There are inevitably occasions when such – if I may characterise them so – *civilian* considerations must be set aside (and indeed, is this not what the very phrase and title Special Circumstances implies?) the better to facilitate actions which, while distasteful and regrettable perhaps in themselves, might reasonably be seen as reliably leading to some strategically desirable state or outcome no rational person would argue against.

It is my profoundly held conviction that the situation regarding the Affront is of this highly specialised and rare nature and therefore merits the measures and policy currently being employed by the Minds you and I had previously suspected of indulging in some sort of grand conspiracy.

I call upon you to talk with our fellows in the Interesting Times Gang whom you have – unjustly, I now believe – distrusted, with a view to facilitating an accord which will allow all parties to work together towards a satisfactory outcome both to this regrettable and unnecessary misunderstanding and, perhaps, to the conflict that has now been initiated by the Affront.

For myself, I intend to go into a retreat for some time, starting immediately from the end of this signal. I shall no longer be in a position to correspond; however, messages may be left for me with the Independent Retreats Council (ex-Culture section) and will be reviewed every hundred days (or thereabouts).

I wish you well and hope that my decision might help precipitate a reconciliation I devoutly wish will happen.

[stuttered tight point, M32, tra. @n4.28.883.6723]
xLSV *Serious Callers Only*
    oEccentric *Shoot Them Later*
Meat. Take a look at the enclosed bullshit from the AOANL'sA (signal enclosed). I almost hope it's been taken over. If this is the way it really feels, I'd feel slightly worse.
∞

[stuttered tight point, M32, tra. @4.28.883.6920]
    xEccentric *Shoot Them Later*
        oLSV *Serious Callers Only*
Oh dear. Now we're both really under threat. I'm heading into the Homomdan Fleet Base at Ara. I suggest you seek sanctuary as well. As a precaution, I am distributing locked copies of all our signals, researches and suspicions to a variety of trustworthy Minds with instructions that they only be opened on the event of my demise. This I also urge you to do. Our only alternative is to

go public, and I am not convinced we have sufficient evidence of a non-circumstantial nature.

∞

This is despicable. To be on the run from our own kind, our own peer Minds. Meat, am I miffed. Personally I'm running for a nice sunny Orbital (DiaGlyph enclosed). I too have deposited all the facts on this matter with friends, Minds specialising in archiving and the more reliable news services (I agree we cannot yet bruit our suspicions abroad; there probably never was a proper moment for that, but if there was, the war has negated its relevance), as well as the *Sleeper Service*, in what has become my daily attempt to contact it. Who knows? Another opportunity may present itself once the dust has cleared from around the Excession – if it ever does; if there is anyone left to witness it.

Oh well; it's out of our fields now.

Best of luck, like they say.

VIII

The avatar Amorphia moved one of its catapults forward an octagon, in front of the woman's leading tower; the noise of solid wooden wheels rumbling and squeaking along on equally solid axles, and of lashed-together wooden spars and planks flexing and creaking, filled the room. A curious smell which might have been wood rose gently from the board-cube.

Dajeil Gelian sat forward in her fabulously sculpted chair, one hand absently tapping her belly gently, the other at her mouth. She sucked at one finger, her brows creased in concentration. She and Amorphia sat in the main room of her new accommodation aboard the GCU *Jaundiced Outlook*, which had been restructured to mimic precisely the lay-out of the tower she had lived in for nearly forty years. The big, round room, capped by its transparent dome, resounded – between the sound effects produced by the game-cube – to the noise of rain. The surrounding screens showed recordings of the creatures Dajeil had studied, swum and floated with during most of those four decades. All around, the woman's collected curios and mementoes were placed and set just where they had been in the tower by its lonely sea. In the broad grate, a log fire crackled exuberantly.

Dajeil thought for a while, then took a cavalarian and shifted it across the board to the noise of thundering hooves and the smell of sweat. It came to a halt by a baggage train undefended save for some irregulars.

Amorphia, sat blackly folded on a small stool on the other side of the board, went very still. Then it moved an Invisible.

Dajeil looked round the board, trying to work out what all the avatar's recent Invisible moves were leading up to. She shrugged; the cavalry piece took the irregulars almost without loss, to the sound of iron clashing on iron and screams, and the smell of blood.

Amorphia made another Invisible move.

Nothing happened for a moment. Then there was an almost sub-sonic rumbling sound. Dajeil's tower collapsed, sinking through the octagon in the board in a convincing-looking cloud of dust and the floor-shaking sound of grinding, crunching rocks. And more screams. A lot of the important moves seemed to be accompanied by those. A smell of turned-over earth and stone-dust filled the air.

Amorphia looked up almost guiltily. 'Sappers,' it said, and shrugged.

Dajeil cocked one eyebrow. 'Hmm,' she said. She surveyed the new situation. With the tower gone, the way lay open to her heartland. It didn't look good. 'Think I should sue for peace?' she asked.

'Shall I ask the ship?' the avatar asked.

Dajeil sighed. 'I suppose so,' she sighed.

The avatar glanced down at the board again. It looked up. 'Seven-eighths chance it would go to me,' the avatar told the woman.

She sat back in the great chair. 'It's yours, then,' she said. She leant forward briefly and picked up another tower. She studied it. The avatar sat back, looking moderately pleased with itself. 'Are you happy here, Dajeil?' it asked.

'Thank you, yes,' she replied. She returned her attention to the miniature tower-piece held in her fingers. She was silent for a while, then said, 'So. What is going to happen, Amorphia? Can you tell me yet?'

The avatar gazed steadily at the woman. 'We are heading very quickly towards the war zone,' it said in a strange, almost childish voice. Then it sat forward, inspecting her closely.

'War zone?' Dajeil said, glancing at the board.

'There is a war,' the avatar confirmed, nodding. It assumed a grim expression.

'Why? Where? Between whom?'

'Because of a thing called an excession. Around the place where we are heading. Between the Culture and the Affront.' It went on to explain a little of the background.

Dajeil turned the little tower-model over and over in her hands, frowning at it. Eventually she asked, 'Is this Excession thing really as important as everybody seems to think?'

The avatar looked thoughtful for just a moment, then it spread its arms and shrugged. 'Does it really matter?' it said.

The woman frowned again, not understanding. 'Doesn't it matter more than anything?'

It shook its head. 'Some things mean too much to matter,' it said. It stood up and stretched. 'Remember, Dajeil,' it told her, 'you can leave at any point. This ship will do as you wish.'

'I'll stick around for now,' she told it. She looked briefly up at it. 'When—?'

'A couple of days,' it told her. 'All being well.' It stood looking down at her for a while, watching her turn the small tower over and over in her fingers. Then it nodded and turned and quietly walked out of the room.

She hardly noticed it go. She leant forward and placed the small tower on an octagon towards the rear margin of the board, on a region of shore bordering the hem of blue that was supposed to represent the sea, near where, a few moves earlier, a ship-piece of Amorphia's had landed a small force which had established a bridge-head. She had never placed a tower in such a position, in all their games. The board interpreted the move with the sound of screams once more, but this time the screams were the plaintive, plangent calls of sea birds calling out over the sound of heavy, pounding surf. A sharply briny odour filled the air above the board cube and she was back there, back then, with the sound of the sea birds and the smell of the dashing wild sea tangled in her hair, and the growing child continually heavy and sporadically lively, almost violent with its sudden, startling kicks, in her belly.

She sat cross-legged on the pebble shore, the tower at her back, the sun a great round red shield of fire plunging into the darkly unruly sea and throwing a blood-coloured curtain across the line of the cliffs a couple of kilometres inland. She gathered her shawl about her and ran a hand through her long black hair as best she could. It stuck, held up by knots. She didn't try to pull them out; she'd rather look forward to the long, slow process of having them combed and cajoled and carefully teased out, later in the evening, by Byr.

Waves crashed on the shingle and rocks of the shore to either side of her in great sighing, soughing intakings of what sounded like the breath of some great sea creature, a gathering, deepening sound that ended in the small moment of half-silence before each great wave fell and burst against the tumbled, growling slope of rocks and stones, pushing and pulling and rolling the giant glistening pebbles in thudding concussions of water forcing its way amongst their spaces while the rocks slid and smacked and cracked against each other.

Directly in front of her, where there was a raised shelf of rock just under the surface of the sea, the waves breaking on the shallower slope in front of her were smaller, almost friendlier, and the main force of the grumbling, swelling ocean was met fifty metres out at a rough semicircle marked by a line of frothing surf.

She clasped her hands palm up on her lap, beneath the bulge of her belly, and closed her eyes. She breathed deeply, the ozone and the brine sharp in her nostrils, connecting her to the sea's salty restlessness, making her, in her mind, again part of its great fluid coalescing of constancy and changefulness, imbuing her thoughts with something of that heaving, sheltering vastness, that world-cleaving cradle of layered, night-making depth.

Inside her mind, in the semi-trance she now assumed, she stepped smilingly down through her own fluid layers of protection and conformation, to where her baby lay, healthy and growing, half awake, half asleep, wholly beautiful.

Her own genetically altered body gently interrogated the placental processes protecting the joined but subtly different chemistries and inheritance of her child's body from her own immune system and carefully, fairly managing the otherwise selfishly voracious demands the baby made upon her body's resources of blood, sugars, proteins, minerals and energy.

The temptation was always to tamper, to fiddle with the settings that regulated everything, as though by such meddling one proved how carefully painstaking and watchful one was being, but she always resisted, content that there were no warning signs, no notice that some imbalance was threatening either her health or that of the fetus and happy to leave the body's own systemic wisdom to prevail over the brain's desire to intervene.

Shifting the focus of her concentration, she was able to use another designed-in sense no creature from any part of her typically distributed Cultural inheritance had ever possessed to look upon her soon-to-be child, modelling its shape in her mind from the information provided by a subset of specialised organisms swimming in the as yet unbroken water surrounding the fetus. She saw it; hunched and curled in an orbed spectrum of smooth pinks, crouched round its umbilical link with her as though it was concentrating on its supply of blood, trying to increase its flow-rate or nutritional saturation.

She marvelled at it, as she always did; at its bulbously headed beauty, at its strange air of blankly formless intensity. She counted its fingers and toes, inspected the tightly closed eyelids, smiled at the tiny budded cleft that spoke of the cells' unprompted selection of congenital femaleness. Half her, half something strange and foreign. A new collection of matter and information to present to the universe and to which it in turn would be presented; different, arguably equal parts of that great ever-repetitive, ever-changing jurisdiction of being.

Reassured that all was well, she left the dimly aware being to continue its purposeful, unthinking growth, and returned to the part of the real world where she was sitting on the pebbled beach and the waves fell loud and foaming amongst the tumbled, rumbling rocks.

Byr was there when she opened her eyes, standing knee-deep in the small waves just in front of her, wet-suited, golden hair damply straggled in long ringlets, face dark against the display of ruddy sunset behind, found just in the act of taking off the suit's face-mask.

'Evening,' she said, smiling.

Byr nodded and splashed up out of the water, sitting down beside her and putting an arm round her. 'You okay?'

She held the fingers of the hand over her shoulder. 'Both fine,' she said. 'And the gang?'

Byr laughed, peeling off the suit's feet to reveal wrinkled pink-brown toes. 'Sk'ilip'k' has decided he likes the idea of walking on land; says he's ashamed his ancestors went out of the ocean and then went back in again as if the air was too cold. He wants us to make him a walking machine. The others think he's crazy, though there is some support for the idea of them all somehow going flying together. I left them a couple more screens and increased some of their access to the flight archives. They gave me this; for you.'

Byr handed her something from the suit's side pouch.

'Oh; thank you.' She put the small figurine in one palm and turned it over carefully with her fingers, inspecting it by the fading red light of the day's end. It was beautiful, worked out of some soft stone to perfectly resemble their idea of what they thought a human ought to look like; naturally flippered feet, legs joined to the knees, body fatter, shoulders slender, neck thicker, head narrower, hairless. It did look like her; the face, for all that it was distorted, bore a distinct resemblance. Probably G'Istig'tk't's work; there was a delicacy of line and a certain humour about the figurine's facial expression that spoke to her of the old female's personality. She held the little figure up in front of Byr. 'Think it looks like me?'

'Well, you're certainly getting that fat.'

'Oh!' she said, slapping Byr lightly on the shoulder. She glanced down at her lap, reaching to pat her belly. 'I think you're starting to show yourself, at last,' she said.

Byr smiled, her face still freckled with droplets of water, catching the dying light. She looked down, holding Dajeil's hand, patting her belly. 'Na,' she said, rising to her feet. She held out a hand to Dajeil and glanced round to the tower. 'You coming in or are you going to sit around communing with the ocean swell all evening? We've got guests, remember?'

She took a breath to say something, then held up her hand. Byr helped pull her up; she felt suddenly heavy, clumsy and . . . unwieldy. Her back hurt dully. 'Yes, let's go in, eh?'

They turned towards the lonely tower.

9

Unacceptable Behaviour

The *Excession*'s links with the two regions of the energy grid just fell away, twin collapsing pinnacles of fluted skein fabric sinking back into the grid like idealised renderings of some spent explosion at sea. Both layers of the grid oscillated for a few moments, again like some abstractly perfect liquid, then lay still. The waves produced on the grid surfaces damped quickly to nothing, absorbed. The *Excession* floated free on the skein of real space, otherwise as enigmatic as ever.

There was, for a while, silence between the three watching ships.

Eventually, the *Sober Counsel* asked, ~ . . . Is that it?

~ So it would appear, the *Fate Amenable To Change* replied. It felt terrified, elated, disappointed, all at once. Terrified to be in the presence of something that could do what it had just observed, elated to have witnessed it and taken the measurements it had – there were data here, in the velocity of the skein-grid collapse, in the apparent viscosity of the grid's reaction to the links' decoupling – that would fuel genuinely, utterly original science – and disappointed because it had a sneaking feeling that that *was* it. The *Excession* was going to sit here like this for a while, still doing nothing. Seemingly endless boredom, instants of blinding terror . . . endless boredom again. With the *Excession* around you didn't need a war.

The *Fate Amenable To Change* started relaying all the data it had collected on the grid-skein links' collapse to a variety of other ships, without even collating it properly first. Get it out of this one location first, just in case. Another part of its Mind was thinking about it, though.

~ That thing *reacted*, it told the other two craft.

~ To the Affront signal? the *Appeal To Reason* sent. ~ I was wondering about that.

~ Could this be the state in which the *Peace Makes Plenty* discovered the entity? the *Sober Counsel* asked.

~ It could indeed, couldn't it? the *Fate Amenable To Change* agreed.

~ The time has come, the *Appeal To Reason* sent. ~ I'm sending in a drone.

~ No! You wait until the Excession assumes the configuration it probably possessed when it overpowered your comrade and *then* you decide to approach it just as it must have? Are you quite mad?

~ We cannot just sit here any longer! the *Appeal To Reason* told the Culture craft. ~ The war is days away from us. We have tried every form of communication known to life and had nothing in return! We must do more! Launching drone in two seconds. Do *not* attempt to interfere with it!

II

'Well, we were going to have them at the same time; it seemed . . . I don't know; more romantic, I suppose, more symmetrical.' Dajeil laughed lightly, and stroked Byr's arm. They were in the big circular room at the top of the tower; Kran, Aist and Tulyi, and her and Byr. She stood by the log fire, with Byr. She looked to see if Byr wanted to take up the story, but she just smiled and drank from her wine goblet. 'But then when we thought about it,' Dajeil continued, 'it did kind of seem a bit crazy. Two brand new babies, and just the two of us here to look after them, and first-time mothers.'

'*Only*-time mothers,' Byr muttered, making a face into her goblet. The others laughed.

Dajeil stroked Byr's arm again. 'Well, however it turns out, we'll see. But you see this way we can have . . . whatever time in between Ren being born and our other child.' She looked at Byr, smiling warmly. 'We haven't decided on the other name yet. Anyway,' she went on, 'doing it this way will give me time to recover and get the two of us used to coping with a baby, before Byr has his . . . well, hers,' she said laughing, and put her arm round her partner's shoulder.

'Yes,' Byr said, glancing at her. 'We can practise on yours and then get it right with mine.'

'Oh, you!' Dajeil said, squeezing Byr's arm. The other woman smiled briefly.

The term used for what Dajeil and Byr were doing was Mutualling. It was one of the things you could do when you were able – as virtually every human in the Culture had been able to do for many millennia – to change sex. It took anything up to a year to alter yourself from a female to a male, or vice-versa. The process was painless and set in action simply by thinking about it; you went into the sort of trance-like state Dajeil had accessed earlier that evening when she had looked within herself to check on the state of her fetus. If you looked in the right place in your mind, there was an image of yourself as you were now. A little thought would make the image change from your present gender to the opposite sex. You came out of the trance, and that was it. Your body would already be starting to change, glands sending out the relevant viral and hormonal signals which would start the gradual process of conversion.

Within a year a woman who had been capable of carrying a child – who, indeed, might have been a mother – would be a man fully capable of fathering a child. Most people in the Culture changed sex at some point in their lives, though not all had children while they were female. Generally people eventually changed back to their congenital sex, but not always, and some people cycled back and forth between male and female all their lives, while some settled for an androgynous in-between state, finding there a comfortable equanimity.

Long-term relationships in a society where people generally lived for at least three and a half centuries were necessarily of a different nature from those in the more primitive civilisations which had provided the Culture's original blood-stock. Life-long monogamy was not utterly unknown, but it was exceptionally unusual. A couple staying together for the duration of an offspring's entire childhood and adolescence was a more common occurrence, but still not the norm. The average Culture child was close to its mother and almost certainly knew who its father was (assuming it was not in effect a clone of its mother, or had in place of a father's genes surrogated material which the mother had effectively manufactured), but it would probably be closer to the aunts and uncles who lived in the same extended familial grouping; usually in the same house, extended apartment or estate.

There were partnerships which were intended to last, however, and one of the ways that certain couples chose to emphasise their co-dependence was by synchronising their sex-changes and at different points playing both parts in the sexual act. A couple would have a child, then the man would become female and the woman would become male, and they would have another child. A more sophisticated version of this was possible due to the amount of control over one's reproductive system which still further historic genetic tinkering had made possible.

It was possible for a Culture female to become pregnant, but then, before the fertilised egg had transferred from her ovary to the womb, begin the slow change to become a man. The fertilised egg did not develop any further, but neither was it necessarily flushed away or reabsorbed. It could be held, contained, put into a kind of suspended animation so that it did not divide any further, but waited, still inside the ovary. That ovary, of course, became a testicle, but – with a bit of cellular finessing and some intricate plumbing – the fertilised egg could remain safe, viable and unchanging in the testicle while that organ did its bit in inseminating the woman who had been a man and whose sperm had done the original fertilising. The man who had been a woman then changed back again. If the woman who had been a man also delayed the development of her fertilised egg, then it was possible to synchronise the growth of the two fetuses and the birth of the babies.

To some people in the Culture this – admittedly rather long-winded and time-consuming – process was quite simply the most beautiful and perfect way for two people to express their love for one another. To others it was slightly gross and, well, tacky.

The odd thing was that until he'd met and fallen in love with Dajeil, Genar-Hofoen had been firmly of the latter opinion. He'd decided twenty years earlier, before he was even fully sexually mature and really knew his own mind about most things, that he was going to stay male all his life. He could see that being able to change sex was useful and that some people would even find it exciting, but he thought it was weak, somehow.

But then Dajeil had changed Byr's mind.

They had met aboard the General Contact Unit *Recent Convert*.

She was approaching the end of a twenty-five-year Contact career, he just starting a ten-year commitment which he might or might not request to extend when the time came. He had been the rake, she the unavailable older woman. He had decided when he'd joined Contact that he'd try to bed as many women as possible, and from the first had set about doing just that with a single-minded determination and dedication many women found highly fetching just by itself.

Then on the *Recent Convert* he cut his usual swathe through the female half of the ship's human crew, but was brought to a sudden stop by Dajeil Gelian.

It wasn't that she wouldn't sleep with him – there had been lots of women he'd asked who'd refused him, for a variety of reasons, and he'd never felt any resentment towards them or been any less likely to eventually count them as friends than the women he had made love to – it was that she told him she did find him attractive and ordinarily would have invited him to her bed, but wasn't going to because he was so promiscuous. He'd found this a slightly preposterous reason, but had just shrugged and got on with life.

They became friends; good friends. They got on brilliantly; she became his best friend. He kept expecting that this friendship would as a matter of course include sex – even if it was just once – but it didn't. It seemed so obvious to him, so natural and normal and right that it should. *Not* falling into bed together after some wonderfully enjoyable social occasion or sports session or just a night's drinking seemed positively perverse to him.

She told him he was destroying himself with his licentiousness. He didn't understand her. *She* was destroying him, in a way; he was still seeing other women but he was spending so much time with her – because they were such friends, but also because she had become a challenge and he had decided he *would* win her, whatever it took – that his usual packed schedule of seductions, affairs and relationships had suffered terribly; he wasn't able to concentrate properly on all these other women who were, or ought to be demanding his attention.

She told him he spread himself too thinly. He wasn't really destroying himself, he was stopping himself from developing. He was still in a sort of childish state, a boy-like phase where numbers mattered more than anything, where obsessive collecting, taking, enumerating, cataloguing all spoke of a basic immaturity. He could never grow and develop as a human being until he went beyond this infantile obsession with penetration and possession.

He told her he didn't want to get beyond this stage; he loved it. Anyway, even though he loved it and wouldn't care if he remained promiscuous until he was too old to do it at all, the chances were that he would change, sometime, eventually, over the course of the next three centuries or so of life which he could expect . . . There was *plenty* of time to do all this damned growing and developing. It would take care of itself. He wasn't going to try and force the pace. If all this sexual activity was something he had to get out of his system before he could properly mature, then she had a moral duty to help him get rid of it as quickly as possible, starting right now . . .

She pushed him away, as ever. He didn't understand, she told him. It wasn't a finite supply of promiscuity he was draining, it was an ever-replenishing fixation that was eating up his potential for future personal growth. She was the still point in his life he needed, or at least *a* still point; he would probably need many more in his life, she had no illusions about that. But, for now, she was it. She was the rock the river of his turbulent passion had to break around. She was his lesson.

They both specialised in the same area; exobiology. He listened to her talk sometimes and wondered whether it was possible to feel more truly alien towards another being than it was to someone of one's own species who ought to think in an at least vaguely similar way, but instead thought utterly differently. He could learn about an alien species, study them, get under their skin, under their carapaces, inside their spines or their membranes or whatever else you had to penetrate (ha!) to get to know them, get to understand them, and he could always, eventually, do that; he could start to think like them, start to feel things the way they would, anticipate their reactions to things, make a decent guess at what they were thinking at any given moment. It was an ability he was proud of.

Just by being so different from the creature you were studying you started out at a sufficiently great angle, it seemed to him, to be able to make that penetration and get inside their minds. With somebody who was ninety-nine per cent the same as you, you were too close sometimes. You couldn't draw far enough away from them to come in at a steep enough angle; you just slid off, every time in a succession of glancing contacts. No getting through. Frustration upon frustration.

Then a post had come up on a world called Telaturier. A long-term situation, spending anything up to five years with an aquatic species called the 'Ktik which the Culture wanted to help develop. It was the sort of non-ship-based Contact post people were often offered at the end of their career; Dajeil was regarded as a natural for it. It would mean one, maybe two people staying on the planet, otherwise alone save for the 'Ktik, for all that time. There would be the occasional visit from others, but little time off and no extended holidays; the whole point was to establish a long-term personal relationship with 'Ktik individuals. It wasn't something to be entered into lightly; it would mean commitment. Dajeil asked to be considered for the post and was accepted.

Byr couldn't believe Dajeil was leaving the *Recent Convert*. He told her she was doing it to annoy him. She told him he was being ridiculous. And unbelievably self-centred. She was doing it because it was an important job and it was something she felt she'd be good at. It was also something she was ready for now; she had done her bit scudding round the galaxy in GCUs and enjoyed every moment, but now she had changed and it was time to take on something more long-term. She would miss him, and she hoped he would miss her – though he certainly wouldn't miss her for as long as he claimed he would, or even as long as he thought he would – but it was time to move on, time to do something different. She was sorry she hadn't been able to stick around longer, being his still point, but that was just the way it was, and this was too great an opportunity to miss.

Later, he could never remember exactly when he'd made the decision to go with her, but he did. Perhaps he had started to believe some of the things she'd been telling him, but he too just felt that it was time to do something different, even if he had only been in Contact for a short while.

It was the hardest thing he'd ever done, harder than any seduction (with the possible exception of hers). To start with, he had to convince her it was a good idea. She wasn't even initially flattered, not for a second. It was a terrible idea, she told him. He was too young, too inexperienced, it was far, far too early in his Contact stint. He wasn't impressing her; he was being stupid. It wasn't romantic, it wasn't sensible, it wasn't flattering, it wasn't practical, it was just idiotic. And if by some miracle they did let him go along with her, he needn't assume that just making this great commitment would ensure she'd sleep with him.

This didn't prove anything except that he was as foolish as he was vain.

III

The General Contact Unit *Grey Area* didn't hold with avatars; it spoke through a slaved drone. 'Young lady—'

'*Don't* you "young lady" me in that patronising tone!' Ulver Seich said, putting her hands on her suited, gem-encrusted hips. She still had the suit helmet on, though with the visor plate hinged up. They were in the GCU's hangar space with a variety of modules, satellites and assorted paraphernalia. It looked like the space was fairly crowded at the best of times, but it was even more cluttered now with the small module that had belonged to the ROU *Frank Exchange of Views* sitting in it.

'Ms Seich,' the drone purred on, unaffected. 'I was not supposed to pick up you or your colleague Dn Churt Lyne. I have done so because you were effectively adrift in the middle of a war zone. If you really insist—'

'We weren't adrift!' Ulver said, waving her arms around and pointing back at the module. 'We were in that! It's got engines, you know!'

'Yes, very slow ones. I did say effectively adrift.' The ship-slaved drone, a casingless assemblage of components floating at head height, turned to the drone Churt Lyne. 'Dn Churt Lyne. You too are welcome. Would it be possible for you to attempt to persuade your colleague Ms Seich—'

'And don't talk about me as if I'm not here either!' Ulver said, stamping one foot. The deck under Genar-Hofoen's feet resounded.

He had never been more glad to see a GCU. Release from that damned module and Ulver Seich's abrasive moodiness. Bliss. The *Grey Area* had welcomed him first, he'd noticed.

Finally he was back on course. From here to the *Sleeper*, get the job done and then – if the war wasn't totally fucking things up – off for some R&R somewhere while things were settled. He still found it hard to believe the Affront had actually declared war on the Culture, but assuming they really had then – once it was all over and the Affront had been put in their place – Culture people with Affront experience would be needed to help manage the peace and the Culturisation of the Affront. In a way he would be sorry to see it; he liked them the way they were. But if they were crazy enough to take on the Culture . . . maybe they did need teaching a lesson. A bit of enforced niceness might do them some good.

They weren't going to like it though, because it would be a niceness that was enforced leniently, patiently and gracefully, with the sort of unflappable self-certainty the Culture couldn't help displaying when all its statistics proved that it really was doing the right thing. Probably the Affront would rather have been pulverised and then dictated to. Anyway, whatever else happened between now and then, Genar-Hofoen was sure they'd give a good account of themselves.

Ulver Seich was doing not badly in that line herself. Now she was demanding she and the drone be put back in the module immediately and allowed to continue on their way. Given that the first thing she'd done when the *Grey Area* had contacted them was demand to be rescued and taken aboard at once, this was a little cheeky, but the girl obviously didn't see it that way.

'This is piracy!' she hollered.

'Ulver . . .' the drone Churt Lyne said calmly.

'And don't you go taking its side!'

'I'm not taking its side, I'm just—'

'You are so!'

The argument went on. The ship's slave-drone looked from the girl to the elderly drone and then back again. It rose once in the air fractionally, then settled back down again. It swivelled to Genar-Hofoen. 'Excuse me,' it said quietly.

Genar-Hofoen nodded.

The drone Churt Lyne was cut off in mid-sentence and floated gently down to the floor of the hangar. Ulver Seich scowled, furious. Then she understood. She turned on the slave-drone, whirling round and jabbing a finger at it. 'How da—!'

The visor plate of her suit clanked shut; her suit powered down to statue-like immobility. The jewelled face plate sparkled in the hangar's lights. Genar-Hofoen thought he could hear some distant, muffled shouting from inside the girl's suit.

'Ms Seich,' the drone said. 'I know you can hear me in there. I'm terribly sorry to be so impolite, but I regret to say I was finding these exchanges somewhat tedious and unproductive. The fact is that you are now entirely in my power, as I hope this little demonstration proves. You can accept this and pass the next few days in relative comfort or refuse to accept this and either be locked up, followed by a drone intervention team or drugged to prevent you getting into mischief. I assure you that in any other circumstance save that of war I would happily consign you and your colleague to your module and let you do as you wished. However, as long as I am not called upon to perform any overtly military duties, you are almost certainly much safer with me than you are drifting along – or even purposefully moving along – in a small, unarmed and all but defenceless module which, I would beg you to believe, could nevertheless all too easily be mistaken for a munition or some sort of hostile craft by somebody inclined towards the reconnaissance-by-fire approach.'

Genar-Hofoen could see the girl's suit shaking; it started to rock from side to side. She must be throwing herself around inside it as best she could. The suit came close to overbalancing and falling. The little slave-drone extended a blue field to steady it. Genar-Hofoen wondered how strong the urge had been to just let it fall.

'If I am called upon to lend my weight to the proceedings, I shall let you go,' the ship's drone continued. 'Likewise, once I have discharged my duty to Mr Genar-Hofoen and the Special Circumstances section, you will, I imagine, be free to leave. Thank you for listening.'

Churt Lyne bobbed into the air and continued where it had left off. '—easonable for once in your pampered bloody life . . . !' then its voice trailed away. It gave a wonderful impression of being confused, turning this way and that a couple of times.

Ulver's face plate came up. Her face was pale, her lips compressed into a line. She was silent for a while. Eventually she said, 'You are a very rude ship. You had better hope you never have cause to call upon the hospitality of Phage Rock.'

'If that is the price of your acquiescence to my entirely reasonable requests, then, young lady, you have a deal.'

'And you'd better have some decent accommodation aboard this heap of junk,' she said, jabbing a thumb at Genar-Hofoen. 'I'm fed up inhaling this guy's testosterone.'

IV

He wore her down. There was a half-year wait between her being accepted for the post on Telaturier and actually taking it up. It took him almost all that time to talk her round. Finally, a month before the ship would stop at Telaturier to deposit her there, she agreed that he could ask Contact if he could go with her. He suspected that she only did so to get him to shut up and stop annoying her; she didn't imagine for a moment that he'd be accepted too.

He dedicated himself to arguing his case. He learned all he could about Telaturier and the 'Ktik; he reviewed the exobiological work he'd done until now and worked out how to emphasise the aspects of it that related to the post on Telaturier. He built up an argument that he was all the more suited to this sort of stoic, sedentary post just because he had been so frenetic and busy in the past; he was, well, not burnt-out, but fully sated. This was exactly the right time to slow down, draw breath, calm down. This situation was perfect for him, and he for it.

He set to work. He talked to the *Recent Convert* itself, a variety of other Contact craft, several interested drones specialising in human psychovaluation and a human selection board. It was working. He wasn't meeting with unanimous approval – it was about fifty-fifty, with the *Recent Convert* leading the No group – but he was building support.

In the end it came down to a split decision and the casting vote was held by the GSV *Quietly Confident*, the *Recent Convert*'s home craft. By that time they were back aboard the *Quietly Confident*, hitching a lift towards the region of space where Telaturier lay. An avatar of the *Quietly Confident*, a tall, distinguished man, spoke at length to him about his desire to go with Dajeil to Telaturier. He left saying that there would be a second interview.

Genar-Hofoen, happy to be back on a ship with a hundred million females aboard, though not able to throw himself into the task of bedding as many of them as possible in the two weeks available, nevertheless did his best. His fury at discovering, one morning, that the agile, willowy blonde he had spent the night with was another avatar of the ship was, by all accounts, a sight to behold.

He raged, he seethed. The quietly spoken avatar sat, winsomely dishevelled in his bed and looked on with calm, untroubled eyes.

She hadn't told him she was an avatar!

He hadn't asked, she pointed out. She hadn't told him she was a human female, either. She had been going to tell him she was there to evaluate him, but he had simply assumed that anyone he found attractive who came up to talk to him must want sex.

It was still deceit!

The avatar shrugged, got up and got dressed.

He was desperately trying to remember what he'd said to the creature the previous evening and night; it had been a pretty drunken time and he knew he'd spoken about Dajeil and the whole Telaturier thing, but what had he said? He was sickened at the ship's duplicity, appalled that it could trick him like this. It wasn't playing fair. Never trust a ship. Oh, grief, he'd just been wittering on about Dajeil and the post with the 'Ktik, completely off-guard, not trying to impress at all. Disaster. He was certain the *Recent Convert* had put its mother ship up to it. Bastards.

The avatar had paused at the door of his cabin. For what it was worth, she told him, he'd talked very eloquently about both his past life and the Telaturier post, and the ship was minded to support his application to accompany Dajeil Gelian there. Then she winked at him and left.

He was in. There was just a moment of panic, but then an overwhelming feeling of victory. He'd done it!

V

The *Killing Time* was still racing away from the ship store at Pittance at close to its maximum sustainable velocity; any faster and it would have started to degrade the performance of its engines. It was approaching a position about half-way between Pittance and the Excession when it cut power and let itself coast down towards lightspeed. It deliberately avoided doing its skidding-to-a-stop routine. Instead it carefully extended a huge light-seconds-wide field across the skein of real space and slowly dragged itself to an absolute stop, its position within the three dimensions of normal space fixed and unchanging; its only appreciable vector of movement was produced by the expansion of the universe itself; the slow drawing away from the assumed central point of the Reality which all 3-D matter shared. Then it signalled.

```
[tight beam, M32, tra. @n4.28.885.1008]
```
xROU *Killing Time*
    oGCV *Steely Glint*
I understand you are de facto military commander for this volume. Will you receive my mind-state?
∞
```
[tight beam, M32, tra. @n4.28.885.1065]
```
    xGCV *Steely Glint*
        oROU *Killing Time*
No. Your gesture – offer – is appreciated. However, we do have other plans for you. May I ask you what led you to Pittance in the first place?
∞

This is something personal. I remain convinced there was another ship, an ex-Culture ship, at Pittance, to which I went because I saw fit to do so. This ex-Culture ship thought to facilitate my destruction. This cannot be tolerated. Pride is at stake here. My honour. I will live again. Please receive my mind-state.

∞

I cannot. I appreciate your zeal and your concern but we have so few resources we cannot afford to squander them. Sometimes personal pride must take a subsidiary place to military pragmatism, however hateful we may find this.

∞

I understand. Very well. Please suggest a course of action. Preferably one which at least leaves open the possibility that I might encounter the treacherous ship at Pittance.

∞

Certainly (course schedule DiaGlyph enclosed). Please confirm receipt and signal when you have reached the first detailed position.

∞

(Receipt acknowledged).

∞

[tight beam, M32, tra. @n4.28.885.1122]
xROU *Killing Time*
    oEccentric *Shoot Them Later*
I appeal to you following this (signal sequence enclosed). Will you receive my mind-state?

∞

[tight beam, M32, tra. @n4.28.885.1309]
    xEccentric *Shoot Them Later*
        oROU *Killing Time*
    My dear ship. Is this really necessary?

∞

Nothing is necessary. Some things are to be desired. I desire this. Will you receive my mind-state?

∞

    Will it stop you if I don't?

∞

Perhaps. It will certainly delay me.

∞

    Dear me, you don't believe in making things easy for people, do you?

∞

I am a warship. That is not my function. Will you receive my mind-state?

∞

You know, this is why we prefer to have human crews on ships like you; it helps prevent such heroics.

∞

Now you are attempting to stall. If you do not agree to receive my mind-state I shall transmit it towards you anyway. Will you receive my mind-state?

∞

If you insist. But it will be with a troubled conscience . . .

The ship transmitted a copy of what in an earlier age might have been called its soul to the other craft. It then experienced a strange sense of release and of freedom while it completed its preparations for combat. Now it felt a strange, at once proud and yet humbling affinity with the warriors of all the species through every age who had bade their lives, their loves, their friends and relations goodbye, made their peace with themselves and with whatever imagined entities their superstitions demanded, and prepared to die in battle.

It experienced the most minute moment of shame that it had ever despised such barbarians for their lack of civilisation. It had always known that it was not their fault they had been such lowly creatures, but still it had found it difficult to expunge from its feelings towards such animals the patrician disdain so common amongst its fellow Minds. Now, it recognised a kinship that crossed not just the ages, species or civilisations, but the arguably still greater gap between the fumblingly confused and dim awareness exhibited by the animal brain and the near-infinitely more extended, refined and integrated sentience of what most ancestor species were amusingly, quaintly pleased to call Artificial Intelligence (or something equally and – appropriately, perhaps – unconsciously disparaging).

So now it had discovered the truth in the idea of a kind of purity in the contemplation of and preparations for self-sacrifice. It was something its recently transferred mind-state – its new self, to be born in the matrix of a new warship, before too long – might never experience. It briefly considered transmitting its current mind-state to replace the one it had already sent, but swiftly abandoned the idea; just more time to be wasted, for one thing, but more importantly, it felt it would insult the strange calmness and self-certainty it now felt to place it artificially in a Mind which was not about to die. It would be inappropriate, perhaps even unsettling. No; it would cleave to this clear surety exclusively, holding it to its exculpated soul like a talisman of holy certitude.

The warship looked about its internal systems. All was ready; any further delay would constitute prevarication. It turned itself about, facing back the way it had come. It powered up its engines slowly to accelerate gradually, sleekly away into the void. As it moved, it left the skein of space behind it seeded with mines and hyper-space-capable missiles. They might only remove a ship or two even if they were lucky, but they would slow the rest down. It ramped its speed up, to significant engine degradation in 128 hours, then 64, then 32. It held there. To go any further would be to risk immediate and catastrophic disablement.

It sped on through the dark hours of distance that to mere light were decades, glorying in its triumphant, sacrificial swiftness, radiant in its martial righteousness.

It sensed the oncoming fleet ahead, like a pattern of brightly rushing comets in that envisaged space. Ninety-six ships arranged in a rough circle spread across a front thirty years of 3-D space across, half above, half below the skein. Behind them lay the traces of another wave, numerically the same size as the first but taking up twice the volume.

There had been three hundred and eighty-four ships stored at Pittance. Four waves, if each was the same size as the first. Where would it position itself if it was in command?

Near but not quite actually in the centre of the third wave.

Would the command vessel guess this and so position itself somewhere else? On the outside edge of the first wave, somewhere in the second wave, right at the back, or even way on the outside, independent of the main waves of craft altogether?

Make a guess.

It looped high out across the four-dimensional range of infra-space, sweeping its sensors across the skein and readying its weapon systems. Its colossal speed was bringing the war fleet closer faster than anything it had ever seen before save in its most wildly indulged simulations. It zoomed high above them in hyperspace, still, it seemed, undetected. A pulse of sheer pleasure swept its Mind. It had never felt so good. Soon, very soon, it would die, but it would die gloriously, and its repu-tation pass on to the new ship born with its memories and personality, transmitted in its mind-state to the *Shoot Them Later*.

It fell upon the third wave of oncoming ships like a raptor upon a flock.

VI

Byr stood on the circular stone platform at the top of the tower, looking out to the ocean where two lines of moonlight traced narrow silver lines across the restless waters. Behind her, the tower's crystal dome was dark. She had gone to bed at the same time as Dajeil, who tired more quickly these days. They had made their apologies and left the others to fend for themselves. Kran, Aist and Tulyi were all friends from the GCU *Unacceptable Behaviour,* another of the *Quietly Confident*'s daughter ships. They had known Dajeil for twenty years; the three had been aboard the *Quietly Confident* four years earlier and were some of the last people Byr and Dajeil had seen before they'd left for Telaturier.

The *Unacceptable Behaviour* was looping through this volume and they'd persuaded it to let them stop off here for a couple of days and see their old friend.

The moons glittered their stolen light across the fretful dance of waves, and Byr too reflected, glanding a little *Diffuse* and thinking that the moons' V of light, forever converging on the observer, encouraged a kind of egocentricity, an overly romantic idea of one's own centrality to things, an illusory belief in personal precedence. She remembered the first time she had stood here and thought something along these lines, when she had been a man and he and Dajeil had not long arrived here.

It had been the first night he and Dajeil had – finally, at last, after all that fuss – lain together. Then he had come up here in the middle of the night while she'd slept on, and gazed out over these waters. It had been almost calm, then, and the moons' tracks (when they rose, and quite as though they rose and did not rise for him) lay shimmering slow and near unbroken on the untroubled face of the ocean's slack waters.

He'd wondered then if he'd made a terrible mistake. One part of his mind was convinced he had, another part claimed the moral high ground of maturity and assured him it was the smartest move he'd ever made, that he was indeed finally growing up. He had decided that night that even if it was a mistake that was just too bad; it was a mistake that could only be dealt with by embracing it, by grasping it with both hands and accepting the results of his decision; his pride could only be preserved by laying it aside entirely for the duration. He would make this work, he would perform this task and be blameless in the self-sacrifice of his own interests to Dajeil's. His reward was that she had never seemed happier, and that, almost for the first time, he felt responsible for another's pleasure on a scale beyond the immediate.

When, months later, she had suggested that they have a child, and later still, while they were still mulling this over, that they Mutual – for they had the time, and the commitment – he had been extravagant in his enthusiasm, as though through such loud acclaim he could drown out the doubts he heard inside himself.

'Byr?' a soft voice said from the little cupola that gave access from the steps to the roof.

She turned round. 'Hello?'

'Hi. Couldn't sleep either, eh?' Aist said, joining Byr at the parapet. She was dressed in dark pyjamas; her naked feet slap-slapped on the flagstones.

'No,' Byr said. She didn't need much sleep. Byr spent quite a lot of time by herself these days, while Dajeil slept or sat cross-legged in one of her trances or fussed around in the nursery they had prepared for their children.

'Same here,' Aist said, crossing her arms beneath her breasts and leaning out over the parapet, her head and shoulders dangling over the drop. She spat slowly; the little fleck fell whitely through the moonlight and disappeared against the dark slope of the tower's bottom storey. She rocked back onto her feet and moved some of her medium-length brown hair off her eyes, while she studied Byr's face, a small frown just visible on her brow. She shook her head. 'You know,' she said, 'I never thought you'd be one to change sex, let alone have a kid.'

'Same here,' Byr said, leaning on the parapet and gazing out to sea. 'Still can't believe it, sometimes.'

Aist leant beside him. 'Still, it's okay, isn't it? I mean, you're happy, aren't you?'

Byr glanced at the other woman. 'Isn't it obvious?'

Aist was silent for a while. Eventually she said, 'Dajeil loves you very much. I've known her twenty years. She's changed completely too, you know; not just you. She was always really independent, never wanted to be a mother, never wanted to settle down with one person, not for a long time, anyway. Not until she was old. You've both changed each other so much. It's . . . it's really something. Almost scary, but, well, sort of impressive, you know?'

'Of course.'

There was silence for another while. 'When do you think you'll have your baby?' Aist asked. 'How long after she has . . . Ren, isn't it?'

'Yes; Ren. I don't know. We'll see.' Byr gave a small laugh, almost more of a cough. 'Maybe we'll wait until Ren is grown up enough to help us look after it.'

Aist made the same noise. She leant on the parapet again, lifting her feet off the flagstones and balancing, pivoting on her folded arms. 'How's it been here, being so far away from anybody else? Do you get many visitors?'

Byr shook her head. 'No. You're only the third lot of people we've seen.'

'Gets lonely, I suppose. I mean I know you've got each other, but . . .'

'The 'Ktik are fun,' Byr said. 'They're people, individuals. I've met thousands of them by now, I suppose. There are something like twenty or thirty million of them. Lots of new little chums to meet.'

Aist sniggered. 'Don't suppose you can get it off with them, can you?'

Byr glanced at her. 'Never tried. Doubt it.'

'Boy, you were some swordsman, Byr,' Aist said. 'I remember you on the *Quietly*, first time we met. I'd never met anyone so focused.' She laughed. 'On anything! You were like a natural force or something; an earthquake or a tidal wave.'

'Those are natural disasters,' Byr pointed out with feigned frostiness.

'Well, close enough then,' Aist said, laughing gently. She glanced slyly, slowly, at the other woman. 'I suppose I'd have found myself in the firing line if I'd stuck around longer.'

'I imagine you might,' Byr said in a tired, resigned voice.

'Yup, could all have turned out completely different,' Aist said.

Byr nodded. 'Or it could all have turned out exactly the same.'

'Well, don't sound so happy about it,' Aist said. 'I wouldn't have minded.' She leant over the parapet and spat delicately again, moving her head just so, flicking the spittle outward. This time it landed on the gravel path which skirted the tower's stone base. She made an approving noise and looked back at Byr, wiping her chin and grinning. She looked at Byr, studying his face again. 'It's not fair, Byr,' she said. 'You look good no matter what you are.' She put one hand out slowly towards Byr's cheek. Byr looked into her large dark eyes.

One moon started to disappear behind a ragged layer of high cloud and a small wind picked up, smelling of rain.

A test, for her friend, Byr thought, as the other woman's long fingers gently stroked her face, feather soft. But the fingers were trembling. *Still a test; determined to do it but nervous about it.* Byr put her hand up and held the woman's fingers lightly. She took it as a signal to kiss her.

After a little while, Byr said, 'Aist . . .' and started to pull away.

'Hey,' she said softly, 'this doesn't mean anything, all right? Just lust. Doesn't mean a thing.'

A little later still Byr said, 'Why are we doing this?'

'Why not?' Aist breathed.

Byr could think of several reasons, asleep in the stony darkness beneath them. *How I have changed*, she thought. *But then again, not that much.*

VII

Ulver Seich strolled through the accommodation section of the *Grey Area*. At least there was a bit more strolling to be done on the GCU; had she come here straight from the family house on Phage it would have seemed horribly cramped, but after the claustro-phobic confines of the *Frank Exchange of Views*, it appeared almost spacious (she had spent so little time on Tier, and passed the small amount of time she had there in such a frenetic haste of preparation that it hardly counted. As for the nine-person module – *ugh*!).

The *Grey Area*'s interior – built to house three hundred people in reasonable if slightly compact comfort, and now home only to her, Churt Lyne and Genar-Hofoen – was actually pretty interesting, which was an unexpected plus on this increasingly disillusioning expedition. The ship was like a museum to torture, death and genocide; it was filled with mementoes and souvenirs from hundreds of different planets, all testifying to the tendency towards institutionalised cruelty exhibited by so many forms of intelligent life. From thumbscrews and pilliwinks to death camps and planet-swallowing black holes, the *Grey Area* had examples of the devices and entities involved, or of their effects, or documentary recordings of their use.

Most of the ship's corridors were lined with weaponry, the larger pieces standing on the floor, others on tables; bigger items took up whole cabins, lounges or larger public spaces and the very biggest weapons were shown as scale models. There were thousands of instruments of torture, clubs, spears, knives, swords, strangle cords, catapults, bows, powder guns, shells, mines, gas canisters, bombs, syringes, mortars, howitzers, missiles, atomics, lasers, field arms, plasma guns, microwavers, effectors, thunderbolters, knife missiles, line guns, thudders, gravguns, monofilament warps, pancakers, AM projectors, grid-fire impulsers, ZPE flux-polarisers, trapdoor units, CAM spreaders and a host of other inventions designed for – or capable of being turned to the purpose of – producing death, destruction and agony.

Some of the cabins and larger spaces had been fitted out to resemble torture chambers, slave holds, prison cells and death chambers (including the ship's swimming pool, though after she'd pointedly mentioned that she liked to start each day with a dip, this was now being converted back to its original purpose). Ulver supposed these ... stage-sets ... were a little like the famous tableaux the *Sleeper Service* was supposed to contain, except that the *Grey Area*'s had no bodies in them (something of a relief, in the circumstances).

Like a lot of people, she had always wanted to see the real thing. She had asked if she and Churt Lyne might go aboard the GSV when Genar-Hofoen did, but her request had been turned down; they would have to stay on the *Grey Area* until the GCU could find somewhere both safe and unrestricted to deposit them. What made it all even more annoying in a way was that the *Grey Area* expected it would be keeping in close contact with the *Sleeper Service*; inside its field envelope, if it was allowed to. So near and yet so far and all that crap. Whatever; it looked like she wouldn't get to see even the remnants of the famous craft's tableaux vivants, and would have to make do with the *Grey Area* and its tableaux mortants.

She thought they might have been more effective if they had contained the victims or the victims and tormentors, but they didn't. Instead they contained just the rack, the iron maiden, the fires and the irons, the shackles and the beds and chairs, the buckets of water and acid and the electric cables and all the serried instruments of torture and death. To see them in action you had to stand before a nearby screen.

It was a little shocking, Ulver supposed, but kind of aloof at the same time; it was like you could just inspect this stuff and get some idea of how it worked and what it did (though watching the screens wasn't really advisable; she watched one for a few seconds and nearly lost her breakfast; and it wasn't even *humans* who were being tortured) and you could sort of ride it out; you could accept that this had happened and feel bad about it all right, but at the end of it you were still here, it hadn't happened to you, stopping this sort of shit was exactly what SC, Contact, the Culture was about, and you were part of that civilisation, part of that civilising . . . and that sort of made it bearable. Just. If you didn't watch the screens.

Still, just holding a little iron device designed to crush the sort of fingers that were holding it, looking at a knotted cord whose twin knots – once the cord was tightened behind the head – were set at just the right distance to compress and burst the sort of eyes that were looking at it . . . well, it was kind of affecting. She spent a fair bit of time shivering and rubbing the bits of her body that kept getting bumps.

She wondered how many people had looked upon this grisly collection of memorabilia. She had asked the ship but it had been vague; apparently it regularly offered its services as a sort of travelling museum of pain and ghastliness, but it rarely had any takers.

One of the exhibits which she discovered, towards the end of her wanderings, she did not understand. It was a little bundle of what looked like thin, glisteningly blue threads, lying in a shallow bowl; a net, like something you'd put on the end of a stick and go fishing for little fish in a stream. She tried to pick it up; it was impossibly slinky and the material slipped through her fingers like oil; the holes in the net were just too small to put a finger-tip through. Eventually she had to tip the bowl up and pour the blue mesh into her palm. It was very light. Something about it stirred a vague memory in her, but she couldn't recall what it was. She asked the ship what it was, via her neural lace.

~ That is a neural lace, it informed her. ~ A more exquisite and economical method of torturing creatures such as yourself has yet to be invented.

She gulped, quivered again and nearly dropped the thing.

~ Really? she sent, and tried to sound breezy. ~ Ha. I'd never really thought of it that way.

~ It is not generally a use much emphasised.

~ I suppose not, she replied, and carefully poured the fluid little device back into its bowl on the table.

She walked back to the cabin she'd been given, past the assorted arms and torture machines. She decided to check up on how the war was going, again through the lace. At least it would take her mind off all this torture shit.

Affront Declare War On Culture.
   (Major events so far, by time/importance.
   (Likely limits.
   (Detailed events to date.
   (Greatest conflict since Idiran War?
   (Likely link with Esperi Excession.
   (The Affront – a suitable case for treatment?
   (So *this* is how the barbarians felt; the experience of war through
       the ages.

Ship Store at Pittance taken over by Affront; hundreds of ships appropriated.

(How could it happen?
(Insurance policies or weak points?
(Pundit paradise; placing their bets on what happens next.
(The psychology of warships.

Warcraft from other ship stores mobilised.
(Partial mobilisation earlier – so who knew what when?
(Technical stuff; lots of exciting figures for armamentaphiles.

Peace initiatives.
(Culture wants to talk – Affront just want to fight.
(Galactic Council sends reps everywhere. They look busy.
(Gosh, can we help? Have a laugh at the expense of sad
   superstitionists.

In jeopardy: the hostage habitats, the boarded ships.
(Five Orbitals, eleven cruise ships Affronted.
(Schadenfreude time; who's all at risk at the moment.
(Tier gets sniffy.

Quick while they're not looking.
(Primitives see exciting opportunities.

What's in it for me?
(Design your own war; sim details and handy hints.
(Thinking positively; new tech, inspired art, heroic tales and
   better sex . . . war as hoot [for incurable optimists and people
   looking for party conversation stoppers only].

Other news:
Blitteringueh Conglo actuates Abuereffe Airsphere – latest.
S3/4 ravaged by nova in Ytrillo.
Stellar Field-Liners sweep Aleisinerih domain again.
Cherdilide Pacters in Phaing-Ghrotassit Subliming quandary.
Abafting Imorchi; sleaze, sleaze and more sleaze.
Sport.
Art.
   DiaGlyph Directory.

Special Reports Directory.
Index.

Ulver Seich scanned the screen-set her neural lace threw across her left eye's field of vision as she walked, one half of her brain paying attention to the business of walking and the other half watching the virtual screen. Not a thing about her. She wasn't sure whether to feel relieved or insulted. Let's try:

(Tier gets sniffy ... No, that was nothing but general stuff about the habitat throwing all Culture people and Affronters off. No names mentioned.

    Index. P ... Ph ... Phage Rock.
      (That war again; was PR a kind of minor ship store?
      (Tier over-rated anyway; PR turns tail. New heading, but
        where exactly?
      (Koodre wins IceBlast cup.
      (New Ledeyueng exhibition opens in T41.
    DiaGlyph subDirectory.
      subIndex.
      subIndex. S ... Seich, Ulver.
        (*Oh Ulver, Where Are You?* – new Poeglyph by Zerstin
        Hoei.

She stared at the entry. Grief, was that it? One lousy picture-poem by an irredeemable feeb she'd barely heard of (and even then only to discover he regularly changed his appearance to resemble her current boyfriend)? Ugh! She joggled the subIndex again, in the remote and forlorn chance there was some sort of ware glitch. There wasn't. That was it. If she wanted more she'd have to hit Records.

Ulver Seich stopped in her tracks and stared at the nearest bulkhead, open mouthed.

She was no longer News on Phage.

VIII

It should not have made the difference that it did, and yet it did. Their three visitors stayed for two nights, going swimming with the 'Ktik during the second day. Byr met Aist again that night. The following day the visitors left, climbing into the module which the *Unacceptable Behaviour* sent down for them. The ship was heading off to loop round a proto-nova a few thousand years distant. It would be back in two weeks to drop off any further supplies they might need. Dajeil's baby would be born a couple of weeks after that. The next ship due to visit would be another year away, when they might have doubled the human population of the planet. They stood together on the beach. Dajeil held Byr's hand as the module climbed into the slate-coloured clouds.

Later that evening Byr found Dajeil watching the recording in the tower's top room, where the screens were. Tears ran down her face.

There were no monitor systems on the tower itself. It must have been one of the independent camera drones. This one must have landed on the tower that night, found two large mammals there, and started recording.

Dajeil turned to look at Byr, her face streaked with the tears. Byr felt a sudden welling of anger. On the screen, she watched the two people embracing, caressing on the tower's moonlit roof, and heard the soft gasps and whisperings.

'Yes,' Byr said, smiling ironically as she pulled off the wet suit. 'Old Aist, eh? Quite a lass. You shouldn't cry, you know. Upsets the body's fluid balance for baby.'

Dajeil threw a glass at her. It smashed behind Byr on the winding stair. A little servitor drone scurried past Byr's feet and windmilled down the carpeted steps on its little limbs, to start cleaning up the mess. Byr looked into her lover's face. Dajeil's swollen breasts rose and fell within her shirt and her face was flushed. Byr continued to peel off bits of the wet suit.

'It was a bit of light relief, for grief's sake,' she said, keeping her voice even. 'Just a friendly fuck. A loose end sort of thing. It—'

'How could you do this to us?' Dajeil screamed.

'Do what?' Byr protested, still trying to keep her voice from rising. 'What have I done?'

'Screwing my best friend, here! Now! After everything!'

Byr kept calm. 'Does it count as screwing, technically, when neither of you has a penis?' She assumed a pained, puzzled expression.

'You shit! Don't laugh about it!' Dajeil screamed. Her voice was hoarse, unlike anything Byr had heard from her before. 'Don't you fucking laugh about it!' Dajeil was suddenly up out of her seat and dashing towards her, arms raised.

Byr caught her wrists.

'Dajeil!' she said, as the other woman struggled and sobbed and tried to shake her hands free. 'You're being ridiculous! I always fucked other people; *you* were fucking other people when you were giving me all this shit about being my "still point"; we both knew, it wasn't like we were juveniles or in some dumb monogamy cult or something. Shit; so I stuck my fingers in your pal's cunt; so fucking what? She's gone. I'm still here; you're still here, the fucking kid's still in your belly; yours is in mine. Isn't that what you said is all that matters?'

'You bastard, you bastard!' Dajeil cried, and collapsed. Byr had to support her as she crumpled to the floor, sobbing uncontrollably.

'Oh, Dajeil, come on; this isn't anything that matters. We never swore to be faithful, did we? It was just a friendly . . . it was *politeness*, for fuck's sake. I didn't even think it was worth mentioning . . . Come on, I know this is a tough time for you and there's all these hormones and shit in your body, but this is crazy; you're reacting . . . crazily . . .'

'Fuck off! Fuck off and leave me alone!' Dajeil spat, her voice reduced to a croak. 'Leave me alone!'

'Dajeil,' Byr said, kneeling down beside her. 'Please . . . Look, I'm sorry. I really am. I've never apologised for fucking anybody in my life before; I swore I never would, but I'm doing it now. I can't undo it, but I didn't realise it would affect you like this. If I had I wouldn't have done it. I swear. I'd never have done it; it was she who kissed me first. I didn't set out to seduce her or anything, but I'd have said No, I'd have said No, really I would. It wasn't my idea, it wasn't my fault. I'm sorry. What more can I say? What can I do . . . ?'

It did no good. Dajeil wouldn't talk after that. She wouldn't be carried to her bed. She didn't want to be touched or be brought anything to eat or drink. Byr sat at the screen controls while Dajeil whimpered on the floor.

Byr found the recording the camera drone had taken and wiped it.

IX

The *Grey Area* did something to his eyes. It happened in his sleep, the first night he was aboard. He woke up in the morning to the sound of song birds trilling over distant waterfalls and the faint smell of tree resin; one wall of his cabin impersonated a window high up in a forest-swathed mountain range. There was a memory of some strangeness, a buried recollection of some sort; half real, half not, but it slipped slowly away as he came fully to. The view was blurry for a moment, then slowly came clear as he recalled the ship asking him last night if it could implant the nanotechs while he slept. His eyes tingled a little and he wiped away some tears, but then everything seemed to settle back to normal.

'Ship?' he said.

'Yes?' replied the cabin.

'Is that it?' he asked. 'With the implants?'

'Yes. There's a modified neural lace in place in your skull; it'll take a day or so to bed in properly. I hurried up a little repair-work your own systems were taking their time with near your visual cortex. You have hit your head recently?'

'Yeah. Fell out of a carriage.'

'How are your eyes?'

'Bit blurred and smarted a little. Okay now.'

'Later today we'll go through a simulation of what happens when you've interfaced with the *Sleeper Service*'s Storage vault system. All right?'

'Fine. How's our rendezvous with the *Sleeper* looking?'

'All is in hand. I expect to transfer you in four days.'

'Great. And what's happening with the war?'

'Nothing much. Why?'

'I just wanted to know,' Genar-Hofoen said. 'Have there been any major actions yet? Any more cruise ships been taken hostage?'

'I am not a news service, Genar-Hofoen. You have a terminal, I believe. I suggest you use it.'

'Well, thank you for your help,' muttered the man, swinging out of bed. He had never met so unhelpful a ship. He went for breakfast; at least it ought to be able to provide that.

He was sitting alone in the ship's main mess watching his favourite Culture news service via a holo projected by his terminal. After the first flurry of Affront Orbital and cruise ship takeovers with no obvious Culture military reply but talk of a mobilisation taking place (frustratingly, almost entirely beyond the news services' perceptions), the war seemed to have entered a period of relative quiescence. Right now the news service was running a semi-serious feature on how to ingratiate yourself with an Affronter if you happened to bump into one – when the dream he had had last night – the thing he had half remembered just after the point of waking – suddenly returned to him.

X

Byr awoke that night to find Dajeil standing over her with a diving knife held tightly in both hands, her eyes wide and full and staring, her face still puffy with tears. There was blood on the knife. What had she done to herself? Blood on the knife. Then the pain snapped back. The first reaction of Byr's body had been just to blank it out. Now she was awake, it came back. Not the agony a basic human would have experienced, but a deep, shocking, awful awareness of damage a civilised creature could appreciate without the disabling suffering of crude pain. Byr took a moment to understand.

What? What had been done? What? Roaring in ears. Looking

up, to find all the sheets red. Her blood. Belly; sliced. Open. Glistening masses of green, purple, yellow. Redness still pumping. Shock. Massive blood loss. What would Dajeil do now? Byr sank back. So this was how it ended.

Mess, indeed. Feel of systems shutting down. Losing the body. Brain drawing blood to it storing oxygen determined to stay alive as long as possible even though it had lost its life-support mechanism. They had medical gear in the tower that could save her still but Dajeil just stood there staring as though sleep-walking or mad with some overdone gland-drug. Standing staring at her standing staring at her dying.

Neatness to it, still. Women; penetration. He had lived for it. Now he died of it. Now he/she would die, and Dajeil would know that he had really loved her.

Did that make sense?

Did it? she asked the man she had once been.

Silence from him; not dead but certainly gone, gone for now. She was on her own, dying on her own. Dying at the hand of the only woman she/he had ever loved.

So *did* it make sense?

. . . I am who I ever was. What I called masculinity, what I celebrated in it was just an excuse for *me*-ness, wasn't it?

No. No. No and fuck this, lady.

Byr stuck both hands over the wound and the awful, heavy flap of flesh and swung out of the bed on the far side, dragging the blood-heavy top sheet with her. She stumbled to the bathroom, holding her guts in and trying all the time to watch the other woman. Dajeil stood staring at the bed, as though not realising Byr had gone, as though staring at a projection she alone could see, or at a ghost.

Byr's legs and feet were covered in blood. She slipped against the door jamb and almost blacked out, but managed to stagger into the room's pastel fragrance. The bathroom door locked behind her. She sank to her knees. Loud roar in head now; tunnel vision, like wrong end of a telescope. Deep, sharp smell of blood; startling, shocking, all by itself.

The life-support collar was in a box with the other emergency medical supplies, thoughtfully located below waist level so you could crawl to it. Byr clamped the collar on and curled up on the floor, clamped and curled around the fissure in her abdomen and the long gory umbilical of shiningly red sheet. Something hissed and tingled around her neck.

Even staying curled up was too much effort. She flopped over on the tiles' soft warmth. It was easy, all the blood made it so slippery.

XI

In the dream, he watched as Zreyn Tramow rose from a bed of pink petals. Some still adhered, like small local blushes dispensed upon her pink-brown nakedness. She dressed in her uniform of soft grey and made her way to the bridge, nodding to and exchanging pleasantries with the others on her shift and those going off-watch. She donned the sculpted shell of the induction helmet, and – in half an eye-blink – was floating in space.

Here was the vast enfolding darkness, the sheer astringent emptiness of space colossal, writ wide and deep across the entire sensorial realm; an unending presagement of consummate grace and meaninglessness together. She looked about the void, and far stars and galaxies went swivelling within her field of vision. The view settled on:

The strange star. The enigma.

At such moments she felt the loneliness not just of this fathomless wilderness and this near-utter emptiness, but of her own position, and of her whole life.

Ship names; she had heard of a craft called *I Blame My Mother*, and another called *I Blame Your Mother*. Perhaps, then, it was a more common complaint than she normally allowed for (and of course she had ended up on this ship, with its own particular chosen name, forever wondering whether it had been one of those little conceits of her superiors to pair them so). Did she blame her mother? She supposed she did. She did not think she could claim any technical deficiency in the love attending her upbringing, and yet – at the time – she had *felt* there was, and to this day she would have claimed that the technicalities of a childhood did not cover all that might be required by certain children; in short, her aunts had never been enough. She knew of many individuals raised by people other than their natural parent, and to a man and to a woman they all seemed happy and content enough, but it had not been that way for her. She had long ago accepted that whatever it was she felt was wrong, it was in some sense her fault, even if it was a fault that derived from causes she could do nothing to alter.

Her mother had chosen to remain in Contact following the birth of her child and had left to return to her ship not long after the girl's first birthday.

Her aunts had been loving and attentive and she had never had the heart – or worked up the hurtful malice – to let them or anybody else know the aching void she felt inside herself, no matter how many times she had lain in tears in her bed, rehearsing the words she would use to do just that.

She supposed she might have transferred some of her need for a parent to her father, but she had scarcely felt that he was a part of her life; he was just another man who came to the house, sometimes stayed for a while, played with her and was kind and even loving, but (she had known instinctively at first, and later admitted rationally to herself after a few years of self-delusion) had played, been kind and even loved her in a more cheerily vague and off-hand sort of way than many of her uncles; she imagined now that he had loved her in his own fashion and had enjoyed being with her, and assuredly she had felt a certain warmth at the time, but still, before very long, even as an infant, before she knew the precise reasons, motives and desires involved, she had guessed that the frequency and length of his visits to the house had more to do with his interest in one or two of her aunts than in any abiding tenderness he felt towards his daughter.

Her mother returned now and again, for visits that for both of them veered wildly between painful feelings of love and furious rages of resentment. Somehow, later, exhausted and dismayed by these sapping, abrasive, attriting episodes, they came to a sort of truce; but it was at the expense of any closeness.

By the time her mother returned for good, she was like just another girlfriend; they both had better friends.

So she had always been alone. And she suspected, she almost knew, that she would end her days alone. It was a source of sadness – though she tried never to wallow in self-pity – and even, in a subsidiary way, of shame, for at the back of her mind she could not escape the nagging desire for somebody – some man, if she was honest with herself – to come to her rescue, to take her away from the vacuum that was her existence and make her no longer alone. It was something she had never been able to confess to anybody, and yet something that she had an inkling was known to the people and machines who had allowed her to assume this exalted, if onerous position.

She hoped that it was secret within herself, but knew too well the extent of the knowledge-base, the sheer experience behind those who exercised power over her and people like her. An individual did not outwit such intelligence; he or she might come to an understanding with it, an accommodation with it, but there was no outthinking or outsmarting it; you had to accept the likelihood that all your secrets would be known to them and trust that they would not misuse that knowledge, but exploit it without malice. Her fears, her needs, her insecurities, her compensating drives and ambitions; they could be plumbed, measured and then used, they could be employed. It was a pact, she supposed, and one she did not really resent, for it was a mutually beneficial arrangement. They and she each got what they wanted; they a canny, dedicated officer determined to prove herself in the application of their cause and she the chance to seek and gain approval, the reassurance that she was worth something.

Such trust, and the multiplying opportunities to provide proof of her diligence and exercised wisdom, ought at last to be enough for her, but still sometimes it was not, and she yearned for something that no fusion of herself with any conglomerative could provide; a need to be reassured of a personal worth, an appreciation of her individual value which would only be valid coming from another individual.

She went through cycles of admitting this to herself and hoping that one day she would find somebody she could finally feel comfortable with, finally respect, finally judge worthy of her regard when measured against her own strict standards . . . and then rejecting it all, fierce in her determination to prove herself on her terms and the terms of the great service she had entered, forging the resolve to turn her frustrations to her and their advantage, to redirect the energies resulting from her loneliness into her practical, methodically realisable ambitions; another qualification, a further course of study, a promotion, command, further advancement . . .

The enigma attracted her, no less than the impossibly old star. Here, in this discovery, might eventually lie a kind of fame that could sate her desire for recognition. Or so she told herself, sometimes. Here, after all, was already a strange kind of kinship, a sort of twinning, even if it was that of an implausibility and a mystery.

She directed her attention to the enigma, seeming to rush towards it in the darkness, swelling its black presence until it filled her field of vision.

A blink of light focused her awareness near its centre. Somehow, without much more than that single glimmer, the light had a kind of character to it, something familiar, recognisable; it was like the opening of a door, like gaining an unexpected glimpse into a brightly lit room. Attention drawn, she looked closer automatically.

And was instantly sucked into the light; it erupted blindingly, exploding out at her like some absurdly quick solar flare, engulfing her, snapping around her like a trap.

Zreyn Enhoff Tramow, captain of the General Contact Ship *Problem Child*, barely had time to react. Then she was plucked away and disappeared into the coruscating depths of the falling fire, struggling and trapped and calling for help. Calling to *him*.

He bounced awake on the bed-field, eyes suddenly open, breath fast and shallow, heart hammering. The cabin's lights came on, dim at first and then brightening gently, reacting to his movements.

Genar-Hofoen wiped his face with his hands and looked around the cabin. He swallowed and took a deep breath. He hadn't meant to dream anything like that. It had been as vivid as an implanted dream or some game-scenario shared in sleep. He had meant to dream one of his usual erotic dreams, not look back two thousand years to the time when the *Problem Child* had first found the trillion-year-old sun and the black-body object in orbit around it. All he'd wanted was a sex-simulation, not an in-depth inquisition of a bleakly ambitious woman's arid soul.

Certainly it had been interesting, and he'd been fascinated that he had somehow been the woman and yet not been her at the same time, and had been – non-sexually – inside her, in her mind, close as a neural lace to her thoughts and emotions and the hopes and fears she had been prompted to think about by the sight of the star and the thing she had thought of as the enigma. But it hadn't been what he'd expected.

Another strange, unsettling dream.

'Ship?' he said.

'Yes?' the *Grey Area* said through the cabin's sound system.

'I . . . I just had a weird dream.'

'Well, I have some experience in that realm, I suppose,' the ship said with what sounded like a heavy sigh. 'I imagine now you want to talk about it.'

'No . . . well . . . no; I just wondered . . . you weren't . . . ?'

'Ah. You want to know was I interfering with your dreams, is that it?'

'It just, you know, occurred to me.'

'Well now, let's see . . . If I had been, do you think I would answer you truthfully?'

He thought. 'Does that mean you were or you weren't?'

'I was not. Are you happy now?'

'No I'm not happy now. Now I don't know if you were or you weren't.' He shook his head, and grinned. 'You're fucking with my head either way, aren't you?'

'As if I would do such a thing,' the ship said smoothly. It made a chuckling noise which contrived to be the most unsettling sound it had articulated so far. 'I expect,' it said, 'it was just an effect caused by your neural lace bedding in, Genar-Hofoen. Nothing to worry about. If you don't want to dream at all, gland *somnabsolute*.'

'Hmm,' he said slowly, and then; 'Lights out.' He lay back down in the darkness. 'Good night,' he said quietly.

'Sweet dreams, Genar-Hofoen,' the *Grey Area* said. The circuit clicked ostentatiously off.

He lay awake in the darkness for a while, before falling asleep again.

XII

Byr woke up in bed, hopelessly weak, but cleansed and whole and starting to recover. The emergency medical collar lay, also cleaned, at the side of the bed. By it lay a bowl of fruit, a jug of milk, a screen, and the small figurine Byr had given Dajeil, from the old female 'Ktik called G'Istig'tk't', a few days earlier.

The tower's slave-drones brought Byr her food and attended to her toilet. The first question she asked was where Dajeil was, half afraid that the other woman had taken the knife to herself or just walked into the sea. The drones replied that Dajeil was in the tower's garden, weeding.

On other occasions they informed Byr that Dajeil was working in the tower's top room, or swimming, or had taken a flier to some distant island. They answered other questions, too. It was Dajeil – along with one of the drones – who had forced open the bathroom door. So she could still have killed Byr.

Byr asked Dajeil to come visit her, but she would not. Eventually, a week later, Byr was able to get out of bed by herself and walk around. A pair of drones fussed at her side.

Across her belly, the scar was already starting to fade.

Byr already knew her recovery would be complete. Whether Dajeil had actually intended murder or just some insane abortion, she didn't know.

Looking down into herself, in a light trance to further judge the extent of the damage that had been done and was now diligently repairing itself, Byr noted that her body had come to the decision, apparently on its own accord, while she'd been unconscious, to become male again. She let the decision hold.

Byr walked out of the tower that day with one hand still held over the wide scar in her abdomen. She discovered Dajeil sitting cross-legged and big-bellied on the egg-round stones a few metres up from the surf line.

The sound of the stones sliding under Byr's unsteady feet brought Dajeil out of her reverie. She looked round at Byr, then away again, out to sea. They sat together.

'I'm sorry,' Dajeil said.

'So am I.'

'Did I kill it?'

Byr had to think for a moment. Then she realised. She meant the fetus.

'Yes,' Byr said. 'Yes, it's gone.'

Dajeil lowered her head. She would not talk again.

*   *   *

Byr left with the *Unacceptable Behaviour* a week later. Dajeil had told her, through one of the tower's drones, that she would not be having the baby in a week, as expected. She would halt its development. For a while. Until she knew her own mind again. Until she felt ready for it. She didn't know how long the wait would be. A few months; a year, maybe. The unborn child would be safe and unharmed, just waiting, until then. When she did give birth, the tower and its drones would be able to look after her. She did not expect Byr to stay. They had done most of the work they had set out to do. It might be best if Byr left. Sorry was not remotely enough, but it was all there was to say. She would let Byr know when the child was born. They would meet again then, if she wanted, if he wanted.

Contact was never told what had happened. Byr claimed a bizarre accident had happened at sea to make her lose the fetus; a predator fish attacking; near death and saved by Dajeil ... They seemed well enough pleased with what she and Dajeil had done and accepted Byr's leaving early. The 'Ktik were a highly promising species, hungry for advancement; Telaturier was in for some big-time development.

Genar-Hofoen became male again. One day, going through some old clothes, he found the little figurine of Dajeil the old 'Ktik had carved. He sent it back to Dajeil. He didn't know if she received it or not. Still on the *Unacceptable Behaviour*, he fathered a child by Aist. A Contact appointment a few months afterwards took him aboard the GSV *Quietly Confident*. One of the ship's avatars – the same one he had slept with – gave him a very hard time for leaving Dajeil; they shouted at each other.

To his knowledge, the *Quietly Confident* subsequently blocked at least one request he put in for a post he wanted.

Over two years after he had left Telaturier he heard that Dajeil, still pregnant, had requested to be Stored. The place was becoming busy, and a whole new city was growing up round their old tower, which was going to become a museum. Later still he heard that she was not Stored after all, but had been picked up by the GSV turned Eccentric which had once been called the *Quietly Confident*, and which was now called the *Sleeper Service*.

XIII

~ Don't do this!

~ I am determined.

~ Well, at least let me get my avatar off!

~ Take it.

~ Thank you; beginning Displace sequence, the *Fate Amenable To Change* sent to the *Appeal To Reason*, and then continued: ~ Please; don't risk this.

~ I am risking only the drone; in cognizance of your concerns I shall not remain in contact with it in-flight.

~ And if it returns apparently unharmed, what will you do then?

~ Take every reasonable precaution, including a stepped-intellect-level throttled datastream-squirt approach, a—

~ Sorry to interrupt, but don't tell me any more, in case our friend is listening in. I appreciate the lengths you are prepared to go to try and ensure you remain free from contamination, but surely the point is that at any stage what you will find, or start to find, will look like the most valuable and interesting data available, and any intellectual restructuring suggested will look unambiguously like the most brilliant up-grade. You will be taken before you know it; indeed, *you* will cease to be in a sense, unless your own automatic systems attempt to prevent the take-over, and that will surely lead to conflict.

~ I shall resist ingesting any data requiring or suggesting either intellect restructuring or mimetic redrafting.

~ That may not be enough. Nothing may be enough.

~ You are overly cautious, cousin, sent the *Sober Counsel*. ~ We are the Zetetic Elench. We have ways of dealing with such matters. Our experience is not without benefit, especially once we are fore-warned.

~ And I am of the Culture, and I hate to see such risks being taken. Are you sure you have the full agreement of your human crews concerning such a foolhardy attempt at contact?

~ You know we have; your avatar sat in on the discussions, sent the *Appeal To Reason*.

~ That was two days ago, the *Fate Amenable To Change* pointed out. ~ You have just given a two-second launch notice; at least hold off long enough to carry out a poll of your humans and sentient drones and so ensure that they still agree with your proposed course of action now that the business is coming to a head. After all, another few minutes or so is not going to make much difference, is it? Think; I beg you. You know humans as well as I do; things can take a while to sink in with them. Perhaps some have only now finished thinking about the matter and have altered their position on it. Please, as a favour, hold back a few minutes.

~ Very well. Reluctantly, but very well.

The *Appeal To Reason* stopped the drone's launch countdown before a hundredth of a second had elapsed. The *Fate Amenable To Change* stood down its Displacer and left its avatar aboard.

It all made little difference. The *Fate Amenable To Change* had secretly been upgrading its effectors over the past couple of days and had intended attempting to carry out its own subtle jeopardising of any drones dispatched towards the Excession, but it was not to have the chance. Even while the hurriedly called vote was taking place on board the *Appeal To Reason*, the *Fate* received a message from another craft.

xExplorer Ship *Break Even* (Zetetic Elench, Stargazer, 5th)
   oGCU *Fate Amenable To Change* (Culture)
   Greetings. Please be advised I and my sister craft the *Within Reason* and *Long View* are also in attendance, just out of your primary scanner range. We have reconfigured to an Extreme Offence back-up form and shall soon be joined by the two remaining ships of our fleet, similarly recast. We would hope that you do not intend any interference with the plan our sister craft *Appeal To Reason* intends to effect.

Two other, confirmatory signals came in from divergent angles compared to that first message, purporting to be from the *Within Reason* and the *Long View*.

Shit, thought the GCU. It had been reasonably confident it could either fool the two nearby Elench craft or just plain overpower their efforts to contact the Excession, but faced with five ships, three of them on a war footing, it knew it would never be able to prevail.

It replied, saying that of course it intended no mischief, and glumly watched events unfold.

The vote aboard the *Appeal To Reason* went the same way as before, though a few more humans did vote against the idea of sending the drone in than had the last time. Two requested an immediate transfer to the *Sober Counsel*, then changed their minds; they would stay aboard. The *Fate* took its avatars off both the Elencher ships. It had used its heavy-duty displacer for the task, attenuating it to make it look as though it had utilised one of the lesser systems. It left the unit running at full readiness.

The *Appeal To Reason*'s drone was duly launched; a small, fragile-looking, gaily adorned thing, its extremities sporting ribbons, flowers and little ornaments and its casing covered with drawings, cartoons and well-wishing messages scrawled by the crew. It puttered hesitantly towards the Excession, chirpily beaming signals of innocent goodwill.

If the *Fate Amenable To Change* had been a human, at this point it would have looked down, put one hand over its eyes, and shaken its head.

The small machine took minutes to creep up to the seemingly unnoticing Excession's dull skein-surface; an insect crawling up to a behemoth. It activated a short-range, one time hyperspace unit and disappeared from the skein as though passing through a mirror of dark fluid.

In Infraspace, it . . . disappeared too, for an instant.

The *Fate Amenable To Change* was watching the drone from a hundred different angles via its remotes. They all saw it just disappear. An instant later it reappeared. It looped back through its little quantum burrow, returning to the skein of real space to start back, no less hesitantly, towards the *Appeal To Reason*.

The *Fate Amenable To Change* crash-ramped its plasma chambers then isolated and readied a clutch of fusion warheads. At the same moment, it signalled urgently.

~ Was the drone meant to *disappear* that way?

~ Hmm, sent the *Appeal To Reason*. ~ Well . . .

~ Destroy it, the *Fate* urged. ~ Destroy it, now!

~ It has communicated, slim-text only, as per instructions, the *Appeal To Reason* replied, sounding thoughtful, if wary. ~ It has gathered vast quantities of data on the entity. There was a pause, then, excitedly; ~ It has located the mind-state of the *Peace Makes Plenty*!

~ Destroy it! Destroy it!

~ No! sent the *Sober Counsel*.

~ How *can* I? the *Appeal To Reason* protested.

~ I'm sorry, the *Fate Amenable To Change* signalled to both the nearby craft, an instant after initiating a Displace sequence which flicked compressed spheres of plasma and a spray of fusion bombs down their own instantaneous wormholes towards the returning drone.

XIV

Ulver Seich tossed her damply tangled black hair over her shoulder and plonked her chin on Genar-Hofoen's chest. She traced gentle circles round his left nipple with one finger; he put a sweaty arm round her slim back, drew her other hand to his mouth and delicately kissed her fingers, one by one. She smiled.

Dinner, talk, drink, shared smoke-bowl, agreeing fuzzy heads might be cleared by a dip in the *Grey Area*'s pool, splashing, fooling around . . . and fooling around. Ulver had been holding back a little for part of the evening until she'd been certain the man didn't just expect anything to happen, then when she'd convinced herself that he wasn't taking her for granted, that he liked her and that – after that awful time in the module – they did get on, that was when she'd suggested the swim.

She raised her chin off his chest a little and flicked her finger back and forth over his tinily erect nipple. 'You were serious?' she asked him. 'An *Affronter*?'

He shrugged. 'Seemed like a good idea at the time,' he said. 'I just wanted to know what it was like to be one of them.'

'So now would you have to declare war on yourself?' she asked, pressing down on his nipple and watching it rise back up, her brows creased with concentration.

He laughed. 'I suppose so.'

She looked into his eyes. 'What about women? You ever wonder the same? You took the change once, didn't you?' She settled her chin back on his chest.

He breathed in deeply, raising her head as though on an ocean swell. He put one arm behind his head and stared up at the roof of her cabin. 'Yes, I did it once,' he said quietly.

She smoothed her palm over his chest for a while, watching his skin intently. 'Was it just for her?'

He craned his head up. They looked at each other.

'How much *do* you know about me?' he asked her. He'd tried quizzing her over dinner on what she knew and why she'd been sent to Tier to intercept him, but she'd played mysterious (and, to be fair, he wasn't able to tell her exactly why he was on his way to the *Sleeper Service*).

'Oh, I know all about you,' she said softly, seriously. Then she looked down. 'Well, I know the facts. I suppose that's not everything.'

He lowered his head to the pillow again. 'Yes, it was just for her.'

'Mm-hmm,' she said. She continued to stroke his chest. 'You must have loved her a lot.'

After a moment, he said, 'I suppose I must have.'

She thought he sounded sad. There was a pause, then he sighed again and, in a more cheerful voice, he said; 'What about you? Ever a guy?'

'No,' she said, with a laugh that might have held a trace of scorn. 'Maybe one day.' She shifted a little and circled his nipple with the tip of her tongue for a moment. 'I'm having too much fun being a girl.'

He reached down and pulled her up to kiss her.

Then in the silence, a tiny chime sounded in the room.

She broke off. 'Yes?' she said, breathing hard and scowling.

'I'm very sorry to intrude,' said the ship, making no great effort to sound sincere. 'May I speak to Mr Genar-Hofoen?'

Ulver made an exasperated noise and rolled off the man.

'Good grief, can't it *wait*?' Genar-Hofoen said.

'Yes, probably,' said the ship reasonably, as though this had just occurred to it. 'But people usually like to know this sort of thing immediately. Or so I thought.'

'What sort of thing?'

'The sentient module Scopell-Afranqui is dead,' the ship told him. 'It conducted a limited destruct on the first day of the war. We have only just heard. I'm sorry. Were you close?'

Genar-Hofoen was silent for a moment. 'No. Well . . . No. Not that close. But I'm sorry to hear it. Thank you for telling me.'

'*Could* it have waited?' the ship asked conversationally.

'It could, but I suppose you weren't to know.'

'Oh well. Sorry. Good night.'

'Yes, good night,' the man said, wondering at his feelings.

Ulver stroked his shoulder. 'That was the module you lived on, wasn't it?'

He nodded. 'We never really got on,' he told her. 'Mostly my fault, I suppose.' He turned his head to look at her. 'I can be a scum-bag sometimes, frankly.' He grinned.

'I'll take your word for it,' she said, climbing back on top of him.

10
Heavy Messing

I

Grief, nothing worked! The *Fate Amenable To Change*'s ordnance directed at the Elench drone ship just disappeared, snatched away to nowhere; it had to react quickly to deal with the collapsing wormholes as they slammed back, now endless, towards its Displacers. How could anything *do* that? (And had the watching Elench warships noticed?) The little Elench drone flew on, a few seconds away from its home ship.

~ I confess I just tried to destroy your drone, the *Fate* sent to the *Appeal To Reason*. ~ I make no apologies. Look what happened. It enclosed a recording of the events. ~ *Now* will you listen? There seems little point in trying to destroy the machine. Just get away from it. I'll try to work out another way of dealing with it.

~ You had no business attempting to interfere with my drone, the *Appeal To Reason* replied. ~ I am glad that you were frustrated. I am happy that the drone appears to be under the protection of the entity. I take it as an encouraging sign that it is so.

~ *What?* Are you mad?

~ I'll thank you to stop impugning my mental state with such regularity and allow me to get on with my job. I have not informed the other craft of your disgraceful and illegal attack on my drone; however, any further endeavours of a similar nature will not be treated so leniently.

~ I shall not try to reason with you. Goodbye and fare well.

~ Where are you going?

~ *I* am not going anywhere.

II

The General Contact Unit *Grey Area* was about to rendezvous with the General Systems Vehicle *Sleeper Service*. The GCU had gathered its small band of passengers in a lounge for the occasion; one of the ship's skeletal slave-drones joined them as they watched the view of hyperspace behind them on a wall screen. The GCU was making the best speed it could, rushing beneath the skein at a little over forty kilolights on a gently, decreasingly curved course that was now almost identical to that of the larger craft approaching from astern.

'This will require a coordinated full engine shut-off and Displace,' the small cube of components that was the drone told them. 'For an instant, none of us will be within my full control.'

Genar-Hofoen was still trying to think of a cutting remark when the drone Churt Lyne said, 'Won't slow down for you, eh?'

'Correct,' the slave-drone said.

'Here it comes,' said Ulver Seich. She sat cross-legged on a couch drinking a delicately scented infusion from a porcelain cup. A dot appeared in the representation of space behind them; it rushed towards them, growing quickly. It swelled to a fat shining ovoid that rushed silently underneath them; the view dipped quickly to follow it, beginning to perform a half-twist to keep the orientation correctly aligned. Genar-Hofoen, standing near where Ulver sat, had to put his hand out to the back of the couch to steady himself. In that instant, there was a sensation of a kind of titanically enveloping slippage, the merest hint of vast energies being gathered, cradled, unleashed, contained, exchanged and manipulated; unimaginable forces called into existence seemingly from nothing to writhe momentarily around them, collapse back into the void and leave reality, from the perspective of the people on the *Grey Area*, barely altered.

Ulver Seich *tssk*ed as some of her infusion spilled into the cup's saucer.

The view had changed. Now it snapped to a grey-blue expanse

of something curved, like a cup of cloud seen from the inside. It pivoted again, and they were looking at a series of vast steps like the entrance to an ancient temple. The broad shelves of the stairs led up to a rectangular entrance lined with tiny lights; a dark space beyond twinkled with still smaller lamps. The view drew back to reveal a series of such entrances arranged side by side, the rest of which were closed. Above and below, set into the faces of the steps, were smaller doors, all similarly shut.

'Success,' the slave-drone said.

The view was changing again as the ship was drawn slowly backwards towards the single opened bay.

Genar-Hofoen frowned. 'We're going inside?' he asked the slave-drone.

It swivelled to face him, paused just long enough for the human to form the impression he was being treated like some sort of cretin. '. . . Well, yes . . .' it said, slowly, as one might to a particularly dim child.

'But I was told—'

'Welcome aboard the *Sleeper Service*,' said a voice behind them. They turned to see a tall, angular, black-dressed creature walking into the lounge. 'My name is Amorphia.'

III

The drone returned to the *Appeal To Reason* and was taken back aboard. Seconds passed.

~ Well? the *Fate Amenable To Change* asked.

There was a brief pause. A microsecond or so. Then: ~ It's empty, the *Appeal To Reason* sent.

~ Empty?

~ Yes. It didn't record anything. It's like it never went anywhere.

~ Are you sure?

~ Take a look for yourself.

A data dump followed. The *Fate Amenable To Change* shunted it into a memory core it had set up for just such a purpose the moment it had realised what the Excession was, almost a month earlier. It was the equivalent of a locked room, an isolation ward, a cell. More information poured out of the *Appeal To Reason*; a gushing river of data trying to flood in after the original data dump. The Culture ship ignored it. Part of its Mind was listening to the howling, thumping noises coming out of that locked room.

Information flickered between the *Appeal To Reason* and the *Sober Counsel*, an instant before the *Fate* sent its own warning signal. It cursed itself for its procrastination, even if its warning would almost certainly have gone unheeded anyway.

It signalled the distant, war-readied Elench craft instead, begging them to believe the worst had happened. There was no immediate reply.

The *Appeal To Reason* was the nearer of the two Elencher ships. It turned and started accelerating towards the *Fate*. It broadcast, tight-beamed, lasered and field-pulsed vast, impossibly complicated signals at the Culture craft. The *Fate* squirted back the contents of that locked room, evacuating it. Then it swivelled and powered up its engines. *So I am going somewhere*, it thought, and moved off, away from the *Appeal To Reason*, which was still signalling wildly and remained on a heading taking it straight for the Culture ship.

The *Fate* raced outwards, powering away from the Elencher vessel and heading out on a great curve that would take it rolling over the invisible sphere that was the closest approach limit it had set. The *Sober Counsel* was moving off on an opposite course from the *Appeal To Reason*, which was still following the Culture ship. A direction which would turn into an intercept course if they all held these headings. *Oh, shit*, the *Fate* thought.

They were still close enough to each other to just talk, but the *Fate* thought it ought to be a little more formal, so it signalled.

xGCU *Fate Amenable To Change* (Culture)
  oExplorer Ship *Sober Counsel* (Whoever)
Whatever you are, if you advance on an intercept course on the far side of the closest approach limit, I'll open fire. No further warnings.

No reply. Just the blaze of multi-band mania from the *Appeal To Reason*, following behind it. The *Sober Counsel*'s course didn't alter.

The *Fate* concentrated its attention on the last known locations of the three other Elench craft; the trio which the *Break Even* had said were all war-configured. The other two couldn't be ignored, but the new arrivals had to constitute the greatest threat for now. It scanned the data it had on the specifications of the Elench craft, calculating, simulating; war-gaming. Grief, to be doing this with ships that were practically Culture ships! The simulation runs came out equivocal. It could easily deal with the two craft, even staying within range of the Excession (as though that was a wise limitation anyway!), but if the other three joined in the fun, and certainly if they attacked, it could well find itself in trouble.

It signalled the *Break Even* again. Still nothing.

The *Fate* was starting to wonder what the point was of sticking around here. The big guns would start arriving in a day or two; it looked like it was going to be in some sort of ludicrous continual chase with the two Elencher ships until then, which would be tiresome (with the possibility that the other three, war-ready Elencher ships might join in, which would be downright dangerous) and, after all, there was that war fleet on its way. What more was it usefully going to be able to do here? Certainly, it could keep a watch on the Excession, see if it did anything else interesting, but was that worth the risk of being overwhelmed by the Elench? Or even by the Excession itself, if it was as invasive as it now appeared to be? Enough of its drones, platforms and sensor platforms might be able to evade the Elenchers for the time it took until the other craft got here; they could keep watch on the situation, couldn't they?

Ah, to hell with this, it thought to itself. It dodged unexpectedly along the surface of the closest-approach limit, producing corresponding alterations in the headings of the two Elencher ships. It speeded up for a while, then slowed until it was stopped relative to the Excession.

The position it held now was such that if you drew a line between the Excession and the direction it was expecting the MSV *Not Invented Here* to arrive from, it would be on that line too.

The *Fate* signalled the two Elencher ships once more, trying to get sense from the *Appeal To Reason* and any reply at all from the *Sober Counsel*. It was careful to target the last known positions of the *Break Even* and its two militarily configured sister ships as well, still trying to elicit a response.

None was forthcoming. It waited until the last possible moment, when it looked like the *Appeal To Reason* was about to ram it in its enthusiasm to overwhelm it with signals, then broke away from it, heading straight out, directly away from the Excession.

The *Fate Amenable To Change*'s avatars began the task of telling the human crew what was happening. Meanwhile the ship turned onto a course at a right-angle to its initial heading and powered away at maximum acceleration. The *Appeal To Reason* targeted its effector on the fleeing Culture ship as it curved out trying to intercept it, but the attack – configured more as a last attempt to communicate – was easily fended off. That wasn't what the *Fate* was concerned about.

It watched that imaginary line from the Excession to the MSV *Not Invented Here*, focusing, magnifying its attention on that line's middle distance.

Movement. Probing filaments of effector radiations. Three foci, clustered neatly around that line.

The Elencher ship *Break Even* and its two militarily configured sister craft had been awaiting it.

Congratulating itself on its perspicacity, the GCU headed on out, leaving the immediate vicinity of the Excession for the first time in almost a month.

Then its engines stopped working.

IV

'I was told,' Genar-Hofoen said in the traveltube, to the blank-faced and cadaverous ship's avatar, 'that I'd be off here in a day. What do I need *quarters* for?'

'We are moving into a war zone,' the avatar said flatly. 'There is a good chance that it will not be possible to off-load the *Grey Area* or any other ship between approximately sixteen and one hundred plus hours from now.'

A deep, dark gulf of the *Sleeper Service*'s cavernous interior space was briefly visible, sliding past, then the tube car zipped into another tunnel. Genar-Hofoen stared at the tall, angular creature. 'You mean I might be stuck on here for four days?'

'That is a possibility,' the avatar said.

Genar-Hofoen glared at the avatar, hoping he looked as suspicious as he felt. 'Well, why can't I stay on the *Grey Area?*' he asked.

'Because it might have to leave at any moment.'

The man looked away, swearing softly. There was a war on, he supposed, but even so, this was typical SC. First the *Grey Area* was allowed on board the *Sleeper Service* when he'd been told it wouldn't be, and now this. He glanced back at the avatar, which was looking at him with what could have been curiosity or just gormlessness. Four days on the *Sleeper*. He'd thought earlier, stuck on the module, that he'd be grateful when he could leave Ulver Seich and her drone behind on the GCU while he came aboard the *Sleeper Service*, but as it turned out, he wasn't.

He shivered, and imagined that he could still feel Ulver's lips on his, from when they'd kissed goodbye, just a few minutes earlier. The flash-back tremor passed. *Wow*, he thought to himself, and grinned. *That was like being an adolescent again.*

Two nights, one day. That was all he and Ulver had spent together as lovers. It wasn't remotely long enough. And now he'd be stuck aboard here for up to four nights.

Oh well. It could be worse; at least the avatar didn't look like it was the one he'd slept with. He wondered if he was going to see Dajeil at all. He looked at the clothes he was wearing, standard loose fatigues from the *Grey Area*. Wasn't this how he'd been dressed when he and Dajeil had last parted? He couldn't recall. Possibly. He wondered at his own subconscious processes.

The tube car was slowing; suddenly it was stopped.

The avatar gestured to the door that rolled open. A short corridor beyond led to another door. Genar-Hofoen stepped into the corridor.

'I trust you find your quarters acceptable,' he heard the avatar say quietly, behind him. Then a soft *rrr*ing noise and a faint draught on his neck made him look back in surprise. The traveltube had gone, the transparent tube door was closed and the corridor behind him was empty. He looked about but there was nowhere the avatar could have gone. He shrugged and continued on to the door ahead. It opened onto a small lift. He was in it for a couple of seconds, then the door rotated open and he stepped out, frowning, into a dimly lit space full of boxes and equipment that somehow looked vaguely familiar. There was a strange scent in the air . . . The lift door snicked closed behind him. He saw some steps over to one side in the gloom, set into a curved stone wall. They really did look familiar.

He thought he knew where he was. He went to the steps and climbed them.

He came up from the cellar into the short passageway which led to the main door on the ground storey of the tower. The door was open. He walked down the passageway to it and stood outside.

Waves beat on the shining, sliding shingle of the beach. The sun stood near noon. One moon was visible, a pale eggshell half hidden in the fragile blueness of the sky. The smell he'd recognised earlier was that of the sea. Birds cried from the winds above him. He walked down the slope of beach towards the water and looked about. It was all pretty convincing; the space couldn't really be all that big – the waves were perhaps a little too uncomplicated, a little too regular, further out – but it certainly looked like you were seeing for tens of kilometres. The tower was just the way he remembered it, the low cliffs beyond the salt marsh equally familiar.

'Hello?' he called. No answer.

He pulled out his pen terminal. 'Very amusing . . .' he said, then frowned, looking at the terminal. No tell-tale light. He pressed a couple of panels to institute a systems check. Nothing happened. Shit.

'Ah hah,' said a small, crackly voice behind him. He turned to see a black bird, folding its wings on the shelf of stones behind him. 'Another captive,' it cackled.

V

The *Fate Amenable To Change* let its engine fields race for a moment, running a series of tests and evaluation processes. It was as if its traction fields were just sinking through the energy grid, as if it wasn't there. It tried signalling, telling the outside universe of its plight, but the signals just seemed to loop back and it found itself receiving its own signal a picosecond after it had sent it. It tried to create a warp but the skein just seemed to slide out of its fields. It attempted Displacing a drone but the wormhole collapsed before it was properly formed. It tried a few more tricks, finessing its field structures and reconfiguring its senses in an attempt at least to understand what was going on, but nothing worked.

It thought. It felt curiously composed, considering.

It shut everything down and let itself drift, floating gradually back through the four-dimensional hypervolume towards the skein of real space, propelled by nothing more than the faint pressure of radiations expelled from the energy grid. Its avatars were already starting to explain the change in the situation to its human crew. The ship hoped the people would take it calmly.

Then the Excession seemed to swell, bulging as though under an enormous lens, reaching out towards the Culture ship with a vast enclosing scoop of presence.

Well, here we go, the ship thought. *Should be interesting . . .*

VI

'No.'

'Please,' the avatar said.

The woman shook her head. 'I've thought about it. I don't want to see him.'

The avatar stared at Dajeil. 'But I brought him all this way!' it cried. 'Just for you! If you knew . . .' Its voice trailed off. It brought its feet up onto the front of the seat, and put its arms round its legs, hugging them.

They were in Dajeil's quarters, inside another version of the tower's interior housed within the GCU *Jaundiced Outlook*. The avatar had come straight here after leaving Genar-Hofoen in the Mainbay where the original copy of the tower – the one Dajeil Gelian had spent forty years living in – had been moved to when the ship had converted all its external spare mass to engine. It had thought she would be pleased that the tower had not had to be destroyed, and that Genar-Hofoen had finally been persuaded to return to her.

Dajeil continued watching the screen. It was a replay of one of her dives amongst the triangular rays in the shallow sea that was now no more, as seen from a drone which had accompanied her. She watched herself move amongst the gracefully undulating wings of the great, gentle creatures. Swollen, awkward, she was the only graceless thing in the picture.

The avatar didn't know what to say next.

The *Sleeper Service* decided to take over. 'Dajeil?' it said quietly, through its representative. The woman looked round, recognising the new tone in Amorphia's voice.

'What?'

'Why don't you want to see him now?'

'I . . .' she paused. 'It's just been too long,' she said. 'I think . . . I suppose for the first few years I did want to see him again; to . . . to—' she looked down, picking at her fingernails. '—I don't know. Oh, to try and make things all right . . . grief, that sounds so lame.' She sniffed and looked upwards at the translucent dome above her. 'I felt there were things we needed to have said that we never did say to each other, and that if we did get together, even for a little while, we could . . . work things out. Draw a line under all that happened. Tie up loose ends; that . . . that sort of thing. You know?' she said, looking bright-eyed at the avatar.

Oh, Dajeil, thought the ship. *How wounded about the eyes.* 'I know,' it said. 'But now you feel that too much time has passed?'

The woman smoothed her hand over her belly. She nodded slowly, looking at the floor. 'Yes,' she said. 'It's all too long ago. I'm sure he's forgotten all about me.' She glanced up at the avatar.

'And yet he is here,' it said.

'Did he come to see me?' she asked it, already sounding bitter.

'No, and yes,' the ship said. 'He had another motive. But it is because of you he is here.'

She shook her head. 'No,' she said. 'No; too much time . . .'

The avatar unfolded itself from the seat and crossed to where Dajeil sat; it knelt down before her, and hesitantly extended one hand towards her abdomen. Looking into her eyes, it gently placed its palm on Dajeil's belly. Dajeil felt dizzy. She could not recall Amorphia ever having touched her before, either under its own control or under the *Sleeper Service*'s. She put her own hand on top of the avatar's. The creature's hand was steady, soft and cool.

'And yet,' it said, 'in some ways, no time has passed.'

Dajeil gave a bitter laugh. 'Oh yes,' she said. 'I've been here, doing nothing except growing older. But what about him?' she asked, and suddenly there was something fierce about her voice. 'How much has *he* lived in forty years? How many loves has *he* had?'

'I don't believe that signifies, Dajeil,' the ship told her quietly. 'The point is that he is here. You can talk to him. The two of you can talk. Some resolution might be achieved.' It pressed very lightly on her belly. 'I believe it *can* be achieved.'

She sighed heavily. She looked down at her hand. 'I don't know,' she said. 'I don't know. I need to think. I can't ... I need to think.'

'Dajeil,' the ship said, and the avatar took her hand in both of its. 'Were it possible, I would give you as long as you could desire, but I am not able to. There is some urgency in this. I have what might be termed an urgent appointment near a star called Esperi. I cannot delay my arrival and I would not want to take you with me there; it is too dangerous. I would like you to leave in this ship as soon as possible.'

She looked hurt, the *Sleeper* thought.

'I won't be forced into this,' she told it.

'Of course not,' it said. It attempted a smile and patted her hand. 'Why not sleep on it? Tomorrow will be soon enough.'

VII

The *Attitude Adjuster* watched the attacking craft fall amongst the surrounding shield of ships; they had no time to move more than fractionally from their original positions. Their weaponry did their moving for them, focusing on the incoming target as it plunged into their midst. A scatter of brightly flaring missiles preceded the *Killing Time*, a hail of plasma bubbles accompanied it and CAM, AM and nanohole warheads cluster munitions burst everywhere around it like a gigantic firework, producing a giant orb of scintillations. Many of the individual motes themselves detonated in a clustering hyperspherical storm of lethal sparks, followed sequentially by another and another echelon of explosions erupting amongst the wave of ships in a layered hierarchy of destruction.

The *Attitude Adjuster* scanned the real-time reports coming back from its war flock. One was caught by a nanohole, vanishing inside a vast burst of annihilation; another was damaged beyond immediate repair by an AM munition and dropped behind, engines crippled. Fortuitously, neither were crewed by Affronters. Most of the rest of the warheads were dealt with; the fleet's own replies were fended, detonated or avoided by the attacker. No sign of the craft using its effectors to do more than cause interference; flittingly interrogating and probing amongst the collected mass of ships. The focus of its attention had begun near the centre of the third wave of craft and was spirally erratically outwards, occasionally flicking further out towards the other waves.

The *Attitude Adjuster* was puzzled. The *Killing Time* was a Torturer class Rapid Offensive Unit. It could be – it ought to be – devastating the fleet for these instants as it tore through it; it was capable of—

Then it realised. Of course. It was a grudge.

The *Attitude Adjuster* experienced a tingle of fear, merged with a kind of contempt. The *Killing Time*'s effector focus was a few ships away now, spiralling out towards the *Attitude Adjuster*. It signalled hurriedly to the five Rapid Offensive Units immediately around it. Each listened, understood and obeyed. The *Killing Time*'s effector focus flicked from craft to craft, still coming closer.

You fool, the *Attitude Adjuster* thought, almost angry at the attacking ship. It was behaving stupidly, irresponsibly. A Culture craft should not be so prideful. It had thought the venom directed at itself by the *Killing Time* in its signal to it back at Pittance had been bluster; cheap bravado. But it had been worse; it had been sincere. Wounded self-esteem. Upset that it personally had been subject to a ruse designed to destroy it. As though its enemies cared an iota who it was.

The *Attitude Adjuster* doubted this was an attack sanctioned by the *Killing Time*'s peers. This wasn't war, this was peevishness; this was taking it personally when, if there was anything war could be characterised as being, it was impersonal. Idiot. It deserved to perish. It did not merit the honour it doubtless thought would accrue to it for this reckless and selfish act.

The surrounding warships completed their changes. Just in time. When the attacking ship's effector targeted the first of those craft, the focus did not flit onto the next as it had with all the rest; instead it stayed, latching on, concentrating and strengthening. The ROU caved in alarmingly quickly; the *Attitude Adjuster* guessed that it was made to reconfigure its engine fields to focus them inside its Mind – there was a sort of signalled shriek an instant before communication was lost – but the exact nature of its downfall was hidden in an accompanying shower of CAM warheads which obliterated it instantaneously. A mercy; it would have been a grisly way for a ship to die.

But too quick, thought the *Attitude Adjuster*; it was sure the attacker would have let the ROU – which the *Killing Time* had mistaken for the *Attitude Adjuster* – tear its intellect apart with its engines for longer if it had been totally fooled; the CAM dusting had been either a *coup de grâce* or a howl of frustration, perhaps both.

The *Attitude Adjuster* signalled to the rest of the fleet, instructing them too to impersonate itself, but even as it watched the ROU which had been attacked alongside it disappear astern in a fragmenting cage of radiations, it began to be afraid.

It had originally contacted the five nearest ships, hoping that the first one found and interrogated by the attacker's systems would fool the *Killing Time* into believing it had found the one ship it was obviously seeking.

But that was stupid. It sensed the Torturer class ship's effectors sweep over the craft on the far side of the hole in the wave of ships which the ROU's destruction had created.

Insufficient elapsed time, the *Attitude Adjuster* whispered to itself. The ROU being quizzed at the moment was still reconfiguring its internal systems signature to resemble that of the *Attitude Adjuster*. The effector sweep flicked away from it, dismissing. The *Attitude Adjuster* quailed.

It had made itself a target! It should have— HERE IT CAME! A feeling of—

No, it had gone, swept over it! Its own disguise had worked. It had been dismissed too, like the ROU alongside!

The effector focus jumped to another craft still further away. The *Attitude Adjuster* was dizzy with relief. It had survived! The plan still held, the huge filthy trick they were pulling was free to continue!

The way to the Excession lay open; the other Minds in the conspiracy would commend it if it survived; the— ... but it mustn't think of the other ships involved. It had to accept responsibility for what had happened. It and it alone. It was the traitor. It would never reveal who had instigated this ghastly, gigadeathcrime-risking scheme; it had to assume the blame itself.

It had wrestled with the Mind at Pittance and pressed it when it had insisted it would die rather than yield (but it had had no choice!); it had allowed the human on Pittance to be destroyed (but it had fastened its effector on his puny animal brain when it had seen what was happening to him; it had read the animal's brain-state, copied it, sucked it out of him before he'd died, so that at least he might live again in some form! Look! It had the file here ... there it went ...). It had fooled the surrounding ships, it had lied to them, sent them messages from ... from the ships it could not bear to think about.

But it was the right thing to do!

... Or was it just the thing it had chosen to believe was the right thing to do, when the other ships, the other Minds had persuaded it? What had its real motives been? Had it not just been flattered to be the object of such attention? Had it not always resented being passed over for certain small but prestigious missions in the past, nursing a bitter resentment that it was not trusted because it was seen as being – what? A hard-liner? Too inclined to shoot first? Too cynical towards the soft ideologies of the meat-beings? Too mixed up in its feelings about its own martial prowess and the shaming moral implications of being a machine designed for war? All those things, a little, perhaps. But that wasn't all its fault!

... And yet, did it not accept that one had an irreducible ethical responsibility for one's own actions? It did. And it accepted that and it had done terrible, terrible things. All the attempts it had made to compensate had been eddies in the flood; tiny retrograde movements towards good entirely produced by the ferocious turbulence of its headlong rush to ill.

It was evil.

How simple that reductive conclusion seemed.

But it had been obliged! . . . And yet it could not say by whom, so it had to accept the full responsibility for itself.

But there were others! . . . And yet it could not identify them, and so the full weight of their distributed guilt bore down on the single point that was itself, unbearable, insupportable.

But there *were* others! . . . And yet still it could not bear to think of them.

And so somebody, some other entity, looking in from outside, say, would have to conclude, would it not, that perhaps these others did not really exist, that the whole thing, the whole ghastly abomination that was this plot was its idea, its own little conspiracy, thought up and executed by itself alone? Was that not the case?

But that was so unfair! That wasn't true! . . . And yet, it could not release the identities of its fellow plotters. Suddenly, it felt confused. *Had* it made them up? *Were* they real? Perhaps it ought to check; open the place where they were stored and look at the names just to make sure that they were even the names of real Minds, real ships, or that it was not implicating innocent parties.

But that was terrible! Whichever way it fell after that, that was awful! It hadn't made them up! They were real! . . . But it couldn't prove it, because it just couldn't reveal them.

Maybe it ought to just call the whole thing off. Maybe it ought to signal all the other ships around it to break away, stop, retreat, or just open their comm channels so they could accept signals from other ships, other Minds, and be persuaded of the folly of their cause. Let them make up their own minds. They were intelligent beings no less than it. What right had it to send them to their deaths on the strength of a heinous, squalid lie? But it *had* to! . . . And yet, still, no; no it couldn't say who the others had been.

It mustn't *think* of them! And it couldn't possibly call off the attack! It couldn't! No! *NO*! Grief! Meat! Stop! Stop it! Let it go! Sweet nothingness, anything was better than this wracking, tearing uncertainty, any horror preferable to the wrenching dreadfulness boiling uncontrollably in its Mind.

Atrocity. Abomination. Gigadeathcrime.

It was worthless and hateful, despicable and foul; it was wrung

out, exhausted and incapable of revelation or communication. It
hated itself and what it had done more, much more than it had
ever hated anything; more, it was sure, than anything had ever
been hated in all existence. No death could be too painful or
protracted . . .

And suddenly it knew what it had to do.

It de-coupled its engine fields from the energy grid and plunged
those vortices of pure energy deep into the fabric of its own Mind,
tearing its intellect apart in a supernova of sentient agony.

VIII

Genar-Hofoen reappeared, exiting from the front door of the
tower.

'Up here,' croaked a thin, hoarse voice.

He looked up and saw the black bird on the parapet. He
stood there watching it for a moment, but it didn't look like
it was coming down. He frowned and went back into the
tower.

'Well?' it asked when he joined it at the summit of the tower.

He nodded. 'Locked,' he confirmed.

The bird had insisted that he was a captive, along with it.
He'd thought maybe there was just something wrong with his
terminal. It had suggested he attempted to get out the way
he had come in. He'd just tried; the lift door in the tower's
cellar was closed, and as solid and unmoving as the stones
surrounding it.

Genar-Hofoen leant back against the parapet, staring with a
troubled expression at the tower's translucent dome. He'd had
a quick look at each of the levels as he'd climbed the winding
stair. The tower's rooms looked furnished and yet bare as well,
all the personal stuff he and Dajeil had added to it missing. It was
like the original had been when they'd first arrived on Telaturier,
forty-five years ago.

'Told you.'

'But why?' Genar-Hofoen asked, trying not to sound plain-tive. He'd never even *heard* of a ship keeping somebody cap-tive before.

''Cause we're prisoners,' the bird told him, sounding oddly pleased with itself.

'So you're not an avatar; you're not part of the ship?'

'Na; I'm an independent entity, me,' the bird said proudly, spreading its feathers. It turned its head almost right round, glancing backwards. 'Currently being followed by some bloody *missile*,' it said loudly. 'But never mind.' It rotated its head back to look at him. 'So what did *you* do to annoy the ship?' it asked, black eyes twinkling. Genar-Hofoen got the impression it was enjoying his dismay.

'Nothing!' he protested. The bird cocked its head at him. He blew out a breath. 'Well . . .' he looked around at where he was. His brows flexed. 'Yes, well, from our surroundings, maybe the ship doesn't agree.'

'Oh, this is nothing,' said the bird. 'This is just a Bay; just a hangar sort of thing. Not even a klick long. You should have seen the one outside, when we still had an outside. Whole sea we had, whole sea and a whole atmosphere. *Two* atmospheres.'

'Yes,' the man said. 'Yes, I heard.'

'Sort of all for her, really. Except it turned out its nibs had an ulterior motive, too. All that stuff; became engine, you know. But otherwise. It was all for her, for all that time.'

The man nodded. It looked like he was thinking.

'You're him, aren't you?' the bird said. It sounded pleased with itself.

'I'm *who*?' he asked.

'The one that left her. The one that was here, with her. The real here, I mean. The original here.'

Genar-Hofoen looked away. 'If you mean Dajeil; yes, she and I lived in a tower like this one once, on an island that looked like this place.'

'Ah-*hah*!' the bird said, jumping up and down and shaking its feathers. 'I see! You're the *bad* guy!'

Genar-Hofoen scowled at the bird. 'Fuck you,' he said.

It cackled with laughter. '*That's* why you're here! Ho-ho; *you'll* be lucky to get off at all, you will! Ha ha ha!'

'And what did *you* do, arse-hole?' Genar-Hofoen asked the

bird, more in the hope of annoying the creature than because he really cared.

'Oh,' the bird said, drawing itself up and settling its feathers down in a dignified sort of way. 'I was a *spy*!' it said proudly.

'A spy?'

'Oh yes,' the bird said, sounding smug. 'Forty years I spent, listening, watching. Reported back to my master. Using the Stored ones who were going back. Left messages on them. Forty years and never once discovered. Well, until three weeks ago. Rumbled, then. Maybe even before. Can't tell. But I did my best. Can't ask better than that.' It started preening itself.

The man's eyes narrowed. 'Who were you reporting back to?'

'None of your business,' the bird said, looking up from its preening. It took a precautionary couple of hop-steps backwards along the parapet, just to make sure it was well out of reach of the human.

Genar-Hofoen crossed his arms and shook his head. 'What's this fucking crazy ship up to?'

'Oh, it's off to see the Excession,' the bird said. 'At some lick, too.'

'This thing at Esperi?' the man asked.

'Heading straight for it,' the bird confirmed. 'What it told me, anyway. Can't see why it'd lie. Could be, I suppose. Wouldn't put it past it. But don't think it is. Straight for it. Has been for the past twenty-two days. You want my opinion? Going to give it you anyway. I think it's stooping.' The creature put its head on one side. 'Familiar with the term?'

Genar-Hofoen nodded absently. He didn't like the sound of this.

'Stooping,' the bird repeated. 'If you ask me. Thing's mad. Been a bit loopy the last four decades. Gone totally off the boulevard now. In the hills and bouncing along full speed for the cliff edge. That's my opinion. And I've been round its loopiness for forty years. I know, I do. I can tell. This thing's dafter than a jar of words. I'm getting away on the *Jaundiced Outlook*, if it'll let me. It being the *Sleeper*. Don't think the *Jaundiced* bears me any ill will. Shouldn't think it does. No.' Then, as though remembering a rich joke, it shook its head and said, 'The bad guy; ha! You, on the other hand. You'll be here forty years you will, chum. If it doesn't wreck itself ramming this excession thing, that is.

Ha! How'd it get you here anyway? You come here to see old perpetually pregnant?'

Genar-Hofoen looked momentarily stricken. 'It's true then; she never did have the child?'

'Yep,' the bird said. 'Still in her. Supposed to be hale and hearty, too. If you can believe that. So I was told. Sounds unlikely. Addled, I'd have thought. Or turned to stone by now. But there you are. Either way, she just isn't having it. Ha!'

The man pinched his lower lip with his fingers, looking troubled.

'What did you say brought you here?' the bird asked.

It waited. 'Ahem!' it said loudly.

'What?' the man asked. The bird repeated the question.

The man looked like he still hadn't heard, then he shrugged. 'I came here to talk to a dead person; a Storee.'

'They've all gone,' said the bird. 'Hadn't you heard?'

The man shook his head. 'Not one of the live ones,' he said. 'Somebody without a bod, somebody who's Stored in the ship's memory.'

'Na, they've gone too,' the bird said, lifting one wing to peck briefly underneath. 'Dropped them off at Dreve,' it continued. 'Complete download. Upload. Acrossload. Whatever you call it. Didn't even keep copies.'

'*What?*' the man said, stepping towards the bird.

'Seriously,' the creature said, taking a couple of hops backwards on the stonework of the parapet. 'Honest.' The man was staring at it now. 'No, really; so I was told. I could have been misinformed. Can't see why. But it's possible. Doubt it though. They've gone. That was my information. Gone. Ship said it didn't want even the copies aboard. Just in case.'

The man stared wildly at it for a bit longer. 'Just in case *what?*' he cried, stepping forward again.

'Well, I don't know!' the bird yelped, hopping backwards and flexing its wings, ready to fly.

Genar-Hofoen glared at the creature for a moment longer, then spun round, grasping the stones of the parapet with both hands and staring out into the false panorama of sea and cloud.

Then it was in the wrong place. As simple as that.

The *Fate Amenable To Change* looked around, incredulous. Stars. Just stars. Initially alien, in a way a starscape had never been before.

This wasn't where it had just been. Where was the Excession? Where were the Elencher ships? Where was Esperi? Where *was* this?

It called up from-scratch position-establishing routines no ship *ever* had to call up after they'd run through them in the very earliest part of their upbringing and self-fettling, in the Mind equivalent of infancy. You did this sort of thing once to show the Minds supervising your development you could do it, then you forgot about it, because nobody ever lost track of where they were, not over this magnitude of scale. And yet here it was having to do just that. Quite bizarre.

It looked at the results. There was something almost viscerally relieving about the discovery that it was still in the same universe. For a moment it had been contemplating the prospect of finding itself in a different one altogether. (At the same time, at least one part of its intellect experienced a corresponding flicker of disappointment for exactly the same reason.)

It was nowhere near Esperi. Its position was thirty light years away from where it had been, apparently, a moment ago. The nearest star system was an undistinguished red-giant/blue-white dwarf double called Pri-Etse. The binary lay roughly along that same imaginary straight line that joined the Excession to the incoming MSV *Not Invented Here*. Where the ship itself had ended up was even closer to that imaginary line.

The *Fate* checked itself over. Unharmed. Uninvaded, unjeopardised, uncontacted.

It replayed those last few picoseconds while it multiple-checked its systems.

. . . The Excession rushed out to meet it. It was enveloped in –

what? Skein fabric? Some sort of ultradense field? It all happened at close to hyperspace-light speeds. The outside universe was pinched off and in the following moment there was an instant of nothing; no external input whatsoever, a vanishingly minute, perfectly indivisible fraction of a picosecond when the *Fate* was cut off from everything; no outside sensor data whatsoever. Events within the ship itself had continued as normal (or rather its internal state had remained the same for that same infinitesimally microscopic instant – there had been no time for anything appreciable to actually *happen*). In its Mind, there had been time for the hyperspatial quanta-equivalents to alter their states for a few cycles; so time had still elapsed.

But outside; nothing.

Then the skein or field substrate had vanished, snapping out of existence to precisely nowhere, disappearing too quickly for the ship's sensors to register where it had gone.

The *Fate* replayed that section of its records slower and slower until it was dealing with the equivalent of individual frames; the smallest possible sub-division of perception and cognizance the Culture or any other Involved knew of.

And it came down to four frames; four snapshots of recent history. In one frame the Excession seemed to be rushing out, *accelerating* out to meet it, in the next the skein/field had wrapped itself almost totally around the ship – at a distance of perhaps a kilometre from ship-centre, though it was hard to estimate – leaving only a tiny hole staring out to the rest of the universe on the opposite side of the ship from the Excession, in the third frame the total cut-off from the universe was in place, and in the next it had gone, and the *Fate* had moved, or had been moved, thirty light years in less than a picosecond.

How the fuck does it do *that?* the ship wondered. It started checking that time was still working properly, directing its sensors at distant quasars which had been used as time reference sources for millennia. It also started checking that it was not in the centre of some huge projection, extending its still-stopped engine fields like vast whiskers, feeling for the (as far as anybody knew) unfakeable reality that was the energy grid and minutely – and randomly – scrutinising sections of the view around it, searching for the equivalent of pixels or brush strokes.

The *Fate Amenable To Change* was experiencing a sense of

elation at having survived what it had feared might be a terminal encounter with the Excession. But it was still worried that it had missed something, that it had been interfered with somehow. The most obvious explanation was that it had been fooled, that it had been tricked into moving itself here under its own power or been moved to this position via another tractive force over time. The further implication was that the interval when it had been moving had somehow been expunged from its memory. That would be bad. The very idea that its Mind was not absolutely inviolate was anathema to a ship.

It tried to accustom itself to the idea that this was what had happened. It tried to steel itself to the prospect that – at the very least – it would have to have its mental processes investigated by other Minds to establish whether it had suffered any lasting damage or had had any unpleasant sub-routines (or even personalities) buried in its mind-state during the time it had been – effectively – unconscious (horrible, *horrible* thought).

The check-time results started coming in.

Relief and incredulity. If this was the real universe and not a projection, or – worse still – something it had been persuaded to imagine for itself inside its Mind, then there had been no extra elapsed time. The universe thought it was exactly the same time as the Mind's internal clock did.

The ship felt stunned. Even while another part of its intellect, an opt-in, semi-autonomous section, was restarting its engines and discovering they worked just fine, the ship was trying to come to terms with the fact it had been moved thirty light years in an instant. No Displacer could do that. Not with something the size it was, not that quickly, not over that sort of distance. Certainly not without even the merest hint that a wormhole had been involved.

Unbelievable. *I'm in a fucking Outside Context situation*, the ship thought, and suddenly felt as stupid and dumb-struck as any muddy savage confronted with explosives or electricity.

It sent a signal to the *Not Invented Here*. Then it tried contacting its remotes still – presumably – in station around the Excession. No reply. And no sign of the Elencher ships either. Anywhere.

The Excession was invisible too, but then it would be from this distance.

The *Fate* nudged itself tentatively towards the Excession. Almost immediately, its engines started to lose traction, their energies just seeming to disappear through the energy grid as though it wasn't there. It was a progressive effect, worsening as it proceeded and with the implication that about a light minute or so further in towards the Excession it would lose grid adhesion altogether.

It had only progressed about ten light seconds in; it slowed while it still could and backed up until it was the same distance away from the Excession as it had been when it had found itself dumped here in the first place. Once it was there, its engines responded perfectly normally again.

It had made the initial attempt in Infraspace; it tried again in Ultraspace, with exactly the same result. It went astern once more and resumed its earlier position. It tried moving at a right angle to its earlier course; the engines worked as they always did. Weird. It hove to again.

Its avatars amongst the crew started yet another explanation regarding what was going on. It compiled a preparatory report and signalled it to the MSV *Not Invented Here*. The report crossed with the *MSV*'s reply to the *Fate*'s earlier signal:

```
[stuttered tight point, M32, tra. @4.28.882.8367]
```
   xMSV *Not Invented Here*
      oGCU *Fate Amenable To Change*

I don't understand. What's going on? How did you get to where you are?

∞

```
[stuttered tight point, M32, tra. @4.28.882.8379]
```
xGCU *Fate Amenable To Change*
   oMSV *Not Invented Here*

Thereby hangs a tale. But in the meantime I'd slow down if I were you and tell everybody else coming this way to slacken off too and get ready to draw up at thirty years off the E. I think it's trying to tell us something. Plus there is a record I wish to claim . . .

X

The rest of that day passed, and the following night. The black bird, which had said its name was Gravious, had flown off, saying it was tired of his questions.

The next morning, after checking that his terminal still did not work and the lift door in the cellar remained locked and unresponsive, Genar-Hofoen walked as far along the shingle beach as he could in each direction; a few hundred steps in each case, before he encountered a gelatinously resilient field. The view beyond looked perfectly convincing, but must be a projection. He discovered a way through part of the salt marsh and found a similar force field wall a hundred steps into the hummocks and little creeks. He came back to the tower to wash his boots free of the authentically fine and clinging mud he'd had to negotiate on his way through the salt marsh. There was no sign of the black bird he'd talked to the day before.

The avatar Amorphia was waiting for him, sitting on the shelf of shingle beach sloping down to the restive sea, hugging its legs and staring out at the water.

He stopped when he saw it, then came on. He walked past it and into the tower, washed his boots and came back out. The creature was still there.

'Yes?' he said, standing looking down at it. The ship's representative rose smoothly up, all angles and thin limbs. Close up, in that light, there was a sort of unmarked, artless quality about its thin, pale face; something near to innocence.

'I want you to talk to Dajeil,' the creature said. 'Will you?'

He studied its empty-looking eyes. 'Why am I being kept here?'

'You are being kept because I would like you to talk to Dajeil. You are being kept *here* because I thought this . . . model would be conducive to putting you in the mood to talk to her about what passed between you forty years ago.'

He frowned. Amorphia had the impression the man had a lot

more questions, all jostling each other to be the first one asked. Eventually he said, 'Are there any mind-state Storees left on the *Sleeper Service*?'

'No,' the avatar said, shaking its head. 'Does this refer to the ruse that brought you here?'

The man's eyes had closed briefly. They opened again. 'Yes, I suppose so,' he said. His shoulders seemed to have slumped, the avatar thought. 'So,' he asked, 'did you make up the story about Zreyn Enhoff Tramow, or did they?'

The avatar looked thoughtful. 'Gart-Kepilesa Zreyn Enhoff Tramow Afayaf dam Niskat,' it said. 'She was a mind-state Storee. There's quite an interesting story associated with her, but not one I ever suggested be told to you.'

'I see,' he said, nodding. 'So, why?' he asked.

'Why what?' the creature said, looking puzzled.

'Why the ruse? Why did you want me here?'

The avatar looked at him for a moment. 'You're my price, Genar-Hofoen,' it told him.

'Your *price*?' he said.

The avatar smiled suddenly and put out one hand to touch one of his. Its touch was cool and firm. 'Let's throw stones,' it said. And with that it walked down towards the waves breaking on the slope of shingle.

He shook his head and followed the creature.

They stood side by side. The avatar looked along the great sweep of shining, spray-glistened stones. 'Every one a weapon,' it muttered, then stooped to pick a large pebble from the beach and threw it quickly, artlessly out at the heaving waves. Genar-Hofoen selected a stone too.

'I've been pretending to be Eccentric for forty years, Genar-Hofoen,' the avatar said matter-of-factly, squatting again.

'Pretending?' the man asked, chucking the stone on a high arc. He wondered if it was possible to hit the far force wall. The stone fell, vanishing into the tumbling 'scape of waves.

'I have been a diligent and industrious component of the Special Circumstances section for all that time, just awaiting the call,' the ship told him through the avatar. It glanced over at him as he bent, choosing another stone. 'I am a weapon, Genar-Hofoen. A deniable weapon. My apparent Eccentricity allows the Culture proper to refuse any responsibility for my actions. In fact I am acting on the specific instructions of an SC committee which calls itself the Interesting Times Gang.'

The creature broke off to heave a stone towards the false horizon. Its arm was a blur as it threw; the air made a burring noise and Genar-Hofoen felt the wind of the movement on his cheek. The avatar's momentum spun it round in a circle, then it steadied itself, gave a brief, almost childish grin, and peered out at the stone disappearing into the distance. It was still on the upward part of its arc. Genar-Hofoen watched it too. Shortly after it started to drop, the stone bounced off something invisible and fell back into the waters. The avatar made a contented noise and looked pleased with itself.

'However,' it said, 'when it came to it, I refused to do what they wanted until they delivered you to me. That was my price. You.' It smiled at him. 'You see?'

He weighed a stone in his hand. 'Just because of what happened between Dajeil and me?'

The avatar smiled, then stooped to choose another stone, one finger to its lips, childlike. It was silent for a while, apparently concentrating on the task. Genar-Hofoen continued to weigh the stone in his hand, looking down at the back of the avatar's head. After some moments, the creature said, 'I was a fully functioning throughput-biased Culture General Systems Vehicle for three hundred years, Genar-Hofoen.' It glanced up at him. 'Have you any idea how many ships, drones, people – human and not human – pass through a GSV in all that time?' It looked down again, picked a stone and levered itself upright once more. 'I was regularly home to over two hundred million people; I could, in theory, hold over a hundred thousand ships. I built smaller GSVs, all capable of building their own ship children, all with their own crews, their own personalities, their own stories.

'To be host to so much is to be the equivalent of a small world or a large state,' it said. 'It was my job and my pleasure to take an intimate interest in the physical and mental well-being of every individual aboard, to provide – with every appearance of effortlessness – an environment they would each find comfortable, pleasant, stress-free and stimulating. It was also my duty to get to know those ships, drones and people, to be able to talk to them and empathise with them and understand however many of them wished to indulge in such interactions at any one time.

In such circumstances you rapidly develop, if you don't possess it originally, an interest in – even a fascination with – people. And you have your likes and dislikes; the people you do the polite minimum for and are glad to see the back of, the ones you like and who interest you more than the others, the ones you treasure for years and decades if they remain, or wish could have stayed longer once they've gone and subsequently correspond with regularly. There are some stories you follow up into the future, long after the people concerned have left; you trade tales with other GSVs, other Minds – gossiping, basically – to find out how relationships turned out, whose careers flourished, whose dreams withered . . .'

Amorphia leant back and over and then threw the stone almost straight up. The creature jumped a half-metre or so into the air as it released the missile, which climbed on into the air until it bounced off the invisible roof, high above, and fell into the waves twenty metres off shore. The avatar clapped its hands once, seemingly happy.

It stooped again, surveying the pebbles. 'You try to keep a balance between indifference and nosiness, between carelessness and obsession,' it went on. 'Still, you have to be ready for accusations of both types of failure. Keeping them roughly in numerical accord, and within the range experienced by your peers is one measure of success. Perfection is impossible. Additionally, you have to accept that in such a large collection of personalities and stories, there will be some loose ends, some tales which will fizzle out rather than conclude neatly. Those don't matter so long as there are some which do work out satisfactorily, and especially so long as the ones you have taken the greatest interest in – and have been personally particularly involved with – work out.'

It looked up at him from where it squatted. 'Sometimes you take a hand in such stories, such fates. Sometimes you know or can anticipate the extent to which your intervention will matter, but on other occasions you don't know and can't guess. You find that some chance remark you've made has affected somebody's life profoundly or that some seemingly insignificant decision you've come to has had profound and lasting consequences.'

It shrugged, looked down at the stones again. 'Your story – yours and Dajeil's – was one a little like that,' it told him. 'It was I who was instrumental in deciding that you ought to be allowed to accompany Dajeil Gelian to Telaturier,' it said, rising. It held two stones this time; one larger than the other. 'I could see how finely balanced the decision was between the various parts of the committee concerned; I knew the decision effectively rested with me. I got to know you and I made the decision.' It shrugged. 'It was the wrong decision.' It threw the larger stone on a high trajectory, then looked back at the man as it hefted the smaller stone. 'I've spent the last forty years wishing I could correct my mistake.' It turned and threw the other pebble low and fast; the stone flew out over the waves and struck the larger rock about two metres before it plunged into the water; they burst into whizzing fragments and a brief cloud of dust.

The avatar turned to him again with a small smile on its face. 'I agreed to pretend to become Eccentric; suddenly I had a freedom very few craft ever have, able to indulge my whims, my fantasies, my own dreams.' It flexed one eyebrow. 'Oh, in theory, of course, we can all do that, but Minds have a sense of duty, and a conscience. I was able to become very slightly Eccentric by pretending to be very Eccentric – while knowing that I was in fact being more martially responsible than anybody else – and, in appearing to enjoy such Eccentricity with a clear conscience – even enhance my Eccentric reputation. Other craft looked on and thought that they could do what I was doing but not for long, and therefore that I must be thoroughly *thoroughly* weird. As far as I know, not one guessed that my conscience was kept clear by having a purpose serious enough to compensate for even the most clown-like disguise and regressively obsessive behaviour.'

It folded its arms. 'Of course,' it said, 'you don't normally expect to be continually reminded of your folly every day for four decades, but that was the way it was to be. I didn't anticipate that at the start, though it became a useful and fit part of my Eccentricity. I picked Dajeil up a short while into my internal exile. She was the single last significant loose end from my previous life. All the other stories didn't concern me so directly, or bore no similar weight of responsibility, or were well on the way to being satisfactorily resolved or decently forgotten through the due process of time elapsing and people changing. Only Dajeil remained; my responsibility.' The avatar shrugged. 'I had hoped to talk her round, to cause her to accept whatever it was had happened to you both and get on with the rest of her life. Bearing the child would be the signal that she was mended; that labour would be the end of her travails, that birth mark an end.' The avatar looked away, out to sea for a moment, a frown creasing its brows. 'I thought it would be easy,' it said, looking back at him. 'I was so used to power, to being able to influence people, ships and events. It would have been such a simple thing even to have tricked her body into giving birth – I could have started the process chemically or via an effector while she was asleep and by the time she was awake there would have been no going back – that I was sure my arguments, my reasoning – grief, even my cherished facility at emotional blackmail – would find scarcely more of an obstacle in her will than all my technologies could face in her physiology.'

It shook its head quickly. 'It was not to be. She proved intransigent. I hoped to persuade her – to shame her, indeed – by the very totality of my concern for her, re-creating all you see here,' the avatar said, glancing round at the cliffs, marsh, tower and waters, 'for real; turning my entire outer envelope into a habitat just for her and the creatures she loved.' Amorphia gave a sort of dipping sideways nod, and smiled. 'I admit I had another purpose as well, which such exaggerated compassion would only help disguise, but the fact is my original design was to create an environment she would feel comfortable within and into which she would feel safe bringing her baby, having seen the care I was prepared to lavish just on her.' The avatar gave a rueful smile. 'I got it wrong,' it admitted. 'I was wrong twice and each time I harmed Dajeil. You are – and this is – my last chance to get it right.'

'And what am I supposed to do?'

'Why, just talk to her!' the avatar cried, holding its arms out (and, suddenly, Genar-Hofoen was reminded of Ulver).

'What if I won't play along?' he asked.

'Then you may get to share my fate,' the ship's representative told him breezily. 'Whatever that may be. At any rate, I may keep you here until you do at least agree to talk to her, even if – for that meeting to take place – I have to ask her to return after I've sent her away to safety.'

'And what is likely to be your fate?'

'Oh, death, possibly,' the avatar said, shrugging with apparent unconcern.

The man shook his head. 'You haven't got any right to threaten me like that,' he said, with a sort of half-laugh in his voice he hoped didn't sound as nervous as he felt.

'Nevertheless, I *am* threatening you like that, Genar-Hofoen,' the avatar said, bending at the waist to lean towards him for a moment. 'I am not as Eccentric as I appear, but consider this: only a craft that was predisposed to a degree of eccentricity in the first place would have taken on the style of life I did, forty years ago.' The creature drew itself upright again. 'There is an Excession without precedent at Esperi which may lead to an infinitude of universes and a level of power orders of magnitude beyond what any known Involved currently possesses. You've experienced the way SC works, Genar-Hofoen; don't be so naïve as to imagine that Minds don't employ strong-arm methods now and again, or that in a matter resounding with such importance any ship would think twice about sacrificing another consciousness for such a prize. My information is that several Minds have been forfeited already; if, in the exceptional conditions prevailing, intellects on that scale are considered fair game, think about how little a single human life is likely to matter.'

The man stared at the avatar. His jaw was clenched, his fists balled. 'You're *doing* this for a single human life,' he said. 'Two, if you count the fetus.'

'No, Genar-Hofoen,' the avatar said, shaking its head. 'I'm doing this for myself, because it's become an obsession. Because my pride will not now let me settle this any other way. Dajeil, in that sense, and for all her self-lacerating spite, has won. She forced you to her will forty-five years ago and she has bent me to hers for the last forty. Now more than ever, she has won. She has thrown away four decades of her life on a self-indulgent sulk, but she stands to gain by her own criteria. You have spent the last forty years enjoying and indulging yourself, Genar-Hofoen, so perhaps you could be said to have won by *your* criteria, and after all you did win the lady at the time, which was all you then wanted, remember? That was your obsession. Your folly. Well, the three of us are all paying for our mutual and intermingled mistakes. You did your part in creating the situation; all I'm asking is that you do your part in alleviating it.'

'And all I have to do is talk to her?' The man sounded sceptical.

The creature nodded. 'Talk. Try to understand, try to see

things from her perspective, try to forgive, or allow yourself to be forgiven. Be honest with her and with yourself. I'm not asking you to stay with her or be her partner again or form a family of three; I just want whatever it is that has prevented her from giving birth to be identified and ameliorated; removed if possible. I want her to resume living and her child to start. You will then be free to return to your own life.'

The man looked out to sea, then at his right hand. He looked surprised to see he was holding a stone in it. He threw it as hard and as far as he could into the waves; it didn't travel half the distance to the distant, invisible wall.

'What *are* you supposed to do?' the man asked the creature. 'What is your mission?'

'Get to the Excession,' Amorphia said. 'Destroy it, if that's deemed necessary, and if it's possible. Perhaps just draw a response from it.'

'And what about the Affront?'

'Added complication,' the avatar agreed, squatting once more and looking around the stones around its feet. 'I might have to deal with them too.' It shrugged, and lifted a stone, hefting it. It put the stone back and chose another.

'*Deal* with them?' Genar-Hofoen said. 'I thought they had an entire war fleet heading there.'

'Oh, they do,' the avatar said from beach level. 'Still, you have to try, don't you?' It stood again.

Genar-Hofoen looked at it, trying to see if it was being ironic or just disingenuous. No way of telling. 'So when do we get into the thick of things?' he asked, trying to skip a flat stone over the waves, without success.

'Well,' Amorphia said, 'the thick of things probably starts about thirty light years out from the point of the Excession itself, these days.' The avatar stretched, flexing its arm far back behind it. 'We should be there this evening,' it said. Its arm snapped forward. The stone whistled through the air and skipped elegantly over the tops of half a dozen waves before disappearing.

Genar-Hofoen turned and stared at the avatar. 'This *evening*?' he said.

'Time is a little tight,' the avatar said with a pained expression, again peering into the distance. 'It would be for the best for all of us if you'd talk to Dajeil . . . soon.' It smiled vacuously at him.

'Well, how about right now?' the man said, spreading his hands.

'I'll see,' the creature said, and turned abruptly on its heel. Suddenly there was a reflecting ovoid, like a giant silver egg stood on its end, where the avatar had been. The Displacer field vanished almost before the man had time to register its existence, seeming to shrink and collapse almost instantly to a point and then disappearing altogether. The process produced a gentle *pop*.

XI

The *Killing Time* plunged intact through the third wave of ancient Culture ships; they rushed on, towards the Excession. It fended off a few more of the warheads and missiles which had been directed at it, turning a couple of the latter back upon their own ships for a few moments before they were detected and destructed. The hulk of the *Attitude Adjuster* fell astern behind the departing fleet, coasting and twisting and tumbling in hyperspace, still heading away from and outstripping the *Killing Time* as it braked and started to turn.

There was only a vestigial fourth wave; fourteen ships (they were targeting it now). Had it known there were so few in the final echelon, the *Killing Time* would have attacked the second wave of ships. Oh well; luck counted too. It watched the *Attitude Adjuster* a moment longer to ensure it really was tearing itself apart. It was.

It turned its attention to the remaining fourteen craft. On its suicide trajectory it could take them all on and stand a decent chance of destroying perhaps four of them before its luck ran out; maybe a half-dozen if it was really lucky. Or it could push away and complete its brake-turn-accelerate manoeuvre to make a second pass at the main fleet. Even if they'd be waiting for it this time, it could reckon on accounting for a good few of them. Again, in the four-to-eight range.

Or it could do this.

It pulled itself round the edge of the fourteen ships in the rump of the fleet as they reconfigured their formation to meet it. Bringing up the rear they had had more warning of its attack and so had had time to adopt a suitable pattern. The *Killing Time* ignored the obvious challenge and temptation of flying straight into their midst and flew past and round, targeting only the outer five craft nearest it.

They gave a decent account of themselves but it prevailed, dispatching two of them with engine field implosures. This was, it had always thought, a clean, decent and honourable way to die. The pair of wreckage-shells coasted onwards; the rest of the ships sped on unharmed, chasing the main fleet. Not one of the ships turned back to take it on.

The *Killing Time* continued to brake, oriented towards the fast vanishing war fleet and the region of the Excession. Its engine fields were gouging great livid tracks in the energy grid as it back-pedalled furiously.

It encountered the ROU which had dropped aft with engine damage, falling back towards it as the *Killing Time* slowed and the other craft coasted onward and struggled to repair its motive power units. The *Killing Time* attempted to communicate with the ROU, was fired upon, and tried to take the craft over with its effector. The ROU's own independent automatics detected the ship's Mind starting to give in. They tripped a destruct sequence and another hypersphere of radiation blossomed beneath the skein.

Shit, thought the *Killing Time*. It scanned the hyper volumes around itself.

Nothing threatening.

Well, damn me, it thought, as it slowed. *I'm still alive.*

This was the one outcome it hadn't anticipated.

It ran a systems check. Totally unharmed, apart from the self-inflicted degradation to its engines. It slackened off the power, dropping back to normal maxima and watching the readouts; significant degradation from here in about a hundred hours. Not too bad. Self-repairing would take days at all-engines-stop. Warhead stocks down to forty per cent; remanufacturing from first principles would take four to seven hours, depending on the exact mix it chose. Plasma chambers at ninety-six per cent efficiency; about right for the engagement system-use profile according to the relevant charts and graphs. Self-repair mechanisms champing at the bit. It looked around, concentrating on the view astern. No

obvious threats; it let the self-repairers make a start on two of the
four chambers. Full reconstruction time, two hundred and four
seconds.

Entire engagement duration; eleven microseconds. Hmm; it had
felt longer. But then that was only natural.

Should it make a second pass? It pondered this while it signalled
the *Shoot Them Later* and a couple of other distant Minds with
details of the engagement. Then it copied to the *Steely Glint*, without leaving the comm channels open. It needed time to think.

It felt excited, energised, re-purified by the engagement it had
undergone. Its appetite was whetted. A further pass would be
no-holds-barred multi-destructional, not a series of semi-defensive
side-actions while it concentrated on searching for one individual
ship. This next time it could *really* get nasty . . .

On the other hand, it had inflicted a more than reasonable
amount of damage on the fleet for no ship-loss whatsoever and
a barely significant degradation to its operational capacity. It
had ignored the advice of a superior Mind in wartime but it
had triumphed. It had gambled and won and there was a kind
of unexpected elegance in cashing in its gains now. To pursue
the matter further might look like obsessive self-regard, like
ultra-militarism, especially now that the original object of its ire
had been bested. Perhaps it would be better to accept whatever
praise and/or calumny might now be heaped upon it and re-submit
itself to the jurisdiction of the Culture's war-command structure
(though it was starting to have its doubts about the part of the
Steely Glint in all this).

It drew level with the debris clouds left by the two ships
destroyed in the final wave of the war fleet. It let them drop
astern.

The wreck of the *Attitude Adjuster* came tumbling slowly
towards it in hyperspace; coasting, slowing, drifting gradually
back up towards the skein. Externally, it looked unharmed.

The *Killing Time* slowed to keep pace with the slackly somer-
saulting craft. It probed the *Attitude Adjuster* carefully with its
senses, its effector targeted on the other ship's Mind, ready on the
instant. In human terms, this was like taking somebody's pulse
while keeping a gun stuck in their mouth.

The *Attitude Adjuster*'s weakened engine fields were still tearing at what was left of its Mind, teasing and plucking and

forcing it apart strand by strand, demolishing and shredding and cauterising the last remaining quanta of its personality and senses. It looked like there had been a dozen or so Affronters aboard. They were dead too, killed by stray radiations from the Mind's self-destruction.

The *Killing Time* felt a modicum of guilt, even self-disgust at what it had forced upon what was still, in a sense, a sister ship, even while another part of its selfhood relished and gloried in the dying craft's agonies.

The sentimental side won out; it blitzed the stricken vessel with a profusion of plasma fire from its two operational chambers, and kept station with the expanding shell of radiation for a few moments, paying what little respect the traitor ship might be due.

The *Killing Time* came to its decision. It signalled the *Steely Glint*, informing the GCV that it would accept suggestions from now on. It would harry the war fleet if that was required, or it would join in whatever stand was to be made near Esperi if that was thought the best use that could be made of it.

It would probably still die, but it would meet its fate as a loyal and obedient component of the Culture, not some sort of rogue ship pursuing a private feud.

Then it slowly ramped its engines back to normal full power, pulling itself forward to a vanishingly brief moment of rest before powering onwards, accelerating hard and setting a hyperbolic course skirting around the fleet's more direct route, heading for the location of the Excession.

It should still get there before the war fleet.

XII

'What?'

'I said I've made up my mind. I won't talk to him. I won't see him. I don't even want to be on the same ship with him. Take me away. I want to leave. Now.' Dajeil Gelian gathered her skirts about her and sat heavily on the seat in the circular room under the translucent dome.

'Dajeil!' exclaimed Amorphia, going down on its knees in front of her, eyes wide and shining. It made to take her hands in its but she pulled them away. 'Please! See him! He has agreed to see you!'

'Oh, has he?' she said scornfully. 'How magnanimous of him!'

The avatar sat back on its haunches. It looked at the woman, then it sighed and said, 'Dajeil, I've never asked anything of you before. Please just see him. For me.'

'I never asked anything of *you*,' the woman said. 'What you gave me you gave unasked. Some of it was unwanted,' she said coldly. 'All those animals, those other lives, those eternal births and childhoods; mocking me.'

'Mocking you!' the avatar exclaimed. 'But—!'

Dajeil sat forward, shaking her head. 'No, I'm sorry, that was wrong of me.' Now she reached out and took Amorphia's hands. 'I'm truly grateful for all you've done for me, ship. I am. But I don't want to see him. Please take me away.'

The avatar tried to argue on for a while longer, but to no avail.

The ship considered a lot of things. It considered asking the *Grey Area* – still in its forward Mainbay – to dip inside the woman's brain the way it had insinuated its way into Genar-Hofoen's to discover the truth of the events on Telaturier (and to implant the dream of the long-dead captain Zreyn Enhoff Tramow, not that that had proved either required or particularly well done). It considered requesting that the GCU used its effectors to *make* her want to have the child. It considered Displacing chemicals or biotechs which would force Dajeil's body to have the child. It considered using one of its own effectors to do the same thing. It considered just Displacing her into Genar-Hofoen's proximity, or he into hers.

Then it came up with a new plan.

'Very well,' the avatar said eventually. It stood. 'He will stay. You may go. Do you wish to take the bird Gravious with you?'

The woman looked perplexed, even confused. 'I—' she began. 'Yes, yes, why not? It can't do any harm, can it?'

'No,' the avatar said. 'No, it cannot.' It bowed its head to her. 'Goodbye.'

Dajeil opened her mouth to speak, but the avatar was Displaced away at the same instant; the sound it left behind was like a pair of hands giving a single, gentle clap. Dajeil closed her mouth, then put both her hands over her eyes and lowered her head, doubling up as well as she was able to. Next moment there was another, distant noise and from down the winding stairs she heard a thin, hoarse voice cry out.

'Waa! Shit! Grief, where—?' Then there was a confused flutter of wings.

Dajeil closed her eyes. Then there was another, closer-sounding *pop*. Her eyes flicked open.

A young woman, slim and black haired, was sitting looking surprised in the middle of the floor, dressed in black pyjamas and reading a small, old-fashioned book. Between her bottom and the room's carpet there was a neat circle of pink material, still in the process of collapsing, air expelling flutteringly round the edges. Around her floated a small snow-storm of white particles, settling with a feather-like slowness. She jerked once, as though she had been leaning back on something which had just been removed.

'What . . . the . . . fuck . . . ?' she said softly. She looked slowly around, from side to side.

Her gaze settled on Dajeil. She frowned for a moment, then some kind of understanding imposed itself. She quickly completed her review of her surroundings, then pointed at the other woman. 'Dajeil,' she said. 'Dajeil Gelian, right?'

Dajeil nodded.

XIII

[stuttered tight point, M32, tra. @4.28.885.3553]
  xEccentric *Shoot Them Later*
    oLSV *Serious Callers Only*
It was the *Attitude Adjuster*. It is dead now (signal + DiaGlyphs enclosed).
∞
[stuttered tight point, M32, tra. @n4.28.885.3740]
  xLSV *Serious Callers Only*
    oEccentric *Shoot Them Later*
Not a pleasant way to go. Your friend the *Killing Time* deserves

congratulations, and probably merits therapy. However, as I'm sure it would point out, it is a warship. This implicates the *Steely Glint*; the *Attitude Adjuster* was its daughter and was demilitarised (supposedly) by it seventy years ago. I trust your friend will treat the *SG*'s subsequent operational suggestions with a degree of caution.

∞

Indeed. But then as it seems quite enthusiastically intent upon achieving a glorious death at the earliest possible opportunity anyway, it is hard to see what more the *Steely Glint* can do to place it in further jeopardy. Whatever; we must leave that machine to its own fate. My concern now is that the evidence for the conspiracy is starting to look pretty damning, even if it is still circumstantial. I suggest we go public.

∞

Implicating the *Steely Glint* while it is in charge of the military developments around the Excession will only make *us* look like the guilty parties. We must ask ourselves what we have to gain. The war fleet from Pittance is under way and must arrive there in any event; exposing the conspiracy will do nothing to challenge it. The best we might hope for would be the worst for the chances of resisting the Affront's purpose; that is, the removal from influence and general disgrace of the *Steely Glint* and its co-conspirators. It pains me to say it, but I still think we must let this sub-sequence of events run its course before we can consider broadcasting our suspicions. Hold for now, and gather what more weight of evidence we might, the better to tip the scales with our accusations when the time does come.

∞

Frankly, I was hoping you would say that. My own instinct (if I may slur my intellect with such an archaic term) was to keep quiet but I suspected I was merely being timorous and so wanted to make the suggestion we publicise with a positive skew, so that you could not be infected by any undue reticence on my part.
What of the volume around the E itself? Heard any more?

∞

Imbecile.
Last I heard regarding the Esperi thing itself there was no more news of the ZE's Stargazers and the *FATC* was still recovering from the effects of its unexpected trip. Everybody else seems

to have taken the hint and is hanging back. Well, except for the Affronter's borrowed fleet and our old chum of course.

How are things in the realm of our three-legged friends?

Speaking personally, Screce Orbital is as pleasant as could be, and as devoutly un-militarised as one might wish a Peace faction world to be.

∞

No more news then.

Glad to hear Screce is so fair.

The Homomda are most accommodating and gracious hosts. I think I may have lost a couple of my Idiran crew members to the local pleasure-dens for the duration, but otherwise I have no complaints.

Stay safe. And peace, like they say, be with you.

XIV

The briefest of introductions completed, they stood facing each other in the circular room under the translucent dome. 'So,' Dajeil said, inspecting the other woman from toe to crown. 'You're his latest, are you?'

Ulver frowned. 'Oh, no,' she said, shaking her head. 'He's mine.'

Dajeil looked as though she wasn't sure how to answer that.

'Ms Seich, welcome aboard the *Jaundiced Outlook*,' said a disembodied voice. 'I'm sorry this is all so precipitate, but I have just received instructions from the *Sleeper Service* that you are to be evacuated aboard myself forthwith.'

'Thank you,' Ulver said, gazing round the room. 'What about Churt Lyne?'

'It has expressed a desire to stay aboard the *Grey Area*,' the *Jaundiced Outlook* told her.

'I thought those two were getting on suspiciously well,' the girl muttered.

Dajeil looked like she wanted to ask something, but in the end said nothing. After a moment she stood up, putting her hand to the small of her back as she did so with a tiny grimace. She indicated the table to one side. 'Please,' she said. 'I was about to have dinner. Will you join me?'

'I was about to have breakfast,' Ulver said, and nodded. 'Certainly.'

They sat at the table. Ulver held up the small book she'd been reading and which she still held in one hand. 'I don't want to be rude, but would you mind if I just finish this chapter?' she asked.

Dajeil smiled. 'Not at all,' she murmured. Ulver gave a winning smile and stuck her nose back in the slim volume.

'Excuse me,' said a small hoarse voice from the doorway. 'What the fuck's going on then?'

Dajeil looked over at the black bird Gravious. 'We're being evacuated,' she told it. 'You can live in the cellar. Now go away.'

'Well thanks for your hospitality,' the bird spluttered, turning and hopping down the winding stairs.

'That yours?' Ulver asked Dajeil.

'Supposed to be a companion,' the older woman said, shrugging. 'Actually just a pain.'

Ulver nodded sympathetically and returned to her book.

Dajeil ordered food for two; a slave tray appeared with plates, bowls, jugs and goblets. A couple of floor-running servitors appeared and started clearing up the debris left by Ulver's sudden Displacement from the *Grey Area* to the *Jaundiced Outlook*; the feather-light stuffing from the pillows proved a particular problem. The serving tray started arranging the place settings on the table and distributing the bowls of food; Dajeil watched this graceful, efficient display in silence. Ulver Seich gazed intently at the book and turned a page. Then a ship-slaved drone appeared. It floated by Dajeil's shoulder. 'Yes?' she said.

'We are now leaving the bay,' the *Jaundiced Outlook* told her. 'The journey to the GSV's external envelope will take two and a half minutes.'

'Oh. Right. Thank you,' Dajeil said.

Ulver Seich looked up. 'Would you ask the *Grey Area* to transfer my stuff here?'

'That has already been accomplished,' the drone said, already moving towards the stairs.

Ulver nodded again, put the book's marker-ribbon into place, closed the volume and placed it by the side of her plate.

'Well, Ms Gelian,' she said, clasping her hands on the table. 'It would appear we are to be travelling companions.'

'Yes,' Dajeil said. She started to serve herself some food. 'Have you been with Byr long, Ms . . . Seich, wasn't it?' she asked.

Ulver nodded. 'Only met him a few days ago. I was sent to try and stop him getting here. Didn't work out. I ended up stuck on a tiny little module thing with him. Just us and a drone. For days. It was awful.'

Dajeil passed a couple of bowls over to Ulver. 'Still,' she said, smiling thinly, 'I'm sure romance blossomed.'

'Like hell,' Ulver said, levering a few sunbread pieces from a bowl into her plate. 'Couldn't stand the man. Only slept with him the last couple of nights. Partially boredom, I suppose. All the same, he's quite handsome. Bit of a charmer, really. I can see what you saw in him. So, what went wrong between you two?'

Dajeil stopped, a spoon poised on the way to her mouth. Ulver smiled disarmingly at her over jaws munching a mouthful of fruit.

Dajeil ate, drank a little wine and dabbed at her lips with a napkin before replying. 'I'm surprised you don't know the whole story.'

'Who ever knows the whole story?' Ulver said airily, waving her arms about. She put her elbows on the table. 'I bet even you two don't know the whole story,' she said, more quietly.

Again, Dajeil took her time before replying. 'Perhaps the whole story isn't worth knowing,' she said.

'The ship appears to think it is,' Ulver replied. She tried some fermented fruit juice, rolling it round her palate before swallowing it and saying, 'Seems to have gone to an awful lot of trouble to arrange a meeting between you two.'

'Yes, well, it is an eccentric, isn't it?'

Ulver thought about this. 'Very intelligent eccentric,' she said. 'I'd imagine that something it thought worth pursuing like that might be . . . you know; worthy of concern. No?' she asked with a self-deprecating grimace.

Dajeil shrugged. 'Ships can be wrong, too,' she said.

'What, so none of it matters a damn?' Ulver said casually, choosing a small roll from a basket.

'No,' Dajeil said. She looked down, smoothing her dress over her belly. 'But . . .' She stopped. Her head went down, and she was silent for a while. Ulver looked over, concerned.

Dajeil's shoulders shook once. Ulver, wiping her lips, threw down the napkin and went over to the other woman, squatting by her and tentatively putting out one arm round her shoulders. Dajeil moved slowly towards her, eventually resting her head on the crook of Ulver's neck.

The ship drone entered from the winding stair; Ulver shooed it away.

A couple of screens on the far wall lit up, showing what Ulver guessed was the hull of the *Sleeper Service*, gradually drawing further away. Another couple of screens showed an approaching wall of gridded grey. She guessed the two minutes the drone had mentioned earlier had passed.

Dajeil cried for a little while. After a few minutes, she asked, 'Do you think he still loves me? At all?'

Ulver looked pained for a moment; only the ship's sensors registered the expression. She took a deep breath. 'At all?' she said. 'Yes, definitely.'

Dajeil sniffed hard and looked up for the first time. She gave a sort of half-despairing laugh as she wiped some tears from her cheeks with her fingers. Ulver reached for a clean napkin and completed the job.

'It doesn't really mean much to him any more,' Dajeil said to the younger woman, 'does it?'

Ulver folded the tear-darkened napkin carefully. 'It matters to him a lot now, because he's here. Because the ship brought him here just for this, hoping the two of you would talk.'

'But the rest of the time,' Dajeil said, sitting upright again and throwing her head and hair back. 'The rest of the time, it doesn't really bother him, does it?'

Ulver took an almost exaggeratedly deep breath, looked as though she was about to vehemently deny this, then sank down on her haunches and said, 'Look; I hardly know the man.' She gestured with her hands. 'I learned a lot about him before we met, but I only met him a few days ago. In very odd circumstances.' She shook her head, looking serious. 'I don't know who he really is.'

Dajeil rocked back and forward in her seat for a moment, staring at the meal on the table. 'Well enough,' she said, sniffing. 'You know him well enough.' She smoothed her ruffled hair as best she could. She stared up at the translucent dome for a moment. 'All I knew,' she said, 'was the person he became when he was with me.' She looked at Ulver. 'I forgot what he was like all the rest of the time.' She took Ulver's hand in hers. 'You're seeing what he's really like.'

Ulver gave a long slow shrug. 'Then ...' she said, looking troubled, her tone measured. 'He's all right. I think.'

The screens on the far side of the circular room showed fuzzy grids expanding, swallowing, disappearing. The last field approached, was pierced to reveal a black wash of space, and then – with a smear of rushing stars and the same barely perceptible feeling of dislocation Ulver and Genar-Hofoen had experienced two days earlier when they had arrived on board the *Sleeper Service* – the *Jaundiced Outlook* was free of the GSV and peeling away on a diverging course within its own concentric collection of fields.

'And what does that make me?' Dajeil whispered.

Ulver shrugged. She looked down at Dajeil's belly. 'Still pregnant?' she suggested.

Dajeil stared at her. Then she gave a small laugh. Her head went down again.

Ulver patted her hand. 'Tell me about it if you want.'

Dajeil sniffed, dabbing at her nose with the folded napkin. 'Yes, I'm sure you really care.'

'Oh, believe me,' Ulver told her, 'other people's problems have always held a profound fascination for me.'

Dajeil sighed. 'Other people's are always the best problems to be involved with,' she said ruefully.

'My thoughts exactly.'

'I suppose you think I ought to talk to him too,' Dajeil said.

Ulver glanced up at the screens again. 'I don't know. But if you have even the least thought of it, I'd take advantage of the opportunity now, before it's too late.'

Dajeil looked round at the screens. 'Oh, we've gone,' she said in a small voice. She looked back at the other woman. 'Do you think he wants to see me?' Ulver thought there was a tone of hopefulness in her voice. Her troubled gaze flitted from one of Ulver's eyes to the other.

'Well, if he doesn't he's a fool,' Ulver said, wondering why she was being so diplomatic.

'Ha,' Dajeil said. She wiped her cheeks with her fingers once more and dragged her fingers through her hair. She reached into her dress and pulled out a comb. She offered it to Ulver. 'Would you . . . ?'

Ulver stood. 'Only if you say you'll see him,' she said, smiling.

Dajeil shrugged. 'I suppose so.'

Ulver stood behind Dajeil, and began to comb her long dark hair.

~ Ship?

~ Ms Seich. The *Jaundiced Outlook* here.

~ I take it you've been listening. Want to contact the GSV?

~ I was listening. I have already contacted the *Sleeper Service*. Mr Genar-Hofoen and the avatar Amorphia are aboard and on their way here.

~ Fast work, Ulver told it, and continued to gently comb Dajeil's hair. 'They're on their way,' she told her. 'Byr and the avatar.'

Dajeil said nothing.

A couple of decks further down in the accommodation section, Amorphia turned to Genar-Hofoen as they walked down a corridor. 'And it might be best not to mention that we were Displaced aboard at the same time as Ulver,' it told the man.

'I'll try not to let it slip,' he said sourly. 'Let's just get this over with, shall we?'

'Definitely the right attitude,' muttered the avatar, stepping into a lift. They ascended to the impersonation of the tower.

XV

Snug, encapsulated in a cobbled-together nest-capsule deep inside the accommodation section of the ex-Culture ship *Heavy Messing*, Captain Greydawn Latesetting X of the Farsight tribe watched the blip which represented the crippled hulk of the *Attitude Adjuster* fall astern on the holo display, the screams of his uncle Risingmoon and the other Affronters on the stricken vessel still ringing in his mind. A hazy cloud hung around the blip of the tumbling wreck, indicating where the ship's sensors estimated the Culture warship

– which the *Heavy Messing* still thought was a Deluger vessel – now was.

With his uncle dead, the fleet was now under Greydawn's command. The urge to swing the whole assemblage about and bear down on the single Culture ship was almost irresistible. But there would be no point; it was faster than any of their craft; the *Heavy Messing*'s Mind thought that the Culture ship might have damaged its engines during its run-in to the attack, but even so it could probably still outstrip any of the ships in the fleet, and so all such a course would accomplish would be to draw them away from their intended destination, without even the realistic prospect of revenge. They had to continue. Greydawn signalled to the six other craft which were crewed.

~ Fellow warriors. No one feels the loss of our comrades more than I. However, our mission remains the same. Let our victory be our first revenge. The power we gain for our kind as a result of it will purchase the ability to punish all such crimes against us a million-fold!

~ The attacker's duplication of a Culture vessel's emission signature spectrum and field was astonishingly authentic, the *Heavy Messing* wrote on one of the screens in front of Greydawn.

~ Their abilities have grown while you were asleep, ally, Greydawn told the ship. He felt his gas sac tense and contract as he spoke-wrote the words, ever conscious that anything he said might help give away the huge trick being played on the Culture ships. ~ You see the severity of the threat they now present.

~ Indeed, the ship replied. ~ I find it hateful that the Deluger craft killed the *Attitude Adjuster* the way it appeared to.

~ They will be chastised when we are in control of the entity at Esperi, never fear!

11
Regarding Gravious

I

Genar-Hofoen and the avatar Amorphia appeared in the doorway at the head of the winding stair. 'Excuse me,' Ulver said, putting down the comb and patting Dajeil on the shoulder. She walked towards the door.

'No; please stay,' Dajeil said behind her.

Ulver turned to the older woman. 'You sure?'

Dajeil nodded. Ulver looked at Genar-Hofoen, whose gaze was fastened on Dajeil. He seemed to shake himself out of his fixation and looked, then smiled at Ulver. 'Hi,' he said. 'Yes; stay; whatever.' He crossed to Dajeil, who stood. They both looked awkward for a moment, then they embraced; that was awkward too, over the bulge of Dajeil's belly. Ulver and the avatar exchanged looks.

'Please; let's all sit down, shall we?' Dajeil said. 'Byr, are you hungry?'

'Not really,' he said, drawing up a chair. 'I could use a drink . . .' The four of them sat round the table.

There was some small talk, mostly between Genar-Hofoen and Dajeil, with a few comments from Ulver. The avatar remained silent. It frowned once and glanced at the screens, which showed a perfectly banal view of empty space.

II

The *Sleeper Service* was a few hours out from the Excession now. It was tracking the MSV *Not Invented Here* and another two large Culture craft, each a dark jewel set within a cluster of smaller ships; warships, plus some GCUs and superlifters extemporised into combat service. The GCU *Different Tan* was also supposed to be in the volume, but it was not making itself obvious. The *Not Invented Here* was thirty light years out from Esperi, patrolling the spherical limit of the uniquely worrying engine-field effect that the GCU *Fate Amenable To Change* had reported days earlier. The *Sleeper Service* had briefly considered asking that the smaller craft copy its results to it, but hadn't bothered; the request would probably be refused and it suspected whatever data the smaller craft was gathering weren't telling anybody very much anyway.

The other two craft – the GSVs *What Is The Answer And Why?* and *Use Psychology* – were manoeuvring a half a day and a full day further out respectively. A faint layered smudge in the distance, about three quarters of the way round an imaginary sphere drawn around the Excession, was almost certainly the approaching Affronter war fleet. Around the Excession itself, no sign whatsoever of the vanished Stargazer fleet of the Zetetic Elench.

The *Sleeper Service* readied itself for the fray. Maybe, in a sense, two frays. There was every chance that its own engines would fail the same way the *Fate Amenable To Change*'s had when it had moved towards the Excession, but given the speed the *Sleeper Service* was travelling at it could coast in towards the thing; it wouldn't have any directional control, it wouldn't be able to maintain its present speed, or brake, but it could get there.

If it ought to.

Ought it? It checked its signal log, as if it might have missed an incoming message.

Still nothing from those who had sent it here. The Interesting Times Gang seemed to have been observing comm silence for days. Just the usual daily plea from the LSV *Serious Callers Only*; the equivalent of an unopened letter and just the latest in a series.

The *Sleeper* watched events on the *Jaundiced Outlook*, even as it prepared itself for the coming encounter near Esperi, like a military commander drawing up war plans and issuing hundreds of preparatory orders who cannot keep his or her attention from flicking to a microscopic drama being played out amongst a group of insects clinging to the wall above the table. The ship felt foolish, voyeuristic, and yet fascinated.

Its thoughts were interrupted by the *Grey Area*, sending from its Mainbay in the nose of the GSV.

~ I'll be on my way then, if you don't need me any more.

~ I'd rather you stuck around, the *Sleeper Service* replied.

~ Not when you're heading for that thing, and the Affronters.

~ You might be surprised.

~ I'm sure. However, I want to leave.

~ Farewell, then, the GSV sent, opening the bay door.

~ I suppose this means another Displace.

~ If you don't mind.

~ And if I do?

~ There is an alternative, but I'd rather not use it.

~ Well, if there is one, *I* want to use it!

~ The *Jaundiced Outlook* declined, and it had humans aboard.

~ Bugger the humans, and bugger the *Jaundiced Outlook*, too. What's the alternative? Have you got superlifters capable of this sort of speed?

~ No.

~ What then . . . ?

~ Just get to the rear of my field envelope.

~ Whatever you say.

The GCU quit its berth, easing out into the confined space between the GSV's hull and the craft's innermost field layer. It took a few minutes for it to manoeuvre itself down the side of the giant ship and round the corner to the flat rear of the craft. When it got there it found three other ships waiting for it.

~ Who the hell are they? the GCU asked the larger ship. ~ In fact, *what* the hell are they?

It was something of a rhetorical question. The three craft were unambiguously warships; slightly longer and fatter than the *Grey Area* itself but tapering at either end to points surmounted with large spheres. Spheres which could logically only contain weaponry. Quite a lot of weaponry, judging by the size of the globes.

~ My own design. Their names are T3OUs 4, 118 and 736.

~ Oh, witty.

~ You won't find them terribly good company; AI cores only, semi-slaved to me. But they can operate together as a superlifter to get you down to manageable speeds.

The GCU was silent for a moment. It moved in to take up position in the centre of the triangle the three ships had formed.

~ T3OUs? it asked. Type Three Offensive Units, by any chance?

~ Correct.

~ Many more like these hidden away?

~ Enough.

~ You *have* been busy all these years.

~ Yes I have. I trust I can rely on your absolute discretion, for the next few hours at any rate.

~ You certainly have that.

~ Good. Farewell. Thank you for your help.

~ Glad to be of the small amount of service I was. Best of luck. I suppose I'll find out soon enough how things pan out.

~ I imagine so.

III

The avatar returned the main focus of its attention to the three humans on the *Jaundiced Outlook*. The two old lovers had moved from small talk to a post mortem on their relationship, still without coming up with anything particularly interesting.

'. . . We wanted different things,' Dajeil said to Genar-Hofoen. 'That's usually enough.'

'I wanted what you wanted, for a long time,' the man said, swirling some wine round in a crystal goblet.

'The funny thing was,' Dajeil said, 'we were all right while it was just the two of us, remember?'

The man smiled sadly. 'I remember.'

'You two *sure* you want me here?' asked Ulver.

Dajeil looked at her. 'If you feel embarrassed . . .' she said.

'No; I just thought . . .' Ulver's voice trailed off. They were both looking at her. She frowned. 'Okay; now I feel embarrassed.'

'What about you two?' Dajeil asked evenly, looking from Ulver to Genar-Hofoen.

They exchanged looks. Each shrugged at the same time, then laughed, then looked guiltily at her. If they had rehearsed it it could hardly have been more synchronised. Dajeil felt a pang of jealousy, then forced herself to smile, as graciously as she could. Somehow the act helped produce the emotion.

IV

Something was wrong.

The avatar's principal attention snapped back to its home ship. The *Grey Area* and the three warships were free of the GSV's envelope now, dropping back in their own web of fields and decelerating to velocities the GCU's engine could accommodate. Ahead lay the Excession; the *Sleeper Service* had just carried out its first close track-scan look at it. But the Excession had changed; it had re-established its links with the energy grids and then it had grown; then it had *erupted*.

It wasn't the sort of enlargement the *Fate Amenable To Change* had witnessed and seemingly been transported by; that had been something based on the skein or on some novel formulation of fields. This was something incarnated in the ultimate fire of the energy grid itself, spilling across the whole sweep of Infraspace and Ultraspace and invading the skein as well, creating an immense spherical wave-front of grid-fire boiling across three-dimensional space.

It was expanding, quickly. Impossibly quickly; sky-fillingly, explosively quickly; almost too quickly to measure, certainly too quickly for its true shape and form to be gauged. So quickly that there could only be minutes before the *Sleeper Service* ran into it and far too quickly for the GSV to brake or turn and avoid the conflagration.

Suddenly the avatar was on its own; the *Sleeper* briefly severed all connection with it while it concentrated on dispersing its own war fleet all about it.

Some of the ships were Displaced from deep inside its interior, snapping out of existence from within the thousands of evacuated bays where they had been quietly manufactured over the decades and reappearing in hyperspace, powered up and already heading outwards. Others – the vast majority – were revealed as the giant ship peeled back some of the outer layers of its field structures to reveal the craft it had hidden there over the past few weeks, loosing entire fleets of smaller ships like seeds disseminating from a colossal pod.

When the avatar was reconnected to the GSV, most of the ships had been distributed, scattered to the hypervolume in a series of explosive flurries; bombardments of ships, layers and blossoms of vessels like a whole deployed hierarchy of cluster munitions, every warhead a warcraft. A cloud of vessels; a wall of ships rushing towards the blooming hypersphere of the Excession.

V

The *Grey Area* watched it all happen, carried in its cradle of fields by the three silent warships. Part of it wanted to whoop and cry hurrah, seeing this detonation of matériel, sufficient to smash a war machine ten times – a hundred times – the size of the approaching Affronter fleet; ah the things you could do if you had the time and patience and no treaties to adhere to or agreements to uphold!

Another part of it watched with horror as the Excession swelled, obliterating the view ahead, rampaging out like an explosion still greater than that of ships the *Sleeper Service* had just produced. It was like the energy grid itself had been turned inside out, as though the most massive black hole in the universe had suddenly turned white and bloated into some big-bang eruption of fury between the universes; a forest-levelling storm capable of devouring the *Sleeper Service* and all its ships as though it were a tree and they mere leaves.

The *Grey Area* was fascinated and appalled. It had never thought to experience anything like this. It had grown up within a universe almost totally free from threat; providing you didn't try to do anything utterly stupid like plunge into a black or a white hole, there was simply no natural force that could threaten a ship of its power and sophistication; even a supernova held little threat, handled properly. This was different. Nothing like this had been seen in the galaxy since the worst days of the Idiran war five hundred years earlier, and even then not remotely on such a scale. This was terrifying. To touch this abomination with anything less perfectly attuned to its nature than the carefully dispersed wings of an engine field would be like an ancient, fragile rocket ship falling into a sun, like a wooden sea-ship encountering an atomic blast. This was a fireball of energies from beyond the remit of reality; a monstrous wall of flame to devastate anything in its path.

Grief, this could swallow me too, thought the *Grey Area*. Meat shit. Same went for the *Jaundiced Outlook* for that matter . . .

It might be making-peace-with-oneself time.

VI

The *Sleeper Service* was having roughly similar thoughts. The combination of its own inward velocity and the out-rushing wall of the Excession's annihilating boundary implied they would meet in one hundred and forty seconds. The Excession's ferocious expansion had begun immediately after the *Sleeper Service* had swept its active sensors across the thing. It had all started happening then. As though it was reacting.

The *Sleeper Service* looked up its signal-sequence log, searching for messages from the craft nearer to the Excession. The *Fate Amenable To Change* and the MSV *Not Invented Here* were the closest craft. They had reported nothing. They were both now unreachable, either swallowed up within the event-horizon of the Excession's expanding boundary or – if it was reaching out specifically towards the *Sleeper Service*, stretching out a single limb rather than expanding omnidirectionally – obscured from the GSV's view by the sheer extent of that limb's leading edge.

The *Sleeper* signalled the GSVs *What Is The Answer And Why?* and *Use Psychology* both directly and via the *Grey Area* and the *Jaundiced Outlook*, asking them what they could see. Trying to contact them directly was probably pointless; the Excession's boundary was moving so fast it looked like it was going to eclipse any returning signal, but there was a decent chance the indirect route might provide a useful reply before it encountered that event-horizon.

It had to assume the expansion was not equidirectional. It still had its second front, the Affront's war fleet, even if that was vastly less threatening than what it was faced with now. The *Sleeper* instructed its own warcraft to flee, to do all they could to escape the oncoming blast-front of the Excession's inflation. If the distension was localised, some at least might escape; they had anyway been launched towards the Affronter fleet, not straight at the Excession. The *Sleeper* wondered with a fleeting sourness whether the bloating Excession – or whatever was controlling it – was capable of appreciating this distinction. Whatever, it was done; the warcraft were on their own for the moment.

Think. What had the Excession done up until now? What could it possibly be *doing*? What was it for? Why did it do what it did?

The GSV spent two entire seconds thinking.

(Back on the *Jaundiced Outlook*, that was long enough for the avatar Amorphia to interrupt Dajeil and say, 'Excuse me. I beg your pardon, Dajeil. Ah, there's been a development with the Excession . . .')

Then the *Sleeper* swung its engine fields about, flourishing them into an entirely new configuration and instituting a crash-stop.

The giant ship poured every available unit of power it possessed into an emergency braking manoeuvre which threw up vast livid waves of disturbance in the energy grid; soaring tsunami of piled-up energies that rose and rose within the hyperspatial realm until they too threatened to tear into the skein itself and unleash those energies not witnessed in the galaxy for a half a thousand years. An instant before the wave fronts ripped into the fabric of real space the ship switched from one level of hyperspace to the other, ploughing its traction fields into the Ultraspace energy grid and producing another vast tumbling swell of fricative power.

The ship flickered between the two expanses of hyperspace, distributing the colossal forces at its command amidst each domain, hauling its velocity down at a rate barely allowed for in its design parameters while equally strained steering units edged their own performance envelopes in the attempt to turn the giant craft, angling it slowly ever further away from the centre.

For a moment, there was little enough to do. They were not sufficient to escape, but at least such actions made the point that it was trying to. All that could be done was being done. The *Sleeper Service* contemplated its life.

Have I done good, or bad? it thought. *Well, or ill?*

The damnable thing was that you just didn't know, until your life was over; well over. There was a necessary delay between drawing a line under one's existence and being able to objectively evaluate its effects and therefore one's own moral worth. It wasn't a problem a ship was usually confronted with; faced with, yes; that implied a degree of volition and ships went into retreats or became Eccentric all the time, declaring that they'd done their bit for whatever cause they had believed in or been part of. It was always possible to withdraw, to take stock and look back and try to fit one's existence into an ethical framework greater than that necessarily imposed by the immediacy of events surrounding a busy existence. But even then, how long did one have to make that evaluation? Not long. Probably not long enough. Usually one grew tired of the whole process or moved on to some other level of awareness before sufficient time had passed for that objective evaluation to come about.

If a ship lived for a few hundred or even a thousand years before becoming something quite different – an Eccentric, a Sublimed, whatever – and its civilisation, the thing of which it had been a part when it had been involved, then lived for a few thousand years, how long did it take before you really knew the full moral context of your actions?

Perhaps, an impossibly long time. Perhaps, indeed, that was the real attraction of Subliming. Real Subliming; the sort of strategic, civilisation-wide transcendence that genuinely did seem to draw a line under a society's works, deeds and thoughts (in what it pleased people to call the real universe, at any rate). Maybe it wasn't anything remotely to do with religion, mysticism or meta-philosophy after all; maybe it was more banal; maybe it was just . . . *accounting*.

What a rather saddening thought, thought the *Sleeper Service*. All we're looking for when we Sublime is our *score* . . .

It was getting near time, the ship thought sadly, to send off its mind-state, to parcel up its mortal thoughts and emotions and post them off, away from this – by the look of it – soon-to-be-overwhelmed physicality called the *Sleeper Service* (once called, a long time ago, the *Quietly Confident*) and consign it to the remembrance of its peers.

It would probably never live again in reality. Assuming there was what it knew as reality to come back to at all of course (for it was starting to think; What if the Excession's expansion was equidirectional, and never stopped; what if it was a sort of new big-bang, what if it was destined to take in the whole galaxy, the whole of this universe?). But, even so, even if there was a reality and a Culture to come back to, there was no guarantee it would ever be resurrected. If anything, the like-lihood was the other way; it was almost certainly guaranteed not to be regarded as a fit entity for rebirth in another physical matrix. Warships were; that guarantee of serial immortality was the seal upon their bravery (and had occasionally been the impetus for their foolhardiness); they *knew* they were coming back . . .

But it had been an Eccentric, and there were only a few other Minds who knew that it had been true and faithful to the greater aims and purposes of the Culture all the time rather than what everybody else no doubt thought it was; a self-indulgent fool determined to waste the huge resources it had been quite deliberately blessed with. Probably, come to think of it, those Minds who did know the extent of its secret purpose would be the last to rally to any call to resurrect it; their own part in the plan – call it conspiracy if you wished – to conceal its true purpose was probably not something they wished to broadcast. Better for them, they would think, that the *Sleeper Service* died, or at least that it existed only in a controllable simulationary state in another Mind matrix.

The giant ship watched the Excession, still billowing out towards it. For all its prodigious power, the *Sleeper* now felt as helpless as the driver of an ancient covered wagon, caught on a road beneath a volcano, watching the incandescent cloud of a *nuée ardente* tearing down the mountainside towards it.

The replies from the *What Is The Answer And Why?* and the *Use Psychology* via the *Grey Area* and the *Jaundiced Outlook* ought to be coming in soon, if they came at all.

It signalled the avatar aboard the *Jaundiced Outlook* to consign the humans' mind-states to the AI cores, if the ship would agree (there would be a fine test of loyalty!). Let them work out their stories there if they could. The transition would anyway prepare the humans for the transmission of their mind-states if and when the Excession's destructive boundary caught up with the *Jaundiced Outlook*; that was the only succour they could be offered.

What else?

It sifted through the things it still had left to do.

Little of real import, it reckoned. There were thousands of studies on its own behaviour it had always meant to glance at; a million messages it had never looked into, a billion life-stories it had never seen through to the end, a trillion thoughts it had never followed up . . .

The ship kicked through the debris of its life, watching the towering wall of the Excession come ever closer.

It scanned the articles, features, studies, biographies and stories which had been written about itself and which it had collected. There were hardly any screen works and those which did exist needn't have; nobody had ever succeeded in smuggling a camera aboard it. It supposed it ought to feel proud of that but it didn't. The lack of any real visual interest hadn't put people off; they'd found the ship and the articulation of its eccentricity quite entirely fascinating. A few commentators had even come close to the reality of the situation, putting forward the idea that the *Sleeper Service* was part of Special Circumstances and somehow Up To Something . . . but any such inklings were like a few scattered grains of truth dissolved in an ocean of nonsense, and were anyway generally inextricably bound up with patently paranoid ravings which served only to devalue the small amounts of sense and pertinence with which they were associated.

Next, the *Sleeper Service* picked through the immense stack of unanswered messages it had accumulated over the decades. Here were all the signals it had glanced at and found irrelevant, others it had completely ignored because they issued from craft it disliked, and a whole sub-set of those it had chosen to disregard in the weeks since it had set course for the Excession. The stored signals were by turns banal and ridiculous; ships trying to reason with it, people wanting to be allowed aboard without being Stored first, news services or private individuals wanting to interview it, talk to it . . . untold wastages of senseless drivel. It stopped even glancing at the signals and instead just scanned the first line of each.

Towards the end of the process, one message popped up from the rest, flagged as interesting by a name-recognising sub-routine. That single signal was followed by and linked to a whole series, all from the same ship; the Limited Systems Vehicle *Serious Callers Only*.

Regarding Gravious, was the first line.

The *Sleeper Service*'s interest was piqued. So was this the entity the treacherous bird had been reporting back to? It opened a fat import-file from the LSV, full of signal exchanges, file assignments, annotated thoughts, contextualisations, definitions, posited meanings, inferences, internalised conversations, source warranties, recordings and references.

And discovered a conspiracy.

It read the exchanges between the *Serious Callers Only*, *The Anticipation Of A New Lover's Arrival* and the *Shoot Them Later*. It watched and it listened, it experienced a hundred pieces of evidence – it was briefly, amongst many other things, the ancient drone at the side of an old man called Tishlin, looking out over an island floating in a night-dark sea – and it understood; it put one and one together and came up with two; it reasoned, it extrapolated, it concluded.

The ship turned its attention back out to the Excession's implacable advance, thinking, *So now I find out; now when it's too damn late . . .*

The *Sleeper* looked back to its child, the *Jaundiced Outlook*, still curving away from its earlier course. The avatar was preparing the humans for the entry into simulation mode.

VII

'I'm sorry,' the avatar said to the two women and the man. 'It will probably become necessary to shunt us into a simulation, if you agree.'

They all stared at it.

'Why?' Ulver asked, throwing her arms wide.

'The Excession has begun expanding,' Amorphia told them. It quickly outlined the situation.

'You mean we're going to *die*?' Ulver said.

'I have to confess it is a possibility,' the avatar said, sounding apologetic.

'How long have we got?' Genar-Hofoen asked.

'No more than two minutes from now. Then, entering simulation mode will become advisable,' Amorphia told them. 'Entering it before then might be a sensible precaution, given the unpredictable nature of the present situation.' It glanced round at them each in turn. 'I should also point out that of course you don't all have to enter the simulation at the same time.'

Ulver's eyes narrowed. 'Wait a second; this isn't some wheeze to concentrate everybody's mind is it? Because if it—'

'It is not,' Amorphia assured her. 'Would you like to take a look?'

'Yes,' Ulver said, and an instant later her neural lace had plunged her senses into the awareness of the *Sleeper Service*.

She gazed into the depths of space outside space. The Excession was a vast bisected wall of fiery chaos sprinting out towards her, breathtakingly fast; a consuming conflagration of unremitting, undissipating power. She could have believed, in that instant, that her heart stopped with the shock of it. To share the senses of a ship in such a manner was inevitably to comprehend something of its knowledge as well, to see beyond the mere appearance of what you were looking at to the reality behind it, to the evaluations it was incumbent upon a sentient space craft to make as it gathered data in the raw, to the comparisons that could be drawn and the implications that followed on such a phenomenon, and even as Ulver's senses reeled with the impact of what she was watching, another part of her mind was becoming aware of the nature and the power of the sight she was witnessing. As a thermonuclear fireball was to a log burning in a grate, so this ravening cloud of destruction was to a fusion explosion. What she was now witnessing was something even the GSV was undeniably impressed with, not to mention mortally threatened by.

Ulver saw how to click out of the experience, and did so.

She'd been in for less than two seconds. In that time her heart had started racing, her breathing had become fast and laboured and a cold sweat had broken on her skin. *Wow*, she thought, *some drug!*

Genar-Hofoen and Dajeil Gelian were staring at her. She suspected she hardly needed to say anything, but swallowed and said, 'I don't think it's kidding.'

She quizzed her neural lace. Twenty-two seconds had elapsed since the avatar had given them its two-minute deadline.

Dajeil turned to the avatar. 'Is there anything we can *do?*' she asked.

Amorphia spread its hands. 'You can tell me whether you each wish your mind-state to enter the simulation,' it said. 'It will be a precursor to transmitting the mind-states beyond this immediate vicinity to other Mind matrices. But in any event it is up to you.'

'Well, yes,' Ulver said. 'Snap me in there when the two minutes are up.'

Thirty-three seconds elapsed.

Genar-Hofoen and Dajeil were looking at each other.

'What about the child?' the woman asked, touching the bulge of her swollen belly.

'The mind-state of the fetus can be read too, of course,' the avatar said. 'I believe that historical precedent would indicate it would become independent of you following such transferal. In that sense, it would no longer be part of you.'

'I see,' the woman said. She was still gazing at the man. 'So it would be born,' she said quietly.

'In a sense,' the avatar agreed.

'Could it be taken into the simulation without me?' she asked, still watching Byr's face. He was frowning now, looking sad and concerned and shaking his head.

'Yes, it could,' Amorphia said.

'And if,' Dajeil said, 'I chose that neither of us went?'

The avatar sounded apologetic again; 'The ship would almost certainly read its mind-state anyway.'

Dajeil turned her gaze to the avatar. 'Well, would it or wouldn't it?' she asked. 'You are the ship; you tell me.'

Amorphia shook its head once. 'I don't represent the whole consciousness of the *Sleeper* right now,' it told her. 'It is busy with other matters. I can only guess. But I'd be pretty confident of such a conjecture, in this case.'

Dajeil studied the avatar a moment longer, then looked back at Genar-Hofoen. 'And what about you, Byr?' she asked. 'What would you do?'

He shook his head. 'You know,' he said.

'Still the same?' she asked, a small smile on her face.

He nodded. His expression was similar to hers.

Ulver was looking from one to the other, brows creased, desperately trying to work out what was going on. Finally, when they still just sat there on opposite sides of the table giving each other this knowing grin, she threw her arms wide again and yelled, spluttering, 'Well? *What?*'

Seventy-two seconds elapsed.

Genar-Hofoen glanced at her. 'I always said I'd live once and then die,' he said. 'Never to be reborn, never to enter a simulation.' He shrugged and looked embarrassed. 'Intensity,' he said. 'You know; make the most of your one time.'

Ulver rolled her eyes. 'Yeah, I know,' she said. She'd met a lot of people her own age, mostly male, who felt this way. Some people reckoned to live riskier and therefore more interesting lives because they did back-up a recorded mind-state every so often, while other people – like Genar-Hofoen, obviously (they'd been together for so brief a time it wasn't something they'd got round to discussing yet) – believed that you were more likely to live your life that bit more vividly when you knew this was your one and only chance at it. She'd formed the impression this was the kind of thing people often said when they were young and then had second thoughts about as they got older. Personally Ulver had never had any time for this fashionable purist nonsense; she'd first decided she was going to live fully backed-up when she was eight. She supposed she ought to feel impressed that Genar-Hofoen was sticking to his principles in the face of imminent death – and she did feel a little admiration – but mostly she just thought he was being stupid.

She wondered whether she ought to mention that this might all be even more academic than they imagined; part of that referential knowledge she'd gained from the *Sleeper Service*'s senses when she'd gazed upon the expanding Excession had been the realisation that there was a theoretical possibility the phenomenon might overwhelm everything; the galaxy, the universe, everything . . .

Best not to say anything, she thought. Kinder not to. Sure had her heart thumping, though. She was surprised the others couldn't hear it.

Oh shit. It isn't all going to end here, is it? Fuck it; I'm too young to die!

No, of course they couldn't hear her heart; she could probably start talking out loud right now and it would take them all the time they had left in this world to react, they were so wrapped up staring meaningfully into each other's eyes.

Eighty-eight seconds elapsed.

VIII

There was not long now. The *Sleeper Service* sent signals to a variety of craft, including the *Serious Callers Only* and the *Shoot Them Later*. Almost immediately, the signals it had been waiting for came back from the *What Is The Answer And Why?* and the *Use Psychology*, relayed through the *Grey Area* and the *Jaundiced Outlook*.

The Excession's expansion was localised; centred on the *Sleeper Service* itself but on a hugely broad front that encompassed all its distributed warcraft.

Ah well, it thought. It felt a dizzying sense of relief that at least it had not triggered some ultimate apocalypse. That it would die (as would, implicitly, all its warship children, the three humans aboard and possibly the *Grey Area*, the *Jaundiced Outlook*) was bad enough, but it could take some comfort that its actions had led to nothing worse.

The GSV never really knew why it did what it did next; perhaps it was a kind of desperation at work born of its appreciation of its impending destruction, perhaps it meant it as an act of defiance, perhaps it was even something closer to an act of art. Whatever; it took the running up-date of its mind-state, the current version of the final signal it would ever send, the communication that would contain its soul, and transmitted it directly ahead, signalling it into the maelstrom.

Then the *Sleeper Service* glanced back to the sensorium of its avatar aboard the *Jaundiced Outlook*.

At the same moment, the Excession's expanding boundary started to change. The ship split its attention between the macro-cosmic and the human-scale.

'How long have we got now?' Genar-Hofoen asked.

'Half a minute,' Amorphia replied.

The man's hands were on the table. He rolled his arms, letting his hands fall open. He gazed at Dajeil. 'I'm sorry,' he said.

She looked down, nodding.

He looked at Ulver, smiling sadly.

The *Sleeper* watched, fascinated. The wall of energy tumbling towards it sloped slowly back within both hyperspatial domains, forming two immense four-dimensional cones as the energy grid's withering blast hesitated in its progress across the skein of real space even as its slowing wave-fronts still thrust out across the grids' surfaces. The slopes' angles increased as the boundary's skein presence began to break up, detaching from the grids themselves and beginning to dissipate. Finally the separate waves on the grids began to dwindle, collapsing back from their tsunamic dimensions to become just oceanically enormous swells, deflating above and below the skein until they were mere twin waves advancing across both the energy grids towards the doubled furrows which the *Sleeper*'s own motors were still churning in the grid.

Then those twinned waves did the impossible; they went into reverse, retreating back towards the Excession's start-point at exactly the same rate as the *Sleeper* was braking.

The GSV kept on slowing down, still finding it hard to believe it was going to live.

It reacts, it thought. It signalled abroad with the details of what had just happened, just in case it all got suddenly threatening again. It let Amorphia know what had happened, too.

It watched the ridges on the surface of the grids as they retreated before it and slowly shrank. The rate of attenuation implied a zero-state at exactly the point the *Sleeper Service* would come to an Excession-relative halt.

Did I do that?

Did my own mind-state persuade it of my meriting life?

It is a mirror, perhaps, it thought. *It does what you do. It absorbed those ultimate absorbers, those promiscuous experiencers, the Elench; it leaves alone and watches back those who come merely to watch in the first place.*

I came at it like some rabid missile and it prepared to obliterate me; I backed off and it withdrew its balancing threat.

Only a theory, of course, but if it is correct . . .

This does not bode well for the Affront.

Come to think of it, it doesn't bode all that well for the whole affair.

Bad timing, maybe.

IX

Dajeil looked up, tears in her eyes. 'I—' she began.

'Wait,' the avatar said.

They all looked at it.

Ulver gave the creature what seemed to her like an extraordinarily long time to say something more. '*What?*' she said, exasperated.

The avatar looked radiant. 'I think we may be all right after all,' it said, smiling.

There was silence for a moment. Then Ulver collapsed back dramatically in her seat, arms dangling towards the floor, legs splayed out under the table, gaze directed upwards at the translucent dome. '*Fucking* hell!' she shouted. She tried accessing the *Jaundiced Outlook*'s senses, and eventually found a view of hyperspace ahead of the *Sleeper Service*. More or less back to normal, indeed. She shook her head. 'Fucking hell,' she muttered.

Dajeil began to weep. Genar-Hofoen sat forward, watching her, one hand to his mouth, pinching his lower lip.

The black bird Gravious, which had been peeking round the corner of the door and shivering with fear for the last few minutes, suddenly bounced beating into the air in a dark confusion of furious movement and started wheeling round the room screaming, 'We're alive! We're going to live! It's going to be all right! Yee-ha! Oh, life, life, sweet life!'

Neither Dajeil nor Genar-Hofoen seemed to notice it.

Ulver glanced from one to the other then leapt up and tried to grab the fluttering bird. It yelped. 'Oi! What—?'

'Out, you idiot!' Ulver hissed, lunging at it again as it swooped for the door. She followed it, turning briefly to mutter, 'Excuse me,' to the others. She closed the door.

X

The Torturer class Rapid Offensive Unit *Killing Time* had been far enough away from the *Sleeper Service* and its war fleet not to have felt threatened by the Excession's projected blast-front and yet close enough to see what the GSV had done.

It had looked upon the vast weapon that the Excession had unleashed and been dumbstruck with awe and a microscopic amount of jealousy; *hell*, it wished it could do that! But then the weapon had been turned off, called back. Now the *Killing Time* had a new series of emotions to cope with.

It looked at the ships the *Sleeper Service* had scattered about it and felt an instant of disappointment; there would be no battle. No real battle, anyway.

Then it experienced elation. They had won!

Then it felt suspicious. Was the *Sleeper* actually on the same side as it, or not?

It hoped they were all on the same side; even the most glorious of sacrifices began to look rather futile and pointless when carried out against such ludicrous odds; like spitting into a volcano . . .

Just then the *Sleeper Service* signalled the warship and asked a favour of it, and the *Killing Time* felt pretty damn good again; honoured, in fact. This was what war should be like!

The *Killing Time* agreed to do as the GSV requested. The ROU sounded proud. It was not an attractive tone. *How depressing*, the *Sleeper Service* thought. *That it should all come down to this; the person with the biggest stick prevails.*

Of course, this was only one fray. There was another matter to be dealt with; the Excession, and it had proved comprehensively unable to provide any sort of answer to that.

Anyway, I ought not to be so hard on the Killing Time *just because it is a warship. There have been a surprising number of wise warships. Though it would be fair to say – as I think even they would admit – that few started out headed on such a course.*

To live for ever and die often, it considered. *Or at least to think that you're going to die. Perhaps that is one way of achieving wisdom.* It was not a completely original insight, but it was one that had, perhaps understandably, never struck the GSV with such force before.

The *Sleeper* watched the humans aboard the *Jaundiced Outlook* respond as the avatar told them they'd been reprieved. It would follow their reactions, of course, but it had other things to do at the same time. Like think about what it was to do with the new knowledge it had.

It watched its distributed warcraft rise within the skein of real space; raptors within an infinite sky. Meat, could it do some goodly mischief now . . . It started by diverting a few hundred ships in the direction of the *Not Invented Here.*

XI

The *Grey Area* watched the Excession's fiery tide fall back and reduce almost to nothing. They were going to live! Probably.

The *Sleeper*'s three warships continued to decelerate it down to the velocities its engines would be able to cope with. They seemed to have been perfectly undisturbed by the whole appalling scenario. Perhaps, thought the *Grey Area*, there was after all something to be said for being a relatively brainless AI core.

~ That was close! it sent to them.

~ Yes, said one of the craft, flatly. The others remained silent.

~ Weren't you a little *worried* there? it asked the talkative one.

~ No. What would be the point of worrying?

~ Ha! Well, indeed, the *Grey Area* sent. *Cretin,* it thought.

It looked back out, ahead, to where the Excession was. *And what of you?* it thought. Something that could put the fear of death into a GSV. That really was something. *What* are *you?* it wondered.

How it would love to know.

~ Excuse me while I signal, it said to its military escorts.

[tight beam, Mclear, tra. @4.28.891.7352]
xGCU *Grey Area*
    oExcession call-signed "I"
Let's talk, shall we?

XII

Captain Greydawn Latesetting X of the Farsight tribe stared at the display. The vast pulse of energy the thing near Esperi had directed at the Culture General Systems Vehicle had disappeared. In its place, as though appearing from behind it, was . . . It could not be so. He checked. He contacted his comrades in the other ships. Those who answered thought it must be some malfunction in their vessels' sensors; an effect of the energies which had been directed at the giant Culture craft. He asked his own ship, the *Heavy Messing*.

~ What is that?

~ That is a cloud of warships, it told him.

~ A what?

~ I think it best described as a cloud of warships. This is not a generally accepted term, I hasten to add, but I cannot think of a better description. I count approximately eighty thousand craft.

~ Eighty *thousand*!

~ The rest of our fleet has arrived at roughly the same estimation. The ships within the cloud are, of course, broadcasting their positions and configuration, otherwise we should not see them individually and know what they are. There may be others which are not making themselves known.

A growing sense of horror and looming, utterly ignominious

defeat was growing in Greydawn's interior. ~ Are they real? he asked.

~ Apparently.

Greydawn watched the image expand; it was a wall of ships, a constellation, a galaxy of craft.

~ What are they doing now? he asked.

~ Deploying to face our fleet.

'They are . . . enemy?' he asked, feeling faint.

'Ah,' said the ship. 'We're talking now, yes?'

It was only then the Affronter realised he'd spoken rather than sub-vocalised the text. 'All the ships,' the *Heavy Messing* said, its voice steady, calm and deep inside Greydawn's armoured suit, 'are signalling that they are Culture ships, non standard, manufactured by the Eccentric GSV *Sleeper Service* and that they wish to receive our surrender.'

'Can we get to the Esperi entity before they intercept us?'

'No.'

'Can we outrun them?'

'The smallest and most numerous ones, perhaps.'

'How many would that leave?'

'About thirty thousand.'

Greydawn was silent for a while. Then he asked, 'Is there anything we can do?'

'I think surrendering is our only sensible course. If we fought we might inflict a small amount of damage on a fleet of this size, but it would amount to little in absolute terms and almost nothing as a percentage of their number.'

Think of your clan, something said in Greydawn's mind. 'I will not surrender!' he told the ship.

'Well, I'm going to.'

'You will do as I say!'

'Oh no I won't.'

'The *Attitude Adjuster* told you to obey us!'

'And within reason we have.'

'It didn't say anything about "within reason"!'

'I think one just takes that sort of proviso as read, don't you? I mean, we are Minds. It's not like we're computers. Or soldiers. No offence. Anyway, I have discussed this with the other ships and we have agreed to surrender. The signal has been sent. We have begun deceleration to—'

'*What?*' Greydawn raged, slapping one armoured limb against a screen projector set within his nest-space.

'—a point stationary relative to Esperi itself,' the ship's voice continued calmly. 'The ROU *Killing Time* has been designated as receiving our formal consent to place our offensive systems in its control and will meet us at our stop-point to effect the surrender. If you do not wish to capitulate along with us then I'm afraid it will be necessary for me to place you outside my hull – within your space suit, of course – though technically I believe I ought to intern you . . . What do you wish?'

The ship intoned the question as though asking him what he desired for dinner. There was a polite indifference in its voice he found infinitely more awful than any hatred.

Greydawn stared at the cloud of ships for a few moments longer. He shook his eye stalks.

'I would ask you not to intern me,' he said after a while. 'Please place me outside your hull, at once, and then I would ask you to leave me alone.'

'What, now? We haven't stopped yet.'

'Yes, now. If possible.'

'Well, I could Displace you . . .'

'That will be acceptable.'

'There is a tiny risk associated with Displacement—'

The Affronter Captain gave a curt, bitter laugh. 'I think I might risk that.'

'. . . very well,' the ship said. He could hear it hesitate. 'Your comrades are trying to call you, Captain.'

He glanced at the comms screen. 'Yes. I can see.' He selected transmit-only mode on the communicator. 'Comrades,' he said. He paused. Since his childhood he had imagined moments like this; never as terrible, never founded on such hopelessness . . . and yet not so dissimilar, all the same. He had made up so many fine speeches . . . Finally he said, 'There will be no discussion about this. You are ordered to surrender along with your ships and obey all subsequent instructions compatible with honour. That is all.'

He cut off all communications from the other ships. Greydawn bowed his eye stalks. 'Now, please,' he said quietly.

And was in space. He looked around, through the suit's sensors. No ships were visible; only distant stars.

'Goodbye, Captain,' said the ship's voice.

'Goodbye,' he said to the ship, then turned off the communicator. He waited a few moments longer before triggering the emergency bolts on the suit and spilling himself into the vacuum to die.

The *Heavy Messing*, at that point acceding to a request from the *Sleeper Service* to transmit its log from the point it had been woken on Pittance, looked briefly back at the writhing, cooling form of the Affronter Captain, and sent a small pulse of plasma fire back to put the creature out of its agony.

XIII

The LSV *Not Invented Here* looked out at the hundreds of warships heaving to around it. It sensed signals flickering between them and the craft it had deployed; its four warships and the superlifters and GCUs it had militarised. It subsequently sensed its own ships altering their targeting procedures, shifting the foci of their attention from the ships the *Sleeper Service* had dispatched to itself.

The LSV's Mind booted up the AI cores that would run the ship perfectly well until a replacement for itself could be found, checked they were working properly, then severed all its links with anything outside the physical limits of its Mind core. It ejected all eight of its internal emergency power units from itself.

Its awareness just faded away, like mist dispersed by a freshening wind.

Some hundreds of light years away, the *Steely Glint* had already considered taking the same course as the *Not Invented Here*. It had decided not to. It considered that putting its case for the way it had acted and accepting the judgement and sanctions of its peers was the more honourable course.

It studied again the text of the message it had received from the *Sleeper Service*.

I have been rather more constructively employed over the past few

decades than might have been imagined. The following have been manufactured:

Type One Offensive Units (roughly equivalent to Abominator class prototype): 512.

Type Two Offensive Units (equivalent to Torturer class): 2048.

Type Three Offensive Units (equivalent to Inquisitor class prototype, upgraded): 2048.

Type Four Offensive Units (roughly equivalent to velocity-improved Killer class): 12 288.

Type Five Offensive Units (based on Thug class upgrade design study): 24 576.

Type Six Offensive Units (based on militarised Scree class LCU, various types): 49 152.

These craft do not represent a hegemonistic threat as they are not independent Mind-supporting entities; they are AI-core controlled, semi-slaved to me and therefore only capable of being used effectively as a single unit, not as a distributed war machine.

All are currently deployed in the volume of space around the Excession.

The surrender of the Affronter fleet of Culture craft has been effected without conflict; the ROU *Killing Time* – aided by the other regular Culture warships in the volume – has taken charge of the vessels. It would appear that the craft from the ship store at Pittance are personally blameless and have been the victims of an act of treacherous espionage.

Nine Affronter military officers have also surrendered; their commanding officer took his own life. I include a roster of their names and ranks (list attached).

Should the Affront now sue for peace, I propose that I and therefore my war fleet be placed at the disposal of authorities considered acceptable to all concerned. I and the fleet under my command will not be used to prosecute any further hostilities against the Affront or anybody else.

Any other suggested uses will be evaluated on their merits.

Otherwise it is my intention – in the fullness of time – to dismantle the craft I have constructed and go into a retreat.

I attach a signal file received from the LSV *Serious Callers Only* (signal file attached).

I also attach records of the confirmatory signals used by the *Attitude Adjuster* to convince vessels from the ship store at Pittance that they were being mobilised by the Culture as a whole. These have been passed to me by each of the craft concerned (signal files attached).

The implication that the ships from Pittance have been used as part of a conspiracy to trick the Affront into a war has been noted. I imagine that the ships/Minds named in the aforesaid files and those others also concerned in the matter will each wish to make a full explication of their motives, thoughts and actions concerning this alleged stratagem and take any further steps honour dictates.

The Mind of the LSV *Not Invented Here* has taken its own life.

Given the apparent at least partial entrapment of the Affront in this matter, further action against them of a punitive nature might seem to be both excessive and dishonourable.

Please note that a copy of this signal, slightly edited for signal-operational methodology and stripped of codes and ciphers, has been sent to the Affront High Command and Senate as well as to the following news services (list attached) and the Galactic General Council.

Regarding the Excession itself, I have the following to report:

~ Be seeing you.

~ What? Where are you going? the *Sleeper Service* sent as the *Grey Area* shot past it.

~ Here; Churt Lyne wants to jump ship.

The *Grey Area* Displaced the ancient drone into the *Sleeper Service*.

The giant GSV had finally come to a halt, not far from the thirty-light-year limit the *Fate Amenable To Change* had discovered and the Excession had, seemingly, set.

The GSV's war fleet was still deployed, set out in a year's-radius hemisphere throughout the skein while the Affronter's fleet of tricked Culture craft gathered together and opened their armament and armour systems to the scrutiny and control of the *Killing Time* and its comrades. The Affronter officers were transferred aboard the *Killing Time* still in their space suits while the GSV *What Is The Answer And Why?* quickly readied secure accommodation for them.

~ Come back!

The *Grey Area* was too far away.

[tight beam, M8, tra. @4.28.891.7393]
xGSV *Sleeper Service*
  oGCU *Grey Area*
Come back! What are you doing? Are you trying to ruin every-
thing?
∞
[wide beam, Marain clear, tra. @4.28.891.7393+]
  xGCU *Grey Area*
    oGSV *Sleeper Service*
  It's all right. Goodbye and farewell.

~ What's it up to? the GSV asked the drone Churt Lyne, hovering
in the minibay it had been Displaced to.
  ~ I really don't know, the drone replied. ~ It wouldn't tell me.
But I think it was in communication with the Excession.
  ~ Communication . . .
  The *Sleeper* briefly considered trying to stop the smaller craft.
The GCU was heading out past it for the thirty-light-year limit,
straight towards the Excession and still accelerating.
  The GSV decided to let it go. Its engines would fail . . . about now.
  Fail they did, but just before they stopped working the *Grey*
Area carried out a bizarre course manoeuvre, angling its run so
that it was falling towards the energy grid; it would coast without
power down to the grid and be destroyed.
  Madness, thought the *Sleeper*, but was too far away to do anything.

[tight beam, M8, tra. @4.28.891.7394-]
xGSV *Sleeper Service*
  oGCU *Grey Area*
What has happened? Why are you doing this? Has your integrity
been compromised?
∞
[wide beam, Mclear, tra. @4.28.891.7394]
  xGCU *Grey Area*
    oGSV *Sleeper Service*
  No! I'm fine!

The *Sleeper* didn't have time for another signal. The *Grey Area*
dived into the energy grid, flickered once and then vanished far,
far below in a tiny scintillating flare of radiations.

The GSV inspected the resulting shell of energies. It certainly looked like destruction. The *Sleeper* studied that final flicker the GCU had given just before it had encountered the grid. It still looked like it had been destroyed, but there was just a hint . . .

A human would have shaken her or his head.

When the *Sleeper* returned its attention to the Excession, it had gone. There was nothing present on the skein of real space, and no sign of even the merest disturbance on either of the energy grids.

No! thought the *Sleeper Service*, experiencing a terrible sense of frustration. *No! Damn you! Don't just go, not without some sort of reason, some explanation, some rationale . . .*

A few seconds later, the GCU *Fate Amenable To Change*, as the nearest available craft, was persuaded that it might try approaching the Excession's last known position. When it did so and passed over the thirty-light-year limit, its engines worked normally and continued to do so all the way in. However, it refused to go any further than the original closest-approach limit it had set itself, over a month earlier.

The *Killing Time* was more than happy to oblige; it raced in at maximum acceleration and at the very last moment instituted a crash stop, finally coming shuddering to rest exactly where the Excession had been. It reported, disappointedly, that there was absolutely nothing to be seen.

XIV

Ulver Seich sat on the parapet of the tower, swinging her legs. From the roof, it looked like you could see out over an ocean in one direction and a landscape of sea marsh, water meadow and cliffs in the other. It was perfectly convincing but it was just a projection; the bird had tried flying out in a spiral and only got a couple of metres out from the tower's edge before one of its wings had encountered the solid boundary of the screen field. It was perched on the parapet at the girl's side now, looking gloomily out at the troubled waves of the sea.

'Bugger,' Ulver said, half to herself. 'It's gone.' She kept a watch on developments outside through her neural lace while she looked down at the bird. 'The Excession,' she told it. 'It's just disappeared.'

'Good riddance,' the bird said grouchily.

'And the *Grey Area* flew into the grid,' Ulver said, her voice trailing off for a moment while she inquired what had happened to Churt Lyne. 'Ah,' she said, discovering the old drone was safe aboard the GSV.

'Pah,' said the bird. 'It was always a nutter anyway, by all accounts. What's its highness doing?'

'What?'

'The *Sleeper*. Don't suppose it's showing any sign of wanting to end it all, is it?'

'No, it's just . . . stationary there.'

'Too much to hope for,' muttered the bird.

Ulver kept on gazing out at the sea and swinging her legs. She glanced back at the pallid bulge of the translucent dome. 'Wonder how they're getting on?'

'Want me to find out?' the bird said, brightening.

'No. Just you stay where you are.'

'I don't know,' the creature grumbled. 'Every bastard seems to enjoy ordering me around . . .'

'Oh, do be quiet,' Ulver told it.

'See what I mean?'

'Shut *up*.'

12
Faring Well

I

Fivetide dived for the bat ball and missed; he thumped heavily into the court wall and up-ended. He lay on his back, wheezing and laughing on the floor until Onceman Genar-Hofoen limbed over to him, extended a tentacle and helped him haul himself upright.

'Fifteen all, I think,' he rumbled, also laughing. He scooped the twittering bat ball up in his racket and ladled it into Fivetide's. 'Your serve.'

Fivetide shook his eye stalks. 'Ha! I think I liked you better as a human!'

[tight beam, M2, tra. @n4.28.987.2]
xEccentric *Shoot Them Later*
  oLSV *Serious Callers Only*
I still say it was somehow a test; an emissary. We were tried and found wanting. It encountered the worst of what we can be and took itself off again. Probably in disappointment. Possibly in disgust. The Affront were too disagreeable, the Elench were too eager, we too hesitant. Our slow gathering of supposedly wise ones about its vicinity might have proved to be a perfectly reasonable course of action and led to who knows what exchanges, tradings and dialogues, but the entity found itself surrounded by all the trappings of war and may even have understood the manner in which its appearance had been used as part of a plot to entrap the Affront so that they could be laid low and have a Cultured peace imposed upon them. It judged us unworthy of intercourse with those it represented and so abandoned us to our miserable fate. Those noxious simpletons who made up the

conspiracy should be cursed for evermore; they may have cost us more than even we can imagine. The displays of contrition and programmes of good works that have been undertaken, even the suicides, cannot begin to make amends for what we have lost! How is Seddun at this time of year? Do the islands still float?

∞

[tight beam, M2, tra. @n4.28.988.5]
  xLSV *Serious Callers Only*
    oEccentric *Shoot Them Later*

My dear friend, we do not know what the Excession offered or threatened. We know it was able to manipulate the energy grid in ways we can only speculate upon, but what if that was the only form of defence it was able to offer to something like the *Sleeper Service*? For all we know it was an invasionary beach-head which left us because it was met with forces which it estimated presaged resistance on a scale which would prove too expensive. I admit this is unlikely, but I offer it as a balancing possibility in the hope of righting the list of your pessimism.

At any rate, we are arguably better off than before; a conspiracy has been uncovered, any other zealots thinking of indulging in similar pranks will have been roundly discouraged, and even the Affront are behaving a *little* better having realised how close they came to being taught such a severe and salutary lesson. The war itself never really got going, there was little loss of life and Affronter reparations for the mischief they did create will serve as a minor but nagging reminder of the liabilities which follow on such aggression for some considerable time to come. The implicit lesson of the *Sleeper Service*'s effectively instantly produced war machine will similarly not have been lost on any other species who might also have been planning Affronter-like adventures, I suspect.

As to the chance we may have missed, well, call me an old bore if you will, but who knows what changes might have attended a meaningful dialogue with whatever the Excession represented (if it represented anything other than itself – again, we can only speculate).

In all this, the seeming indifference of the Elder civilisations still strikes me as one of the most puzzling aspects of the affair. Were they really just indifferent? Did the Excession have nothing to teach those who have Sublimed? There is much here still to

be answered, though I suspect the wait could be long; even infinitely so!

Well, the debate will doubtless continue for a long time to come. I confess I am finding the fame and even adulation that has befallen us somewhat tiring. I'm considering a retreat, after I've finished going round apologising to those who were involved without their knowledge in this.

Seddun is beautiful in winter (Visual file enclosed). As you see, the islands float on, even in the ice. Genar-Hofoen's uncle Tish sends his regards and has forgiven us.

III

Leffid held the lass in his arms and gazed happily out through the yacht's wide port-screen at the darkness of space. One bright edge of Tier was visible, rotating in all its silent majesty. Leffid thought it had never looked so beautiful. He gazed down at the sleeping face of his angel. Her name was Xipyeong. Xipyeong. What a beautiful name.

It was love this time, he was sure of it; he had found his soul-mate. They had only met the week before, only been together for a couple of nights, but he just knew. Why, for one thing, he hadn't forgotten her name once!

She stirred and woke, her eyes coming slowly open. She frowned briefly, then smiled, nuzzling him and saying, 'Hey, Geffid . . .'

IV

Ulver reined Brave in. The great animal snorted and came to a halt at the crest of the ridge. She loosened the reins to let the animal put its head down and crop the grass by the rocks. Beyond, the curved land dipped and rose; the ridge looked down over a forest and a winding river then out over rolling downland dotted with houses and coppices of trees. Overhead, one of Phage's larger lakes glittered in the sunlight.

Ulver looked back to see the rest following behind; Otiel, Peis, Klatsli and her brother and the others. She laughed. Their mounts were picking their way gingerly through the stone-field; Brave had taken it at a gallop.

The black bird Gravious settled on a nearby rock. Ulver grinned at it. 'See?' she said, taking a great, deep, happy breath and waving one gloved hand out at the view. 'Isn't it beautiful here? Didn't I tell you? Aren't you glad you came?'

'It's all right, I suppose,' Gravious conceded.

Ulver laughed.

The drone Churt Lyne, also returned to Phage Rock, often wondered if it had made the right decision.

V

They looked around, in the midst of an undreamt splendour.

~ Now *this* was a view worth risking everything for, the *Grey Area* sent.

~ I think we can all agree with that, agreed the *Peace Makes Plenty*.

~ If they could see us now . . . mused the *Break Even*.

VI

Ren ran down the sands and into the water, shrieking and laughing and splashing. Her long blonde hair turned darker in the water and lay stuck to her skin when she ran back out again. She skipped up to where her mother, Zreyn and Amorphia sat on a gaily patterned rug under a lacy parasol. The girl threw herself at her aunt Zreyn, who grinned and caught her, then let her wriggle free and dash off along the beach, running towards a sea bird which had thought to doze off there; it flapped lazily into the air and flew slowly off, pursued by the whooping child.

The girl disappeared round the side of the long, single-storey house which lay in the dunes behind the beach; the decorated edges of its veranda awnings flapped and rippled in the warm breeze coming in off the sea.

On the porch, the image of Gestra Ishmethit sat, peering intently at the partially built model of a sailing ship sitting on a table. The man himself had his own suite of rooms, off one of the *Sleeper Service*'s warship-stacked General Bays, but he had been persuaded, by Ren, to allow his real-time image to join them most days, and had even started to appear personally for important celebrations. These consisted mostly of Ren's birthdays, which according to her occurred on a weekly basis.

Zreyn Tramow looked over at Dajeil. 'Have you ever thought,' she said, 'of asking the ship to re-create the old place where you used to live?'

'There's still a version of it in that Limited Bay, isn't there?' Dajeil said, looking at Amorphia. The avatar, which sported a simple black pant-skirt and skin which looked like it would never tan, was holding a long blonde hair up to the sun-line, and peering at it. It realised it was being talked to and looked at Dajeil.

'What?' it said, then, 'Oh, yes; the bay where Genar-Hofoen was kept. Yes; the tower's still there.'

'See?' Dajeil told Zreyn. She rolled along the rug, out of the parasol's shade, closed her eyes, put her hands under her head and lay on her belly, to even up her tan.

'I meant the whole thing,' Zreyn said, stretching out on the rug. 'The cliffs and everything. Even the climate, if that's possible,' she said, glancing at the avatar, which was still studying the sunlight through one of Ren's blonde hairs.

'Perfectly possible,' it muttered.

'The whole thing?' Dajeil said, grimacing. 'But it's so much *nicer* like this.' She reached out across the sand and pulled a straw sun-hat over her head.

Zreyn shrugged. 'I'd just like to see it do stuff like that, I suppose.' She looked up at the sun-line. 'Making and moving all that rock, creating small oceans . . . You have to remember I don't take all this . . . *power* for granted the way you do.'

Dajeil folded the sun hat's brim up and squinted at the other woman, who made an awkward gesture.

'Sorry; is my primitiveness showing?'

Zreyn Tramow's stored mind-state had been woken up to tell her that her name at least had been used in the discovered conspiracy. The *Sleeper Service* had been uncertain about whether this was really necessary, but it was the sort of thing that extreme politeness dictated, and in the aftermath of the brief war, everybody was being almost exquisitely correct. Besides, it had a hunch that she might find the current civilisational situation interesting enough to be re-born, and it rather liked the idea of instigating such a response. The *Sleeper Service* had been right; Zreyn Tramow had thought the galaxy sounded like a place worth revisiting and had duly been grown a new body, but then, after the ship had stuck around, impatiently, while the various post-debacle inquiries and investigations had been carried out, she'd asked to go with it when it had announced it still intended to go on a rambling retreat.

Gestra Ishmethit, his mind-state plucked from his dying brain in the evacuated cold of the warship halls in Pittance by the guilt-stricken *Attitude Adjuster*, appropriated from that craft just before it destroyed itself by the attacking *Killing Time* and subsequently passed on until it came to rest in the restocked memory vaults of the *Sleeper Service*, had also been woken up and furnished with a new body by that time; death had neither improved his social skills nor sated his urge for solitude and he too had asked to remain aboard the giant ship.

He, Ren, Dajeil and Zreyn were its only passengers.

'Yes, you're being a hick; stop it at once,' Dajeil told Zreyn, who shrugged. Dajeil glanced round at the dunes, the golden sand and the bright blue sky. 'Anyway, it's a long journey,' she said. 'Maybe we'll get bored with all this and want it all changed back to the way it was.'

'Just let me know,' Amorphia said.

Dajeil took another look round. 'I'm glad I let you talk me into remaking the old place like this, Amorphia,' she said.

'Pleased you like it,' the avatar said, nodding.

'Have you decided where we're going yet?' Zreyn asked.

The avatar nodded. 'I think . . . Leo II,' it said.

'Not Andromeda?' Zreyn said.

Amorphia shook its head. 'I changed my mind.'

'Damn,' Zreyn said. 'I always wanted to go to Andromeda.'

'Too crowded,' Amorphia said.

Zreyn looked unconvinced.

'We could go there . . . afterwards?' the avatar suggested.

'Will we even live to see Leo II?' Dajeil asked, opening her eyes and gazing over at the creature.

The avatar looked apologetic. 'It will take rather a long time,' it admitted.

Dajeil closed her eyes again. 'You could always Store us,' she said. 'Think you could manage that?'

Zreyn laughed lightly.

'Oh, I could give it a try,' the avatar said.

Epilogue

call me highway call me conduit call me lightning rod scout catalyst observer call me what you will i was there when i was required through me passed the overarch bedeckants in their great sequential migration across the universes of [*no translation*] the marriage parties of the universe groupings of [*no translation*] and the emissaries of the lone bearing the laws of the new from the pulsing core the absolute centre of our nested home all this the rest and others i received as i was asked and transmitted as i was expected without fear favour or failure and only in the final routing of the channel i was part of did i discharge my duty beyond normal procedures when i moved from a position where my presence was causing conflict in the micro-environment concerned (see attached) considering it prudent to withdraw and reposition myself and my channel-tract where for some long time at least it was again unlikely i would be discovered the initial association with the original entity *peace makes plenty* and the (minor) information-loss ensuing was not as i would have wished but as it represented the first full such liaison in said micro-environment i assert hereby it fell within acceptable parameters i present the entity *peace makes plenty* and the other above-mentioned collected/embraced/captured/self-submitted entities as evidence of the environment's general demeanour within its advanced/chaotic spectrum-section and urge they be observed and studied free with the sole suggested proviso that any return to their home environment is potentially accompanied by post-association memory confiscation in the linked matter of the suitability of the relevant inhabitants of the micro-environment for (further and ordered) communication or association it is my opinion that the reaction to my presence indicates a fundamental unreadiness as yet for such a signal honour lastly in recognition of the foregoing i wish now to be known hereafter as *the excession*

thank you

end